Wounded

By Nick Mann

Strategic Book Publishing and Rights Co.

Strategic Book Publishing and Rights Co., LLC
USA | Singapore
www.sbpra.com

For information about special discounts for bulk purchases, please contact Strategic Book Publishing and Rights Co., LLC. Special Sales, at bookorder@sbpra.net.

ISBN: 978-1-68181-302-8

Review Requested:
If you loved this book, would you please provide a review at Amazon.com?
Thank You

To Marion

Prepare for what one character in Nick Mann's *Wounded* calls "a serious case of disaccustomcy." In his new novel, *Wounded*, author Nick Mann challenges readers' perceptions even as he sucks them in with his serious flair for storytelling. He weaves together a powerful narrative of loyalty and friendship, told with a rich perspective through the intertwined stories of three African American men who grew up together in DC. Both historical and contemporary, this is a story of the black experience in the nation's capital. Reading about the pain experienced by characters as fully realized as these may not be easy, but *Wounded* deserves a wide readership, especially today, and especially among those who may not otherwise be "accustomed" to its tough but essential message.

Karen Lyon (The Literary Hill editor for the *Capital Hill Rag*)

***

As a Vietnam vet, I was totally absorbed by Nick Mann's description of the war from two very different perspectives, that of an Army Band member at the huge Long Binh base, and that of a young officer with an elite special operations team in the northern highlands. With vivid detail, the author authentically recreates the experience "in-country" as well as the inner turmoil of the protagonists. The fast-paced exploits of Tracy Brown's recon team are sprinkled with fascinating historical details, all making for a great read.

Bill King, 5th Special Forces Group, Vietnam, 1966-68

***

It's said that addiction is a family disease, because the person who suffers from a substance use disorder rarely hurts only himself or herself. Nick Mann's *Wounded* explores, in riveting detail, the extraordinary power of an alcohol use disorder to destroy life's potential, impose suffering on those within its sphere of influence, and sink individuals into an ever-darker hole from which escape becomes less and less possible. Conversely, *Wounded* also demonstrates the remarkable courage required by all affected to recover from its ravages. Mann demonstrates how a unique "family" network helps protagonist Levi Chance on his journey to become whole again. *Wounded* is a must-read for anyone who's been touched by a substance use disorder—and, I believe, that includes us all!

Bill Beard, a retired project manager for nationwide substance use treatment and prevention programs and a person in long-term recovery.

***

The detail with which novelist Nick Mann describes Marva Chance's sojourn from Aiken, SC to Washington, DC had to be a God-Thing! On a recent visit to Aiken to visit my Cousins Lily and Wilhelmina, Nick and I heard about my Grandmother, Rhoda Kitchens Duncan. Nick's manuscript for Wounded was already at the publisher when this visit occurred. Yet, when you read about the fictitious Marva's journey and the reasons behind it, you could put a ditto for Grandmother Rhoda. That's the first God-Thing.

Nick and I also heard about how Cousin Lily was forced to pick cotton and do other hard labor tasks as a young girl. Nick had thought he was writing fiction, but here was another ditto between the character Marva; this time with Cousin Lily. Another God-Thing.

Lastly, Marva's son, Levi Chance is the protagonist in Wounded. The tale of Levi's lifelong struggle with alcoholism in this book is sometimes painful to read. But eerily my father was introduced to alcohol at a very early age by his father, who made some of the best Moonshine in Aiken County. My father struggled with alcoholism all of his life in many of the same ways as Levi. I want to express to readers that I think this book is an act of Divine Intervention. I hope you will be touched by it, as I am.

Katherine Leni Duncan Warner

Table of Contents

Author's Note

I find the genre of historical fiction (with primarily African American characters) extremely challenging. It's about mindset. How much do the characters need to be blended in seamlessly to the way it actually happened from a historical perspective? Or how much latitude does the author have to tell the story of the characters and set those stories in scenes that approximate but do not necessarily comport to historical facts? Over the course of more than three years writing *Wounded*, this author found himself continually challenged by this conundrum. I hope readers will find that the history-inspired references spice up what I hope will be an interesting tale.

Nick Mann

Prologue

National Capital Housing Authority

Washington, DC

February 21, 1955

Dear Resident,

The National Capital Housing Authority intends to purchase and remove the buildings from approximately five blocks in the Southwest section of Washington, located between Second and Third Streets, Eye and M Streets, and Delaware Avenue and Canal Street, and to build on the cleared site 456 low-rent houses and apartments for low-income families. The building in which you are now living is one of those which will be removed and the Authority will begin negotiating for its purchase.

To aid you in locating other living quarters, the Authority has opened a Relocation and Site Management Office at 400 L Street, Southeast, telephone – Lincoln 4-1355. This office, under the supervision of Mr. Omar Rogers, will be open to serve you every day except Saturdays, Sundays, and holidays, from 9:00 a.m. to 4:30 p.m. Employees of the Relocation Office will visit your home within the next few days and ask you certain questions. We shall appreciate your cooperation with the staff, for this will help you and your neighbors.

Often strange stories are started about the supposed action of a government agency which buys property and plans to tear it down so as to build on the cleared land. If you are worried by any such stories, or if you have any questions as to the Authority's work in this neighborhood, please let Mr. Rogers or other members of his staff know about them, in order that you can be given the correct information.

Low-income families who are to move from the houses bought by the Authority will have an equal chance for vacancies in public housing with families who are being removed from old houses in the Southwest by the Redevelopment Land Agency and with families displaced by other public action. If your income is too high to allow you to become a tenant of public housing, our Relocation Office – with the cooperation of the Redevelopment Land Agency – will assist you wherever possible in finding a vacancy in good private housing.

The Relocation Office also will tell you about the arrangements that the Authority will make after it acquires the property for your continued use of your present home until you move. These arrangements will include an agreement with you for the payment of a fair rent. If you decide to make your own arrangements for another place to live, please let our Relocation Office know, either in person or by phone, and send your keys to the office at 400 L Street, SE.

We are sure that you will find the Relocation staff and other employees of the Authority ready to assist with your relocation problems. With your cooperation, the Authority will be able to successfully carry out its plans for rehousing you and your neighbors.

Sincerely,

John Greely, Executive Director

A Prequel to *Forgetful*

South of museums
A place cherished and reviled
Still the loss lingers.

Chapter 1
Like Frankie

Spring 1956

Twelve-year-old Levi Chance saw his Saint John Island born and Aiken County, South Carolina raised mom pacing up and down in the front of the house on F Street SW and knew he was in trouble. It was way after dark, and Marva Chance had told Levi over and over to be home before the sun went down. She swatted him as he ran into the house. In her dialect born on the Sea Islands of her home state, Marva asked, "Where you been?"

"Simple City, Ma."

"Simple what? What you talking bout, boy?"

"You know, Ma. Simple City. Over by First and Q."

"What? First and Q? Das cross M Street. I swanit I told you not ta cross M Street after school. You sposed ta stay close ta home after school and come in fo dark. What you doing dere at First and Q?"

"I was listening to Marvin, Ma. He was singing with the big boys under the lamppost."

"Marvin? Marvin who, boy?"

"I don't know his last name, Ma. Marvin goes to Randall. He's famous, Ma. He can sing."

"You can sing too, but you not supposed ta be cross M Street hanging round some big boys singing under no lamppost after dark."

"But, Ma. He lets me sing 'Why Do Fools Fall in Love' with them. You know that new song by Frankie Lymon. It's the best song out. Frankie's just a little older than me, and my voice is high like his. Marvin says I got it."

"I swanit, if you don't git up da stairs and wash up fo dinner, you gone git it all right. Child, you worry me ta death."

15

"Yes, Ma."

Little Levi shot up the stairs, grateful for his reprieve.

Later at the dinner table, he asked, "Ma, can y'all call me Shawty from now on?"

"What?"

"Shawty, Ma."

"Shawty. What kind a name Shawty? Yo name Levi. Yo name in da Bible. No, you ain't gone be called no Shawty."

"Aw, Ma. Shawty's a cool name. That's what Marvin calls me."

"Fa true? Now some big boy dat I don't know name Marvin, he's gone and rename my son. Lawd Jesus, what I gonna hear next?"

"Can I, Ma? Can I be Shawty?"

"No, you cain't be no Shawty. Not today. Not tomorrow. Not never."

Chapter 2
On the Way to the Bayou

September 1996

Ben Parks came back into a groggy consciousness. What happened? He was on the side of the road. Then the pain in his face brought him back a few minutes. That's when he started to remember. He'd been furious. *What's up with this guy tailgating me?* he'd thought.

The George Washington Parkway in Virginia skirts the Potomac River through some beautiful scenery, with Washington, DC on the left coming into Georgetown. He had been heading toward the Key Bridge, which came across the river and spilled into M Street, NW. But it was foggy that night, and Ben's 1985 Toyota Cressida didn't have fog lamps. He was straining to see. For a while he'd been aware that he was developing cataracts. Glare of any kind was difficult for him at night and terrifying in fog. And this jerk behind him with the bright yellow fog lamps had been right on his bumper for, it seemed, miles. Why didn't he go around?

Ben, from the Michigan Park neighborhood in Northeast Washington, DC, had already been driving slowly, about forty miles per hour. He honked his horn and when nothing happened, he flipped the bird in his rearview mirror. From the direction of the bright lights came a loud sustained horn. He slowed to thirty, then to twenty, then to fifteen. The car still stayed on his bumper. There was almost no traffic on the two-lane road. Why didn't he go around? Had Ben done something to him earlier on the trip that he didn't realize? Had he cut him off or something? If so, he was unaware.

Ben had spotted a cutout on the side of the parkway and had pulled over. The bright yellow lights had pulled in behind.

"Damn! I can't get rid of you," Ben muttered to himself.

He'd opened the door and approached the vehicle behind, still not being able to make out what kind it was. As he reached the front of the car, still bathed in bright light, the passenger door opened and Ben hurled an insult, "Are you having fun, you jerk? There's all the road in the world and you want to blind me with those damn fog lights. What the fuck's wrong with—"

That's all Ben could remember getting out of his mouth before the punch came from the direction of the bright lights. He must have gone straight down, because he didn't remember anything further. Now he was getting to his feet and brushing himself off. The throbbing in his face was intense. The guy had landed a good one, and Ben hadn't even seen it coming. Why? Who? Ben had no clue.

A lone car whizzed by. Ben looked around and saw his car with the driver's door still open with the bell chime ringing incessantly. As he looked down, he spotted tire tracks where another vehicle had backed up and pulled away. Staggering, he made it back into the Cressida and just sat in the driver's seat until his head cleared. Then, pulling back onto the road, in less than a mile he saw the cloverleaf exit to come across the Key Bridge into Georgetown.

When Parks stumbled into the Bayou at Wisconsin and K Streets just before the main act was coming on, his almost lifelong friend Levi Chance saw him and waved. As Ben got close to the one seat Levi was saving in the packed room, Ben's friend gasped, "What the hell happened to you?"

"Man," said Ben breathlessly, "I don't even know. I was trying to get down here from Rockville."

Ben told the story of his harrowing episode, finishing with, "The dude coldcocked me. I never even saw the punch."

"What do you mean?"

"The dude had these yellow lights in my face. The punch came out of the lights. I never saw the punch. I never saw him. By the time I got off the ground, there was nothing left but this gong ringing in my head."

Levi was with his on-again and off-again squeeze, Janice Westbrook. She, Levi, and Ben had all met in high school in the late 1950s. Janice got up, and when she came back to the table she had ice in a towel from the bar for Ben's face. The cold temperature gave some quick relief. Levi caught a barmaid by the arm and shouted over the din, "Bring him a cold Fosters, sweetheart."

Both Janice and Levi were drinking ginger ale. Ben had seen Janice with a mixed drink once in a while, but never when she was with Levi. Just as Ben's Fosters arrived, the lights dimmed. The place immediately got still with anticipation. Would this be the main act? This special tribute night would be historic.

As Ben swigged the Fosters, he thought, *That dude on the side of the road would have had to kill me for me to miss this.*

Then, after one or two more warm-up groups, *she* slowly walked out on stage. She settled herself, placing both booted feet on a rung of a stool before whispering into the microphone her breathy, "Good evening!"

And the rest of the night was hers.

Chapter 3
The Warrior

December 1967

Second Lieutenant Tracy Tolliver Brown had just returned from his first long-range reconnaissance patrol, or LLRP mission, in Vietnam. Neh, one of the Montagnard members of the eight-man recon team, had two nonlethal wounds. He was being hurriedly off-loaded from the helicopter that had just landed at the Phu Bai base camp. Tracy had been grazed on his butt and had taken another round that entered his left cheek, collided with a molar, and exited out of his open mouth. The tough-as-nails, six-foot-five, 238-pound behemoth had functioned for the rest of the mission without a blip. He'd hardly noticed the blood from the slugs after being hit. A medic on the ride back to Phu Bai had cleaned the butt wound and used petrolatum gauze in the cheek wound. Tracy's wounds were already starting to scab a little by the time the chopper landed.

Angel, the team's communications specialist, had been KIA. He'd taken an AK-47 slug through the back of his head that had come out through his right eye. Tonight, all the recon soldiers plus other troops stationed at Phu Bai would gather in the NCO club to sing "Hey Blue" for him:

I had a dog and his name was Blue.

Bet you five dollars he's a good dog too.

Hey, Blue! Hey, Blue!

You're a good dog too.

Then after several more verses detailing the bravery, loyalty, and friendship of the dog, the final verse would intone Angel's name:

Our friend Stavros Angelopoulos too,

Bet you five dollars he's a brave one too,

Hey, friend! Hey, friend!

You were a good guy too.

Tracy was a West Point graduate and from the Michigan Park neighborhood in Northeast Washington, DC. He'd been noticed immediately about six or seven weeks ago as he'd pulled his duffle bags out of the helicopter that delivered him to the base. He'd been immediately drafted into reconnaissance team Samoa, strictly on the basis of his massive size, but he'd backed the first impression by acquitting himself well on the mission.

"How'd the big black guy do?" asked Zeke Austin, a commando running over to speak with Whit Wattlington, who'd been team leader.

Whit simply replied, "He's good in the woods."

This was all he had to say. In commando speak, the phrase meant that a soldier had a unique combination of bravery and skills.

"Is he injured?"

"He took a couple of little hits, but you can't tell by the way he's acting. I think he lost a tooth."

"Good! I'm about to go out on a snatch into Laos and I need him."

Zeke had been about to load up his team for another mission. He caught up with Tracy, who was walking beside Ksor's stretcher.

"Soldier, how'd you like to go out again in about an hour?"

Tracy stopped and grasped Neh's hand. The small in stature but powerfully built tribesman squeezed back and said, "Neh's okay."

Tracy thought a moment before responding, "Do I have time to get a shot, a shower, and a meal?"

"Shot, yes. You need antibiotics for that cheek. Shower, yes. Meal, no. We'll get you a meal from the mess while you see the doc and shower. You can eat on the chopper. I'll brief you on the mission once we're on the way. It's a snatch, similar to the one you just finished, but this time we're going to take a truck driver off the Ho Chi Minh Trail. That'll be a gold mine for enemy transport info. We monitored your comms in the field, and everybody thinks these snatches might become your specialty. What do you say?"

Tracy hesitated. He'd heard tales of the "Hey Blue" ceremony but had never participated. He wanted to say a proper goodbye to Angel, but Tracy could feel the rush and knew he'd miss singing "Hey Blue" for his fallen comrade.

"See you in forty-five minutes," said Tracy, running toward his barracks.

Chapter 4
Marva's Journey

In the late summer of 1943, tall, wiry, strong, brown-faced, and pretty Marva Doucette had come to DC totally by happenstance. At seventeen, she was poor and had very little schooling, but she knew that picking cotton in Aiken County, South Carolina, was not the kind of life she wanted to live. Besides, a man had come upon her, forced himself on her in a way that she'd never experienced. After that, she knew that the feelings she was starting to feel inside herself meant that something was happening, and she didn't want it to happen there.

So, she did something that no little black girl of the South should have done. Without warning or saying goodbye to the older brother who looked after her, she left early one morning and walked out to the road with a hatbox full of all her worldly belongings. Marva came to a little one-pump gas station known to all the local coloreds. She wore brown brogan shoes and a long, flowered calico skirt she had found in an empty shack near the one that she and her brother Homer lived in. Her faded blue shirt hung low over her skirt, and her hair was tied up in a white bandana. The only other clothing she had with her was a floppy hat, some underthings, and a tattered blue wool sweater that she had folded tight and stuffed into her hatbox along with the worn toothbrush, hair brush, spare socks, and two soap bars she'd been saving for this occasion. The night before she had snuck out of their little sharecropper's shack while her brother was visiting his 'lil' gal' across the way. She'd burned the clothes she'd worn in the fields every day for as long as she could remember.

At the gas station, she positioned herself where cars pulling out would see her, and she stuck her thumb out. After a while, she had caught the first ride that stopped. Since she didn't have a destination in mind, wherever they were going was fine with her.

It was a black couple driving a black four-door Ford. Medgar and Susie Gray were heading from Augusta, Georgia, up to the nation's capital for the funeral of one of their relatives. The couple was friendly and asked about her. And when she told her story they became concerned that her brother would be worried.

"He name Homer. He won't care. Homer Doucette tired of me. My fingers hurt all day from picking. Homer pick fast. But end of day, I don't have much. He always has ta use some of he money ta feed me. He always complain I cain't pick faster. But I jus cain't. He maybe wonder where I gone. But soon, ain't nobody gone worry wid me."

The Grays were silent for a long time. Then Susie Gray swallowed hard and turned around toward the back seat. "We're glad to have you riding with us, child. We'll do what we can for you. We're going to Washington, DC. Is that all right with you?"

"Yes, ma'am," said Marva. "Dat far?"

"We'll be there sometime tonight or early tomorrow."

They stopped for gas or to eat from their picnic basket, or to use one of the "colored" restrooms they found along the way. Marva was surprised that the Grays switched drivers on several stops and that Susie seemed to drive just as well as Medgar. Then, 450 miles later, up the old Route One that ran from Florida to Maine, they arrived in the nation's capital. She didn't know anyone in this strange northern town and had no place to stay. When they entered DC, they drove through town until they came to the corner of 13th and T Streets, NW. Marva looked up at the building and read the sign Whitelaw Hotel as Medgar navigated into an alley to a small parking lot in the back. Early in the morning, Medgar got out and went around to the front. After a few minutes, he came back with a key. Susie and Marva had waited in the car. As Medgar came back toward the car and Susie opened her door, Marva experienced a sense of dread.

"Can I just sleep in yo car tonight and den I make my way in da morning?"

"You're coming inside, young lady!" said Susie with her most commanding tone.

Marva slept on the couch in the Gray's hotel room that night. All the occupants of room 310 were sound asleep ten minutes after entering.

In the morning, Susie Gray invited Marva to come with them. Marva protested, feeling she'd imposed more than enough, but Susie insisted. At 734 First Street SW, the three travelers walked up to the Friendship Baptist Church. Marva was wearing her same travel clothes, though the Grays were more dressed up than they'd been on the trip. Feeling awkward and clutching her hatbox, Marva looked for a way to excuse herself. But she didn't have any place to go.

Luckily Susie's family had the presence of mind to welcome Marva warmly despite their time of grief. They invited Marva downstairs into the basement fellowship hall. There she was served a hearty breakfast by elderly church women who bustled around a small kitchen on the side. Then Marva was left sitting alone and the Grays and their family went upstairs. Soon Marva heard a sound she'd never heard before. She was startled by its depth and richness, and she shot up from her chair.

Seeing her reaction, one of the women came in from the kitchen and said, "Sorry, child, but our organist turns up the sound too loud sometimes. We're used to it. After a while, you'll get used to it too."

Marva had never heard an organ before. She sat down and listened and began to fall in love with the majesty of the music upstairs. After the music stopped, there were various voices, the most prominent coming much later as the booming eulogy was delivered by the Reverend Benjamin Harrison.

Then the funeral was over. The Grays reappeared and hustled Marva upstairs and outside to their car, where a line of cars was forming. Eventually they began to drive together for a long while before they turned into what Marva recognized as a cemetery, but much larger than the little ones she'd seen in the country.

After the burial, the procession came back to Friendship, and there was another meal in the Fellowship Hall. Finally, as the home-going activities were wrapping up, Susie's older sister, Alma Stokes, who worked as a census punch card worker for the government, was huddling with Susie. The family was recognizing the plight of this poor little Southern girl and trying to decide what they could do. Finally, Alma called her husband, Bundy, who had been taking trash and garbage bags out to the row of aluminum cans behind the church. Shortly she had persuaded Bundy to do everything he could to find Marva somewhere to stay.

Marva spent another evening with the Grays, ending with her sleeping again on the couch in their hotel room. But when everyone was up the following morning there was a different mood in the room. Marva sensed a mood of purpose and mission, though she couldn't have described it at the moment. Medgar Gray drove them from their hotel in the Northwest section of town back down to the Southwest section, where Friendship Church was located. There, just a few blocks away, they came to the tidy little home of Alma and Bundy Stokes. The address was 49 Eye Street SW. It was small, but immaculately clean. The Grays, accompanied by Marva, stepped through the door and were met by the noise of youngsters coming from upstairs, but the ruckus was playful and Marva's heart lifted at their sounds.

Soon Susie and Medgar, Marva, Bundy, Alma, and the two teenaged Stokes boys, Bart and Brian, were all bunched together in the vicinity of a too-small, oval-shaped table in the middle of the front room of their house. Most were perched on wooden chairs, but Bundy, Medgar, and the older boy Bart pulled up milk crates to sit on at the table. Marva had never experienced this kind of meal. For one thing, there was the food: ham, grits, eggs, biscuits, coffee, and Kool-Aid. Then there was the genuinely warm conversation around the room, the likes of which Marva had never been exposed. After eating, Marva asked if she could help with the dishes. Hearing the request, Suzie and Alma smiled approvingly at each other.

"You got good manners, child," said Alma.

Bundy Stokes and Medgar Gray had left the house right after breakfast. The women busied themselves with chitchat for an hour or more until the men came back around ten. Bundy Stokes motioned for Marva to come outside with him. Both Alma and Susie looked concerned, but Marva went out after Bundy.

"My wife has taken a liking to you, child," said Bundy out on the walkway in front of the house. "Matter of fact, I kind of like you too. Sorry we just don't have room for you at our place, what with my wife and me and our boys. There is a place that's not grand, but there's a cot that you could rent. Do you want to go see it?"

"Thank you, Mr. Stokes."

"I have to ask, do you have any money at all?"

Marva tightened, but then nodded. Bundy didn't probe further. He drove Marva over to Dixon's Court in a section nicknamed Hell's Half Acre. Dixon's Court was really just a wide cobblestone alley. Around the alley one could see door after door panning around in a square-cornered U-shape. The first thing Marva was aware of was the smell. It was not unbearable but insistent, faintly pungent, not quite of rot, but more of sweat and age, and something else; the smell was vaguely familiar to Marva. Walking from the car, they came to the third door on the right. Two steps led up to this and every other door, and these doors opened up into the alleyway dwellings of Dixon's Court.

Bundy ascended the two steps and knocked. Then, without waiting, he turned the knob and opened the door. Marva followed Bundy up the steps and walked in. Her first impulse was to back out of the dimly lit space, and she actually took one step back. But then she caught herself. She could make out ten cots along three walls and a table and some wooden chairs positioned by the fourth wall. Another table and a few folding chairs were in the middle of the room. Assorted metal pans and plates, tin pails, and stacks of various cloths and rags were visible on and around this middle table. On many of the cots there appeared to be stacks of folded clothing.

Looking around the room, on one of the cots Marva could make out the silhouette of a person under some tattered covers, evidently still asleep at about ten thirty in the morning. Directly across from this cot on the other side of the room, a young woman of about Marva's age was sitting on a folding chair like the ones in the middle of the room, brushing her pressed hair while looking into a small, round mirror she had propped up on a suitcase standing longwise on her cot. Around other cots, Marva noticed cardboard boxes, tattered suitcases, pairs of shoes, or other possessions showing that someone slept there. All these cots were neatly made up. That is, all but the first cot on the left side of the room, which was devoid of any cover.

"That must be the one Johnny told me about," said Bundy.

"Johnny King runs three or four of these dwellings for Mr. Clyde Bushrod, Esquire. Johnny said one was open, so that must be it."

At that point, a small dark shape appeared from under the bed on the far side of the opposite wall from the empty bed. The mouse paused and then scurried across the room and ducked under a little table by one of the beds. After a beat, Bundy and Marva heard the distinct snapping noise of a trap springing. The sleeping shape moaned softly and then turned over, still under her covers. The young woman brushing her hair looked over, let out a laugh, and then went back to her fastidious grooming. Bundy looked at Marva to gauge her reaction.

"When I was trying to think of a place for you, I worried about the rats and mice. There's more expensive places than this in homes that rent out rooms. They charge as much as twenty dollars or more per month. But money aside, I didn't take you to one of those because most of them do bed sharing. I personally wouldn't want to be in a place where I'd have to share a bed with someone I didn't know. There's bed sharing all over town because of so many new workers coming here to support the war. Guess I should have asked you if you'd mind."

Marva's nose turned up. "Wouldn't want ta be in a bed wid nobody, woman no man. Rather have a cot by myself."

"Good, I thought I'd made the right call."

"You ought ta see da mices in da country. Thousands a mices in da country where I come from. Rats is just cousins. Dey ain't gone bother me, and if dey get too close, I'ma bother dem."

Bundy let out a howl of amusement, but that settled the issue.

Chapter 5
Taking the Plunge

Marva's face showed impassive.

"If you take it, I know Alma can spare some sheets, a pillow, and a couple of blankets out of our linen closet at home. And I'll pick up some traps for you if you want. Most of these ladies work down on the water, shucking crabs or scaling fish, or some such. That one who's asleep is a dance hall girl, and I'm not sure about Ms. Goldilocks over there," gesturing toward the woman with the brush. "But the ones who work on the water get to stay here, and Mr. Bushrod takes something from their wages to pay for their rent."

Marva was now staring at the empty cot in the corner.

"If you've got three bucks a week to pay, then you can stay and work or not work or whatever you want. If you don't, we can probably find you a flat for you to rent. But remember, that would run you as much as eighteen to twenty dollars or more every month."

For the first time, Marva thought of the nickels, pennies, quarters, dimes, and two crumpled one dollar bills rolled up in a bandana in the hatbox she had left back at Bundy's house. Before she'd left Aiken County, Marva had counted up. She knew she had $7.14 to her name, and amazingly she hadn't spent a dime during her travels to this point.

Interrupting her contemplation, Bundy said, "I've got an idea. I want to try something when I get to work. But you need to tell me what you want to do about this place, and we'll either take you back to stay with Alma just for today, or we'll go back and get you some provisions for this place. Then when I get back from work, maybe I'll have something else to tell you."

"I have three dollars. I take dis place. I think I need ta be by mysefs ta think 'bout what I gone do. I thank you, Mr. Stokes, but I just needing ta think."

"Sure, girl. Sure. I'm going back now to get you those linens from Alma and pick up some traps. Should I bring back that hatbox of yours on the way?"

"Yes, suh! Thank you so much."

When Bundy was gone, Marva stood still for a moment looking over at the empty cot to her left.

"I'm Gina," came a voice from the right.

"Oh. I's Marva. Nice ta meet you," said Marva, looking over inexpressively.

"I'm from Farmville, down in Virginia. I heard you talking to that man. I seen him around. Seems like a nice man. He don't come after us like a lot of men. I heard you gonna move in with us. It's okay. You'll get used to it."

"Farmville, huh. I don't know there was a town named fo a farm. I from a farm down South Carolina. Me and big brother stay in a shack wida outhouse out back. I guess dis ain't better, but it ain't no worse."

"Well you're really gonna be at home. We got outhouses around the corner in this alley. So it'll be just like South Carolina. Matter of fact, since you'll be the new girl, you'll make the slop crew when our house's turn comes around to clean out the outhouses. I guess you've done that before, too, down in South Carolina."

Gina let out a big laugh, and for the first time Marva smiled, remembering hauling pails of slop from her outhouse back home and taking them out to the road on the days that the slop wagons came by for collection. Then she threw her head back, opened her mouth, and roared a tremendous and refreshing laugh that felt so good she felt a chill.

Next, for the first time since entering the open-spaced room, Marva felt her legs come alive again. She had been frozen in place all this time, but now she turned and walked over to the cot that would be hers. She patted it all over and was surprised that it wasn't dusty. It felt softer in some places than in others. But she decided to test it.

She practically leapt off her feet and landed flat on her back on the cot. And it held.

"Girl, you braver than most folks I seen. You gonna be all right," said Gina from across the room.

"Where erbody?" asked Marva.

"All us alley coloreds that live in Mr. Bushrod's places have to work. Most of the girls in this one are from the South, like you and me. These girls clear out as soon as the sun comes up, 'cept for Sally over there and me. Sally works at night somewhere. I'll be leaving soon to catch the streetcar uptown to Mr. Bushrod's house, where I do the cleaning. I get there at noon and usually be back here 'round ten at night. So about all we do here is sleep. I'm guessing that'll be the case for you too. And speaking of work, what kind of work can you do?"

"All I really know how ta do is pick cotton. But not really."

Gina laughed again. "Ain't no cotton fields in this town."

"But I think I could laan other things."

A loud rap at the door interrupted them, and Bundy Stokes barged in loaded with Marva's hatbox under his arm and two brown paper bags in either hand.

"Here, girl, come help me," said Bundy. "Why don't you take this hatbox of yours over by your cot and then come with me?"

Bundy followed and deposited the brown bags. "I brought you some stuff you might need. You can look through it when you get back."

"Hold up! Don't I need ta give my money fo da first week?"

"Already took care of that. Gave Johnny King six bucks on the way back. That's two weeks. The Grays left town a little while ago going back to Augusta. They told me to say goodbye and to wish you good luck. They also gave me five dollars to give you. I put another one with it and gave it to Johnny. So you've got two weeks before you have to dig into your stash."

From across the room, Gina chimed in. "Girl, I told you that was a nice man. But he's a real sweetie, ain't he? It's a shame he don't seem to want to get frisky with nobody. Don't you wanna to get frisky, sweet man?"

Bundy looked across the room and smiled a big smile before saying, "When I want to get frisky, young lady, I go home to my wife. But thanks for the compliment anyway."

"You welcome, sir," said Gina with a big smile.

"Gina, what should Marva do with her precious things? Are they safe here?"

"I cain't be responsible for saying for sure, mister. But I'll tell you this. I leave stuff here in my suitcase every day, and when I come back, it's all right here. I been here almost four months now, and I don't remember anybody saying anything was missing when they came in at night. We all kind of look out for one another here in Dixon's. We don't have much, but we have each other."

"What do you think about that, Marva?" asked Bundy.

Marva contemplated as she opened her hatbox and felt around for the tied-up bandana that held her money. Then, "Lemme just git two a dees quarter, and den I gonna put dis right back where it come from."

Gina said, "I like that, girl. I told you that you were brave. I think everything's gonna be all right. If you want, come Sunday, I'll take you with me up to my church. You're gonna need a good church. I go to the United House of Prayer. You heard of Bishop Daddy Grace, right? He's the best preacher 'round."

"I already went ta a church fo a funeral. She right over ways from here. If Mr. Bundy don't mind, I like ta go dere on a Sunday."

Now Bundy was showing impatience. "Of course you can come back to Friendship. Nobody can keep you out of church down here. But we need to go. Let's go, Marva. I need to get to work. I want you to come with me and meet someone."

"Who, Mr. Stokes?"

"You'll see when we get there. Hurry up, girl."

"Bye y'all," said Gina with a big smile.

"Bye, Gina," said Marva with a wave as she dropped the two quarters into the front pocket of her long skirt and followed Bundy out to some unknown destination.

Chapter 6
A Job

They drove in Bundy Stokes's humpbacked, black, four-door Buick through the neighborhood past narrow streets till they turned onto the wide vista known as Fourth Street. A major stop on the Underground Railroad during the enslavement of Africans in this country, Southwest DC was one of the oldest parts of the city. It had been settled in the seventeenth century, and by 1790 it was officially incorporated into the District of Columbia. Free black people were attracted to Southwest because of the part it played during the Civil War, and because it was a place where they could find work on the river. A failed escape attempt by enslaved Africans occurred in 1848, and it had been referred to down through the years as "The Pearl Episode," after the ship that was used.

Bundy was conducting a tour. "They used to call this street Four and a Half Street until around 1934," he explained. "Used to be cobblestone, but the stones were all breaking and coming up. Was a big celebration at the renaming ceremony after they paved it and made it more modern. Mostly white people live on this side of the street," said Bundy, gesturing toward the higher numbers.

"And mostly coloreds live over where we're coming from in the lower numbers. The Marine Band plays for the May Day Parade every year. Course, we're not really welcome then. But sometimes we all can meet here on Fourth Street. White people are mostly okay over there. They're just different."

Marva took in Bundy's words and turned them over in her mind. "White mens is devils where I come from. Das what Homer always say."

Bundy didn't respond right away. He studied Marva's face to assess her openness. Then he said, "That's probably true about some of them, Marva. Maybe even many of them, but I bet it's not true about all of them. Even in South Carolina."

Marva took it in.

"You ever hear of Al Jolson? He was a white singer that grew up in this neighborhood and learned how to sing like a colored man. Became famous in a movie called *The Jazz Singer*. That was the first movie that talked."

Marva had never seen a movie, talking or otherwise, and hadn't heard of Al Jolson. She'd attended school until she was twelve, when her mom died. She'd been one of the bright ones among the farm children, and she prided herself on being able to read phonetically, even if she didn't know what a word meant.

Marva read the names as they passed different sites in Bundy's car: the Jewell Theater, Atkin Grocery, Schneider's Hardware, the Ideal Barber Shop, the Minnesota Bar, Dakota Café, 114 Club, Shulman's Market. Bundy corrected her pronunciation as she read aloud. Merchants of all kinds were doing their morning business. They came to a massive gate with guards and signs indicating Fort McNair.

Bundy pointed as he executed a right turn onto Water Street. "Other than West Point, and a post up in Carlyle, Pennsylvania, it's the oldest army base in the country."

Marva nodded and peered down the street until Bundy completed his right turn and a new view opened up. She knew what a fort was. They had forts in South Carolina from the Civil War. She'd never heard of West Point, but she kept that to herself.

The street they turned onto curved and soon opened up onto a sprawling riverside. As they parked and got out, Marva was amazed at the teaming activity surrounding her. She could see the mixture of sailing ships, barges, fishing and oyster boats, ferries, and smaller private boats at various piers out past the square-shaped concrete buildings and warehouses, most with flat roofs. People milled around or walked with purpose in every direction. Bundy had pulled over so she could watch for a while. The whole area smelled of the water and fish and these sensations were reminiscent of her birthplace on St. John Island before her mom's death caused the overseers to send Marva and her brother inland to Aiken County.

Now Bundy continued the impromptu tour. He started up again, swung around back to Fourth Street, and made a left back in the direction from which they had come. This time Marva was able to see more businesses: The Keiser Restaurant, Lifshitz Shocket and Butcher, Morgenstein Bakery, Sperling's Mini Department Store, the Sanitary Grocery, Rubinstein Variety, and the American Filling Station. Finally Marva realized that they were back, approaching the area of Dixon's Court. She looked at Bundy quizzically. But at that very moment, Bundy crossed C Street and pulled over. This time he turned off the car and got out. Marva followed across to the west side of Fourth Street. They walked a few steps up toward Independence Avenue and turned into Bruce Wahl's Restaurant and Beer Garden. Bundy was a bartender there, and one of his stops while he'd left Marva at Dixon's Court was to come talk to Mr. Wahl (everybody called him Bruce).

By now it was about eleven thirty, so the restaurant was open. They walked in through the gathering throng assembled around round metal tables that stretched to the point closest to the stage. A large man was holding court at one of the tables. Bruce was a handsome, dark-chocolate-colored man who wore a black tam and possessed an infectious smile. He was very popular in the community, not only because he was proprietor of the sector's most successful gathering place, but he was also the chairman of the Willow Tree Athletic Club Benevolent Association. Willow Tree sponsored a football team that played at the Randall Junior High field against teams like the Anacostia Troopers. Willow Tree also sponsored outings to the National Zoo, as well as picnics in fun places like Fort Washington, Maryland.

"This is Marva," said Bundy.

The big man turned, looked Marva up and down quickly, and smiled. Then he went back to his conversation without a word.

"Never mind him," said a woman walking up to them quickly. She introduced herself. "I'm Ophelia Wahl. I'm Bruce's wife, and I heard you were coming in. Bruce is the kind, once he said yes to Bundy, he was through. I'm going to show you around," she said, taking Marva by the arm and gently pulling her away from the busy area near the sign that read "Bruce Wahl's Showboat."

"Now the job pays six fifty a week. Is that all right?"

Marva nodded, for the first time realizing that she was being given a job. Marva learned that she would be expected to bus tables, sweep, mop, and do other odd jobs. She learned that the opening had happened just yesterday, when the previous girl didn't show up for work for the third time after having been warned repeatedly. Ophelia Wahl was pleased to see that Marva showed no aversion to the job description as it was being explained.

"First though, child, we got to get you cleaned up. I know where Bundy has you staying and overcharging you for a single cot. You may not know it, but you carrying a smell. We open at ten thirty every morning. I want you here by nine thirty so you can wash up properly; get that Dixon Court smell off you so the customers don't complain. We got a shower back in the locker room with a door that locks because both men and women use it. You'll have a uniform to put on in your locker. Maybe some days you can even wash out your own clothes on our scrub boards and let them dry while you working. Can you do that?"

"Yes, ma'am!"

As they walked together toward the door to the locker room, a waiter carrying a tray over his head tripped. The tray fell with a loud spill. Nobody was hit, but the patrons all turned. Some gasped. Some clapped and laughed. The flustered waiter had started picking up bits of plate. Marva spotted a broom against the wall and left Ophelia's side. She grabbed the broom and started sweeping up bits of food and debris. The smiling Ophelia came over with a heavy metal dust pan and leaned over. Marva looked at her and Ophelia nodded toward the positioned dust pan. Marva immediately got it and began sweeping her pile into the dust pan. Several repetitions of this and the spill was up.

Ophelia said, "Now you wait while I bring a mop from the back."

Soon the mess was clear and the floor had been cleaned. Ophelia was brimming with admiration for this tall Southern girl.

And so, Marva Doucette settled into a daily routine: Up in the morning by five thirty or six with the other girls at the dirty red brick house on Dixon Court, and chatting and getting to know their routines, hopes, fears, and becoming acclimated to life in a city. June, the girl in the cot on the other side of the still-sleeping Mary, the dance hall girl, coughed off and on most nights. She was slight and light skinned, and Marva found out that she had come from a place called Danville.

The closest water spigot was two blocks up on Fourth Street. Marva would walk out with two metal pails each morning and stand in line, as mostly blacks would each take their turns getting water. Long ago, in Aiken County, Marva had perfected the art of the birdbath. So washing in a pail was nothing new, and she used one pail for her first quick wash of the morning, and Marva always left the second pail for June to use. Then she'd walk through the neighborhood and eventually down Fourth Street to the water to watch fishermen and customers transacting their business. But she always turned back north and conscientiously got up to Bruce Wahl's usually before nine and immediately took her second wash of the morning. Marva's first life experience with an actual shower came in the locker room at Bruce Wahl's. She worked at her various tasks until ten at night some days, until midnight some days, and much later some days, and then she'd start the same thing all over the next day.

Marva was off the farm. She didn't dream or hope. Marva was content. She sometimes thought about Homer. She sometimes thought that she might try to write him to let him know where she was. Then she'd usually remember what she told the Grays, that Homer wouldn't care. She didn't know if that was totally true, but she really believed that he was better off not having to watch after her.

Chapter 7

Shame

It wasn't until after the first of the year 1944 that Marva began to experience any noticeable signs of being with child. Gina at Dixon's Court and Ophelia Wahl actually noticed it on the same day. Gina's comment was casual and nonaccusatory, "Hey, I see we're gonna have company sometime soon."

She chuckled as Marva looked over and, noticing that Gina was staring at her belly, covered her face. While setting up for the dinner customers that same day, Ophelia came up beside Marva and whispered, "You're going to have to talk about that bundle you're carrying sooner rather than later, young lady. We're gonna have to start making some plans."

On Marva's next break, Ophelia made a call from the locker room. Alma and Bundy Stokes were parked across the street from Bruce Wahl's that evening when Marva got off work. Back at their home, the three of them stayed up for hours that night trying to decide what to do about Marva's pregnancy.

Marva was distraught. Through her tears, she told the story. "I ain't have no relations wid no man 'cept dat drunk man Zachary dat come on me when Homer were out fo da night. When I woked, he were already on me. I hit him good and he lip go ta bleeding. He fell off me, but fo I could get up he pull out a blade. He told me ta lie back and he held dat blade to my neck while he do what he do. Den he say I was his and he would come back to see me every now and den. He say I shouldn't tell Homer 'cause he gone kill my brother if he cause trouble."

Alma Stokes rocked Marva Doucette as she told the story. She and Bundy had never seen this strong young woman in this state. Their hearts broke as they realized the pain Marva had carried in secret all this time.

"I have to find out something about how Freedman's Hospital will deal with an unmarried woman coming in to have a baby. I don't know if they would take the baby. Pastor will know. I'll talk with him tomorrow."

Alma said, "Not to Reverend Harrison. Sister Maybelle Simms is who we need to talk to. People don't know it, but Sister Simms midwifes when somebody needs it. I don't know about Freedman's Hospital. Only reason to go to Freedman's would be so this baby could get a birth certificate, but they'd just put 'unknown' on the line for the father. Do you want to keep this baby, child?"

Marva had never thought of this. It brought about another round of sobbing that lasted almost a half hour. Finally, she calmed down and said, "Dis baby ain't something ta decide 'bout keeping or not keeping. Dis baby gonna be a person. Gonna be my lil person. I ain't choose it, but das all right. I choosing it now. Das all I wanna say 'bout that."

Silence fell over the room. Marva stiffened her back and sat up for the first time that evening. A mood of resolve fell over her. She had not dealt with this prior to this evening, but now she was clear about what she wanted.

Finally, Alma spoke, "If you agree, we'll keep your baby here until you're living somewhere else, out of Dixon's Court. Is that all right with you, child? You'll have a key to the door and can come and go whenever you want."

Hearing his wife, Bundy stood up and said, "I'm gonna get busy tomorrow and make a little crib. That settles that."

That night, Marva sat upright in the only armed chair that the Stokes's owned. She slept for about two hours and then the dawn came. She silently left the Stokes's house and walked to Dixon's Court. She lay on her cot. Gina came over and sat beside her.

"You want to talk about anything, girl?"

"Marva okay, Gina. Thank you fo being my friend. I be okay."

The two women hugged and then Gina went back to her cot. With her newfound resolve, Marva rose the next morning and began her normal routine, beginning with her trip out to the Fourth Street water spigots.

Chapter 8
Big Sam

Six-foot-two, 265-pound Samuel Chance from Washington, DC, had been drafted into the segregated army in 1942. Wide and muscular, with enormous hands and feet, twenty-year-old Big Sam, as he was called, was the very definition of what it meant to be "big boned." The United States had entered the war in the Pacific against Japan and in Europe against the Nazis in Germany and Mussolini in Italy and North Africa. In response to political pressure as well as the intense need for manpower, President Roosevelt had made three critical appointments: Judge William Hastie of Howard University was appointed assistant director of the War Department, Howard University's Campbell C. Johnson became special aide to the director of the Selective Service, and Benjamin O. Davis was promoted to brigadier general in the Army. These three appointments spurred activity on a number of fronts to provide opportunities for coloreds to serve.

Because he had scored a two on a five-point scale (with one being the best) on the Army General Classification Test (AGCT), Samuel wasn't wait-listed interminably for training like many colored draftees. As soon as the 92nd Infantry Division (Buffalo Soldiers) was reactivated in October 1942, Big Sam was sent to Fort Huachuca, Arizona, for basic training. But early on at Huachuca, a visiting white major's jeep was passing by morning formation one day with smoke seeping from the hood. The jeep stopped right beside the formation. After falling out of formation, Samuel, whose father, Sam Senior, had worked on cars for as long as he could remember, shyly asked his drill sergeant if he could take a look.

"With the Major's permission, one of my troops wants to take a look under the hood of your jeep, sir!" said the sergeant with a snappy salute.

He was given permission, and in no time he'd found the ruptured hose under the hood and told the major's driver what to say when they went to the motor pool. After this incident, the major arranged for the big colored soldier with mechanical aptitude to be transferred to an engineer unit. So instead of fighting with the 92nd, which was the only colored unit to see combat in Europe during World War II, Samuel Chance was sent from Arizona to Camp AP Hill in Virginia to learn how to drive a bulldozer and operate other heavy machinery.

Until Big Sam left the service in December 1944, he served in the 95th Engineer Regiment in Canada, where he worked on building the new Alaska Highway that had just been approved by President Roosevelt. Most of the black soldiers assigned to this project were from the South and hated the cold, but Big Sam had experienced cold in DC and didn't seem to mind it there. He worked long hours moving earth and supporting the road construction. The fact that he'd managed to learn to drive a dozer quickly and with great skill, coupled with his gusto in the cold, brought Big Sam to the attention of several white US Army engineering officers. Under Colonel Heath Twichell's leadership, Big Sam and the colored soldiers of the 95th Engineer Regiment completed a 300-mile stretch of road in British Columbia, from mile zero at Dawson Creek all the way to Fort Nelson.

Roger MacDowell was one of the white officers in the 95th Regiment who took note of Big Sam's prowess and work habits. MacDowell's family had an ice business in Washington, DC, and one day after the war, in 1945, while driving down North Capital Street near Union Station, he spotted a very large colored man on the corner. He pulled over and jumped out. "Chance! Sergeant Chance! Don't you know how to salute anymore?"

The big man looked warily at first, then broke into a big smile. "Captain Mac, what you doing down here? There must be a road you should be building somewhere."

Conscious of their location on a public street, the men refrained from the bear hug both craved. Instead they grabbed hands and held on for more than a two or three count. Then Big Sam said, "Captain Mac, I'm about ready to go back to the engineers. Been back here in Washington for a whole year and can't find a job. Been doing odd jobs, and I make a little money shooting pool. Matter of fact, I'm on my way up to Frank Holiday's Pool Hall up by the Howard Theater right now. Want to see if I can find me someone that hasn't seen me shoot. But luckily, I've got money from the Army. You know I never spent anything, so I saved up a little nest egg."

Through Roger MacDowell, Big Sam got a job as one of the few colored ice truck drivers in DC at that time. He picked up his truck each morning at the Terminal Refrigerating and Warehousing Company at Fourth and D Street SW and quickly learned his route from there over to Uline Arena at Third and L Streets NE for his first load of the day. At each stop on his back-and-forth route, he used the skills he'd honed with the 95th Regiment to establish friendly relations with customers, whether white or black.

While he'd been unemployed in the first part of 1945, before Big Sam ran into Roger MacDowell, he'd done odd jobs fixing things around the neighborhood. One day he went for a bite for lunch near his home in Southwest DC to the restaurant of an old family friend, Bruce Wahl. On that occasion, Samuel Chance noticed a tall, slim-but-muscular young woman bringing three cases of beer from the back over to the bartender, Bundy Stokes. Bundy wasn't in a hurry. The daytime customers didn't drink much. Big Sam watched as he almost lovingly iced the bottles in preparation for the evening customers who'd plunk down thirty-five cents all night for the icy treats.

Twenty years old now, Marva Doucette took Big Sam's breath away. He couldn't take his eyes off her as she worked back and forth in the room. While watching, he took note of the brown brogan shoes she wore under the skirt of her starched blue uniform. When Samuel Chance finished his meal, he paid the waitress and waited by the side door for the lovely young lady to appear. As she went past, he stepped in front of her and she froze.

"Hello, young lady. What size shoes do you wear?"

Marva sputtered.

"What size? I'm thinking you're about a nine."

"I don't know, suh. Scuse me, I cain't be talking ta no customers."

"Sorry to bother you," said Big Sam.

A week later, Big Sam took lunch again at Bruce Wahl's. He had corralled Bruce, asked about Marva, and gotten the details that she was young and alone in the city but that she was very conscientious and smart.

Ophelia walked up while the two friends talked. "Don't bother Marva today, Big Sam. She's upset. A girl named June who lives with her up at Dixon's was taken away in the ambulance wagon yesterday. They say she has the TB."

Big Sam waited another week for his day off. That next time after his meal, he waited again for the young woman to come through the side door. He stepped in front of her, and her face showed alarm. From his side, he held out a bag emblazoned with the name: The Hecht Company. Marva hesitated.

"Please take it."

"What it is?"

"Just take it, please. We'll talk again the next time I come in."

Tentatively Marva reached out for the bag. Big Sam tipped his cap and said, "I hope you like them." Then he left.

Marva rushed back into the locker room and sat on the first chair she came to. In the bag, she found two boxes. In the first was a pair of black shoes with seven lace eyelets and thick, cushioned heels. The insole slanted up in about a ten- to fifteen-degree angle from front to back. The lower section had somewhat of a shine, but not a fine gloss like some of the shoes she'd seen on ladies who came to Bruce Wahl's for dinner or dancing at night. The upper section around the laces were soft and fuzzy, almost like fur. Hurriedly, she put the shoes back in the box. In the second box Marva found a very different pair of shoes. They were black and a light tan. She turned them over and over.

Then Ophelia came back in the locker room, took one look, and said, "Try them on. They're called saddle shoes."

For the first time, Marva noticed that Ophelia was wearing the same type of shoe as the pair in the first box. Now she saw how nice Ophelia's feet looked in them. Marva fumbled to take off her brogans. Ophelia sat by her and waited. Marva was now in her coarse gray work socks, one of two pairs she'd brought from South Carolina and rotated wearing every other day. She was holding the right saddle shoe, about to pull it on.

Ophelia said, "Wait." She went over to her own locker in the next row and then came back with a pair of socks. "The style is to wear bobby socks with saddle shoes. Pull these on first and then turn them down over the top of your shoes."

Marva had seen this style on a lot of ladies walking around the streets of Southwest and knew what Ophelia meant.

"What dat man name?" asked Marva as she stood and walked around in the shoes that seemed to fit her feet perfectly.

"That's Big Sam. He's a friend of mine and Bruce's. He's very nice, and he asked me to go with him to find you some nice shoes."

Marva finished lacing both shoes and then threw her brogans in the bottom of her locker. For the rest of the day, she broke in the saddle shoes, and by the time she got off around one thirty that next morning, Big Sam was waiting outside of the restaurant.

"I'd like to drive you home, Marva, if you'll let me."

"Thank you, sir. I don't know what ta say."

"Please say yes."

"Yes, suh."

"My name is Samuel Chance. I'd like you to call me Samuel."

"Okay, Samuel. Thank you fo da shoes."

They got into Samuel Chance's snazzy two-door black DeSoto automobile, with the tan stripe running back to front almost like an arrow, and the matching tan roof. Big Sam started up the car, worked the clutch, and pulled off.

After about a block, Marva said, "I live Dixon Court."

"I know where you live, Marva."

"But I need ta make a stop ta see my baby befo I go home."

Big Sam paused. This was a surprise he hadn't anticipated. Then he said, "Where?"

He drove Marva to the Stokes home and waited for about twenty minutes as Marva used her key and went in to see her boy, Levi Doucette. When she came back out, she demurred, "I don't know what you think a me, sir, but now I ready ta go home."

Big Sam drove to the opening by the Court, stopped and turned off the engine. "Will you sit a bit with me, Marva?"

"Yes."

Marva looked toward the court, and for the first time noticed a big white-domed building that showed itself behind the court, not very far away.

"What dat building over dere?" she asked.

"That's the Capitol of the United States of America. That's where all the senators and congressmen from all around the country come to make laws."

"Oh, dat sound important."

Then after a while she asked, "Do you think dey know about us over here. We so close."

Big Sam didn't answer right away. "I'm sorry to say, they probably don't, Marva. They probably don't. Or if they do, they don't care. But now, tell me a story about Marva Doucette."

Marva thought for a long time and Big Sam didn't interrupt her train of thought. Then, "Dere's two Marva Doucettes, Samuel. One a cotton-picking farm girl come from Gullah peoples what first live on Saint John Island and den live in Aiken County in South Carolina. She have a brother who took care of her from time she was 'bout ten year old when her ma died from da consumption fever. She miss her brother sometime and feel bad dat she just left him without no word a where she going. But dis Marva afraid a what her brother would say ta her or think a her if he ever seed her again. She also afraid a what her brother do if he find out dat one his men friends takes da liberties wid his lil sister. Homer got a terrible temper. Don't know if he woulda' whupped da man, or whupped me, or whupped da both us."

"And the other Marva Doucette?" prodded Big Sam.

"Da other Marva Doucette like a newborn baby." She laughed, hearing herself. "A baby with a baby."

She stole a glance over at Sam, and seeing no negative in his face, she continued. "Every day she see something she never see befo. Da whole world change fo her and she happy, maybe fo da first time in her lifes. Couldn't be dis without a lot a peoples dat I not even know a couple years ago—Mrs. Stokes and her husband, Ms. Wahl and her husband, dah peoples from Augusta, Georgia, dat brought me up here ta Washington in da first place, dah peoples at da Friendship Church dat takes me in. I be a blessed young lady, and I knows dat."

"That's lovely, Marva."

They sat in silence. Then finally Big Sam Chance spoke. "I'm in love with you. That's all I'll say for now. Good night."

The blushing Marva said good night and quickly exited the car. She walked briskly across the court and up the steps of the third door on the right. Big Sam pulled away after seeing her walk through the door of her alleyway dwelling.

Chapter 9

Reconnection

Samuel Chance had been left a small but well-maintained row house that his grandparents had owned in the 200 block of F Street SW. A little more than two months after that first drive back to Dixon's Court in Big Sam's DeSoto, Marva and Samuel were married at Friendship Baptist Church by the Reverend Benjamin Harrison. The Stokes were all in attendance. Susie and Medgar Gray drove up from Augusta, Georgia, to be there, and Susie was Marva's matron of honor. Many of the staff from Bruce Wahl's were there, and Big Sam, who was an only child, had his parents and many of his friends to support him. Also, Roger MacDowell from Big Sam's army days, who'd gotten him the job with the ice company, was there.

Marva moved out of the Court and into Big Sam's house on F Street. She was so happy with having two bedrooms, her own kitchen, her own bathroom, and all the other features of the small but well-kept little house. Bundy had made a small bed with railings for the toddler, and this was the first piece of furniture installed in the smaller of the two bedrooms.

After making love their first night together on F Street, Big Sam said, "I want to adopt Levi. How would you feel about that, my love?"

Marva's heart burst open. She sobbed and sobbed. Sam Chance was caught by surprise and recanted. "Oh, my sweet Marva, I'm sorry. I didn't mean to upset you."

He held her until she could speak.

"Samuel, you so good ta me. And now you say you want ta give my son a proper name and a real daddy. Das what I want fo him so bad. I love you. I love you. You don't know how much I love you."

In a swift motion, she rolled over and mounted him for a second round of lovemaking for the night. The first had been sweet and tender. This was fierce, and Sam Chance became the target of an animal lust that Marva didn't know was in her. They spent themselves completely and then slept until the morning, when the sound of little Levi playing in his new bed awakened them.

***

Marva also maintained connections with the girls that had become her friends. She often stopped by Dixon's to chat on her walk from Big Sam's house to work in the mornings. Marva reflected on the whirlwind in the world and in her life since the summer of 1942 when she had walked down that road in Aiken County and caught a ride with the Grays. There had been a war in Europe and the Pacific, Marva had gone from picking cotton to being a restaurant worker, and now at age twenty she was a mother and a wife.

Samuel Chance was always full of surprises. On the next weekend after they were married, he came home and announced that he had the week off. Marva was happy for him, but then thought of the workweek ahead of her.

"Guess what," said Sam.

"What?"

"You have the week off too."

"No I don't, Samuel."

"Yes, you do. I worked it out with Bruce. Told him that we needed a proper honeymoon."

After the surprise washed over her, she jumped into his arms. "What we gone do?" she asked.

"Tomorrow we're going on a road trip."

"I cain't go on no road trip. I got ta stay close ta Levi."

"I've already worked it out with Ms. Alma. She and Mr. Stokes are looking forward to you having some time away."

Marva thought. "Where?"

"It'll be a surprise. You pack up some things tonight, and we'll be ready at the crack of dawn."

In the morning, they set out in the DeSoto across the Highway Bridge across the Potomac River into Virginia. Marva was in high spirits and was so in love with this big man who had come into her life as she was transitioning from the young farm girl into a proper city woman.

The trip that Big Sam took Marva on meandered down Route 1, the long highway that ran 2,450 miles up and down the East Coast from Maine to Florida. They drove through Virginia and into North Carolina. Big Sam had brought a basket of all kinds of goodies and sandwiches, so they ate whenever they were hungry. He had three large thermos jugs. One had black coffee and the other two contained Kool-Aid; one was lemon flavored and the other orange. They stopped on the side of the road to picnic and to look at the farms and cold-but-beautiful landscapes. With no sense of direction or distance, Marva was enthralled and just enjoyed the ride.

They stopped late that night and pulled into a motel that had a sign for "Colored Rooms" on one end near Fayetteville. Big Sam had used Victor Green's *The Negro Motorist Green Book* to plot out his route. Mr. Victor Green had been a colored postman in Harlem back in the 1930s. When he realized the problems he and all blacks faced with discrimination while traveling from state to state, he began publishing his guide in 1937. He had tapped into a network of colored mail carriers across the country who knew better than anyone what restaurants, gas stations, state parks, beauty parlors, tourist homes, private homes, and other resources were safely open to colored travelers. Over the years, until it went out of business, the guide had grown from about fifteen pages in the 1937 inaugural issue to over ninety pages in the edition that Big Sam was using. So Sam knew this motel would be right where he found it. In the room that night they made love several times and slept in each other's arms until light came into the room.

On the road again for about an hour, they passed a sign: Welcome to South Carolina. Marva went on alert.

"Where we going, Samuel?" she asked rather sharply.

"Just some ways down the road, sweets," said Big Sam, aware that his secret might be about to be revealed. It had taken him at least a dozen calls back and forth with the Grays over the past week to locate and finally speak to Homer Doucette down in Aiken County.

Marva's brother had been a little testy at first when he had heard from this strange man, who told him a story about his sister living in Washington, DC, and now being Mrs. Marva Chance. But there was something about the way that Big Sam spoke in a heavy-but-kind voice that eventually relaxed Homer, speaking on a wall telephone at the same gas station where Marva had launched her journey back in 1942. Now he was excited that he would see his sister again.

Marva flashed. "You turn this car around, Samuel Chance! I cain't believe you tricking me and taking me back to Aiken County. Ain't nobody dere want ta see me."

"That's not true, sweets. Homer wants to see you. In fact, Homer can't wait to see you."

"You talked wid my brother. How? When? What you been up ta, Samuel?"

"Other than Levi, he's the only family you have, Marva, except that now you've got me. But a brother is blood. It's not right how it's been left between you two. It's time. Really, sweets, it's time."

Marva was quiet. Big Sam left her with her thoughts. Morning turned to afternoon as they rolled through Columbia, and soon Marva thought she recognized the landscape. When Big Sam turned onto the dusty road by a familiar gas station off Route 1, Marva sat up and screamed, "Oh Samuel, I really love you, man!"

Big Sam spotted what he was looking for: a fence ended and there was a cluster of about fifteen wooden shacks off the road. He turned in and found the one with the black Ford with Georgia license tags parked near. It was Medgar and Susie Gray's car. They were standing by the door of a little shack. Between them was Homer Doucette and a tall black woman. The woman was smiling, and Marva saw how beautiful she was.

Big Sam's car came to a stop and Marva threw open her door and tore out in a dead run. Homer let out a whoop and met his sister in a fierce embrace.

"Hey, baby sis. How you, baby sis? Welcome home, baby sis."

"Oh, Homer, I missted you."

"I miss you too, baby sis. You remember Jocelyn. And meet yo nephew and niece. Das Homer Junior riding his lil sister Candy on his back over dere by da fence."

Marva ran over to the children and they tentatively stopped their playing to politely say hi to this new aunt that they didn't know. When Big Sam joined her, they seemed to change their mood. He may have been the biggest man they'd ever seen. When he stooped down to eye level with Homer Jr., the boy smiled for the first time.

"You a giant."

"No, not really."

"You my uncle?"

"Yes, I guess I am."

The boy smiled and ran down the road. The little girl shyly sidled up to Sam and he engulfed her with his big hands. Marva took leave and went back over to her brother, as Homer Jr. came back with two friends to see the new big uncle that had arrived from somewhere up north.

Jocelyn and the Grays were walking together talking. Jocelyn was pointing to this and to that in an impromptu tour of the little community. In a quiet voice, Marva said, "Come sit over on de log."

Homer smiled. "Das da log we use fo serious talking. We gonna have a serious talk?"

"You gone see," said Marva, taking her brother by the hand. Once they were side by side on one of the big logs that had been positioned around a community fire pit, Marva turned to Homer. "I also have a son, Homer. He not my husband's boy, but Big Sam gonna adopt he. He name Levi, an he last name gone be Chance once all da papers go through."

Homer's face constricted. "Who yo baby father?"

Marva couldn't answer right away. Tears welled in her eyes. Then Homer knew.

"Was dat Zachary Deal. Das right! Was he, wasn't it, sister? Dat drunk bastard raped you, didn't he? Full of dat white lightning he did dat ta you, didn't he? Damn, girl, why didn't you tell me? Why you just leave without telling me?"

"I sorry, Homer. I so sorry. I just decided dat it best fo me ta go. I didn't want you ta do something and maybe git kill. And I didn't want you ta kill nobody. I just needed ta leave and go find my own life away from here and away from he. I needed ta, Homer. Can you understand dat?"

Their eyes met. Both were full of tears. They embraced.

"Sho, Marva. I understand."

Then after a moment, Homer had a thought that sent him into uproarious laughter. It caught Marva by surprise.

"What? What, Homer? What funny?"

"You wanna know what happen ta Zachary Deal?"

Marva's eyes flashed. "Something happen ta he? I don't care. I don't care what happen ta he. I never want ta see he again."

"Oh, you won't. He dead. Deh found he stinky body out in da cotton fields one morning. He had stuck heself through da neck wid a knife."

Marva was surprised. She waited.

"Wanna know da funny part?"

"What?"

"Da neck wound what killed he. But dat wasn't da only wound. Dey ran and get Mr. Standpoint ta come out a da big house. When he came, dey show he Zachary's pants dat were full a blood. Mr. Standpoint had dem pull off da pants. Zachary private parts been cut off. Mr. Standpoint try fo few weeks ta find out what really happened, but den he loss interest.

"Finally one night, Jocelyn told me dat Zachary had been raping a young girl down da road. But one night he came fo her and dere were six women from da camp waiting. Jocelyn was one a dem. When he walk in she cabin, da six of dem come out and pull he down on da floor. Dey held he down while da lil girl cut. Den dey pull up he pants and carry he out ta da field where dey left he with a knife in he hand. Befo dey left, dey stuff some a he private parts in he mouth. After dey left, he spit dose out and done de rest. Look like at first he tried ta stab heself in da chest. But everybody figure dat he was too weak ta put da knife through he chest, so he just took da easy way ta stab heself in da throat."

Marva sat for a long while in silence. Then finally she said, "Here come Jocelyn wid Medgar and Susie. Let's go see what Sam and yo kids doing. We going ta have ta get back on da road fo dark."

"But we want you ta stay fo a while. We got catching up ta do."

"Maybe next time, Homer. I need ta go home. I need ta go home. I love you. I need ta go home."

Chapter 10
The Sweetness Ends

Back in DC, the adoption process concluded, and Levi's name change from Levi Doucette to Levi Doucette Chance was completed. Big Sam was elated. They established a routine. He drove the route in his ice truck through DC and nearby Maryland. Marva played with Levi in the mornings. Sometimes at the Stokes house and sometimes wandering the streets of Southwest DC. If she wanted to go by Dixon's Court, she dropped Levi at the Stokes's neighbor's house. Everybody in the neighborhood, including little Levi, loved Ms. Fanny Barkesdale, who was always at home.

Marva never forgot to go and see the girls she already knew at the Court, and to meet new ones that had moved in. Big Sam taught Marva to drive the DeSoto. An early riser, she did all of these roamings in the early morning so that she could arrive at Bruce Wahl's by ten to help set up before the doors opened for the lunch crowd.

Some weekdays she would catch the vendor that everyone called Catman pushing his produce cart down Fourth Street early in the morning. She would buy potatoes, onions, turnips, and collard greens, only to have to rush back home to deposit them before turning around and going to work. Between watching the cooks at Bruce Wahl's and little teaching sessions with Alma Stokes, Marva was learning to be a fine cook. It was Big Sam who asked Alma to teach Marva how to clean and cook chitterlings. As time went on, she became famous for them.

Marva became a frequent customer of many of the businesses to the east of Fourth Street, like Johnson's Pharmacy in the 600 block of Third Street SW. On Fourth Street, she hesitated one morning at the doorstep of Atkin Grocery, still wary of white people. But one of the Jewish clerks came to the door and opened it.

With a heavy accent, he said, "Hello. You're that little girl that Big Sam Chance married, aren't you?"

"Yes, sir."

"Well, what are you waiting for? Come on in. What are you shopping for this morning?"

"I need some ground beef and some spices, sir."

"Well you just look on that shelf over there and I bet you'll find all the spices you want. Then meet me over at that counter and I'll grind you up some fresh meat."

On certain weekends when Bruce Wahl's could spare Marva, she and Big Sam would socialize at events held at Randall Junior High School, go to movies at the Jewell Theater, or enjoy cabarets sponsored by the Willow Tree Social Club. They usually stayed away from Bruce Wahl's on Marva's days off.

Marva also soon received her official driver's license. Her first real distance drive was down to a party at the cottage of one of the Howard University professors whose laboratory was on Big Sam's ice route. The cottage was at Highland Beach in Anne Arundel County, Maryland, on the Chesapeake Bay. Highland Beach had been founded back in the 1890s by the brother of Frederick Douglass as a place where Negroes could go, since they weren't welcome at many other Chesapeake Bay sites. Big Sam gave Marva history lessons as they crossed the streets of the town, many of them named for famous Negroes, like Dunbar Street, Langston Street, and Henson Street.

Marva was starting to really become a big movie fan. One day Big Sam and Marva were driving north on Seventh Street on the way to the Hecht Company Department Store. As they crossed F Street SW, Marva spotted the Ashley Movie House.

"Ooh, Samuel, it's another movies," she shrilled with a giggle.

"No, baby. That one's not for us. We'll just stick with the Jewell."

As they crossed Pennsylvania Avenue, Sam chinned his head down to the left. "There's an area down there called Murder Bay. Has anybody told you about that?"

"Naw."

"There's prostitute houses and dance halls and criminals of all kinds down there. I know you like to walk. I'd just say that you might not want to be walking around over there. They don't want us on their sidewalks. It's dangerous for men and even more dangerous for women, unless they're in the life."

Marva couldn't help but be a little curious. She thought of one of the women at Dixon's Court who'd been described as a dance hall girl. But she said, "Okay, Sam."

Further up Seventh Street into Northwest DC, Marva for the first time saw the elegant Garfinkel's Department Store. This store had originally been in the area of Massachusetts Avenue and Forty-Ninth Street, but had relocated to a newer and bigger building downtown.

"Let's stop at dis one, Samuel," she demurred.

"I'm sorry, but you're really striking out today, my love. That one's not for us either. But anything they have, we'll find even better up at Hecht's. They wouldn't let us eat in their cafeteria, but they sure don't mind us spending our dollars to buy their clothes."

Sometimes, if he had the day off and she didn't, Big Sam held a barstool at Bruce Wahl's just to relax and be near his wife when she was working.

As Levi grew, he and his dad became virtually inseparable. By happenstance, at the age of four, Big Sam and Levi were visiting Marva at Bruce Wahl's where Marva was now a full-blown waitress making $8.00 a week. It was daytime, but the piano player was in early because he had to meet a piano tuner that was due to come in. Joshua Thomas Ogilvie tickled the keys of the out-of-tune instrument and Levi was captivated. He pulled away from his dad and rushed over to join JT on the stool in front of a worn Hobart M. Cable upright piano that sat on a short platform under the sign that read Bruce Wahl's Showboat, and the rest was history. Within a year, the little prodigy with the perfect pitch could play almost anything by ear. On his own time, JT Ogilvie continued to meet Levi for lessons during the day whenever he could for years after that.

***

In February of 1951, Big Sam Chance was turning off Kenilworth Avenue late at night on his way to drop off his truck at the Terminal Refrigerating and Warehousing Company. Marva was waiting in the DeSoto to pick him up and take him home, although he had no problem walking late at night. She'd just wanted to surprise him.

But the night grew long and no Big Sam appeared. Finally, a police car with flashing lights pulled up behind the car. Two white police officers got out and walked toward Marva, and she convulsed in terror. Her mind raced with thoughts of disaster, and her worst fears were realized.

"Evening, miss. Would you roll down your window, please?"

The politeness only added to Marva's fears.

"We went to your house and your neighbor told us we could probably find you here."

"Please, sir. Tell me what you want wid me."

"We need you to drive back home so you can park your car. Then we're going to take you over to Freedman's Hospital. There's been an accident."

By the time Marva arrived in the emergency room, Big Sam had already been pronounced dead. A drunk driver had plowed into him with enough speed and force to push his truck over an embankment. A shard of broken metal gashed his chest open. It took five men to pull Big Sam out of the truck, and he was rushed by these onlookers to the hospital. There the doctors worked hard to stabilize him, but eventually he succumbed.

The idyllic, almost charmed life that had started with her leaving that Aiken County, South Carolina, farm back in 1942 came crashing down around Marva Chance. She grieved deeply at the loss of Big Sam, but because he had properly executed a will, she and little Levi were able to keep his DeSoto and continue to live on F Street until 1957. Urban Development came to Southwest around 1955 or 1956.

For seven-year-old Levi Chance, the winter of 1951 saw a wound open in his soul that he would carry with him for the rest of his life. Thanks to the resilience of youth, he eventually renewed his piano lessons with jamming JT Ogilvie. At school, he found most subjects easy. He made a few friends with the local kids in Southwest, and because of his tall athletic frame and good looks, he attracted young girls everywhere he went. But although he developed a façade of bravado that most people believed and admired, years later incidents would trigger the wound he kept buried inside.

Chapter 11
Urban Renewal

1955

Ten-year-old Levi came home one evening to the little house on F Street Southwest in the District of Columbia. First he had stopped at Henry's Market on the corner for some red licorice, so it was a little after 6 p.m., and although school at Anthony Bowen Elementary School had let out at 3 p.m. as usual, he'd been in a hurry to walk a few blocks. That afternoon, the big kids were playing ball on the Randall Junior High field. Real hardball, too, not that slow-pitch softball that some older teams played that didn't look anything like the games on grandad's black-and-white television at home. Those softball games weren't cool.

But today the big boys were playing baseball in real uniforms, right on the Randall field. The big lanky pitcher for the team in the red-and-gray uniforms had a loopy windup and a big leg kick, and the blue-and-white uniformed team had made only three hits and one run in seven innings. That pitcher could hit too. He and the center fielder and the catcher for the red and grays had all hit homers with men on base.

That had been fun to watch. Even more fun were the girls from Anthony Bowen in the bleachers who had started pestering him to sing something when the game started to get out of hand. He'd said no, and then he'd said he'd sing something after the game was over if they wanted to stick around. He knew they would, and he'd crooned to them about six or eight numbers, with various classmates singing backup. They really weren't important to the girls. They didn't care who was singing backup, as long as Levi Chance was showing off that beautiful boy tenor.

Usually after a performance like this, at least three or four girls would want Levi to walk them home. Some lived in nice, neat houses like Levi's, and others lived in little shanties that didn't even face a street. They faced out onto alleys. Levi was learning the art of French kissing and was developing early signs of becoming a ladies' man. He loved to watch sports, but although very tall for his age, he wasn't good at any. But he didn't need to be. The good Lord had blessed him with pipes, and those rare pipes could get Levi Chance almost anything he wanted. The fact that he was smart—straight A's and B's in school—was just an added blessing. He never worried about a thing.

Except tonight, he knew his mom wouldn't be happy. She always had dinner ready by 5 p.m. and hated to have to keep it warm for anybody. If granddaddy, who'd moved in with them after his father died, was late, she couldn't say much. But if Levi was late, she would pitch a fit. He turned the knob on the door that was always unlocked and opened it slowly to minimize the creaking. As he stepped in lightly with the sack that served as a book bag over his shoulder, Levi expected the screaming to start any second. Still nothing. Around the corner, made by bookshelves positioned so one could see to the back of the house from the front door, was the rustic dining room table. The lamp was on, and Levi thought there was stirring, but no talking—unusual. What was going on?

Levi rounded the bookcase and stopped short. Mamma was sitting there in tears. The next-door neighbor, Ms. Fanny Barksdale, was patting mamma on the back, but was also in tears, and mamma was patting her back. Granddaddy Samuel was at the head of the table, piled high with a plate of mamma's meat loaf, mashed potatoes, gravy, green beans, rolls, and butter. Empty plates were at all the settings, but nobody had touched the food. The normal food aroma wasn't even as strong as usual, signaling to Levi that it had been sitting for a while and was cold.

Samuel Chance Sr. looked at Levi and said only three words, "Sit down, boy."

Levi dropped his bag and took his customary seat. Now he was hungry. "Don't you want me to wash my hands?"

Marva looked at him and opened her mouth to speak, but instead came more tears. Levi looked at the three grown-ups. He looked at his granddaddy, who looked especially displeased.

This was a new way to deal with me coming home late, thought Levi.

He really hadn't been that worried coming home. Levi always could charm his way out of trouble. But tonight was different. Tonight was scary. Something was really wrong. Levi didn't speak a word.

After what seemed like ten minutes of silence and wailing, Samuel Sr. said to Marva, "Hand your boy that paper, daughter. He might as well read it for himself."

Levi took the papers and flipped to the front. He started reading:

In the United States District Court for the District of Columbia

District Court Docket No. 101-22

United States of America, Plaintiff, v. 177 Parcels of Land in the District of Columbia, John W. Green et al., and unknown others, defendants.

Filed June 30, 1955

John Brock

Clerk

To:

Barbara Adams, Tenant, Farr Building

Johnston Adams, Tenant, 187 M Street SW

Clarice Adams, Tenant, 187 M Street SW

Thomas Acheson, 912 E Street SW

Carlton Banks, 100 Eye Street SW

Eugertha Banks, 100 Eye Street SW

Armstead Barksdale, 283 F Street SW

Fannie Barksdale, 283 F Street SW

And the names continued through the B's, then the C's, where Levi's eyes came to:

Marva D. Chance, 281 F Street SW

Samuel Chance Sr., 1377 Half Street SW

Levi's eyes lingered and lingered. Then he read on through the rest of the C's, D's, E's, and F's to the G's, where it picked up with:

Ronald Gabney, Trustee, 2014 3rd Street SW

Addie Gilliam, 709 F Street SW

B. B. Gold, unknown heirs, alienees and divisions of 900 7th Street SW

John W. Green, 1111 Delaware Avenue SW

Kate Green, 1111 Delaware Avenue SW

Margaret Gullatee, 209 2nd Street SW

and further on down the alphabet through the H's, and the M's, and the S's, where Levi spotted:

Bundy Stokes, 49 Eye Street SW

Alma Stokes, 49 Eye Street SW

. . . through the rest of the S's and T's, where it picked up again with:

Alice Vetmer, Tenant, 660 L Street SW

Dorothy Womble, 1244 P Street SW

Brett B. Yastremsky, Major General, US Army National War College

Until a total of 717 names and addresses had been listed. Then the document went on:

You are hereby notified that a complaint in the combination has hereby been filed in the office of the clerk of the above named Court in an action to condemn an estate in fee simple in the property described in Schedule A attached hereto and made a part hereof for public use for the provision of decent, safe and sanitary dwellings for families of low income in the District of Columbia, pursuant to the Act of June 12, 1934, as amended, and the US Housing Act of 1937, as amended.

The authority for the taking is the Act of March 1, 1929, as amended, c. 416, 45 Stat. 1415 et seq. (U. S. Code Title 40 Sec. 361 to 384); the Act of June 12, 1934, c 465, 48 Stat. 930 as amended by the Act of June 25, 1938, c. 691, 52 Stat. 1186 (D.C. Code Title 5 Sec. 103 to 116); and the U. S. Housing Act of 1937, approved September 1, 1937, as amended, c. 896, 50 Stat. 888 (U. S. Code Title 42 Sec. 1501 et seq.).

You are notified that if you have any objection or defense to the taking of your property you are required to serve upon plaintiff's attorney at the address herein designated within twenty days after personal service of this notice upon you, an answer identifying the property in which you claim to have an interest, stating all of your objections and defenses to the taking of your property. A failure to serve and answer shall constitute a consent to the taking and to the authority of the Court to proceed to hear the action and to fix the just compensation and shall constitute a waiver of all defenses and objections not so presented.

You are further notified that at the trial of the issue of just compensation, whether or not you have answered or served a notice of appearance, you may present evidence as to the amount of the compensation to be paid for the property in which you have any interest and you may share in the distribution of the award of compensation.

You are lastly notified that the plaintiff has filed a notice of demand for a jury trial on the issue of just compensation. You are further notified that at the trial of the issue of just compensation, whether or not you have answered or served a notice of appearance, you may present evidence as to the amount of the compensation to be paid for the property in which you have any interest and you may share in the distribution of the award of compensation.

Signed Chauncey P. Teller, Attorney

Lands Division, Room 2545

Department of Justice

Washington DC

Samuel Chance Sr. and Fannie Barksdale had watched in silence as Levi read through the document. Marva Chance's head was on the dining room table and her wet eyes were closed.

Samuel asked, when his grandson looked up, "Did you understand all that, boy?"

"Yes, sir. I mean, no, sir! I mean, I guess so, sir."

"What did you read, boy?"

"The government is going to buy all these people's houses. But I didn't know we wanted to sell this house, Granddaddy."

Marva looked up. "We don't, Levi. None a us do. Da government robbing us. Das all. Dey making robbery legal."

This brought on a new wave of tears, and Fannie Barksdale stood and moved behind Marva, where she encircled her with her arms in a tight embrace.

"God's going to make a way, Marva. He's going to make a way," said Fannie over and over.

"I told you mine came yesterday. Me and Armstead went over to Friendship, and Reverend Harrison prayed with us. He kept saying God's going to make a way."

Samuel Chance Sr. said to Levi, "We've suspected something like this since a letter came for the public housing folks earlier this year, son."

Marva's throat caught. She gasped, then said, "What you mean? I haven't know 'bout da thing."

"Yes, you have, daughter. We even talked about it and expressed our surprise and outrage, same way we feel it now."

"No, Sam! No! I don't know nothing 'bout dis."

"Daughter, I love you like you were my actual blood. I wouldn't lie to you. Back in February, there was a letter sent to some people across M Street. I got a copy from somebody, and we sat right here at this table and read it over together. It said basically the same as this one. When was this date?"

Samuel looked through the documents. "Here it is. February twenty-first, so it was about four months ago when they notified some people we know. I'll have to tell you about the research that I did after I saw that February letter."

Marva screamed, "I don't want ta know 'bout no damn research!"

"I gotta tell you, and I gotta tell this boy what I know."

Marva got up and walked out the front door. She didn't come back from her walk for about forty minutes. When she was out of the room, Sam Sr. asked, "Do you feel like you want to know more about this, boy?"

Levi nodded but didn't speak. Sam Sr. went in the kitchen and opened a drawer, where he found some notes he'd made.

"Well, according to what I dug up back when it was cold this winter, this all started with some white lady named Smith, Cloethiel Smith. Let me think a minute, there was a man too, his name was even stranger . . . I'll find it. Both of them were architects. These two wanted to show everybody how they could make a neighborhood better in the drop of a hat. They weren't interested in nothing that would take a long time. They wanted wham, bam, thank you, ma'am.

"And they found us. Not us, the Stokeses and us—the Chances, in particular. The us's that they found were just stuff that was south of the nation's Capitol Building. So they started talking to the congressmen in the Capitol Building, only to find they'd been talking about doing something about Southwest for ten years or more.

"The folks in the Capitol told them that to the southeast they could see coal smoke pouring out the plant over on New Jersey Avenue. And there were congressmen who would walk out onto the west terrace of the Capitol and, to the southwest, they would see Dixon Court and other alleys where people were living. They'd see railroad yards and tracks running every which way. And beyond that they could just see crowded streets with a lot of colored people and mostly small buildings, before, way over in the distance, they could see the water.

"Mind you, there was always white people down there too, but the ones closest to them were mostly colored folks. They could practically spit over into Dixon Court where you and your mom go to help those ladies she used to live with.

"Those senators didn't like looking at that stuff. Now mind you, they had built temporary buildings all over to the west of them for all the government workers and military workers that kept coming, and coming, and coming to this city, all the way back from the First World War. They called them tempos, but they might as well call them permanent, because they weren't going anywhere for years.

"So these two architects—Justement, here's the other name. Justement was the guy's name that teamed up with Smith, saw an opportunity right here in our town to try out something invented by some French guy. I think they called it unified structure. Basically, it replaces little bitty houses with great big self-contained buildings for the same amount of people or even more. They had a solution, and all they'd needed to find was a place that needed it. We were it."

"But why come after us, Grandpa Sam? We weren't causing no problems."

"If you got a lot of power, son, you decide what's a problem. We ain't got no mayor here in the District of Columbia. Congress runs this city, at least the official part of this city. We were a problem to their eyeballs."

Levi dropped his head and whispered, "Crackers." He wasn't allowed to curse or say certain derogatory words in front of Sam Sr.

Continuing with his lecture, Levi's grandfather said, "So Congress has gotten the city flunkies called the National Capital Park and Planning Commission to target us for an experiment where these two architects can try out their unified structure ideas. The district commissioners don't have no power, so they can't do nothing. But still, first they've got to move all us out. This letter is the first step. That's what this is all about. I was hoping that somebody like A. Phillip Randolph would get interested and help us to stop having our homes taken from us. But I know he's a busy man, so that was wishful thinking."

Levi wasn't hungry anymore. "Can I go upstairs to my room?"

"Okay, boy, you go on upstairs. Nothing you can do down here. Nothing anybody can do. You go on upstairs. Do your homework, you hear me?"

"Yes, sir."

Chapter 12

Giant

1957—Just After Memorial Day

Samuel Chance Sr. had been busy for weeks. The houses at 281 F Street SW, 49 Eye Street SW, and 1377 Half Street SW were piled with packed boxes full of dishes, clothing, bric-a-brac, tools, papers and books, pictures, and various other small items. Except for the beds that the family used on Eye Street, a few chairs, and the dining room table, all the other furniture was wrapped and taped up.

Because of the white flight of the late 1950s, the previously all-white section of Southeast DC known as Anacostia was full of "For Sale" signs. Samuel Sr. had already received his urban renewal check as compensation for the taking of his home on Half Street SW. Actually, since the death of his son, Samuel had lived with his daughter-in-law and his grandson Levi on F Street. But Samuel had used his Half Street funds and some savings to purchase a small home on Maple View Place SE. Whenever he could find some strong young backs to help him, he loaded up furniture and boxes from both Southwest homes and moved them over to Anacostia.

Marva had been sickly lately and had stopped working at Bruce Wahl's Restaurant and Beer Garden. Now thirteen-year-old Levi had been spending a lot of time at Alma and Bundy Stokes's house, because neither Samuel Sr. nor Marva had the energy to supervise him. After dark one Friday evening, just after Memorial Day, Levi ran into the Stokes's house on Eye Street SW with a tale.

"Uncle Bundy, you should have seen it. You should have seen it. He was the biggest man in the world, right over at Randall."

Lighting his pipe, Bundy said, "Slow down, young man. Who's the biggest man in the world?"

"They were calling him Wilt, Uncle Bundy."

Bundy slapped his knee as he interrupted, "Goodness, I forgot all about it. Meant to go over there myself to see our boy Elgin whoop up on Wilt the Stilt."

"What's this all about?" interrupted Alma Stokes.

"It was boss, Aunt Alma. There must have been a thousand people all around the playground after school. All these players that we've never seen before were there. But the big boys and men were talking about the battles between DC players and guys from Philadelphia and New York. Then this long red-and-white Oldsmobile pulled up, and this giant got out of the car. He was the biggest man I'd ever seen. Everybody started yelling, 'Wilt, Wilt. Wilt's here. It's on now.'"

Levi ran into the kitchen, grabbed a glass, and filled it with tap water, which he guzzled down quickly.

"I snuck through the crowd and sat on the ground right on the side of the court. Seems like everybody had been waiting for him, because no games had started up. Guys were just on the court shooting around, but when Wilt came on the court, things got serious. Four other big guys—not as big as him, but still big—they came from the sides and stood behind the giant. The guy they were calling Wilt was eyeballing this other big guy—not as big as him, but still big. And then the other guy pointed in the crowd and four guys came out and stood behind him. And then they started playing whole court."

"That must have been Elgin Baylor," said Samuel Sr.

"It's been all the talk of the town. Wilt Chamberlain has been in town for a couple of weeks. They've been playing pickup games at a lot of playgrounds from Banneker, to Kelly Miller, to Turkey Thicket, and tonight they were coming to Randall."

Alma asked, "Oh, Elgin's that Spingarn High School boy, isn't he, Bundy?"

"That's him. They say he's the smoothest kid on the court that's ever been. So apparently, some guys up in Philly were teasing Wilt

Chamberlain that there was a kid in DC that could take him out. Wilt had to come down and see what they were talking about."

Now turning back to Levi, Bundy asked, "So, what happened, boy? Who won the game?"

"Uncle Bundy, the giant was dunking the ball through the hoop without hardly even jumping. But it wasn't even close. That other big guy, I guess that was Elgin, he was even better. He was shooting jump shots from way, way out. Then somebody on the giant's team would run out at him, and he'd drive around them. Sometimes he'd go all the way to the basket. He even jammed the ball backwards a couple of times. And when he'd jump up, it looked like he would just hang in the air as long as he wanted until the other guy was out of the way.

"Other times he'd hit this other guy named Willie Jones. We'd seen him at Randall a lot of times before. Willie was cussing the giant all game and hitting jump shots. He'd take the pass from Elgin and swish it through. Then he started talking trash to Elgin, his own teammate. That's when Elgin started taking Willie's shots out of the air and dunking them before they went in."

"No, he didn't!" screamed Alma.

"Yes, he did, Aunt Alma. That was really funny."

Bundy asked, "What did Willie do then?"

"He started cussing Elgin just as much as he was cussing Wilt. But at the end, Elgin's team hit thirty before Wilt's got to twenty."

"Hot damn," yelled Bundy. "See? These New York and Philly guys think they have the only good playground players. Hot damn."

"So, this other guy had next. He picked Wilt to stay on the court with some other new guys. And Uncle Bundy, the Elgin team won again. After it happened a third time, I came home 'cause I was getting hungry and it was getting dark. But it was the funnest—"

Alma interrupted, "The most fun."

"It was the most fun time after school all year. I bet they're still playing up there now."

"Well that's wonderful, but now I want you to wash up so I can feed you. Then I'll walk you over to your mom's house. You know she's been feeling poorly, but she called about you just before you came in."

"Don't you want to go back up there with me after we eat, Uncle Bundy?"

Alma gave her husband a stare.

"I don't think so, son, but gimme five," said Bundy. They slapped hands as Levi ran up the stairs to wash.

Chapter 13
The Plaza

October 1959

At Harrison Technical High School, near the Eckington Yards in Northeast DC, all the Michigan Park kids—Benjamin Parks, Arthur Bostic, Clyde Simms, Tracy Brown, Deanna Nance, Lou Bonefant, and Janice Westbrook—were barely one month into life as high school students. Davita Sheridan was there too. She and Ben Parks had been practically inseparable in junior high school, but after that afternoon on Davita's couch, when both had lost their cherries during the first week at Tech, Davita had stood off from Ben for the most part. It had hurt Ben deeply. Davita was truly his first love. He may have been hers also, and certainly she cared about him deeply. But being a serious student, Davita had set boundaries with the immature Ben Parks, and he had finally had to live with the distance.

On the fringes of the MP crew, a tall, wiry tenth grader was standing. He was shifting his feet back and forth in a rhythmic sway and seemed to be humming something. Ben had joined the choir the second day of school, and during their first practice, the teacher, Mrs. Grayson, had complimented him on his smooth tenor voice. Ben had seen this kid recently walking in the MP neighborhood, but was sure that he hadn't grown up there. *He must be new*, thought Ben as he approached.

"Hey."

The boy said, "Yeah, I seen you eyeballing. Can't quite figure me out, huh? Well, I'm Levi, and I'm the baddest singer you ever met."

Ben was taken aback, partly because of the brashness and boastfulness, and partly because Ben had always considered himself one of the "baddest" singers.

"Well, I'm Ben, and if you so bad, hit this."

Ben took a breath and opened up with his best Little Anthony impression. He kept the volume down, so as not to be noticed too far away.

The boy nodded rhythmically until Ben finished, and afterward gave him a little pat on the shoulder.

"Not bad. Not bad at all. But in that 'she wants to be free' part, you ought to try to . . ."

Levi barely seemed to breathe and then let loose in a voice that seemed it couldn't have come from someone so young. For fifty feet around them, everyone turned. Levi completed the verse and Ben's mouth was open.

"Don't worry, you ain't bad. Come on and hit this chorus with me."

Levi got out the first phrase before Ben figured out the second tenor. Then he joined in and they heard someone a few feet away say, "That's bad." A couple of girls that Ben didn't recognize walked up with Davita in between and they whispered as Levi and Ben continued. But they needed something. Right on cue, Clyde Simms stepped through the growing audience.

"Let me hit this with y'all," said Clyde in his deep bass voice. Clyde easily slid into a tight baritone part.

Now the trio was swinging the tune and popping their fingers, but with Levi on lead and the other two holding background, the new kid realized he could cut loose with some extra riffs. Ben knew he'd never heard a voice like this. When they finished, Ben and Clyde waited for Levi to still take the lead. He looked at them and knew what they wanted, so he started again. This time the tune was the Silhouettes "Get a Job." Levi sang the lead and Clyde grinned widely. He was showing off, because on this one he really got a chance to demonstrate his mellow bass. This time an upper classman, Emanuel Freeze, also from MP, slipped in just above Ben's second with a close first tenor harmony.

The plaza was a party for the next fifteen minutes as the impromptu group ranged from one doo-wop song to the next. When the whistles blew, signaling the end of the lunch period, Ben walked with Levi. "You ought to come on join the choir, man. That teacher, Mrs. Grayson, is fine as she wants to be."

"Naw, man. I got my eye on the marching band. I play the slide trombone," he said, emphasizing the slide part with his hand and body gestures. "No, really, I'm about those eighty-eights, but I haven't been able to figure out how to carry one marching in a parade, so I'll slide."

Ben looked totally lost.

Levi laughed. "Come on, pick it up, son. The piano, man. The eighty-eights. The piano."

Ben's expression slowly changed from confusion to embarrassment. Then he started to get tickled and morphed into goofy laughter. Levi continued laughing. When Ben looked up, he spotted Davita at the school door, about to go in. She had turned at the door and was smiling at them. Then she disappeared.

With instant rapport, Ben and Levi slapped hands down low. They went their separate ways to afternoon classes, but after school they met up again. Together they rode the trolley back across Rhode Island Avenue and got off at South Dakota Avenue. From there they walked down toward Michigan Park. As they passed Monroe Street, Ben thought of Davita's house briefly, but Levi was waxing on about his musical prowess and this brought Ben back into the present. They sang as they walked: The Del-Vikings' "Come Go with Me," The Crests' "Sixteen Candles," and finally Levi broke out with Frankie Lymon's "Why Do Fools Fall in Love."

As they turned off South Dakota Avenue onto Randolph, Ben pointed to a house. "You know Emmanuel, that eleventh grader who was singing with us?"

"What's up?"

"That's his house right there."

"That's a bet. I live right up in the next block."

They got to Levi's house on Randolph Street and stopped and stood in front as Levi told Ben about Marvin Gay from back in his old neighborhood of Southwest Washington.

"He used to love to hear me sing that song," said Levi, referring to his impression of Frankie Lymon, once back at First and Q Streets SW under a lamp post. "You ever hear of the Marquees?"

"No."

"That was my man Marvin, this dude Reese Palmer, and some other cats. But now he's out in Chicago. He still calls me sometimes. Says when I get out of high school he wants me to come with him and be his piano player. Marvin plays a little himself, but he ain't got my touch. You heard that new jam "Twelve Months of the Year?"

"Of course," said Ben as he tried to start it up, "Twelve months—"

"Yeah, yeah, yeah," cut in Levi. "That's Marvin singing with Harvey and the Moonglows. Harvey Fuqua let Marvin do that talking part at the beginning. Next time you hear it, you'll see."

"Who's this young man?" interrupted Alma Stokes as she came out of the house and walked down the walkway toward the boys.

"Aunt Alma, this is my best friend, Ben," announced Levi. Ben looked at Levi with a surprised—no, a shocked expression.

"Well, if he's your best friend, how come I've never met him?" asked Alma.

"I'm Benjamin Parks, ma'am," said Ben with his hand outstretched. Alma Stokes took it in both hands warmly.

"Pleased to meet you, young man. You live in the neighborhood?"

"Yes, ma'am, just a couple more blocks that way," said Ben pointing further up Nineteenth Street.

"Well, I'm glad Levi has met someone in the neighborhood. We just moved in here this summer and we don't really know anyone. We'll have to have you and your family over for dinner sometime, but now Levi has to come in and eat. He's got to practice and do his homework every night after school."

Levi looked at Ben and shrugged, turned his back, and walked into the house without a goodbye.

Ben walked the rest of the way home with all kinds of questions about his new neighbor and, apparently, his new best friend. Where had he come from? Was he living with an aunt? Where were his parents? All kinds of questions. Then quickly he thought of his geography homework and ran the rest of the way home.

Back in the neighborhood that weekend, Ben found the little house on Randolph Street. He invited Levi to walk over to the playground with him and they got to talking.

"Tell me where you're from again."

"I told you, I'm from Southwest. I went to Randall. Me and my people just moved in over here in June. I been walking the neighborhood for a couple of months but really haven't met nobody. Been kind of angry."

"Why? You don't like the neighborhood?"

"It's all right, but it's not home. I'm from Southwest."

"You keep saying that. What are you talking about? You from Arizona or New Mexico or somewhere?"

"No, man, I'm from Southwest DC. You know, where the fish market is at. Where Bruce Wahl's, and Friendship Baptist, and Greenleaf, and the boat to Marshall Hall, and—"

"Hold up, sport. I don't know anything about any of that. Slow down. And if that's where you're from and it's all that, why're you here?"

"We got put out."

"Oh, y'all couldn't keep it up. That's not cool."

"Naw, man, it didn't have nothing to do with that. The government put us out. They put all of us out. All my friends. My family. We're spread out all over now. Most of my friends are out at East Capital Dwellings over Sixtieth and East Capital. They call it urban renewal. One day, if you come over my place, I'll show you the papers."

Ben had no idea what he was talking about. That evening he asked Richard Parks about Southwest. Ben's dad relayed the story of urban renewal with the insight of a historian.

Chapter 14

Dinner

Two weekends later, Alma and Bundy Stokes invited Richard and Gillian Parks to their home to break bread. Ben's parents were pleased to meet Levi, who'd called at the house several times, and Gillian had asked Ben about who this new boy was. Richard, Gillian, Ben, and Penelope (Penny) walked over from their house and were greeted at the door by Bundy, who showed them into the living room. It was full of well-worn but highly polished furniture. That room and the adjacent dining room seemed a bit overcrowded with furniture to Gillian's eye. But, of course, she didn't say anything.

"It's so nice to meet people in the neighborhood. Actually, that's kind of the way people in this neighborhood get to know each other, through their kids," said Gillian as she walked through to the kitchen. Bundy, Richard, Levi, Ben, and Penny took seats in the living room.

"Can I help with anything?"

"Well, we're from Southwest. It's just our way. Everybody knew everybody where we came from. Everybody watched out for everybody," replied Alma. "Sure. Why don't you look in the refrigerator and get that pitcher of lemonade and fill the glasses out on the table. Dinner is actually ready."

The dinner was delicious: fried pork chops and onions in rich gravy, creamy mashed potatoes, collard greens, and homemade rolls with butter, with deep-dished peach cobbler for dessert. After dinner, Gillian told Ben and Penny to take the dishes and asked Alma if the kids could do the washing.

"My heaven, yes. Sometimes it's a struggle getting Levi to help out. Maybe your kids can help train him. Go ahead, Levi, show your guests where everything is in the kitchen and help out."

Levi wasn't pleased, being told on like that, but he quietly got up from the table and began to collect plates. Penny and Ben did the same, and soon the adults, who had retired to the living room, could hear sounds of water and clanging plates and playful conversation as the chores were being done.

Bundy pulled out a pipe, lit it, and offered Richard and Gillian drinks. Richard had a Scotch and water. Bundy joined him, but the women didn't partake.

Alma spoke quickly in a rather hushed tone. "We especially wanted to meet you because it looks like Levi and your son have quickly formed a bond. Our Levi puts on a front like he hasn't got a trouble in the world. He's actually gifted. The boy can play just about any instrument you put in front of him. And he gets A's and B's in his subjects. But besides us and JT Ogilvie, who taught him to play the piano, and his uncle Homer down in South Carolina, he really doesn't have anyone. He's actually not our son."

The men sat back and listened as the women spoke.

Gillian said, "Yes, we've gathered that you're the aunt and uncle. We were wondering about the parents."

"Actually, we're not related by blood. Levi calls me aunt and calls Bundy uncle, but we were just friends of his parents, who lived in the neighborhood. We were the first people in DC who met Levi's mother when she came off the farm from down in South Carolina. She was hitchhiking, and my sister and brother-in-law picked her up."

"Nineteen Forty-Two," said Bundy.

"Marva was his mom. She was such as beautiful child. And she was smart as a whip, even though she was uneducated. She died right after we all signed the papers to buy this house. When we all got moved, Levi and his mom and granddaddy went over to Anacostia for a while. Sam Senior is still over there, but he's got high blood pressure, the gout, and other things. The plan was that Marva and us would put the money we got from the government together so we could buy something nice. If you want to know why there's so much stuff in here, it's because there was certain furniture in storage from their house on F Street that Levi wanted to keep. We just couldn't give everything away that reminded him of his mother and daddy."

"Oh, that's sad. Had she been sick, or was it sudden?"

"TB. Marva was a real angel. TB was bad in some parts near where we lived. Before she got married, she stayed for a while in a place called Dixon's Court. All them that lived in her building were mostly girls from the South, like her. But there were also men and families in other buildings. Bundy found the place for her."

Bundy broke in defensively. "It was the only thing I could find on quick notice. Also, the only thing she could afford. But I also got her a job right away."

"Anyway," continued Alma, not paying Bundy's excuse any attention, "After Marva married Levi's stepdaddy, she moved out of Dixon's. But she kept going back. She brought bread, and jam, and cakes to those girls. She sat and talked to them. She combed their hair and helped them wash in tubs or pails. And when they got sick, she'd get off work late at night and go over to Dixon's and just be with them. Big Sam, that was her husband, Sam didn't really like her going there because several of her friends had died. Everybody said it wasn't safe. Sometimes he'd go in there and make her leave. But Marva was just an angel. She kept going for years."

Richard said, "I remember reading in the *Evening Star* or *Post* about tuberculosis in Southwest. Apparently it can lie latent for a long time. And as I recall, about one-quarter of people with prolonged exposure to tuberculosis become infected with the bacteria, and about one in ten of those people with latent infection are likely to develop full-blown TB."

Alma continued, "We don't know when she picked up the bug, but she started coughing and sweating more than a year ago. Finally, she died last spring, just before Levi graduated from Randall and just a couple of weeks before we moved up here. The boy was devastated, as if losing his stepdaddy wasn't enough. The poor thing, he started getting this hard shell around him. We were just about the only ones he'd talk to other than his granddaddy, Big Sam's father. But Sam Senior has been real sick for a few years and couldn't keep Levi for long by himself.

"When we finally got through to him about how much we loved him, he let us in. At first he just sat in the house. We'd tell him to go outside and play, and he'd just walk around a few blocks and then come back. Then we started talking to him about going to Tech. That's when he started putting on airs, getting real cocky. JT started working with him again and that's helped. We think he just wants to show the world that he's all right."

"You say his stepdaddy had died earlier," prodded Gillian.

"Oh, yes. Big Sam Chance drove an ice truck. There was a terrible accident one night."

"Nineteen Fifty-One," said Bundy.

"His truck was hit and rolled over an embankment. Door came off and metal scraps flew everywhere. Ripped him up. Nothing the doctors could do to save him."

Richard and Gillian stared at each other in silence.

"Hey, Aunt Alma," interrupted Levi, coming in from the kitchen with Ben and Penny right on his heels. "They invited me over to their house to see their basement."

Alma looked at her guests.

"Sure, that's fine with us," Richard said to Bundy and Alma.

It was a Saturday night, and the kids weren't expected to do homework or to be in bed early.

"Go ahead, Levi. Be back by midnight," said Bundy.

The kids whooped and rushed out together.

The Stokes and the Parks spent the next few hours in conversation, learning about each other's stories and the stories of their children.

Chapter 15
The Harrison Tech Years

Random thoughts from Ben and Levi, as well as word-markers, that represent their experiences and feelings while going through high school. Their bonds to each other grew stronger, even though their journeys during this period shaped them differently.

1959–1960, Ben Parks:

First sexual encounter with Davita.

Then, estranged from Davita.

Just average in track.

Singing in the choir.

The jazz club.

Friendship with Levi.

DC loses baseball team (first time).

1959–1960, Levi Chance:

Readjustment from Southwest DC.

What happened to my home?

I'm bluffing.

This new guy Ben . . . maybe a friend.

Just sing and they'll like me.

Missing Daddy.

Missing Ma.

The people I love die.

Emmanuel, Arthur, Tracy, Clyde, new friends.

1960–1961, Ben Parks:

Wish I could have gone with the track team. Won high school division of Penn Relays.

Latin. Who speaks Latin?

Singing Frostiana.

Still no action with Davita.

C grades.

1960–1961, Levi Chance:

Missing JT.

Mr. Thompson and band.

Starting to like the trombone.

Emmanuel graduating. Off to the army. Will miss him.

Marvin is now Gaye. No more Gay.

1961–1962, Ben Parks:

College applications. Howard, Grambling? No Middle State in Ohio. Yuk!

Doo-Wopping with the Mystics.

Levi leads, not me.

Good in history. Maybe that'll be my major.

Graduation day.

1961–1962, Levi Chance:

"Stubborn Kinda Fellow," and "Hitch Hike," and "Pride and Joy."

Marvin won't call me back.

Mr. Thompson says I'm a prodigy.

Ben is still my best friend. He's smart but doesn't know it.

Envy Ben for his parents, Dr. Richard Parks and Mrs. Gillian Parks.

Aunt Alma and Uncle Bundy doing the best they can. Not flesh and blood.

Heard the Pershings Own play "1812 Overture" on steps. That's what I want to do.

Army recruiter, Sergeant Taylor. 42S MOS, that's elite. Better than 42R.

Okay, it's graduation day. Here goes the rest of my life.

Chapter 16
Senior Prom

The telephone rang at the Parks' home and Gillian Parks answered. She commenced to having an involved conversation. Observing this, Ben Parks was on his way over to Turkey Thicket playground where he would meet Clyde, Arthur, Tracy, and Lou for a five-on-five run against some guys from Bloomingdale on the other side of North Capital Street.

As he opened the door his mom called out, "Wait a minute, Ben, this is for you. I was just catching up with your friend Davita. Haven't talked with her in forever."

Ben's throat caught. He hadn't spoken with Davita in forever either. He actually kind of avoided her because she avoided him.

"Hello. Hi, Vita. What's up?"

"Well you haven't asked me yet."

Silence. Ben was not only caught off guard, but now he was puzzled. What was Davita talking about?

"I haven't asked you what, Vita?"

"To be your date for the prom."

Silence again. Davita continued, "Are you going with someone else?"

"Well, no. Hadn't thought it through. Hadn't thought of anyone."

"Well?"

"Vita, you chilled me out. You put me on lockdown. What are you talking about?"

"I chilled you out from having sex. But we dance at parties, don't we?"

"Yeah."

"Aren't we still friends, Ben?"

"Yeah, I guess so. I hope so."

"So, what's the problem? I'm just talking about going to the prom, Ben. I'm not talking about jumping in the back of Dr. Parks' Cadillac after it's over. Just going to the prom. Don't you want me to be your date?"

Damn this girl. She always was a step ahead of him. She always knew how to make him crazy. She damn well knew that he'd love for her to be his prom date. She probably knew he wasn't seeing anybody, but this arm's-length relationship they'd had through high school was stressful on him and made him crazy.

"Vita, I'm going to want to kiss you after the prom."

"Okay, maybe one or two kisses. That's all, though."

"Shit, will you be my prom date, Vita?"

"Again, without the curse word, please."

Silence.

"Please."

"Davita Sheridan, would you go to the prom with me?"

"Oh, what a nice surprise. I'd love to, Benjamin Parks. Thanks for asking."

***

The night of the prom, Ben picked Davita up at her house and had a lovely corsage for her dress. She wore a pale orange velvet bodice dress that flared out at the bottom. It scooped down in the front so you could see the tops of her breasts. Ben peeked all through the night. He totally kerfuffled at how to get the corsage on without making contact with those boobs. Davita grabbed the corsage in his hands and guided him to the right spot.

"Now, just pin it, Benjamin."

He did.

***

The dinner dance at the Washington Hilton Hotel, at the intersection of Florida and Connecticut Avenues in Northwest DC, featured the Bobby Felder dance orchestra in rare form. Playing a combination of standards from the American songbook and many of the R&B hits of the day, the room was a spectacle of motion. Ben looked for his friend Levi, who'd said he wasn't coming. Ben had coaxed him and told him that he shouldn't do Janice that way. She was there with her older brother, a sophomore at Howard University. Janice wasn't having a great time.

But the biggest surprise of the day was the arrival of the big man on campus, Tracy Brown, with his date, Deanna Nance. They walked in arm in arm and everyone turned and looked. Tracy was about the coolest guy Ben knew. All A student. Basketball team and track team (miler, shotput, and high jump). Spanish club president. Tracy did it all. Nominated for West Point. The thing was, nobody put these two together. In addition to all his achievements, Tracy had spent his high school (and junior high) years dogging every skirt he came in contact with.

Deanna, on the other hand, had spent her entire high school years focusing on her classwork, editing the high school newspaper, and on the cheerleading squad. Without trying, she made boys drool when she walked down the hallways. Before this she had been untouchable. Every boy's dream, but no boy's reality. Deanna was an astrology buff. As a Scorpio, it had been important for her to put any potential suitor through the compatibility test. The cake was baked for her when she learned that Tracy was Cancer, one of her most compatible signs.

Tracy was dark, six foot five, and muscled. Deanna, resplendent in her white mid-calf gown with shimmering sparkles with a goldish chain piece encircling her waist, was caramel colored, five foot ten and lean, with sexy seriousness exuding from every pore. Now, this night her smile was soft but dazzling. Her skin always looked like it had been polished and buffed. They were striking beyond words, but nobody had put them together. They danced together as if they'd danced many times before, but nobody had ever seen them dance together. They talked comfortably and close to one another, but nobody was privy to their conversations. Classmates were talking about the surprise couple the entire night and for weeks and months afterward.

Ben and Davita stayed on the dance floor most of the night. They spun and whirled to their favorite up-tempo tunes and danced close to the wonderful ballads played by the band. Afterward, kisses underneath the cherry trees near the Tidal Basin across from the Jefferson Memorial were sweet and extended. Ben was on fire. Davita, as she always had been, was in charge. When she eased the passion back and led them back up for air, Ben tried to resist. But then he walked her back to Dr. Richard's car and sat in silence.

"What are you going to do, Ben?"

"I'm going to school out in Ohio. What about you?"

"I'm staying home and going to Howard. I think I'm going to study business and maybe one day take over my parents' restaurant. I mean, I'm staying in DC, but I'll be living on campus, not at home with my parents."

"I've missed you so much. I'm going to miss you."

"Will you write me?"

"Probably not."

"I understand. But if you do, I'll write you back."

"Thanks for tonight, Vita."

Ben drove her home and walked her to the door of her Northeast house on Monroe Street. She turned and touched his cheek. Ben didn't try for another kiss. That pleasure was etched in his mind, but he let go of any hope that it would lead to something more.

"Good night, Vita."

"Good night, my friend. Good night, Benjamin."

A few days later, Levi called Janice, "Hey, girl, how was the prom?"

"Don't ask me about the prom. If you had wanted to know about the prom, you would have been at the prom with me. Don't ask me about the prom, not now and not ever."

The telephone line went dead in Levi's ear.

Chapter 17
Arrival in Nam

December 1967

"Sergeant Chance. Sergeant Chance. Is one of y'all Sergeant Chance?"

Levi had just collected his duffle bag off the Tan Son Nhut airport conveyor and picked up his trombone case. He looked around, befuddled.

"Sergeant Chance?"

The big burly soldier was eying Levi. He was the only soldier in the masses gathered around the conveyor who sported an instrument case.

Levi noticed the stripes: three stripes up and none down, buck sergeant, an E-5, just the same as Levi. The voice came from a grizzled soldier who appeared to be somewhat north of thirty years old. Levi was twenty-three years old, and with five years of service under his belt he felt he was doing all right.

"Right here!" he answered.

He felt some relief. All the other soldiers on the flight seemed to be headed straight for combat units. One of his fears, as he'd hopped on the Lockheed C-130 Hercules configured for troop transporting in Japan after his TWA commercial flight from the States, was that he'd get lost in the sauce and conscripted into some infantry platoon or something. Months later, his band would notice his paperwork and start asking questions about why he hadn't arrived. They'd check and find that he'd swallowed a bullet in a firefight because he'd fumbled trying to take the safety off his rifle.

"Let's go, soldier. You're assigned to the two sixty-sixth. You'd never find us if somebody didn't pick you up. There's a gig tonight at

Long Bihn, so nobody else was around. I'm a mess sergeant, but here I am. Let's go. You can ask questions on the way."

Levi was in data overload but did his best to collect himself by straightening his cap. He remembered the words on his orders. He knew he was being assigned to the 266th Army Band, headquartered in someplace called Long Binh. So he felt like this sergeant was legit; he knew Levi's name and he called out the right unit. Then a little panic. *Where's my axe?* he thought. He'd insisted on keeping his bone with him on his flight, but his piano (Levi's Suitcase Silver Sparkle by Fender Rhodes) had to be shipped out early. Levi later felt foolish, realizing that it wouldn't have been held at the airport, but for this moment this was just another thing for him to worry about.

As for his trombone, although the army furnished the newest instruments to their professional musicians, Levi still preferred the sound of older horns played by greats like Kid Ory, Jack Teagarden, and especially JJ Johnson. He'd been given his Williams Model 8 bone by JT Ogilvie back in 1951. Since then he'd played and lovingly maintained it all these years.

"Do you know if my other axe got here? It was shipped out last week."

"Axe. What the fuck! You musicians speak a foreign language anyway. That's why you'll get along good over here with these gooks."

Levi looked forlorn. The journey over the last five years flashed through his mind. Since that day on the plaza when he met Ben Parks and established himself as a talented musician, cool cat, and true Michigan Park friend, it had all been a blur. In August 1962, the audition had been arranged right in Hamilton Tech's empty auditorium by Sergeant Taylor, the army recruiter. It was a snap. Levi had felt no pressure at all. Sergeant Taylor and Mr. Thompson were there along with this guy they had called the "auditioner." The auditioner had seemed like he wanted to find something Levi couldn't do, especially with his sight reading.

Finally, after two hours of Levi breezing through everything put in front of him, including the difficult trombone part in Rossini's *La Scala di Seta* (the Silk Ladder), Sergeant Taylor had said, "If this recruit were a white kid, you would have been on your knees sucking his dick an hour ago."

The two army sergeants had a big shouting match right there in front of Levi. Mr. Thompson had come up on stage as if ready to jump in between them. But eventually the auditioner had relented. Begrudgingly, he'd said, "I got to admit it. You're a special little colored kid. I can't think of a single one of our bones that can outplay you. Welcome to the US Army Band program."

Then there had been nine weeks of basic training, followed by Advanced Individual Training at the US Army Element School of Music at Camp Lee, Virginia. At the tender age of eighteen, Levi was assigned to the elite band called the Pershings. As time went by, he wanted to play with them at John F. Kennedy's funeral back in November 1963, but his participation wasn't requested. He was also glad that while in high school, Mr. Thompson had insisted that he learn to play the bugle. With that ability, Levi had represented the Pershings countless times over the years playing "Taps" at military funerals, though because he was black he never got that chance at Arlington National Cemetery.

He'd stayed in touch with his civilian buddy, Ben, who had done the college thing and was now in graduate school. But even more, Levi had stayed in touch with another Tech graduate. Janice Westbrook had gone to Howard University after Tech. She and Levi were an item off and on for years. She was some awesome eye candy on his arm when the Army Band had social functions. Janice was about as sexy as any of the band guys had ever seen, and she gave him credibility as more than just a musician. Janice knew he liked pussy, and Levi knew she liked dick. So they didn't crowd each other, but some-kind-of-way Janice was Levi's woman. So, when he'd told her he was volunteering to leave the Pershings and to be assigned to Vietnam, Janice had been devastated.

Through the years, Levi had also been in touch with Emmanuel Freeze, Arthur Bostic, Clyde Simms, and Tracy Brown. All of them were soldiers. Emmanuel and Clyde were really gung ho. They had enlisted right after graduation, even before Levi, but they had gone right into the infantry and both of them had made rank pretty quickly. Emmanuel was an E-6, and Clyde was an E-5 noncommissioned officer now. Both were seeing themselves as career soldiers. And both craved action. Arthur had gone on to play football in college and took ROTC. Tracy went to West Point. Both came into the army after graduation as second lieutenants. Levi loved to write and to get letters, and to various degrees he had regularly corresponded with Ben and all of his soldier buddies for all these years, but the lure of action eventually had reeled him in. He wanted to be a part of it; at least to the extent that a band soldier could be a part of combat action. He wanted to be nearby.

Levi felt in his back pants' pocket. That's where he kept the one-page letter folded up in a cellophane baggy. He didn't have to read it anymore, because he had almost memorized it, but he kept it with him, maybe for good luck. He thought about his friend Benjamin Parks, whose life had taken such a different path since they had graduated from Harrison Tech. Levi had gone up to Ohio in the spring for Ben's college graduation. Alma and Bundy had driven up with him, and they had proudly watched Ben's parents, Richard and Gillian, as they entertained close family and friends at a restaurant near Ben's college campus. As proud as he'd been of Ben, he didn't want to change places. He liked the life he'd had for the past four years with the Pershings. But it was important for him to realize that Ben was proud of him too. The letter in his back pocket, in part, read:

> *You know you've always been a star to me. That probably goes for all of us from the neighborhood, but I don't know if anybody ever told you. And I can't believe how brave you are because I know that nobody is making you go to Nam. You had it made playing with the band in DC. I know you, man. You're volunteering for this shit. Damn, that's the stupidest*

thing I've ever heard of. But it makes me know how special you really are.

You make sure you take care of yourself. I'll keep an eye on Mrs. Alma and Mr. Bundy. You just keep your head down. Can't wait for you to come back.

Your friend forever,

Ben

The mess sergeant was speaking, "Relax, Axeman. I may be a mess sergeant, but I've been around the Two Sixty-Sixth long enough to know what you're talking about. Yes, your piano is here. It arrived day before yesterday. Now let's go!"

Sergeant Scalia took off with a quick pace, and Levi followed along as best he could, encumbered by his duffle and his bone case. His combat boots didn't fit quite right and he thought he was developing a blister. The fancy uniforms worn by the Pershings were a far cry from the jungle fatigues he was wearing now, but he managed. As they walked out of the terminal from Tan Son Nhut Airport outside of Saigon, Vietnam, he spotted a soldier standing by an open jeep at the curb. The sergeant palmed something into the soldier's hand as he grabbed Levi's duffle and slung it into the back seat. Then he walked around, opened the door, and folded his large frame behind the wheel.

"Do you need another invitation, soldier?"

With his bone case safely in his clutches, Levi jumped in. Sergeant Scalia reached below a green blanket and showed Levi an M-16 and an M-79 grenade launcher.

"Take your pick, soldier."

"Hold on, Sarge, you don't understand. I'm just a horn player."

"You may be a horn player, but you're now in a country where, by general orders, we can't be on the roads without being armed. So, again I say to you, take your pick."

Pointing to the M-79, Levi said, "Well, I don't even know what that is, so I guess I'll choose the M-16."

"Thought you'd say that," said Scalia with a smirk.

Off they went out of the airport complex and into the streets of Saigon, the capital city of The Republic of South Vietnam. He'd had no expectations, and yet he was stunned by the visuals as he rode through the city he'd been hearing about. This was the city ruled by the Cambodian Khmer in the seventeenth century and then by Nuyen rulers from Hue in the eighteenth century, until, in 1859, it was conquered by France and Spain. Levi had suffered through a tutorial by his history-buff friend, Ben Parks, before leaving the States. He knew that when Ho Chi Minh and the Viet Minh came to power in the North in the 1940s, Saigon had been named capital in the South by Emperor Bảo Đại. But now dustiness was perhaps the biggest sensation he experienced in riding through this capital. Bicycles, pedicabs, and walking were the overwhelmingly preferred means (or most available) of transportation.

City men seemed to wear various pants and suits, but strikingly topped off with what Levi later came to call "cone hats." These pointed-at-the-top and wide-at-the-bottom hats offered shade from the oppressive sun. Also, Levi later learned the name *"Ao dai,"* for the colorful tunics-over-pants he saw adorning the women on the streets of the capital city. As the sergeant headed northeast out of the city for another thirty-three kilometers, more visuals came to Levi:

Water buffalo!

Yes, water buffalo were everywhere. Water buffalo standing around on the sides of roads and in fields. Water buffalo being led by men walking in front with cone hats. Young boys riding water buffalo. Various kinds of wagons loaded with all manner of things were hitched to water buffalo and being driven like the stagecoaches in American Western movies.

Sandy in appearance, the predominant landscape was covered with a rusty-red laterite type of soil, but was lush green in other places, with clusters of hedgerows in some places, and rocky in still other places. The countryside offered sights and smells that were quite foreign to Levi. The countrymen's two-piece garb shifted from the variety of colors Levi had seen on men in the city. Now they were mostly black, but still offset by their big white cone hats. The women in the country seemed to wear clothes that were closer to the men's shirt and pants combination, but their heads were either not covered or were tied up with what appeared to be bandana-like scarves. Occasionally Levi spotted a woman with the same type of cone hat as the men wore.

Off in the distance, Levi spotted paddy fields and what appeared to be both men and women stooped over with their hands in the water, planting or pulling rice. In more sandy places and closer to the roads, there were chickens and even red-crested roosters walking around seemingly without direction or human supervision. In other places there appeared to be tall enclosures, as many as fifteen to twenty sandbags tall, behind which there might have been GI or ARVN (Army of the Republic of Vietnam) soldiers manning mortars or other munitions.

The twenty-five- to thirty-mile trip took them about one and one-half hours, traveling northeast on Route 316. They crossed the Đồng Nai river and Sergeant Scalia said, "Okay, we're getting close to home."

"Home. Is that Long Bihn? How far are we?"

"Not far."

The sergeant didn't elaborate further. Levi continued looking around. Then, as the sergeant turned left where a road sign pointed to Biên Hòa (both an ancient city and another massive airbase), Levi saw rows and rows of straight trees for as far as he could see.

"What's over there?"

"That's the Ga No Nai rubber plantation. It's huge, but the really big one is the Michelin plantation further east."

Levi had never seen rubber trees. Looking at the acres and acres of rubber trees, it had never occurred to him that an exportable product like rubber would originate in a war-torn place like Vietnam.

Finally, in one hour, Levi and Sergeant Scalia came to Long Binh Army Base, east of the Đồng Nai River and close to Biên Hòa Air Base. Coming in through Long Binh's Gate Six on the southeast side of the massive (Cleveland, Ohio-sized) facility, Levi took in the sights. He found tens of thousands of what fighting troops called REMFs (rear echelon mother fuckers) on the facility. The massive infrastructure was in every way equal to anything at a stateside base. Long Binh was home to services for soldiers, including a hospital, dental clinics, crafts shops, a large Post Exchange stocking clothing and all manner of high quality stereo and photographic equipment and recordings, a library, and educational buildings where soldiers could take college extension courses, and every recreational facility imaginable, from basketball and tennis courts to swimming pools, handball and squash courts, bowling alleys, and of course restaurants and nightclubs for officers, NCOs, and enlisted men.

Chapter 18

The Unit

Levi's initial reception in the 266th wasn't exactly friendly. He'd dropped off his duffle and his bone case on an empty bunk in barracks building 5136. Then he'd been pointed to a large aluminum hanger-looking structure where he spotted a small office or orderly room in the back. Captain Jeffrey Jax looked up from his desk as the new replacement came in. He opened up a file and scanned. Then he barked, "A Forty-Two S, no less. All my soldiers are Forty-Two R. Who the hell did you piss off to be over here?"

"Nobody, sir. I volunteered."

Captain Jax looked stunned. He just stared. "Mother, father, sister, brother! They done sent me a crazy one."

Then he regained some composure.

"What the hell do I need with a piano player in a marching band? Unless you're a lot stronger than you look, soldier. Well, welcome, I guess. Your kit is in the hall outside. Set it up and I'll be in there in a minute. I want to hear what you can do."

Levi walked out from the captain's office into the large hanger used as the band's practice hall. He spotted the well-packaged box containing his Fender, and in about twenty-five minutes, just in time for the captain, he had it set up and plugged into a long extension cord running from a bank along the wall.

"Well, let me hear it."

Thirty minutes later, Captain Jax and about a dozen band members, along with another thirty or more miscellaneous troops, were stomping their feet and clapping their hands to Levi's impromptu concert. Finally, the captain said, "Well you're a badd mothafucker! But I still can't use a piano player in my marching band. Have you ever held a cymbal?"

Levi looked sheepish. "No, sir! But you don't understand. I'm also a bone player. That's what I did with the Pershings. I thought you knew."

"All I knew about you soldier was when that box came for you last week."

"Sorry, sir, about the confusion. I thought there might be some opportunity to play my keyboard here. But for you, I'm a bone player."

"Well, where is this alleged bone, soldier?"

"It's back on my bunk, sir. I didn't know to bring it. I was just told to report to you."

"Germ!" barked Captain Jax to another soldier standing nearby. "Get this guy's bone off his bunk. In the meantime, soldier, can you play 'Georgia on My Mind' on that Fender? Every day I try to hear that tune at least once. Born and raised in Statesboro."

Now the audience of Levi's new bandmates were really blown away. Not only did Levi swing a long introduction for the Hoagy Carmichael standard, with jazzy licks all the way from arpeggios and glissandos to bluesy riffs, but the captain's anticipation for his home state's song was peaking.

"Get to the point, mothafucker!"

Suddenly Levi's voice filled the space in the hangar. As yet, he hadn't sung since he'd started this impromptu concert, but now the fullness of his rich tenor bounced back and forth across the expanse. It wasn't quite the raspy rendition that Ray Charles had done in 1960 on the *Genius Hits the Road* album, but it was just as soulful, albeit in a sweeter and more melancholy style.

Captain Jax closed his eyes and rocked back and forth.

As Levi finished, the soldier who'd been referred to as Germ returned and placed the case next to the Fender. As the final lingering chord echoed, Levi opened up and retrieved his precious Williams. By the time Captain Jax's eyes were opening, Levi was fitting his mouthpiece and tuning. And off he went with the gospel inspired "When the Saints Go Marching In."

Apparently, that was enough to tip the table for everybody listening. Instruments appeared through doorways and out of unnoticed boxes and cases around the hanger. The ensuing jam had all the makings of a New Orleans second line of musicians following up a somber funeral parade or celebratory Mardi Gras march. Various band members (trumpeters, sax players, and clarinetists) took solos. Levi had started it up and felt no need to reestablish his lead. By the time the verse came around for about the fifth time, Captain Jax had pulled out his Conn Shooting Star alto saxophone and was coloring around the melody. Levi noted that he had some skills. He later learned that Captain Jax also played a mean licorice stick (clarinet).

Finally, "Okay, soldier, that's enough," said Captain Jax, with his sax mouthpiece still partially in his mouth. "From now on, whenever you hear me say the word Georgia, you know what I want. You don't even have to have an axe with you. Just vocalize that mothafucker, but for now, you have an appointment in the NCO club at fifteen hundred hours. Something about them wanting you to organize a house band to play on some evenings. So maybe that Fender will come in handy after all."

"Yes, sir!" shouted Levi as he shifted his bone to his left hand and shot up with his right in the most military salute the captain had seen since he left stateside.

Everybody present in the 266th Army Band hangar that day laughed, including Captain Jax.

"You say you were with the Pershings. Well that's a damn fine salute, soldier. I guess they taught you well. But you're in Vietnam now. We don't do that over here. You understand? Now go get showered so you can look pretty at the NCO club."

Chapter 19
Band Life

The guys in the quintet all had day jobs in the 266th Army Band headquartered at the mammoth Long Binh Post. The 17,000-acre Long Binh site was a sprawling command headquarters for the US Army in Vietnam. At its peak, as many as 50,000 to 60,000 soldiers were stationed at Long Binh.

The 266th played marches and pop music several times a week on post or elsewhere. Levi played trombone in the band, but at the Annex 14 NCO Club, he usually stuck to keyboards, shifting between his Fender Rhodes and the club's Kohler & Campbell upright piano.

The drummer was Paul Proudfoot, a full-blooded Keetoowah Cherokee from Chickasha, Oklahoma. Proudfoot was a snare drummer in the marching band and handled the trap set in the quint. The fellas joked that Proudfoot's last name should have been Proudcock, because he had the biggest, fattest one anybody on base had ever seen. Proudcock is what everybody called him. The large Indian was thunder on the skins.

***

It was Proudcock who took Levi on his first jeep tour of Long Bihn, beginning with the basics: the mess hall, several routes to the barracks, and the PX. Then, as they drove some of the more than 150 miles of road that crisscrossed the huge encampment, Proudcock narrated and Levi read the signs. The 266th Army Band was but one small group of soldiers sharing the Long Bihn base with the likes of the 62nd Army Engineers, the 64th Quatermaster, the 79th Maintenance Battalion, the 379th Transportation Company, the US Army Vietnam Installation Stockade, the 1st Aviation Brigade, the 44th Medical Brigade, the 1st Logistical Command, the 24th Evacuation Hospital, the 18th Military Police Brigade, and the 3rd Ordinance Battalion, among many others. They passed a military bus with lettering on the side: 90th Replacement Battalion.

Sensing his question, Proudcock preempted, "They're outside the gates on the road back toward Ben Hoa. One of the reasons we had Sergeant Scalia meet you was we didn't want you scooped up by them. Basically, that's where almost everybody else you flew in with went. From there, they get sent God knows where: First Cav, Americal, on and on, based on what unit has lost the most guys. They might be there a few hours or days or sometimes weeks. They come over here to shop and stuff."

Levi just stared at the soldiers jumping off the bus, knowing that they were "replacements."

What the hell does that feel like? he wondered silently.

Levi observed shirtless GIs carrying huge shells to artillery placements and deuce-and-one-quarter trucks being off-loaded of their cargo of corpses bound for the States. He observed that there was no standard saluting. As a replacement, the middle finger seemed to be the standard greeting for many soldiers stationed at Long Binh. Levi observed all manner of signage, from the impromptu to the planned. The words Reefer Kings were proudly displayed on one barracks they passed. They passed a business and Levi read aloud, "The Loon Foon Restaurant."

Proudcock interjected, "Really good eating there, my man. Really good! Hope you know how to use chopsticks. Ask for a fork and everybody in the place will laugh and stare at you. Now, I think we need to bring this tour to a close. But before we go in, I need to swing you by the armory."

"Not interested. By the way, Sergeant Scalia made me take a rifle on the way from the airport. Something about not being allowed to be out on the road outside of post without being armed. Is that true?"

"Yeah, when we go out in the band bus, there are weapons drawn for us and stored in the back. We might not see them, but they're there in case we drive into some shit. The point is, you need to know where the armory is in case something happens."

***

Six foot three Bobby Fister was called "Fingers." He was from Reno, Nevada, played the tuba by day, and by night thumped on his Engelhardt Kay C1 double bass. He had huge hands and manhandled the upright in a way that Levi had never seen anyone do back home in DC. Bobby said the upright was the only instrument big enough for him to play.

The quintet featured two pieces in the horn section. Akimitsu Lee was a Japanese American who hailed from San Francisco. Nicknamed "Ack," he played trumpet but also doubled on the piano. This was cool, because occasionally Levi would want to pull out his bone, especially for one of those New Orleans bluesy or second-line type numbers. Ack could slide in effortlessly on the ivories whenever a switch seemed to fit the song.

Finally, Robert Scott was from Harlem. He was a stone-cold John Coltrane and Charlie Parker devotee. When not playing, Robert listened incessantly to stereo Trane and Bird records, and when he played jazz he wailed on the tenor and alto as closely to his inspirations as he possibly could. "Harlem" is what everybody called Robert.

One night, an MC took it upon himself to name Levi's quintet the Statesiders. Nobody in the group cared. They started gaining a reputation across Vietnam. If they weren't playing at Long Binh, they often were called on to gig in one of the military facilities in Saigon, or even on the economy in one of the many nightclubs catering to soldiers and local jazz fans. As long as it didn't interfere with the business of the 266th, they had Captain Jax's blessings.

Monday, January 29, 1968, Levi's group was off for the evening. Then they were booked at the Tan Son Nhut NCO for that Tuesday and then back at the Long Binh Annex 14 club for Wednesday through Sunday. So, on Wednesday the 31st, for the first set of the night, the Statesiders fronted an open-mike session where soldiers got up and sang all sorts of R&B and doo wop songs. On a typical night, one might hear a playlist consisting of the Intruder's "Cowboys to Girls" from 1968, the Del-Vikings "Whispering Bells" from 1957, or if there was a bass voice in the room, then the requested song had to be the Marcels "Blue Moon" from 1961. This open microphone set started at 8 p.m. and ran to about nine thirty. One MP always got up when he was off duty and could come in. He liked to sing Gene Chandler's 1962 hit, "Duke of Earl."

"Makes me feel special, like I'm a duke and I'm actually going to get out of this place alive," he said one night when a heckler tried to get him to sing something else.

Every night, the Statesiders would have to backup someone on the 1965 hit "My Girl" from the Temptations.

Proudcock would mouth to Levi, "He ain't got no girl. Probably never had no pussy in his life."

Clyde Simms slipped in one night and sat at the back of the room drinking a beer. He and Levi exchanged looks and pounded on their chests in recognition and respect. But just as quickly, Clyde was gone before the next break.

Around ten or ten thirty, the quintet played their jazz set, which ran until midnight. They were getting toward the end of the last set. They'd just finished a rousing "Night in Tunesia," which everybody said the quintet ought to record because of Ack's virtuoso trumpet driving the track.

For the final number, Levi tickled the keys for the intro of their jazzy rendition of the popular "Gloria," to loud applause. Despite the jazzy rendition, the troops always sung out the letters whenever they heard the familiar changes that signaled the chorus "G, L, O, R, I, A."

When they finished the number, the master sergeant who usually served as MC came on the bandstand and took the mic. "Be careful tonight, everyone," he said. "We all know that there's supposed to be a truce on for the Tết holiday, which started today. It's their New Years. All of a sudden, the enemy isn't transmitting anything. Watch your backs and be ready tonight."

Chapter 20

Homeys

It's a curious thing how soldiers apparently have to have nicknames. Staph Capone (or Germ) was a drummer and usually played the bass drum in the marching band, though he could also play snares if needed. The band's drum major Steve Stephens, whose parents certainly deserved a conviction for felonious naming, was "Twice." After his debut performance in the hangar on his Fender Rhodes, Levi had been dubbed "Liberace," a nickname that he tolerated because he couldn't do anything about it, but he didn't like it. Captain Jax was "The Game" behind his back.

So if you got three guesses with the first two not counting, you'd probably come up with the nickname that stuck to Levi's friend and former Mystics crooner Emmanuel Freeze. One day Levi was reading a magazine on his bunk.

"Hey, Liberace, a couple of dudes named Antifreeze and Bosco are in a jeep asking about you. They're over at the PX."

"Antifreeze? Bosco? I don't know anybody with them fucked-up names . . . oh, yeah. I just might," said Levi, breaking out into a big smile and rushing out of the barracks with his cap not quite sitting on his head correctly. He ran the mile distance from the barracks to the PX and found a jeep idling in front with Arthur Bostic sitting in the driver's seat wearing the subdued insignia of the 1st Cavalry Division.

"Oh, no! I don't believe it. Who in the hell else would it be with a fucked-up name like Bosco? And I'm guessing Antifreeze is Emmanuel. Where the hell is he?" shouted Levi in a booming outside voice.

"He's in the PX. Be back out in a minute. Dudes in the unit needed shaving cream, toothpaste, and razors, shit like that. S-Four sends us over here with vouchers to stock up for the unit. It was just our turn to make the run from camp. We wanted to anyway when we heard your sorry ass was in-country."

Arthur was out of the jeep and he and Levi man-hugged for over a minute.

"All right, soldiers, break that shit up!" came the loud voice of Emmanuel Freeze, also sporting the 1st Cavalry camo patch.

Levi was beside himself. "How'd they let you two mothafuckers get in the same unit."

Bosco spoke, "Ain't that a bitch? Just happened, man. We don't know. Somebody in the Pentagon not paying attention maybe. Or maybe it's not an issue."

Antifreeze followed, "Anyway, it's cool. I get to serve with my homey. And now I get to see another homey. I guess you've seen Clyde. He's around this bitch somewhere."

"Yeah, he's over on the other side of the Post with the Third, guarding all the whole wide world's ammunition and other shit that goes boom. He's a gung-ho mother fucker. Takes that shit real serious. But I guess you two are gun ho too. Me, I just play my music. Clyde comes into the NCO club sometimes. We've got a little combo that plays. Clyde slips in and listens for a while and then slips out. Doesn't say much. Hey, why don't you stay over and see me play tonight?"

"Naw, we got to get back, man. There's a war out there to fight. Can't mess around with you REMFs living in the lap of luxury. But we just wanted to see you, Levi. You look good, man. You feeling good?"

"Yeah, but I'm feeling better now. Thanks for coming to see me."

"Keep your head down, homey."

"You too."

Then, before pulling off, Emmanuel turned, "You ever see Tracy?"

Levi thought about Tracy Brown, another Michigan Park friend from Harrison Tech. A bartender at the Officer's Club, when Levi introduced himself as being from Washington, DC, had talked about having met this fearless Special Forces dude from Washington, DC. The bartender had shrugged.

"I met Lieutenant Brown once when I guess he was taking some time. Haven't seen him since. I hear he's always into something scary. Other people speak his name from time to time. He's kind of like a legend. From what I gather, that dude is always going to be wherever the nasty shit is."

"If you see him, tell him to be safe."

"You got it."

Arthur worked the clutch on the jeep and burned a little rubber as they sped away.

Chapter 21

What's That?

The 275th Việt Cộng Regiment attacked targets from Ben Hoa Airbase along Highway 1 to the Long Binh Army Post in late January and February 1968. Levi Chance had been in-country only a few weeks. He had settled into a routine with the 266th Army Band and with the Statesiders.

One night in mid-February, Levi was awakened from a sound sleep around 2:30 a.m. in Long Binh barracks building 5136. He'd been asleep only about thirty minutes. Groggily he struggled to focus. Another loud explosion.

"What's that?" asked Levi to nobody in particular. Germ was several bunks over from Levi and was already up and pulling on a pair of combat boots.

"Sounds like incoming to me," said Germ.

"What's that mean?"

"Dumb ass! That means we're being shelled. RPGs, or satchel charges, or grenades, or whatever other kind of shit Charley has, it's coming in on us."

Levi realized that he'd never expected to actually come close to combat. He was a band member. He didn't fight. He played.

"What do we do?" said Levi, hitting a lamp by his bunk.

"Not that, you cherry motherfucker," said Germ in a loud whisper. "Turn off that fucking light."

Levi complied.

"Everybody up," came a loud voice at the door. Though he couldn't be seen in the darkened room, Levi knew it was The Game.

"They're trying to figure out what's going on. MPs and combat aviation group soldiers are engaged. We're on standby for a call. If the call comes, we're all hauling ass to the armory to check out weapons. I hope you girls remember something about shooting from your basic training."

This was part of what came to be known as the Tết Offensive. It lasted over two or three months in early 1968. Tết has been described as the bloodiest fighting of the entire Vietnam War. The holiday called Tết Nguyên Đán begins on January 31, marking the first day of the year on a traditional lunar calendar. Some say it's the most important of all Vietnamese holidays. This made it doubly incredulous that a sudden attack was being launched, breaking an unspoken truce that usually settled over Vietnam during Tết.

Despite the huge explosions that were heard for miles outside of Long Binh, the 266th band members never were called to the armory that night or the next day. Later in the aftermath they found that there were over one hundred attacks launched during Tết. And they found that a unit of the NVA's 27th Regiment had been assigned specifically to destroy the large ammunition depot run by the Army's 3rd Ordinance Battalion located right there at the Long Binh Army Base. This was a prize target containing about a hundred ammo bunkers stocked with every imaginable type of Army and Air Force munition.

Clyde Simms from Michigan Park, DC, fought that night with members of the 3rd Ordinance Battalion alongside a detachment of MPs to repel the Việt Cộng attack. Dozens of VC soldiers were killed or captured. But a first lieutenant that Levi had never seen, sporting the patch of the 3rd Ordinance Battalion, showed up the following morning escorted by Captain Jax.

Levi had his back turned as he heard The Game's whispery voice, "That's Sergeant Chance." Then in full voice, "Hey, Liberace."

Levi turned and the officer from the 3rd spoke, "Sergeant Clyde Simms said you guys were from the same neighborhood back in DC."

"Yes, sir."

"Sit down, son."

It was not a request. Levi immediately felt sick to his stomach. The officer got right to it. "Sorry to tell you, he bought it yesterday."

Silence fell over the room as Levi took in this news. Some fellow band members observed Levi, while others suddenly found they needed to straighten their bunks or inspect the shine on their boots.

Levi learned that on the night of the attack, the heavy shelling that had awakened him was from enemy mortars. He learned that around 3 a.m., as the VC broke through the outer perimeter of the ammunition depot, an intense firefight had ensued. It was in this firefight that Clyde had taken a mortal hit through his neck. Several MPs also were killed in the attack before the good guys began to repel their attackers.

"There's a notification team on its way to Sergeant Simms' house back in DC. Do you know his family?"

"Uh. A notification team?"

"Sorry, soldier, that's Army jargon. That's what we call the guys who bring this kind of bad news to parents, wives, sons and daughters, etc."

"Uh-uh."

Levi felt like he wanted to throw up. Finally, "Yeah, I know his folks. His dad's a cop. His mom stays at home. He has an older brother and sister. The sister is in Miami. The brother lives in . . . I think he lives in Nashville."

"That's helpful, son. Thanks. Sergeant Simms had told us about you. Said all you guys from the neighborhood were close. That's why we wanted to come over in person to let you know. Regulations say we have to tell the family first. But that's underway, and we didn't know if his parents would call you or something."

"Uh. I don't know. I don't know if they know I'm here."

"Well just in case, we wanted you to be prepared."

"Uh."

Levi broke down. Now, Proudcock, Twice (the drum major), Harlem, and Ack rushed over.

"Sorry, soldier," said the officer from the 3rd. He gave a nod that Levi didn't see, did an about face, and marched out of the room. Captain Jax remained a few minutes. He stepped forward, and Proudcock held up his hand.

Harlem walked up close. "We got this, Captain."

"Thanks, soldier," said the captain. He too made a quiet exit.

Chapter 22
The Ghost in Training

In the summer of 1954, a set of ten international accords on Indochina were reached at a conference in Geneva, Switzerland. Earlier that year a French military installation near Dien Bien Phu in Vietnam had been overrun. Conference participants were from China, the Soviet Union, the United States, France, the UK, Cambodia, Laos, the Viet Minh, and the State of Vietnam. The major result of this conference was the division of Vietnam along the seventeenth parallel into a northern communist country and a southern country headed by emperor Bảo Đại.

Other provisions of this conference included the guarantee of free elections within a year in neighboring Laos and its neighbor to the south, Cambodia. Both these neighbor countries were to be considered neutral going forward. The tenth of these accords was signed by only some of the nine participating parties. It established that the nations of Poland, India, and Canada would be enlisted to supervise all Vietnam elections to be held in two years for the reunification of the Viet Minh and the State of Vietnam. The United States was one of the parties not agreeing to this tenth accord. As it turned out, the US had designs on turning the State of Vietnam into a democracy.

***

February 1964

Under orders from the Pentagon, General Westmoreland, who was the US military commander in Vietnam, began equipping, staffing, and deploying covert commando units. These units would take over programs previously executed by the Central Intelligence Agency in Vietnam. Air Commandos from the US Air Force, US Army personnel (to include Special Forces and the predecessors to the Delta Force), US Navy Seals, Marine Force Recon personnel, and CIA operatives were all organized together under the umbrella of a newly established Special Operations Group (SOG). Very quickly, however, the group was renamed Studies and Observations Group to make it more innocuous to the curious or prying eyes of the media and/or the US Congress. The ruse became that the group's mission was researching military strategy for academic purposes. General Westmoreland had only field oversight authority for SOG after it was stood up. The first Chief of SOG, Army Paratrooper and Special Forces Colonel Clyde Russell, reported directly to the Joint Chiefs of Staff in the Pentagon back in the States.

***

August 1967

First Lieutenant Tracy Tolliver Brown found his duffle among the piles scattered on the ground outside the 90th Replacement Battalion's orderly room near Long Binh. He was finally here. He'd dreamed about arriving here all through his last two years at West Point.

Having been graduated five months ago from West Point, Lt. Brown felt a sense of destiny. This is what he was meant to do. In the folklore of his family, several elders had told stories of a great-great-great-great-grandfather who was a Creek Indian warrior. Tracy's ancestor had fought Andrew Jackson at the battle of Horseshoe Bend. The African-hating Jackson, of course, would later go on to become the seventh president of the United States. According to these family stories, Tracy's ancestor escaped and later led a raiding party that overran a Georgia plantation, killing the owners and liberating the enslaved workers. As the war party swept down on the plantation, the ancestor had observed a stately and suddenly emboldened woman come to action. The big African woman used her brute force to pull a whip out of the hand of a pale middle-aged overseer. She then turned the whip on the overseer and about a dozen other whites. Sometime later, the Creek warrior had a child with the African woman, who became one of the freed persons assimilated into the Creek Nation.

114

Now, Tracy, having been promoted to first lieutenant because of his assignment to a commando unit, was destined to be a warrior. He was well equipped for it. Tracy was ready to repay his country for the four years of free tuition and board and the first-class military training that had been bestowed upon him at West Point. He was ready to give an account of himself in the tradition of his African American and Creek ancestors. At six foot five and having trimmed himself from his starting weight four years ago of 255 pounds to a lean 242, he was muscled and strong. Yet Tracy could run "for days," as one of his trainers had quipped back at the Point. Tracy Brown had been a two-sport letterman in high school, but eschewed athletics in college in favor of total emersion in the crafts of leadership and war.

A short stint at the 3rd Special Forces group at Fort Bragg, North Carolina, had further sharpened and focused him and convinced him about what he wanted to do in Nam. Tracy wanted to be a commando. He wanted to do long-range reconnaissance. Now he was ready to get busy. After arriving at Tan Son Nhut Airport, Tracy only spent one night at the 90th Replacement Battalion.

The next morning after his arrival, he was scooped up by two soldiers wearing Asian-made "sterile' uniforms" (i.e., with no insignias whatsoever). They motored back to Ton Son Nhut, where they boarded a C-130 transport plane along with about fifty other soldiers and marines, plus several female Red Cross workers and two army nurses. The massive plane lifted off and proceeded to head northeast. About two hours later (about 435 miles, or 700 kilometers as the crow flies), they landed at a rough airport south of the ancient city of Huế, near the Pacific coastline.

Off-loading, Tracy saw most of the passengers being picked up and heading north in the direction of Huế. Not wanting to wait to catch a smaller plane, his two escorts jumped into a jeep they'd parked hours earlier. Now the three headed about five miles south to the encampment known as Phu Bai Combat Base, shared between the Marine and Army units. Tracy learned that he was now officially assigned to SOG, which had a forward operating base at Phu Bai.

When off-loading his duffle that first day at Phu Bai, another sterile uniform-wearing soldier in his mid-thirties had been walking by. Captain Whit Watlington took one look at Tracy and yelled, "Big fellah, have I been waiting for you!"

"What?"

"Come with me. I'm about to make you an offer you can't refuse."

***

The next morning

Training Day One

Tracy met some of the members of RT (reconnaissance team) Samoa. Whit Watlington was One-Zero. One-Zero was code for a recon team leader. To be a One-Zero meant you'd been on at least ten to twenty missions and probably more, and you'd come back alive. You had earned the respect of team members who'd been out with you and usually you'd accomplished your mission. If you hadn't accomplished your mission, there were overwhelming reasons why you hadn't. Finally, you'd more often than not brought your team back with a minimum of KIAs.

Code name One-One on RT Samoa was Specialist Five (Spec-5) Henry "Hot Sauce" Rivera. As assistant team leader, a One-One was considered almost as bad-assed as the One-Zero, but just not as experienced and not with the same reputation.

The One-Two was Marine Master Sergeant Stavros "Angel" Angelopoulos. Angel, on a previous tour, had been with a conventional unit in the 26th Marines. There he became fascinated with the recon missions. He had extended and volunteered for assignment to SOG. Traditionally, One-Twos on recon teams functioned as communications specialists.

Mission planning and training for Tracy began with a target and mission description meeting that next morning. The other team members were cycling through all this for the second time because of Tracy, but didn't seem to mind. Maybe Whit had privately convinced them of the benefits of having the big African American on the team. The Americans were Whit, Angel, Hot Sauce, and Tracy (aka Brownie). They were seated around a rectangular table in one of the bunkers at Phu Bai.

Whit started out doing most of the talking, "Gentlemen, I want you to meet Brownie. He has some other name, but that's what we're going to call him. I took onc look at this fresh meat coming from the States and knew there'd be a greater chance for us meeting our mission with him than without him. Luckily when I briefed the commander on my new thinking, he agreed. I'm going to get right into it.

"Yesterday I went out again for a flyover. We didn't buzz the village. I'm pretty comfortable with how it's laid out, and we'll go over that again for Brownie's benefit. Maybe we'll see something we didn't see the first time around. But I wanted to see, number one, if the LZ[1] that we talked about is still the best bet. And number two, I wanted to see where we might encounter hot stuff between the LZ and the village."

"Oh yeah, you know I like hot stuff," said Hot Sauce.

"The kind of hot stuff I like doesn't come in a bottle," chimed in Angel.

Whit said, "Hold on and let me get through this, okay? Then you can show Brownie the kind of barbarians you are."

Laughs.

"So, let's talk it over again. Here's what we're doing. Our mission will be to infiltrate a Việt Cộng[2] village in the A Lưới district on the edge of the A Shau Valley. We're calling this village, Zebra. Our mission is to snatch one or both of the following bad guys.[2]"

---

[1] Landing zone

[2] While the NVA and PAVN were full-time North Vietnamese soldiers, the Việt Cộng (also known as the People's Liberation Armed Forces) were communists who might be full-time in a formalized Cong unit, or who might be guerilla soldiers by night and ordinary villagers and farmers by day. To the extent that the Cong had any direction from formal communist channels, this direction came from the NLF (National Liberation Front) for South Vietnam.

Whit placed their photos on the table side by side as he said their names, "Phan Đức Trong is Target A, or 'Bowlegs,' for obvious reasons. Nguyễn Quang Hứng is Target B. We call Target B 'Fang' 'cause that gook has one bad set of buckteeth. Most of the time, these two pretend to be ordinary rice farmers. A lot of Cong villages are gated with lookouts and punji stakes all around them. This one isn't. It seems to pretend to be just another village of rice farmers, but below this particular village are tunnels where all the Charlie action goes on. I'll get back to that later."

Hot Sauce said to Tracy, "So you're supposed to ask what's so special about these two dudes."

Tracy took the bait. "What's so special about these two dudes?"

Angel placed an aerial photo down beside those of the two booby makers. "These Charlies are known to produce some of the nastiest shit encountered yet by American GIs. They not only make the booby traps themselves, but run a sort of finishing school for booby trap makers. After their training, these students fan out all over Vietnam, Laos, and Cambodia. So our mission . . ."

Hot Sauce broke in, "Should we decide to accept it."

Without breaking his train of thought, Whit continued, ". . . is to get into the village and capture one or both of these booby-trap geniuses so that the analysts back in Saigon can pick their brains about all manner of things having to do with booby traps and their deployment. Stealth is going to be essential. We're not going in to shoot up or destroy the village. If that's all MACV wanted, they would have given the mission to a conventional unit like Eleventh Armored Cavalry or Twenty-Sixth Marines right here at Phu Bai."

Tracy said, "Sounds like fun."

Whit responded, "Glad you feel that way. Truth is, I took one look at you when you were off-loading from the jeep yesterday and I knew with you there would be a greater chance that we could subdue, and therefore not have to kill, these two master booby trappers."

Angel added, "Shit, they'll take one look at your big ass and volunteer to come along."

Laughs.

Now it was Angel's turn to move the ball forward.

"These two dudes not only make the best boobies our forces have ever run into, but they also have trained maybe hundreds of Charlies to make them just as good. And those hundreds have trained other goo gobs to make them. In other words, you are looking at the two tenured professors of the Charlie Cong Booby Trap University. It's located right smack dab in the middle of that innocent-looking Zebra village right there in the picture."

Angel tapped the picture on the table for emphasis. Then, for a good portion of the rest of the day, the RT Samoa members took Tracy through the collection of mock and actual booby traps. Hot Sauce stood and went to three other tables in the room. He lifted some oily tarpaulins to reveal the collection.

Tracy learned that punji stakes and bamboo spears smeared with poison or feces were what GIs often called "VC toothpicks." He learned about some of the stinging fire ants, scorpions, and vipers that Charlie used in their booby traps. He learned about the different ways these creatures' toxins poisoned the unlucky souls that came in contact with them, and how these creatures were dropped into pits to become some unfortunate GI's worst nightmare.

Tracy learned about the placement of pressure-sensitive explosives on door thresholds, under common household objects, and even at the base of flag poles to surprise over-eager GIs who wanted to replace an NVA or NLF flag with the Stars and Stripes. An especially sinister trick was booby trapping mango trees just as the fruit reached peak ripeness. ARVN soldiers and GIs alike didn't seem to be able to resist climbing for these luscious fruits and getting their asses blown apart.

He learned about spiked swinging logs and falling weight traps that were usually placed over roads and trails. He learned about various types of tree snares and ankle traps that secured but didn't kill unsuspecting GIs. He learned about neck snares that did, in fact, choke and kill. He learned about the sabotaging of abandoned ammunition and/or grenade caches so they would blow when moved.

For the last hour of the late afternoon, they moved into maps and intelligence reports. This session was more intense than any he'd experienced at either West Point or Fort Bragg. As early evening rolled around, Tracy's brain was fried.

Whit gave every one but Tracy the rest of the evening off, saying, "We'll pick it up in the morning, and Tracy, you'll get to meet our other Samoa team members. But before you hit the rack, I want you back here by yourself. I'm going to be quizzing you off and on about this terrain map. You dig?"

"Got it. I'll need to snatch some sleep for an hour or two to get my brain working again. That's all I'll need."

***

Training Day Two

RT Samoa's size doubled the next day, from four to eight. Tracy had been inserted and given the unusual code as One-Three in charge of snatching and manhandling. Rounding out the team were four Montagnard tribesmen. Tracy had learned back at Fort Bragg that one of the things distinguishing US Army Special Forces operations from operations in every other part of the army was the emphasis on training and working with indigenous forces. Whether Montagnards (mountain people from Vietnam's central highlands) or Nungs (ethnic Chinese tribesmen), missions always included these Indigs on recon teams. And these Indigs were loyal to their SOG leaders and were as committed and as brave as any American GI.

The Montagnards were motivated. They were generally stocky and dark-skinned. and the Vietnamese people discriminated against them. They were regarded as *moi* (savages). So, since the Vietnamese people didn't like the Yards, the Yards didn't like the Vietnamese back (neither North nor South). Simple as that. RT Samoa's Yards were Doi, Neh, Ksor, and Glun.

After introductions, Whit picked it up, "Code name Zebra village is on the southeast edge of a densely forested area of the valley. We think that gives us somewhat of an advantage in terms of our ability to drop on the far side of the forest and trek through without being seen. We'll come out on the edge where we can wait until Covey[3] says we should spring. On the southeast side of the village are rice paddies served by a stream that runs down from the mountains. A system of two- to four-foot-wide dykes is used by farmers from the village to walk out into the field. These dykes are splayed out on either side of the stream. The Cong/farmers step off the dykes into the flooded paddies when planting or harvesting their rice.

"On the northeast side of Zebra are tunnels that overlap underneath. Our aerial reconnaissance tells us that Fang and Bowlegs spend days or even weeks playing the role of ordinary rice farmers. Then the tip-off pattern has been observed. Over a period of days, newcomers start arriving at the village. Shortly thereafter, Bowlegs, Fang, and these newcomers disappear into the tunnels for several days. We believe that during these periods, they are conducting the booby training. We know there is a rather large room in one of the tunnels specifically dedicated to training."

Tracy smiled. "So we sneak into the tunnel, find the training room, and snatch the trainers, and at the same time we blow away the trainees."

Silence.

"Uh, Brownie. No, first of all, the students are not targets in this particular mission. But why else do you think we're not going to do it that way?"

Tracy was embarrassed and thought. Then it dawned on him. Sheepishly, he said, "Because the geniuses are more vulnerable

---

[3] Covey was the call sign for SOG recon men (Covey Riders) riding with pilots from the Air Force's 20th Tactical Air Support Group out of Danang and Pleiku. They spotted targets and supported SOG ground operations by overflying high above Vietnam, Laos, and Cambodia. These eyes-in-the-sky saved many American lives with their tactical advice and by calling in evacuations, artillery or close air support.

when they aren't in the tunnels. The best shot at them would be when they're out in the dykes doing their rice farmer impressions outside the village.

The Americans and Yards smiled.

"Bingo again, my very large and dark-skinned brother. Besides, you wouldn't fit in a tunnel in the first place. Actually, at first that was our theory. I'm sure you haven't noticed it yet, but Whit, Angel, and me are not much taller than Doi, Neh, Ksor, and Glun. We're of diminished stature on purpose in this RT."

Everybody except Tracy broke out in loud guffaws. Tracy smiled but kept his mouth shut.

"We thought we were going to all be going into the tunnels. We actually sent Ksor and Glun in to do some recon one night when it seemed that most of the Charlies were out doing mayhem. They went in from the stream through one of the underwater entrances, dressed in their black VC pajamas and their rice paddy hats. What was your verdict, Ksor?"

In surprisingly good English, Ksor said, "Too confusing. Easy to get lost. Easy to get cut off. Some false tunnels with booby traps at end."

"And now that we have your big ass, totally out of the question," said Hot Sauce.

The briefing went back to Whit.

"Ksor also brought back these pictures. If I weren't at war with these guys, I'd be amazed at their ingenuity. Ventilation shafts facing in multiple directions and able to be closed off to prevent flooding. I make this one out to be sleeping quarters. This one seems to be where they store arms and rice. Here's the well. These are definitely firing posts, and this one is definitely a kitchen. But the one that blows me away is this pic of their conference chamber, all decked out in total habitat. On one side, you'd think we were out in the middle of the jungle somewhere, and on the other side, it looks like an ordinary crossroad.

"Anyway, it's possible that MACV will have the Third Marine Division go in after our mission and clear the village and blow as many tunnels as possible. But we have no chance at all at the bomb geniuses if they do this first, because their means of getting away are too many and too sophisticated, so our snatch attempt has priority."

At this point, Doi produced a canvas bag and plopped himself in front of Tracy. Out of the bag he produced a whole array of supplies that proved to be for camouflage.

Whit said, "Brownie, we're going to shift now. We all know how to do this, so we're going to leave you with Doi and Neh for about an hour. We have to figure out what's the best look for you, and then you're going to have to learn to do it yourself."

"Do what?" Tracy yelled at Whit's back as he was walking out of the room.

And just like that, Angel, Hot Sauce, Whit, Ksor, and Glun were gone. Neh rolled over a five-foot-tall mirror. He positioned it behind Doi, who was laying an assortment of tubes out on the table. The jars and brushes were for creating the five shades of green face-covering, known as the frog-skin camouflage pattern. The products had been secretly created for the US military by Revlon, in consultation with horticulturists familiar with the flora and fauna of Southeast Asia.

Doi worked on Tracy, calling for different colors and brushes. He experimented with the combinations and thicknesses that would work with Tracy's dark skin. Neh acted like an emergency room nurse assisting a doctor in surgery. He grabbed and handed over stuff as called for in their native Degar language. Doi finished in about one hour. And right on time, the others appeared to assess and make suggestions. Tracy turned his head back and forth, staring at himself in the mirror. Whit took a Polaroid picture, and when it was processed placed the photo front and center on the table in front of Tracy. Then the five disappeared again. Neh used a bucket of soapy water and cloths to clean Tracy up. Then Doi handed a new makeup brush to Tracy.

"Now you do it, Brownie!"

"You've gotta be shitting me."

"Not shitting you. You have to be able to do self. We have to do ourselves before mission. You go now!"

With a sigh of resignation, Tracy took the brush and began. At some point, Whit came back alone, looked, nodded approvingly, and left again. Then Neh cleaned Tracy up again while Doi took away the mirror.

"Now you do it again. No mirror. Usually we don't have mirrors."

"Fuck, this is getting old."

"You GIs so spoiled. This is what we do. So now this is what you do, Brownie. You start. Neh and Doi come back soon. We bring you back something to eat." Then they disappeared.

After several minutes of hyperventilating, Tracy finally started. He stared at the Polaroid photo in front of him. Finally, he started and found the process painstaking. He was clumsy with the brushes. He tried to replicate what he saw on the photo. Several times he sneak-peeked at the mirror, plunged a rag into the soapy water, cleaned himself up, and started over. After over one hour, Neh and Doi returned with a platter of food and placed it on the table. Tracy ignored the food, now consumed with making himself look exactly like the Polaroid photograph.

Late in the afternoon, all the members reappeared and evaluated Tracy's look. They agreed that he'd done a fine job.

Whit said, "That's enough for today. It's Neh's birthday, and we're going to have a party. See you at the NCO club around eighteen hundred. We're going out at oh seven hundred in the morning. Everybody in full cammo and equipment. We're going to practice patrol walking all day. You too, Brownie, in full cammo and equipment. We'll decide on your armament before we start out, but you need to do the cammo. So whatever time you think you need to be here to start getting ready, that's when you should show up."

***

The raucous party for Neh broke up around midnight, but Tracy turned in around 2200 hours. When he'd arrived around 1830 at the NCO Club (which was two large field tents connected) he walked in on Neh standing on a barstool singing "Secret Agent Man" by Johnny Rivers.

"A man who lives a life of danger . . ."

Whoops and hollers followed every chorus, sung by the entire room.

Tracy found out that the Montagnards had picked up a love of the tune from their GI counterparts because it basically touted badd MFs. They took every opportunity to break out in the song. Neh, Glun, Ksor, and Doi liked to think of themselves as badd MFs too, and by all means, Tracy would soon discover that they were.

***

Training Day Three

Tracy was in the training room at 0430 the next morning. After several tries without looking in the mirror until after he'd finished, he was finally satisfied. At 0630, the other team members started coming in. They were in cammo already.

Deciding on armament was no small task. One of the reasons the SOG consistently held a 1,000-to-1 KIA advantage over the NVA and Viet Cong (versus only 100-to-1 for conventional forces) was that commando teams trained to try to have no weak links. They were better equipped than the enemy in so many ways, but especially in terms of their prowess with superior armament. Where the enemy or even conventional GIs would spray, commandos fired three-round bursts or even single shots. And the enemy went down. Sometimes the enemy sprayed and nobody went down. If commandos sprayed, a whole bunch of the enemy went down.

"I'm seeing stuff that isn't American made. Why?"

Without seeming to hear the question, Whit began, "Well, let's start with our US-made M-79 grenade launchers with both shotgun and rocket shells. That's going to be what Doi and Hot Sauce carry, and you should see them. Poncho Villa would be jealous if he saw these dudes' bandoleers. One will be a twenty-rounder of fragmentation or high explosive shells, and the other will hold ten shotgun shells. Both ladies will also have a couple of frag grenades and some smoke grenades in case we need to get away under cover."

Doi, who usually walked the point on recon patrols, beamed at being mentioned first. Hot Sauce stayed quiet for a change.

"Now you, Angel, and I will carry these US-made Colt CAR-15s. They look like the M-16, but they were modified for guys like us. The barrel is half the length of the M-16, and watch this."

Whit demonstrated collapsing the stock for portability, and then snapping it back out for firing.

RT-Samoa total so far: three CAR-15s and two M-79s.

"But back to your question, traditionally a lot of LRRPs go into areas like Laos and Cambodia where, by treaty, we're not supposed to be. You'll do some of those eventually. As a matter of fact, you'll do a lot of those if we don't get you killed on your first LRRP."

Whit winked and Tracy winked back.

"On those missions, we don't carry Stoners or CAR-15s. If we lose control of a foreign weapon, we can credibly deny being there. For this mission, we're in Vietnamese territory, so I like the CAR-15. But for some reason, some of our Montagnard brothers prefer the longer Stoner 63A, also made in the good old US of A. For Neh and Ksor, that's their choice."

RT-Samoa total so far: two M-79 grenade launchers, plus three CAR-15s, plus two Stoners.

"The question is, what else?"

Hot Sauce took up the lead with the brief. "Me, Ksor, Glun, and Neh will each have four claymores. And for dogs, me and Neh will also each have one of these little bags."

Tracy asked, "What's in them?"

"Red pepper."

"Oh," said Tracy, catching on immediately.

Now Whit took the brief over again. "Whether you carry a CAR-15 or Stoner, everyone will take along twenty extra mags, modified for thirty rounds. We generally stop at twenty-nine rounds, which prevents jamming. Glun will be our Chinese RPD machine gun guy.

Glun broke out into a big grin, did a thumbs-up, and made a spraying gesture. Tracy thought to himself, *Now where would he have ever seen an Audie Murphy movie?*

Whit continued, "Modifications include a chopped barrel and modified drum magazines, so we're talking about twelve pounds of weight instead of over fifteen, delivering one hundred twenty-five-minus-one rounds instead of one hundred. Glun carries five additional mags."

RT-Samoa total so far: two M-79s, plus four CAR-15s, plus two Stoners 63-As, plus one Chinese RPD machine gun, plus sixteen claymores.

"What else? Oh yes, Angel has to lug the PRC-25 radio. Also, I carry this V-42 stiletto, unofficially dubbed the SOG knife, with a six-inch blade. I highly recommend it. I'm even getting better at throwing it. What do you think, Tracy?"

"Give me two."

"What you going to use two for?"

"I'll have one in the small of my back for stand-up fighting or throwing. Then I'll have one on my ankle in case I'm on the ground, though that's unlikely."

"Oh, you never get put on the ground?"

"Frankly, no."

"You ever wrestled?"

Tracy broke out laughing.

"What? You never heard of wrestling."

"Oh, I heard of it. That's a damn boring sport. Tried it at the Point. Got tired of slamming guys; no competition."

Now Whit and the whole room broke out laughing. Whit said, "Didn't I tell you guys I was bringing in a beast? Samoa, meet Brownie the Beast."

While they all guffawed, Whit slid over two of the sheathed knives. Tracy grabbed a stiletto from its sheath, spun, and hurled it, without seeming to aim, straight to the center of a wooden post across the room.

"Damn," said Angel.

"Chalk it up to my Indian ancestry," said Tracy.

"Although I guess I should also give credit to the hundreds of hours I put in at the Point perfecting my throwing skills. In our senior year, when my classmates were sleeping, I was outside every night throwing for at least an hour. Maybe my ancestors just motivated me."

At which point, Glun, Doi, Neh, and Ksor all bent over and pulled big curved blades from scabbards that had been hidden under the weapons table.

"What the hell are those?" asked Tracy with surprise.

Hot Sauce answered, "Oh, you mean those Gurkha Kukri fighting knives?"

The Montagnards waived the blades menacingly toward Tracy, who broke out in a broad grin.

Whit said, "So, is there anything else someone thinks they need?"

Tracy replied, "Yes, I'd like a pistol, especially for when I get in close."

"Boy, have I got a deal for you," said Whit.

"In fact, I bet you already know this Colt M1911 semi-automatic service pistol from your time at the Point."

"Oh yeah! Fires forty-five-caliber slugs that pack a punch; seven-round magazine. That's what I was hoping for, and I'll try two extra mags."

"Only two?"

"Believe me; that's all I'll need. If I have to draw my pistol, it'll be close range. That means one slug, one KIA. Not expecting to have to kill twenty-one all by myself."

"Well, I forgot to mention that Doi and Hot Sauce will also be carrying the same pistols with three extra mags."

"Cool."

Now Whit winked at Hot Sauce, but Hot Sauce frowned. "Damn, Whit, you know I can't wink. You just trying to embarrass me."

At that, all four Montagnards winked and then cracked up laughing. Whit winked back at them. Then, "Okay, that's it for now, boys and girls. We'll take a break and then head on out for our walk. We want to test all this weight we're carrying."

RT-Samoa final armament total: three CAR-15s, plus two Stoner 63-As, plus one Chinese RPD machine gun, two M-79 grenade launchers, plus sixteen Claymores, plus three V-42 stilettos, plus four Gurkha Kukri fighting knives, and three M1911 semi-automatic service pistols.

***

The rest of the day, RT Samoa learned "how to walk." Tracy was incredulous at first. Then on a dry run he was in the fifth position in line, assigned to surveil from 0800 to 1000 hours on the team's perimeter. He watched Neh in front of him and tried to copy everything the Yard did:

Step,

Scan front,

Scan side,

Look for anything out of the norm,

Then look down for your next step.

Use the toe of your foot to test first before placing the whole foot. Pause and listen, look, and smell.

Gradually shift your weight onto the forward foot as you clear the tallest elephant grass or tree branch from in front of your face, but also hold onto it to make sure that it doesn't make a sound crashing into the man behind you.

Now carefully bring the trailing foot up parallel with the lead one.

After more than three hours, Tracy got impatient when he noticed that their one-step-per-minute pace had only moved them a little more than half a click (about 500 meters). In frustration, he stepped forward too hard. A twig snapped loudly, and every member of RT Samoa stopped and their eyes shot darts at the new guy.

Whit said, "What the fuck, Brownie! You couldn't have stepped around that twig? Charlie can hear that kind of snap over one hundred yards away."

"Shit, Whit, I got big feet."

"Well you'd better learn where to place those big feet, or else we'll have to chop them in half. Or I'll get SOG upstairs in Saigon to approve your transfer to any grunt unit you so desire. Your big-ass feet are not going to get my commandos killed. If you can't see a place to step, you've got to stop. Bend over and clear a path with your hands if you have to. The enemy thinks GIs are easy to see in their bright green unis. That's why we don't wear bright green unis. Charlie thinks we are easy to smell. That's why we try our damndest to smear ourselves or otherwise disguise our soaps and other products. He thinks we are easy to hear. That's why we're doing what we're doing right the fuck now. We are commandos. We are ghosts. Is that clear, Brownie?"

Tracy was enraged. All the animal adrenaline burst underneath his skin to lash out. Tracy was good at everything. Nobody had ever admonished Tracy Brown. Why? Because Tracy Brown was good *at everything*. Tracy had always been good at everything. How dare this short-assed motherfucker intimate that he couldn't do something as simple as walking in the woods! *How dare him!* And then it subsided. His eyes softened. He closed them and began to breathe deeply.

"Sorry, Whit. Sorry, man. I can do it. I can walk softly. Let's go. I'll show you. Sorry, team. I'll do it."

Without acknowledging Tracy's apology, Whit said, "While we're stopped, I want to make one more thing clear. We don't talk on patrols. *We don't talk!* One of the reasons why we practice so hard and so much is that we want to know each other's thoughts before they're thought. We use hand signals and gestures if we can't read each other's minds. But this is the last time until we get back to the FOB tonight that anyone will say anything. He signaled Doi, who was on point. The Yard silently stepped off.

***

Two Whole Weeks More

They did the same walk the next day. Then they did a different walk the next day and the next. They did still different walks the next day and for three more consecutive days, and these times another recon team staged some surprise assaults. They did this over and over, day after day, and week after week, until Whit and all the other RT Samoa members, including Tracy, agreed that they were virtually undetectable together. They had practiced their impeccably choreographed IAs (immediate action drills) so much that they didn't even have to think about them.

One evasive technique Tracy learned was the double back. If a Cong tracker or watcher was suspected to be onto the RT, they would return to the starting point and usually strike out on another path; sometimes to evade the tracker and sometimes to flank him. Tracy had to learn Doi's alert hand signal (which could be used by any team member), and Whit's signal for the double back. RT Samoa also practiced ambush and counter-ambush techniques, as well as sniping and counter-sniping. They practiced techniques for hiding in plain sight and for hiding in thin cover without being noticed.

Every day, photos came into the Phu Bai base, and Samoa members were given a stack to study. Bowlegs and Fang were usually photoed from directly above, but occasionally Covey could get an angle so that their faces could be seen. Each member of the team was expected to be able to identify the targets instantaneously and from as far away as possible.

After the second week, RT Samoa started practicing extractions and exfiltrations. This was going to be the heart of their mission. Before going out one morning, Whit said, "We'll bring Bowlegs and Fang back to the FOB with us if we have to, but what we'd really like to do is have a chopper drop a STABO harness, haul them out, and take them straight to Saigon."

The RT also practiced taking the targets out overland, just in case. Their rehearsals included night and day scenarios, and all their scenarios assumed being under fire. By the fourth week, Tracy was itching. Countless LRRP missions had gone out since he'd arrived at Phu Bai FOB, and he'd not yet been out on a mission.

He approached the One-Zero for LT Samoa, "I'm dying here. All we've done since I got here is train. I came here for contact. When are we going out, Whit?"

"In the morning, Brownie. In the morning! This afternoon we did our final weapons testing. Everything and everybody tested out. Now we're ready to go."

Tracy let out a yelp. Whit Watlington, his One-Zero, said, "Before you arrived we were actually ready to go, but when I took one look at your big ass, I knew that I needed you to cap off our team. I actually had to sell the SOG Ops. Finally, when they admitted that this mission wasn't time sensitive, they ran it up to SOG Saigon, who said it was okay to delay. You were green. We can't have green on any LT, and especially not on this one. This is going to be one hairy motherfucker."

"You know, people think us commandos are the baddest SOBs in the war, and we are. But we're badd, not just because we're badd. We train. We prepare. Then we go out and kick ass. You thought you were ready to kick ass when you showed up, but you weren't. Now you are. Get your gear and be ready for the chopper at oh seven hundred."

RT Samoa was ready for action.

Chapter 23
Code Name Boobie-Baby

The Kingbee pilot lifted the H-34[4] chopper off from Phu Bai around 0730 that morning in early December 1967. The lift would take a half hour, over the eastern range and into the A Shau Valley LZ. Thirty miles southeast of Khe Sahn, the twenty-five-mile-long, mile-wide A Shau Valley near the Laotian border was flanked by densely forested 5,000-foot mountains. Not playing for the city championship in basketball at Harrison Tech, not in any of the exercises at West Point, had Tracy experienced such an adrenaline rush.

Whit observed him and violated the no-talk rule, saying, "Breathe, Brownie. Breathe. It'll calm you down. You're totally prepared. We all are. Let that relax you."

Due to their desire to land without incident, RT Samoa's LZ was about two and a half kilometers from Zebra. Villages all over this province were used to hearing helicopter flyovers, so these overflights tended not to draw too much attention unless they were really close. Now it was right at the tail end of the rainiest season in Central and Southern Vietnam. The temperature, eighty degrees Fahrenheit, would be about at the average for this time of year. As Samoa flew into the LZ, they were pleased that it was not raining at the moment. Rain would have made it really difficult to navigate through the tall elephant grass in front of them.

Covey had advised RT Samoa that they shouldn't land too close to the forest abutting the village. Cong patrols might pick them up. By landing where they did, they could approach the dense forest

---

[4] The Sikorsky H-34 helicopter was thought of as obsolete by many conventional units using modern Bell UH-1 "Hueys." But the Vietnamese pilots known as "The Kingbees" who supported SOG operations seemed to prefer them.

carefully and pick their point of entry. The walk through tall elephant grass using their one-step-per-minute procedure was estimated to take many hours. By nightfall (around 2000 hours) that should bring them to a relatively open rise that would crest in about fifty yards. Then, descending the backside of the rise, they would enter the dense mangrove forest with a few open pockets where the soil was too rocky for dense growth. The plan was to walk this stretch (one click) and arrive at its edge in the middle of the night. Then they would rest on the edge of the forest for a few hours of sleep until nearly sunup. That's when they would rise and view the village.

Whit had warned RT Samoa that they should be ready to spring into action that very morning. He'd also said that they might not go for several days. They should be prepared to wait in hiding until Covey told them the targets were in the rice paddies. No word from Covey came that first morning. By evening, they took turns burning the land leeches off each other. The second night, a tiger came within twenty yards of their hiding place in the forest and almost certainly saw at least one of them. The fact that it showed no interest may have been the product of a full belly, or the result of smelling that the odds of multiple adversaries weren't worth the bother.

Eating breakfast at daybreak on the second morning, Angel gave a signal and handed his radio headset to Whit, who listened to the word from Covey. Then he gave the pack-up-and-move signal. By this, everyone knew that the targets had left the village for the rice paddies. When ready, Doi took the point, and the rest of RT Samoa fell in line behind: Whit, Angel, Glun, Tracy, Ksor, Hot Sauce, and Neh.

The crawl and crab-walk around to the east side of the village was painstakingly slow. Then, just as the dykes and rice paddies to the southeast came into view, small arms fire hit around them from Russian AK-47s, SKS carbines, and French 9mm MaT-49 submachine guns. Despite Whit's admonition on the chopper to breathe and calm down, Tracy had been on pins and needles up to this point.

He'd realized how amped up he was, but when the first slugs hit the ground about four feet away, amazingly, Tracy relaxed.

Thank you, grandfather, Tracy thought. *It's finally real, and I hope you'll be proud of me when this day is done.*

Without any words, RT Samoa went into one of its many immediate action drills. From the crawl position, the first group (Whit, Angel, Glun, and Hot Sauce) pivoted right toward the village and their CAR-15s and Stoners returned fire in three-round bursts, while Hot Sauce sent in grenades from his M-79.

The second group (Doi, Tracy, Ksor, and Neh) moved left, half stood, and began an all-out race toward the rice paddies. The Charlies play-acting as farmers in the fields had looked toward the action, but had not yet started to move. Tracy was now in full-out sprint mode across one of the dykes.

Charlies jumped out from tunnel rabbit holes with AK-47s. Two of them sported RPG grenade launchers. Whit was watching the second group's progress from more than forty meters away. He easily knocked these two down with his CAR-15 as they attempted to train their weapons on the group running toward the targets.

Thw-wh, thw-wh came the multi-syllable report and echo of Whit's weapon in single-fire mode. The first man's body fell backward and his AK flew up in the air. The second man was trying to turn to locate where Whit's fire was coming from.

Thw-wh, thw-wh, thw-wh.

The second man's head exploded from the first shell, before his chest burst from the second and third rounds. Whit was an excellent marksman, and his training was paying off in all kinds of ways. He'd given himself the task of covering group two as they went for the targets until they were on the scene. Then he would turn and rejoin Angel, Glun, and Hot Sauce in group one's firefight.

Now, from memory, Tracy spotted both targets as they raced across an intersecting dyke to get some hidden weapons. Whit, still watching group two's progress, saw the targets' trajectories.

"Cut them off before they can get to where their guns are stashed," Whit uncharacteristically shouted. Tracy fired in automatic mode on the run.

Thw-thw-thw-thw-thw-wh.

He'd taken out one bodyguard. The burst caught the man in the front side and then bullets stitched a path up his chest. Then Tracy collapsed the CAR-15 stock, slung it, and drew his pistol, all the while closing the distance between himself and the targets. Ksor was just about five meters behind Tracy. Meanwhile, Doi lobbed grenades into rabbit-hole positions under the dykes.

Thoomp, thoomp, followed by *booom, booom. Thoomp, thoomp,* then *booom, booom.*

The commandos could hear screams coming up from rabbit holes that were being turned into gravesites. Neh's Stoner bursts picked off several Charlies running toward them from various points in the rice paddy.

Tracy was now just ten feet from the targets. He instinctively went against his training, which was to always aim center mass. He aimed low and his pistol sounded.

Pphw-wh.

He was trying to shoot Fang in the left leg to get him off his feet, but his round caught the booby meister through the right knee. Now, while Fang crumpled and writhed in pain, Bowlegs and two other bodyguards were on top of Tracy. Three others looked on at the scrum. They were trying to get a clear shot at the big black commando.

Then these two observing Charlies raised their AK-47s toward Tracy. But they never got to fire. Ksor's Stoner barked its sound and they were down. The Montagnard warrior lowered the rifle and hefted his big knife. With a violent downward swing, he chopped off the shooting arm of the third observing bodyguard. The man screamed and fell. Ksor finished it by swinging a merciful deadly blow into the man's chest as he writhed on the ground.

Two simultaneous firefights were now underway. Running and leaping across dykes, Doi and Neh emptied round after round of Stoner and M-79 shotgun shells down into rabbit holes in the rice paddies. At the same time, group one, with Whit having rejoined them, was starting to wear down the Charlies in the village, who were running between buildings or engaging them from tunnel firing ports.

Without warning, Neh was hit in the left shoulder. The round spun him around just as another caught him from the back on the right side just below his chest cavity. Immediately Ksor was sprinting toward his fellow Montagnard, leaving Tracy to deal with Bowlegs and his two remaining bodyguards. Because the firefight was raging, the no-talk rule was suspended. Speaking in the Degar language of their tribe, Ksor briefly checked with Neh and scanned both wounds, treating them with the quick clot gauze that all the commandos were carrying. Neh assured Ksor he was still in the fight. His shoulder had gone limp down to the elbow, but he found he could still shoot by lifting his forearm parallel to the ground and balancing his Stoner across it. The two tribesmen together with Doi soon prevailed in the rice patty battle.

Meanwhile, Tracy had been left with Bowlegs and his two remaining protectors. Fang was out of commission, writhing on the ground with his knee wound. Tracy flipped one attacker off his back. Using uncommon strength, he grabbed and snapped both this man's arms. He punched the other bodyguard with his massive fist directly in the face. The blow landed with such violence as to knock the Charlie out cold. Blood spattered all over the unconscious man's face as everything flattened, his nose split, and his eyes bulged and bled.

Tracy and Bowlegs eyed one another. Bowlegs was sinuous, but at least a hundred pounds lighter. Tracy instantly knew from this man's stance that not only was he no ordinary farmer, he also was no ordinary fighter. With a slight smile, Tracy thought, *This could be fun. If I had more time, I'd let this guy hit me just to see what kind of load he brings.*

Then Tracy silently chuckled at another thought, *These VCs must know what horrible shots they are, so as long as me and Bowlegs are in close combat, they're not going to risk hitting one of their booby trap teachers.*

Tracy circled, and now Bowlegs was coming at him with a machete. In a quick motion, Tracy stopped and backed up a step. This meant that he wasn't where the Cong thought he'd connect. The man went off balance, and as he did, Tracy jumped forward and slammed him down across the dyke and into the rice paddy. His machete flew out of reach, but quicker than Tracy expected, the soaking-wet adversary sprung up on the side of the dyke and shot him with a field-made cigarette lighter gun. Tracy had momentarily turned away to survey his Montagnard companions. The first shot caught him in the back of the cheek and spun his head around. Amazingly, the molar stayed in place and the round came through his mouth and exited when he yelled in pain. A second shot slammed into his backside as he spun away. A normal man would at least have been knocked off his feet. Tracy, now down to 239 pounds and only six-percent body fat, was no normal man.

Now Bowlegs had Tracy's full attention again. The two-shot cigarette lighter gun being empty now, the booby maker was fishing in the ditch for his machete. Tracy came up behind him and skillfully aimed the knife side of his big hand at the ganglia place low in the back of the man's neck. This particular set of tightly wound nerves impacted not only the neck, but also the thoracic and abdominal cavities. The man began to twitch as his central nervous system started to lock up. Tracy hoisted up the booby trap sensei like a sack of potatoes, threw him over his shoulder, retrieved his CAR-15 and pistol, and retreated to rejoin group one.

Damn, I still haven't had a chance to use my knives, thought Tracy with his ironic sense of humor.

About thirty Cong lay dead across the fields. Now Ksor turned his attention back toward where Tracy was moving. Neh was walking on his own in the same direction. Doi and Ksor trotted over to restrain Fang, who was painfully starting to get up from the trench, despite his knee being a mass of shattered bone and blood. They didn't try to lift the somewhat overweight second target, but, to the man's screaming protests, Doi and Ksor simply dragged him along behind them by his armpits.

Now as group two rejoined the rest of RT Samoa, their targets in tow, Whit eyed Neh's wounds. The tribesman smiled and winked. Whit had seen Tracy get hit in the cheek and butt. Following his One-Zero's eyes, Tracy cracked, "You should probably suck out the infection."

"If that's what you need, then you'll die," said Whit.

With the machine gun, M-79s, CAR-15s, and Stoners all engaging the village, firing from that direction began to wane. The team could see dozens of Cong (men and women) sprawled dead throughout the village. They presumed that noncombatant women and children were probably hiding down in the tunnel system. Unless they came out fighting, Samoa's mission had no interest in them.

Then Whit said, "Angel, get on the horn to Covey for a pickup. We'll take two lines for the targets right here."

In less than five minutes, they heard the *whop, whop, whop* of an H-34's rotors. As they strapped him in, Bowlegs began to kick. Tracy stepped forward and backhanded him. The booby master fell back, unconscious again. Fang was placed in the other STABO line lowered from the chopper. A moment later, the two targets were off the ground and their trip to Saigon was underway. The medic and other chopper crewmen would be able to restrain them, while also keeping them alive.

Now Whit and his commandos regrouped for the *di di mau*[5] back to the LZ. This time they'd be skirting rather than trampling through the forest. Speed rather than stealth would be at a premium now. Coming around the forest and up and down the rise, Samoa was now at the edge of the elephant grass area. Doi held up his

---

[5] GIs colloquialized a common Vietnamese phrase *(di di mau* or get lost!). Sometimes GIs meant "get lost" but other times they just meant "hurry" or "fast exit."

hand, signaling stop. He'd spotted a place where the waist-to-shoulder-length elephant grass seemed to have been disturbed. Now Whit signaled Angel on the radio. He mouthed that he wanted Covey to let them know what was in the grass.

"Charlie's waiting for us in there," mouthed Angel, conveying the word from above.

"Options?" whispered Angel into the receiver. He came back with word from above.

"Back in the woods, there's an open pocket where a chopper could land if we could clear two trees—three hundred and fifty meters."

Whit said, "Get the coordinates."

They were passed along and Doi immediately set off running up and back down the rise again, heading in the direction of the woods. The rest of RT Samoa followed, suspending their normal one-step-per-minute caution. Glun and Ksor, hanging back at the top of the rise, saw a platoon of about forty Charlies break out of the elephant grass at the exact spot where DOI had spotted their sign. With a yelp, the enemy started to sprint after Samoa.

"Bad guys come," Glun yelled, opening up with a shotgun blast. Ksor's Stoner joined in the covering fire for their teammates.

Ten seconds later, Whit was at the edge of the trees and turned to fire back. He yelled to Glun and Ksor to come ahead and that he was covering them. Tracy started to also drop in order to help Whit cover his teammates, but his One-Zero said, "No! You, Doi, and Angel go on and don't stop till you get to the new LZ. Find those trees and call into Covey for something from the air to knock them down."

Bullets whizzed into the mangroves from the pursuing Cong as other Samoa commandos dove in next to their One-Zero. They returned fire for about three minutes, enough for the pursuers to drop to the ground. Then the trailing Samoa commandos stood in a low crouch and started deeper into the woods.

Tracy, Doi, and Angel had found four, not two, trees that prevented the clearing from being a proper LZ. Choppers needed at least fifty to sixty feet of clearance for their rotors to get close to the ground.

Angel called up to Covey. "Work a miracle for us! In the next couple of minutes, we need something to come over and blow the shit out of four trees. Two minutes after that we need a chopper to dust us the hell out of here."

"Will see what I can do. Call you right back."

Tracy looked a question over to Angel, who held up his hand in a "wait a minute" gesture. But in under one minute, Covey was back in touch with amazing news. The word was good.

"They caught an F-105 Thud pilot on his way home from a Ho Chi Minh trail run. He's still half loaded and wouldn't mind using up some more fire juice. Y'all get the hell away from those trees, quick. They're about to go to tree heaven."

Without words, Angel took off across the clearing, back toward where they had first arrived. He waved the others to follow. They could already hear the roar of the F-105 Thunderchief fighter-bomber coming in low and passing directly over the scurrying RT Samoa recon team. The commandos saw it circle back as the pilot lined up his shot. Just as they made the edge, they almost ran into Whit and the teammates, who were about to come into the clearing.

"Stop! Get low!" screamed Angel, awkwardly diving back into the woods.

The Thud came in low, and the commandos heard the whir of the M-61 20mm multi-barrel gun firing at 6,000 rounds per minute. Just like that, the four trees in a cluster shredded, split apart, and fell. The Thud pilot banked to allow himself to see if he'd done the trick. When he saw the trees were down, he tipped his wings and was gone.

Unfortunately, Charlie must have also been hiding and watching the show. As soon as the jet disappeared, Samoa heard them advancing. Whit sprang from his cover in the woods and stepped ten meters into the clearing. He turned and placed his two claymores facing the edge of the woods. The other seven commandos followed suit, spreading and staggering the placement of claymores. As they were doing this, they heard the *whop-whop* sound of H-34 rotors. Turning, they saw Bubba, a beloved and courageous (some said crazy) South Vietnamese pilot, who was known to all but Tracy.

Bubba descended to less than six feet and hovered for the dust off. Running toward where the chopper would descend, they heard the first Charlies break into the clearing firing. Bubba rotated around so his nose faced perpendicular to the wood line. He held it steady but couldn't put the bird on the ground. There was still too much underbrush for a complete landing. The door gunners leaned out and began firing over the commandos' heads as they started piling in. Tracy boosted Neh up and the Montagnard got a hand from the medic.

Then Angel was handing his radio up. He had boosted himself up on the rudder when his head exploded. One round entered under the cranium and came out through his eye. Angel was dead instantaneously. Blood and the milky white gelatinous eye material seeped out all over his face. Before he could fall, the crew chief caught him by the collar and pulled him in. By now, Glun, Hot Sauce, and Neh were in the bird. They were helping the door gunners to ensure the Cong kept their heads down.

Glun, Doi, and Ksor all turned and detonated their claymores just before leaping up into the chopper.

Boom! Boom! Boom!

The last people into the chopper were Whit Wattlington and Tracy Brown. Whit detonated the last claymores as he hauled himself in. As the bird lifted off, one of the door gunners caught a cluster of rounds in his chest. He flew backward across the cabin, unconscious but still alive because of the steel plate body armor that H-14 door gunners wore. The medic saw the blood stains that covered Tracy's ass. He unceremoniously cut away the back of Tracy's pants and used a saline solution to quickly clean the hip wound. As they flew away, the medic hooked up an intravenous for Neh. Now he rested the fallen door gunner out of the way next to Angel's corpse.

"You'll need antibiotics. Other than that, looks like you're a quick clotter, but I'll still put some gauze over the hole in your cheek. That okay with you, soldier?"

Tracy, with his ass exposed, raised his thumb in approval. "Just don't think we're gonna get friendly now," he quipped.

As the helicopter arced over the trees and out of sight from the Charlies, Tracy let his eyes go unfocused in the way that he did when communicating with his ancestor. Using the only phonetic word he remembered from growing up and hearing the passed-down stories about the old warrior, he thought, *Muh-Doe* (Thank you) *Grandfather. I hope you are proud of me. I felt you protecting me and I give you all the blessing and honor that I have. Muh-Doe.*

As for wounds, Tracy discovered over the next few missions that in the world of SOGs, wounds rarely took commandos out of action. Though KIAs were mourned, wounds actually seemed to be badges of honor. And Tracy learned that wounded SOG commandos were usually treated at the FOB, not medevac'd to the rear like normal grunts. Sometimes they went out on their next missions still wounded, as he would soon find out firsthand. During his three tours in Vietnam, Tracy Brown would be wounded in action six more times. None of these took him out of action for more than one month.

Tracy was awarded the Purple Heart for the slugs he took in the ass and in the cheek on the first snatch mission with Whit Watlington. For his bravery in capturing the two valuable targets on that mission, Whit had written him up for the Silver Star. MACV in Saigon downgraded Tracy's award to the Bronze Star for Valor.

Chapter 24
The Ho Chi Minh Trail

SOG LRRP operations in Laos, and later in Cambodia, sustained a higher rate of both kills and casualties than virtually any other type of GI unit in the entire war.

The Ho Chi Minh Trail was a system of roads and paths that began in North Vietnam and progressed south through eastern Laos, until spilling out at various places in South Vietnam. It was used by NVA and PAVN convoys and troop commands to deploy vehicles, tanks, troops, and supplies (especially weapons, ammunition, explosives, and tons and tons of rice), with the benefit of circumventing the stiffer opposition they would have encountered on a direct route from the north to the south. For one thing, US troops, by rules of engagement, were not supposed to be in Laos. Conventional units never went there, so the interdiction activities of SOG could never be reported through any direct channels and certainly had to be hidden from congressional scrutiny and from the media.

The "Trail" was something of an engineering miracle because of the craftiness of its design, and especially because of the amazing ways that it was maintained and camouflaged. If a part of the system was tampered with by SOG missions, that portion would sometimes be up and running again in a few days. Tributaries of the system often could not be seen from overhead due to the way trees and other vegetation were tied together to obscure anything below the canopy.

SOG's missions were inventive and demonstrated a great amount of ballsiness on the part of SOG commandos. SOG directed what became known as "projects," with mysterious names like Bright Lights (for rescues and KIA retrievals), a PsyOps (psychological operations) and an SOG invention called "Radio

Hanoi" (for disinformation), and Daniel Boone (venturing into Cambodia). There was also Humidor (a deception effort, including disinformation leaflet drops), another PsyOps fiction: the Paradise Island mock North Vietnamese village in South Vietnam, and what were known as "poison pen letters" to NVA soldiers. And there was Eldest Son (involving the salting of NVA weapons and ammo to make them blow up in the enemy's face), Urgency (involving SOG agents conducting secret missions in North Vietnam), plus Project Delta (predecessor to the US Army's elite counterterrorism unit known as Delta Force).

Tracy Brown's fourteenth and fifteenth missions happened in late July and early August 1967. They were part of the ultra-secret Commando Lava (CL) project, and they took RT Samoa to highly strategic points along the Ho Chi Minh Trail. CL was a joint operation between SOG and the US Airforce's 374th Tactical Airlift Wing staged out of Ubon Royal Thai Airbase. The Dow Chemical Company had been asked to develop a way to degrade the Ho Chi Minh Trail. Dow came up with a powdered compound of trisodium nitriloacetic acid mixed with sodium tripolyphosphate. It was referred to as "the solution" or "Calgon," rather than with any use of the word "chemical." It was important to avoid the possibility of accusations that the US was conducting chemical warfare. Calgon had no intended use as a weapon against people. Instead, it was designed to be used on roads during Vietnam's monsoon season, particularly on the Ho Chi Minh Trail, to seriously interfere with North Vietnamese troops' ability to move their resources from the north to the fighting in the south.

Specifically, the idea was that the Calgon would bubble up upon making contact with the hardpacked roads during rainy season and turn everything into impassable mud. On mission fourteen, Whit Wattlington's RT Samoa was inserted into a Laotian LZ without being spotted. The team was in place to observe a specially fitted C-130 transport aircraft dropping over nineteen tons of Calgon over a section of the Trail known as the Barrel Roll. All of the CL missions required secret approval from the US Ambassador to Laos.

During the next three days, Tracy and the team members of RT Samoa stayed hidden in plain sight in the jungles around the drop area. They saw some of the Calgon solution seem to slide off the roads in the rain without bubbling up. In other places the bubbles stayed on the road, but the dirt was packed so hard that only surface mud materialized. Fortunately, the team stayed hidden well enough over this period that there were no combat incidents. Overall, before they were exfiltrated, they'd observed very minimal degrading of the hard road surface. They'd witnessed several truck convoys pass with no problems whatsoever. That was the report Whit Wattlington filed upon returning to the FOB.

Other SOG teams apparently filed similar reports, because the Commando Lava project was permanently cancelled. Unacceptable loss of life in some commando teams was one factor. Relatively little impact on the Ho Chi Minh Trail was another. And the risk to the very expensive C-130s making the Calgon drops may have been the most important factor.

On mission fifteen, RT Samoa was tasked with a mission beyond the Ashau Valley, just over the Laotian border. They were to blow up a ZPU-series, multi-barrel, anti-aircraft autocannon camouflaged near a cave. An NVA two-man, LZ watcher team witnessed the insertion of the commandos being dropped. The drop position was around a bend from the bottom of the mountain containing the cave. The watchers radioed the drop-in to their handlers, and almost immediately Samoa was overrun by two, forty-man platoons from the NVA's 7th Division. An intense firefight ensued, and in the process Tracy took three AK-47 rounds across his lower torso and heavily muscled right thigh. He was lucky to have been dragged onto a H-47 for dust off by the two Montagnards (Neh and Glun), who were the only other original team members still alive. The bodies of Whit, Hot Sauce, Ksor, Doi, and Pauley Davis (the One-Two who had replaced Angel) were all subsequently retrieved by a Bright Light mission.

Grandfather. I deeply mourn the deaths of my comrades in arms. And I'm thankful for your strong protecting presence.

Sitting in a wheelchair several nights after his return to the FOB, the heavily bandaged Tracy Brown led multiple rounds of singing of "Hey Blue' in the NCO club for each of his fallen RT Samoa comrades.

Fifteen weeks later, First Lieutenant Tracy Brown was out on his sixteenth mission with his newly adopted RT Christmas. SOG had been considering him for a One-Zero slot prior to his injuries, but out of fear of his loss of confidence, they balked. Tracy grew to admire Zeke Austin, the RT Christmas One-Zero, but the memory and lessons from Whit Watlington and the rest of RT Samoa would last forever for the battle-hardened man from DC's Michigan Park.

After that, for all the action Tracy saw, if he'd had been a conventional soldier he would have probably acquired considerable "fruit salad." The racks across his chest might have included the Republic of Vietnam Campaign Military Award, Vietnam Gallantry Cross, Vietnam Service Ribbon, and the Meritorious Service Ribbon, not to mention a Silver Star or even a Distinguished Service Cross. However, Tracy wore only three ribbons on his trip home at the end of his first tour. The first two were his Ashau Valley Purple Heart and Bronze Star for Valor, and the third ribbon was another Purple Heart for mission twenty-three, also in the A Shau Valley. Under intense fire, he had been grazed across his neck and in the ensuing fall had hit his head on a rock. A bloody mess across his neck and face, and barely able to see, Tracy was still in the fight. He and Zeke Austin held off the enemy with their CAR-15s while the rest of RT Christmas finished blowing up a hidden communications bunker. Missions two through twenty-two generated no medals until 1998, because, before that time, American forces supposedly never were in Laos.

***

When Deanna Nance saw her man coming off the plane at Dulles International Airport outside of Washington, DC, she kissed him, and kissed him, and kissed him. When she saw his bullet scar on his left cheek, her eyes teared up as she turned his head to kiss it. Then she said, "Yes!"

Deanna had written Tracy over thirty times that year. He had written her back three times, but in one of his letters he had asked her to marry him. In April 1969, they became man and wife. Tracy was totally in love with his new wife. He loved the look of her, the feel of her, the smell of her, their history together as members of the unofficial Michigan Park crew, and Tracy was amazed at Deanna's grasp of all manner of things about his life that he imaged a woman just wouldn't be able to comprehend.

And yet Deanna Nance Brown quickly realized that her man was constantly thinking about Vietnam. Though this fact was unspoken between them, she privately understood it. They made love constantly. She doted on him. But there came a time when Tracy needed to get back into the action.

As Tracy Brown's aircraft circled and began to descend into the airport at Tan Son Nhut in October 1969, the newly promoted captain reached over with his right hand and removed the shiny gold band from the third finger of his left hand. He tucked it into an envelope, sealed it, and placed it in his carry bag. By November 1969, Brownie Brown was back in action. He joined RT Tango, and after distinguishing himself as a One-One on four missions, he was asked to take over as One-Zero of RT Puerto Rico, whose previous One-Zero had not returned from a mission in Laos.

***

For the next year through the end of 1970, Tracy's RT Puerto Rico conducted thirty-seven missions in South Vietnam and into Laos, plus four more into the infamous Fishhook section of Cambodia, west of the South Vietnamese cities of Pleiku and Kon Tum. A number of tributaries of the Ho Chi Minh Trail clandestinely ended in Cambodia instead of in South Vietnam, but rules of engagement, enforced by President Lyndon Baines Johnson, to the chagrin of General William Westmorland and other field commanders, held that because of the Geneva Accords, no incursions into Cambodia were permissible, even in instances of hot pursuit.

Prince Norodom Sihanouk was supposedly at least neutral in the fight. However, the Sihanouk government supplied over 60,000 truckloads of rice to the North Vietnamese, not to mention allowing the presence of sanctuaries for some of the NVA to hide its most high-level headquarters outside of North Vietnam. The bunker complex housing the NVA's Central Office for South Vietnam (COSVN) headquarters was just one mile from Cambodia's eastern border with South Vietnam. Actually, in areas of Cambodia where the NVA operated, there were absolutely no Cambodian civilians. Many in the civilian population lived in constant fear, not only because of the farce of their country's neutral status, but also because of the rise of what would become the Khmer Rouge, who would go on to rule and terrorize Cambodia after the Vietnam War ended in 1975.

It was said that if a commando went out on more than fifteen or twenty missions over an entire tour, people in the know would begin to wonder why that soldier was still alive. Many of RT Puerto Rico's missions were of the "snatch" variety, but Tracy's RT also retrieved casualties, took out truck convoys, called in air strikes on hidden targets, tapped into cable lines that were the enemy's communication lifeblood, and destroyed weapons and rice caches.

Chapter 25
Back at Long Binh

Tết was essentially over by sometime in March or April 1968. Although the Tết Offensive was disastrous for the Việt Cộng, in that they eventually lost more than sixteen times the number of casualties as the American forces, it was also a disaster for the US because of the bad publicity at home that flowed from the loss of about 2,600 American lives.

Similarly, the loss of US Marines fighting in Khe Sanh near Quảng Trị Province, was a public relations nightmare, in spite of President Lyndon Johnson's determination that it wouldn't become another disaster like the French had had at Dien Bien Phu back in 1954. President Johnson and General Westmoreland had sent word to US commanders General Wheeler and General Tolson to defend and hold Khe Sahn "at all costs." The "at all costs" phrase in these orders became front-page fodder for major news outlets in the States for months.

The death of Clyde Simms cast a pall over Levi Chance from which he would never really recover. Certainly, this was not the first tragedy to befall the gifted musician. He remained deeply wounded from the accidental death of his father, Big Sam Chance, when he was very young, and from the death of his dear mom, Marva Chance, from tuberculosis when he was a teenager. The tragic loss-of-place that he felt from the so-called urban renewal, which took away the family home on F Street SW in the District of Columbia, still festered in his deep subconscious. His memories occasionally triggered bouts of prolonged sadness bordering on rage and depression.

But Levi had learned to survive. He was skilled with wearing a façade of false bravado and even cockiness. His routine in the aftermath of Clyde's death included rather mundane duties with the

266th Army Band around the base at Long Binh. These were interspersed with band trips off post. Another habit he picked up was slipping off post for a little "sumpn-sumpn" from the local camp followers.

The 266th Army Band was Levi's real gig, but during down times, the Statesiders were in demand. He'd hop on the Chinook with one or both of his axes and fly to various gigs in Biên Hòa or Saigon. Sometimes it was to any one of countless orphanages or convents in or outside of cities like Vung Tau, or small villages with names like Chon Thanh and Lao Bao, or larger cities like Quang Tri and Phan Thiet.

Sometimes the Statesiders played various US army posts like the First Infantry Division's Base Camp at Lai Khe or the 23rd Infantry (Americal Division) post near Chu Lai. The most fun gigs, of course, were over to China Beach, right on South Vietnam's Pacific Ocean coast. This was where many GIs went for some R&R and to ogle the round-eyed women who might even grace their male counterparts by joining them for a swim. Gigs at China Beach were always raucous and fun.

Everywhere Levi went, he asked if anybody knew Tracy Brown from DC. Sometimes a soldier would respond affirmatively, but nobody ever knew where Tracy was or much about what he was doing. Usually it was a bartender who knew something. Their brief comments tended to be something like, "That big mothafucker's a phantom."

Or, "Yeah, he came in with a couple of his boys last week. They mostly slept, but then they wanted booze and women. The next week they were gone again. They never said where they'd been or where they were going."

***

Levi got horny in Vietnam. He reasoned that one doesn't go from the kind of prolific sex life that he'd had to that point in his life to cold celibacy. Eventually Levi caught the clap—twice. It's not that Vietnamese girls were any more or less virtuous than any other girls around the world, but the girls that hung around the military base camps were after money from hookups, and many of them had frequent hookups with many different GIs. Depending on their negotiation skills and the soldiers' desperation, they could get anywhere from $5 to $50 or more for their services. This was big money on the Vietnamese economy.

Levi really didn't like rubbers. After his second time dripping, the doc warned him, "Either your stuff is going to fall off one day, or you're going to be incurable."

Back in the barracks, Levi told Twice what Doc had said. The drum major looked serious. "You know there are rumors of GIs who have been here for years and are never allowed to go back to the States."

"I don't believe it."

"That's just what I heard, Liberace."

From that point on, Levi didn't go off post for pussy. There was a particular Vietnamese woman who cleaned on post. The GIs called these women hooch maids. A lover of both Vietnamese and American music, Thu Minh cleaned in several barracks, including building 5136, and she had a fancy for Levi's music. When Levi started paying attention to her, she became exclusive for him for the rest of his tour. After he'd extended in-country several times, in 1971, just before Levi was due to rotate back for the last time, Thu Mihn brought up the subject of her coming back to the States with him. That led to a falling out between the two of them. After that, Levi left her alone until he was gone.

There was one other noticeable change in Levi Chance that he didn't try to mask: drinking. He'd tasted alcohol in moderation since he was a teenager, but he'd frankly not liked the taste of beer and had never been particularly impressed with wine. He'd taken a brandy with Coke from time to time, and it chilled him out, but he'd never felt a need to drink more than maybe once or twice per week.

Now, if there wasn't an important band practice or gig on a particular day, Levi found himself pouring out a Christian Brothers

VSOP in the morning instead of going to the mess hall for breakfast. If anything is plentiful on a big military base, it's alcohol. If the band was playing off post, he didn't drink much until he got back. But when the Statesiders played the NCO club until midnight, Levi would hang around after the last set and might have two or three doubles before heading back to the barracks. He worried about Tracy Brown almost every day.

Harlem, the sax player, was the first one to notice the change. "Hey, Liberace, you might want to go see Chaplain Peyton. You can't fool me, brother. I know you're hurting. That's why the army pays people like Holy-Holy to help us when we have issues; when we're feeling fucked up."

"Thanks, Harlem. I don't have issues. End of story, okay?"

"Sorry, man. Not trying to get into your business."

Harlem, Ack (trumpet), Proudcock (drums), and Fingers (double bass), talked about Levi privately. They made a group decision never to raise it again, unless Levi started fucking up musically— and he never did.

***

April 1968

It was approximately four months after RT Samoa's first mission in the A Shau Valley. By this time, the valley was held by the People's Army of Vietnam (NVA) and was utilized by them as a huge logistical supply depot. Now fighting in the A Shau Valley with the US Army's airmobile 1st Calvary Division were Emmanuel Freeze and Arthur Bostic from Michigan Park in DC. A Shau was considered of vastly strategic importance. Thus, the First Cav was there with 20,000 men and about 450 helicopters. First Cav brought to bear more firepower than any other division-sized US military unit in Vietnam.

Emmanuel had been one year ahead of Levi at Harrison Tech, but they had become close for a couple of years, singing together with the doo-wop group called The Mystics. Arthur had played varsity football at Tech, and he and Levi had taken numerous classes together over their three years of high school. One morning, in April 1968, Emmanuel and Arthur became two of nearly 150 Americans killed in a series of battles with names like Dong Re Lao Mountain (dubbed Signal Hill) and Operation Delaware.

This time it was different for Levi Chance. He got no direct visit from Captain Jax or any other Army officer. Rather, one day Sergeant Chance was notified that he had a call from the States. He went to the band office, and when he lifted the receiver and said hello, the voice on the other end was that of his Uncle Bundy.

"Hello, Levi," said the voice on the other end of the static-laced phone line.

Levi immediately recognized the voice and was at first happy for the contact, but then just as suddenly he became apprehensive. "Uncle Bundy, is Aunt Alma all right?"

Alma was fine, and that wasn't the news that Bundy Stokes was calling about. This call was about Emmanuel Freeze and Arthur Bostic.

Chapter 26

College

After high school graduation, the lives of Tracy Brown, Levi Chance, and Benjamin Parks took very different paths. Tracy went to West Point and then became a war hero in the futile effort known as Vietnam. Levi enlisted in the Army. He did almost ten years, including time with the elite US Army Band at Fort Meyers, Virginia. He had surprisingly volunteered for reassignment and did several tours in The Republic of South Vietnam. Levi had the pleasure in January 1969 of meeting Johnny Cash. Cash toured Vietnam and played a set live at the Annex 14 NCO Club in Long Binh. Levi went back to Nam for one more tour in 1970.

Benjamin Parks, on the other hand, enrolled at Middle State College in Ohio, and got through in five years with a degree in sociology. During his freshman year at Middle State, Ben's priorities certainly weren't in the right place. First of all, he didn't know how to study, and his grades showed it. Academically, Ben did not do well for the first couple of years at Middle State. What concerned him more was the fact that, come the time for spring pledging, Ben didn't have the grade point average to pledge the Omega Psi Phi fraternity. This really hurt him on a pride level, but he didn't yet get the message that he had to do something differently.

The shy undergrad from DC didn't get a lot of feminine attention at Middle State College. Samantha Porter, a big-breasted blonde from Teaneck, New Jersey, was his only sexual partner in his freshman year. There was a community softball field in a neighborhood near the college. That's where Ben and Samantha started going, first to kiss and pet, and eventually that's where they had sex, in the visitor's dugout.

Leaving the student cafeteria early one morning, Ben was walking down the sidewalk back to his dorm. As he walked he spotted a car door swing open. The big white man stood in front of Ben and said, "Get in."

It was Samantha's dad. Ben got into the passenger seat and the man came around the car to sit beside him in the driver's seat. Upon receiving a call from the dean of students, he'd driven all night from Teaneck to get there before morning classes started. The man had a small snapshot of Ben and Samantha in his hand.

"I'm Mr. Porter."

"Yes, sir. I guessed that."

"Samantha is my baby. She's my only child."

"Yes, sir."

"Why do you think it's a good idea for you two to be dating? A negro boy and a white girl?"

Ben was speechless. Then finally he said, "I don't know, sir."

"I don't want to keep driving back and forth across the country. I want you to do me a favor, boy. Would you leave my little girl alone so she can have a normal college life?"

Rage was now added to the fear that Ben had already been feeling. But then, for some reason, he experienced some guilt. This big man was saying that his daughter couldn't be having a "normal college life" because she'd been with him. Ben didn't have the quickness or sophistication to think that through there on the spot. He just felt bad.

"Yes, sir."

The man got out on the driver's side, walked around the car, and opened the passenger door. Without a word, Ben stepped out. Immediately the man walked back around the car, got in, and drove away. That was the end of Ben and Samantha. Later that day, they had a class together, English Literature. They didn't speak. Samantha looked over several times, but Ben wouldn't make eye contact. He didn't have much appetite for any other white girls on campus for the rest of his time in college.

Ben was totally celibate during his sophomore year. Then he dated Trenice Jackson and Barbara Lofton during his first junior year, sometimes overlapping. Trenice was a sister from Chicago's Cabrini Green projects. Barbara was another sister. She was from Brooklyn, New York. In the following junior, not quite a senior year, he and Trenice were more or less exclusive. Not that they were in love or anything, they just needed wrestling partners from time to time. They both had concluded that being pseudo-monogamous was in their best interest if they were going to have a chance of focusing enough to get decent grades. With his GPA now over 2.0, Ben was able to pledge into his desired fraternity that year.

Trenice was a political science major and wanted to become a lawyer. Ben, at that point, thought he was going to be a social worker. He also understood that he needed to get some pretty good grades to offset his less-than-stellar record at the beginning of his college stint.

Ben's methodical study tendencies began to emerge somewhere in his second junior year. He often thought during this period of Davita Sheridan, his childhood sweetheart. Ben could hear her telling him that he was immature. He made up his mind that he wasn't going to be immature anymore. So Ben started observing what students that did well did. And he started imitating them. When he saw something, he tried it. Sometimes he didn't understand it, so he asked.

In one conversation with his white roommate, Peter Blake, from St. Paul, Minnesota, he said, "You're reading that Social Movements chapter again. I thought you did that yesterday."

The textbook, *Collective Behavior*, was by Ralph Turner and Lewis Killian.

Peter looked up from the pages. "You ever see twice a movie that you liked?"

"Sure."

"Do you normally see things the second time that you didn't see the first time."

"Yeah."

"Same thing with reading."

Ben made a note and pasted it to the mirror over his study desk: Skim it, read it, review it.

At the end of the semester, he was proud of his grade of A-minus in his course on Social Movements. He also had three B's and one C in the second-semester language course that he'd flunked previously. That semester's grade point average was 3.0. In his previous six semesters in college, Ben's grade point average had ranged from a low of 1.6 to a high of 2.4.

The next semester, Ben was in a course on the sociology of communities. The text was *Community Structure and Change* by Lowry Nelson, Charles Ramsey, and Coolie Verner. After several lectures, Ben was reading one of the chapters. He realized that he wasn't getting much on the concept of social stratification, despite his recently acquired reading system. Then he was in the library one morning, sitting at a table with another student (Paula Kriminski from Columbus, Georgia) and noticed all the markings in her text. It was the same text that Ben was having difficulty with. He inched his chair closer to Paula, careful to keep enough distance that she wouldn't get the wrong idea.

"Can I ask, what's all that writing you're doing in your textbook?"

"It depends. I just know that every time I read a chapter, there's important stuff buried in there among the weeds, so I always want to come out of every chapter with five things to focus on that I think are important. If I get to the end of a chapter and I've only made four notes, I go back right away and find another thing to highlight or underline, and then I make a note about it. My notes are basically how I understand what the author is trying to say. Or the other kind of note I write is a question about what the author is saying. If that's the case, I make sure I ask the professor that question at the next lecture."

"Oh," said Ben. "Thanks!"

Ben went back into chapter eight of the Nelson, Ramsey, and Verner textbook. He skimmed first. On the side, he penned terms that jumped out: inequality, power, and social class. Then he went back to those sections and made notes in the margins that were basically rephrasings of the text's definitions of each of those terms.

At this point he was hooked. The third time through, he found three other terms that piqued his interest: prestige, higher and lower standing, and economic position. This led to Ben making additional notations in the margins. One of his longer notes read: "It seems easy for society to talk about class using distinctions like upper, upper-middle, and middle, but there doesn't seem to be common terminology for what comes next. Sometimes people shift to pure economics and talk about poor people. Sometimes they shift to racial designations. At the bottom are colored people or blacks. Seems like there's either discomfort or embarrassment over what to call the folks in the lower classes."

At the end of the spring semester, Ben had a B in his Sociology of Communities course as well as in his other four courses. Again, Ben's semester GPA was 3.0, and his cumulative GPA had for the first time crept up to 2.25 going into his senior year.

In another breakthrough, Ben invented a filing system that he would use for the rest of his life. He realized that when he wanted something, he almost always could remember approximately when he got it, so he dated everything. Filing things alphabetically required that you must remember what a paper or article is called or who its author is, but if you thought of it and remembered when you got it, you could find it in a chronological file. Ben filed papers, notes, articles, and the like chronologically in loose-leaf notebooks. From that point on, he only needed to leaf through the notebook for that particular month to come up with what he was looking for.

At the campus library, Ben spotted someone throwing out a bunch of used three-ring binders. He retrieved the best eight that he could find and entered his senior year confident that there would be no more rooting around in messy piles of paper when he wanted to refer to something he'd been given or read.

In the first semester of Ben's senior year (which was actually his ninth semester in college), Ben was in a course entitled World Philosophies. The textbook was *Philosophic Classics: Bacon to Kant* by Walter Kaufmann. He and Peter were no longer rooming together. Ben had a room off campus, but he and Peter were still friends, and occasionally they studied together, along with Paula and two other female sociology majors. There was a large dining room table that Ben's landlord allowed him to use for study sessions, and so the group most often met at Ben's place. They were studying for the final exam, and the group was assembled around the dining room table grilling each other on various theories and concepts. That is, all but Paula, who was standing and pacing around the others at the table.

"Hey, Paula," said Ben. "We had a chair for you. Sit down; you're kind of making me nervous."

"Well, Ben, I can leave if that's what you want."

"No, that's not what I'm saying at all. I'm just noticing that we're all sitting and paying attention and you don't seem to be with us."

"Believe me, Ben, I'm with you. It's just that I'm not feeling alert, and in order to help me focus, I need to stand. I'm not trying to distract you."

Peter immediately stood and kept standing for the rest of the study session, and by the end of the session, Ben was standing too. He was amazed at the added energy that came to him from simply moving and changing positions as he posed questions to others and answered their questions. Standing for concentration was a habit that stayed with Ben, not just for the rest of his undergrad training, but throughout graduate school also. He was always more alert standing versus sitting.

Perhaps the most significant course that Ben Parks took at Middle State was entitled Organizations as Social Systems. Foreshadowing what would later become a career for Ben, he was fascinated by the notion of systems as "the whole of a thing," as his professor continually said. The text, *The Social Psychology of*

Organizations by Daniel Katz and Robert Kahn, introduced Ben to concepts that would become the core jargon of the field of organization development (OD), terms like systems, leadership, roles, power and authority, effectiveness, and structure. Ben earned an A in this course.

The last dominant feature of Ben Parks' senior years was when he met Addie Sherrie Isles, a lovely freshman coed from Western Pennsylvania. She was beautiful, smart, and fiery. Ben thought he loved that, and was immediately attracted to her. They dated for his two final semesters in college. Their relationship became like a roller coaster: steamy and intense for weeks and then cold and aloof for some more weeks before reverting to steamy again. By the time Ben graduated, he was worn out from the ups and downs. He thought that his goodbye to Addie that June would be the last he would ever see her.

***

At the time of graduation, Ben had raised his overall college GPA to 2.42. Within months after college graduation he was drafted. Ben gave Uncle Sam an extra year over the minimum two, in order to be able go to Officer Candidate School. He spent his overseas duty in Korea and finished his service by late 1970. After service in the army, he applied to graduate school, and his grade point average, buttressed by his status as an army veteran, was enough for him to be accepted at American University in Washington, DC.

Entering American University in 1971, after his discharge in 1970, Ben was a changed man. Actually, it would be more accurate to say that Ben, nearing the age of twenty-six, had finally become a man. Two years earning a master's degree at American were followed by time teaching American and world history in the District of Columbia public school system.

During this period, Ben Parks felt the world was his oyster. He was hopeful and full of excitement about his future.

Chapter 27

The Letter

Janice picked Deanna up that Saturday afternoon for lunch. They had talked on the telephone the previous night, and Janice didn't think Deanna sounded right. She wasn't her normal easy and lighthearted self. They parked on Eighteenth Street in the Adams Morgan section of DC, and after ordering fajitas and sangria at the Mixtec Restaurant, the old girlfriends began to small talk, but that didn't last long. Janice broke the ice.

"Is it Tracy? Has something happened to him?"

That's all it took. Deanna broke down silently. She wasn't about to let it all go, but tears suddenly appeared in her eyes and she lowered her head. Janice reached across the table and cupped Deanna's long, slender fingers. She just let her feel whatever she was feeling for a while. Then, "Tell me, Deanna."

Deanna wiped her eyes and took a deep breath. "Nothing's wrong with Tracy. He's alive. He's not hurt. Girl, I'm happy. These tears aren't sad. I'm grateful. He's leaving that awful place, and he's never going back again. God is so good, Janice. God is so very, very good."

"Halleluiah," shouted Janice, never the one to be shy or reserved.

People at several tables nearby looked over, some with concern and some to echo Janice's praise.

"You've spoken with him?"

"No, my Tracy is usually in places where he doesn't have access to telephones. But I got this letter yesterday when I came home from work. I had just finished reading it for the third time when we talked on the telephone."

"Okay, girlfriend. Spill the beans. What'd he say?"

"I'm not going to tell you. I'm going to let you read it while I work on my salad. I'm about to get so serious about my weight and health, you won't know me, girl."

"Chil', you ain't never had a weight problem. What you talking 'bout?"

"Maybe not that you or anyone else can see, but I see when I'm off. I'm off. I'm about to get back on track."

Deanna reached under her seat and retrieved her purse. She took out a small envelope, closed her eyes, and smelled it. Then she opened her eyes with a look across the table that threw Janice off. She held her gaze. Then, "Janice, I'm going to let you read this letter, but before I do, I'm going to ask you a question, okay?

"Okay."

"Did you ever fuck Tracy?"

"What? Oh my God! What? Deanna, what are you talking about?"

"Did you?"

"Deanna, you don't even curse. What are you talking about?"

"Did you, Janice?"

"Why are you asking me that, Deanna?"

"Because when I get my hands on that big Negro, I'm going to rock his world. I've got to be in shape, because that big pretty black man is going to feel it in his toenails. I was trying to think last night about who might have been the freakiest woman he'd ever fucked, and the answer came to me. It probably was you. And my plan is to go super freak on that niggah beyond what he's ever experienced. So I just wanted to verify that you set the mark, and now I know what my game has to be like, all that *and* six bags of chips."

Janice looked astonished, embarrassed, amazed, embarrassed, shocked, embarrassed, then tickled, and then she broke out in another one of her uproarious laughs. Everybody in the place stopped to watch. Then finally, "Maybe once or twice. Maybe three times, tops. But that was back in high school, girl."

"Thank you. Now read this."

My darling Dee, I miss you. I try not to think about it very often because it throws me off my game. But in the down moments I think of you and miss you so much. So I want you to know that I'm leaving Nam for the last time. I'm going to the 10th Special Forces Group in Germany. I should be there by the end of next month. I want you to pack up and join me.

We could win this Vietnam War, but we won't. And I'm not even sure that's a bad thing. We have no business trying to dictate what kind of government they have over here. Most of the South Vietnamese big shots that I've met seem to be about their own thing and not about what's good for the people. But it's not that we won't win because of the soldiers. If anybody reads this but you, it would probably end my career. A lot of guys over here go into a shell in order to cope. Sometimes it's serious and sometimes not so serious. Some of them have families back home and some don't. I think the ones with families probably handle things a little better.

But for me, I think sometimes that if I didn't have you to come home to I'd be a mad man. This life is a hard thing to go through alone. I thank my lucky stars that I'm not alone. I love you more than you'll ever know.

By the way, I've been put in for the DSC. That stands for Distinguished Service Cross. I think it will go through, but it takes a while. It'll probably be granted by the time I get to Germany. I want you there with me when I get it.

I love you girl.

Tracy

***

Germany, May 1970

"Why, Tracy? Why are you going back there? I want you here. You've done more than three tours, and you're still going back?"

"Because I can, Deanna. I'm good at war. That probably sounds terrible to you, but it's the plain truth. There's stuff that needs to be done to save the lives of very brave GIs over there right now. They need leadership. They need comrades they can count on. For me it's not the war. That war is unwinnable. But it's about the soldier next to you. That's why I have to go back."

***

By the time Captain Brown's fourth tour in Vietnam was completed, he had conducted an impressive ninety-plus LRRP missions. South Vietnamese counterparts working with SOG sent word down the chain that the NVA had placed a bounty on the head of "the big brown soldier." Once SOG missions into Laos and Cambodia were declassified, Tracy's medal count rose after the fact. He was awarded an additional Bronze Star with Oak Leaf Cluster (for valor), a Silver Star, and the DSC (Distinguished Service Cross) that had been shelved earlier, plus four more Purple Hearts. As many as four hundred casualties per month had been reported in US newspapers during the heaviest fighting of the Vietnam War. When US Forces withdrew from Vietnam, in 1974, over 21,000 US troops were KIA.

Chapter 28

Reentry

Levi Chance left the army in 1971. He had served more than eight years in the United States Army. Though he had never experienced a minute of face-to-face combat himself, his homeys (Clyde, Emmanuel, and Arthur) had paid the ultimate price. When Levi returned from overseas, he still had no idea about the fate of Tracy Brown, the ghost. What Levi had developed during the Vietnam years were two coping mechanisms for dealing with anxiety: working on his music to the point of exhaustion, and drinking. He wasn't a loud drunk. He didn't even drink much in public, but he was a drunk, just as sure as anybody.

***

Alma and Bundy Stokes were waiting at National Airport, just outside of DC in northern Virginia, when Levi's plane touched down one morning from a red-eye flight from Seattle. He was in his rumpled Class A army green uniform sporting three up and one down chevrons. This was the designation for an army staff sergeant. Levi was carrying his bone case and a small overnight bag. At the gate, Alma screamed when she saw him coming down the ramp.

"There he is! There he is! Oh, my heaven, look at him."

Bundy put his arm around his wife for reassurance. These two dear souls. They'd raised Bart and Brian, their biological sons, and then doubled back and taken on the child of a near child. Marva Chance had stolen their hearts when she appeared from South Carolina one day in their church. Their devotion to Marva had completely transferred to her son, Levi Chance. Now he was home and trying to get through a throng of protesters about forty feet in front of them. But Sergeant Levi Chance couldn't get though. Alma was suddenly mortified. The throng wouldn't let her Levi through. Then she saw a young white woman spit on her Levi. A man pulled her back, but she was yelling something at him. Levi looked surprised.

"Murderer," the woman yelled. "Murderer!"

What was happening, thought Alma. This was the son of Marva Chance. The sweet boy who'd lost so much. He wasn't even a fighter. He was in the band. What was this young woman talking about?

Then there were a couple of airport policeman escorting Levi through the throng. Now he was putting down his bags in front of them, with tears streaming down his face. Alma reached out and touched Levi's face and wiped back the tears. Then Levi was hugging his adopted aunt and uncle.

"Oh, look at you. Look at you. You've been off in that terrible war, and now you're home. You're not going back there. You hear me? You're not going back any more," said Alma.

"No, ma'am. I'm not going back ever again. I'm home now. When I get to the house, I'm taking off this uniform and you won't ever see it again. Okay?"

"Yes, yes, yes," Alma replied with relief, patting Levi over and over. They were walking toward the baggage claim area. They would need a red cap to handle Levi's duffel bags. The well-travelled suitcase Silver Sparkle by Fender Rhodes had been shipped directly to the Stokes's home.

"How's grandfather?"

Silence.

Levi's mind immediately went to the worst. "When?"

Bundy said softly, "Just before Christmas."

Levi began to sweat, and through his pores came an acrid odor that the Stokeses had never smelled on him, or on anyone. As Levi spotted one of his duffels and stepped to retrieve it, Alma gasped and Bundy grabbed her to keep her from saying anything. He whispered to her, "He's been traveling now from the other side of the world. He's tired and worn and needs to get home and clean up and rest. Let's take one thing at a time."

Outside of the terminal at National Airport, protesters against the war had picket signs and were yelling at every soldier they saw. Levi jumped every time he heard a new voice. His eyes welled with tears again, and Bundy Stokes started yelling back, "This is my boy. He's a hero and you're all jerks."

Finally, this ordeal was over. The moment Levi got through the door back in Michigan Park, he literally tore off his uniform. He walked through the living room to the kitchen, opened the trash can and deposited every stich down to his skivvies. Then, for the next two days, Levi Chance just slept.

Janice Westbrook was working for the United States Labor Department. She came over and stayed with Levi the second night. Alma and Bundy, good Baptists that they were but also pragmatic people, were cordial and said nothing. Out of respect, Levi and Janice kissed and cuddled but refrained from sex. Janice spooned with Levi and rubbed his chest as he mostly slept through the night. She was up and gone to work before anyone else in the house rose the next morning.

As Levi gradually began to acclimate back to the familiar surroundings, he learned many things. He learned that his grandfather had died in his sleep and that Brian Stokes had stopped by one day after work because the family hadn't heard from Sam Sr. in several days. Lastly, he learned that his grandfather's small home on Maple View Place Southeast was now his.

Next, Levi started checking in with the Michigan Park gang of the old days. Benjamin Parks was the first person he wanted to see. The reunion happened on the campus of American University. Walking from class to the parking lot one day, Ben heard a voice, "Hey, little fella, your shoe's untied."

There was the involuntary move to stop and check his shoes. Ben saw that they were tied just fine. Then the recognition area of the brain kicked in and he knew there was only one voice like that. He didn't even turn to look.

"Slap my face and call me ugly. You know, if you're going to surprise a brother, you ought to be able to come up with something that's not so lame. I had sent word to the Việt Cộng to make sure they kept you over there, but I guess they ignored me."

Levi was sitting on a bench that Ben had just walked past. Now he stood, and Ben faced around.

"The Cong told me what you said, but they also knew that you wouldn't know your right from left without me. Actually, what's with this graduate school? We all didn't know whether your dumb ass was going to make it out of high school. So here I am back to reestablish my dominance over my little friend. What's the matter? Can't a true army war hero get some love?"

At first, they high-fived. Then there was a two-handed shake that they pumped up and down, moving each other across the sidewalk and bumping into other students passing by. And finally, they man-hugged and held each other, still and tight. Ben thought of the Mystics, which caused him to step back.

"Man, do you know about Emmanuel and Clyde?"

"Yeah, and Arthur too. Has anybody heard from Tracy?"

"Dude, Captain Brown was here last month sporting his medals. He's all lean and cut, and he's got a couple of bullet scars on his face. He and Deanna Nance got married. They were in Germany for a while, but now he's headed back to Nam for the third or fourth time. Been gone about two weeks ago. Deanna thinks she's got a bun in the oven."

Data overload for Levi. He'd been in-country at the same time as Tracy and never could find him.

"Wait! Tracy and Deanna?"

"Yeah, man. You know, nobody could get with that back at Tech. Everybody tried."

"True that. I know I wanted some."

"But after they were at our high school prom together, Deanna went all the way to the West Coast to study fashion design in San

Francisco. Nobody knows when it started to really get serious. It might have been while she was out there or after she came home and went to New York to work on Madison Avenue. She's all fly and doing her thing, but Tracy won that prize, man. The hero won the prize. Deanna went to New York for a while, but she's back in the neighborhood getting ready for their baby. Tracy promised this would be his last tour."

"Damn! I did a three-spot in Nam, but I strung mine all together. Tracy must have spaced his out. What about you?"

"Korea after college, dude. I dodged that Nam bullet."

"That's good. You wouldn't have been able to hang in the Nam. Too intense."

"So now it's my tour's rougher than your tour. Okay, I admit it. I surrender."

"Just playing with you, my man."

With Ben in the lead, the two old friends started walking toward the parking lot on Nebraska Avenue. Levi asked, "Did you ever see Lou Bonefant after he left Nam for Korea?"

"No. You mean Lou was in Korea?"

"That's right. My understanding is he's still over there. He extended, from what Janice told me."

"I didn't even know. Wish I had known. So you've already seen Janice?"

"Yeah man, she stayed with me my first night back. She's comfortable. You know."

"I guess. How'd you get over here? How'd you know where I was?"

"I walked around to your house and talked to Ms. Gillian. She told me where to find you and what time your class was over."

"Need a ride?"

"Course I do."

"Well, let's go then," said Ben, opening up a two-toned-blue used Volvo parked in the student lot.

The friends traveled over to Adams Morgan, parked, and went to the Red Sea Ethiopian Restaurant on Eighteenth Street, right off Columbia Road. They gorged on the delicious Ethiopian food, pulling up the spongy bread and grabbling lamb and chicken morsels, potatoes, greens, and peas, and cramming their mouths but still somehow talking nonstop around their food. Ben noticed that Levi drank only juice, but didn't know the significance.

Suddenly Ben said, "Whoa, I have an exam tomorrow. Got to get home. You want to stay or go?"

"Ride me back, little fella. I'm with you."

***

Levi could abstain from drinking when he needed to not drink. He'd been home for more than one month and hadn't touched a bottle. Within a few days, the smell that his adopted aunt and uncle smelled had left him and he went about reintegrating. He dropped in on Ben and his parents, Richard and Gillian, and paid his respects to the families of Emmanuel, Arthur, and Clyde. He was invited to Janice's apartment for three straight evenings.

On the fourth evening, Janice said, "Lover, I have an early day in the morning. Can we take tonight off?"

"No problem."

Levi put on his clothes and closed her door behind him. He and Janice had been like this since high school. They were fierce in the sack, but without the emotional attachment that one would expect. After a month, Janice had not called, and neither had Levi called her.

Now it was time to put off the procrastination. He made the call, and surprisingly his boyhood idol answered: Marvin Gay, who was now Marvin Gaye. On the telephone, the short conversation had gone like this, "Hey Marvin, it's Shawty. Remember me from the neighborhood? Shawty. Sounds like Frankie."

"Oh, damn, Levi Chance! Where you been, boy?"

"Oh, man. I been 'round. Matter of fact, I'm just back from Nam."

"Oh, my brother. You been in the war. Glad you made it back. You remember, I couldn't hang with that shit."

"Yeah, I remember. Look, I been listening to that 'What's Going On' joint. That's inspired, man. Sure am proud of you and hope you win a Grammy."

"Thanks, Shawty. Just trying to get down what I'm feeling, you know?"

"Yeah, I know that's right."

"Say, I wanted to see if we could hook up." Levi held his breath.

"Sure! When can you come up?"

The next day Levi caught the Greyhound bus to Detroit. He arrived in the evening and checked into a hotel. That's when he lost his confidence and the self-sabotage began. Levi told himself he was going downstairs in the hotel for just one drink. He stayed in the hotel's bar until the bartender asked him to leave so he could close. The next day when he got together with Gaye, the pop star immediately noticed there was a problem. The thirty-minute visit was pleasant. They caught up on many of the old Southwest associates that had dispersed, mostly to Southeast DC and Prince George's County, Maryland, but at the end, when Levi asked, "Man, when can I come up and start working with you?"

Marvin Gaye took his time. Finally, he shook his head. There was a daunting silence between them. Eventually he quietly said through clinched lips, "Homey, I don't think that's a good idea right now."

Silence.

"Sorry, Shawty, I don't think I can help you with that Jones you got. That liquor is coming out of your pores this morning. Say hello to Ms. Alma and Mr. Bundy for me. Now I got a session to get to."

That was it. Crushed again. Like salt rubbed into wounds of hurt, loss, and an endless sea of disappointment that just goes on and on.

Chapter 29
Music beyond the Army

Now Levi didn't want to drink. His first act upon arriving back in DC from Detroit was go to the bank. He started making withdrawals, and in about ten months he withdrew virtually every penny he'd saved during nine-plus years in the army, plus some insurance money that he had access to from his father and grandfather. From the moment he went into training at Camp Lee, Virginia, he had decided to try to save at least $1,000 every month he was in the military. After all, he had free room and board and uniforms for as long as he stayed in. He was single with no dependents. Why did he have to spend money? All told, his savings and insurance, along with the money he got from Samuel Chance Sr., together came to over $390,000. He used the money wisely as he set about on a project. Levi had decided to convert the basement of the Anacostia house left to him by his deceased grandfather into a state-of-the-art, twenty-four-track recording studio.

Despite his failings, Levi was still brilliant when he applied himself. He could study plans and figure out how to panel, elevate basement floors, and take out portions of the first floor to create a twenty-one-foot vertical section from the basement. Alma Stokes gave him linens and towels and other necessities for settling into the second-floor residence of the house, and he bought a new mattress to fit his grandfather's double bed on the second floor. The second bedroom already had twin beds that were practically new.

He laid the parquet floor tiles, installed the soundproofing on walls and ceilings, and built enclosed vocal and drum booths. He hired a plumber to install an attractive bathroom in the back corner of the basement just behind the two-level sound section of the studio. He did everything himself whenever he could. Brian and Bart Stokes assisted when they could find time from their jobs, as did Ben Parks when he wasn't in class or studying. His next-door neighbor, Stuart Cheeks, a retired postal worker, pitched in too. Levi was a man possessed.

His largest investment was for $29,000 on a used but good-condition, twenty-four-track Rupert Neve mixing console that he found in New York (advertised in a trade magazine). Joe Minolo, the part owner and engineer at Diamond Studio in New York, even travelled back to DC with Levi and kicked in odds and ends (cables, microphones, headphones, monitors, etc.) that were being upgraded back at his Fifty-Ninth Street studio in Manhattan.

Levi had regaled Joe with tales of playing with the 266th in Vietnam, and even more impressive, his stint with the Pershing's Own Band. Joe had a heart murmur that had kept him from military service. He seemed to love the notion of a war veteran coming back and breaking into the record studio business on a shoestring. He'd made a snap judgement that Levi had a shot at success and therefore was worth helping.

Joe stayed with Levi for two days to help him install the new equipment. And Levi got special tutoring from Joe on the fundamentals of sound recording. Ever the quick study, overnight Levi became a whiz behind the soundboard. When he was ready for other purchases, he'd call Joe for advice. About one week after Joe had gone back to New York, a postal truck rolled down Maple View Place and stopped in front of Levi's house. The doorbell rang, and when Levi answered, he saw the driver's helper unloading a large box from the back. He looked at the driver's paperwork and saw that whatever was coming was from New York.

Coming in through the wide basement door, the box was placed in the middle of the shiny wood control room floor. When the delivery crew had left, Levi tore open the box to find an MCI JH24 two-inch, twenty-four-track analog recording machine. Five new rolls of two-inch tape were included in the box. A note was attached:

Thought you might need this stuff too. We don't need it anymore. Send me about $3,000 or $4,000 when you have it (or whatever you can come up with). Good luck! Joe.

Thus was born Levi's EAC Recording Studio. He didn't advertise what the initials stood for. Ben Parks was the first one to figure out they stood for Emmanuel, Arthur, and Clyde.

Levi's final investment was for a ten-foot, wrought-iron security fence and two Doberman pups that he named Chocolate and Vanilla. He worked with a professional animal trainer and became an expert dog handler. Choc and Nilla never misbehaved when Levi was at the house recording by himself, or in sessions with artists or paying clients. When Levi was away, Stu fed them and looked in on them, but they knew their job was to take care of EAC. They did their jobs well. As they grew to well over 120 pounds, they developed their low growls, which they tended to use with suspicious passersby instead of barking. Barking was for friendly greetings or for playing in the park with Levi or Stu.

Word of EAC spread throughout the low-key jazz, burgeoning disco, and early hip-hop communities in the District, Maryland, and Virginia (DMV). Soon Levi was in great demand as the sole engineer at EAC. When he needed a real heavy hitter, he'd ask Joe Minolo to come down from the Big Apple, and Joe usually found a way to adjust his schedule up at Diamond and oblige.

But what Levi really wanted was his own artist. Just one at first, then maybe more. But just one talented singer or player to work with, write for, and groom. Eventually he saw himself as a record producer who would work in the style of Quincy Jones and whose name would convey quality whenever it was associated with a new release.

Chapter 30

Insult

Joe and Levi's mutually supportive relationship progressed over a three- or four-year period. At first, Joe didn't know how talented a keyboardist Levi was, but one day on a break at EAC, Levi left the control room and went into the studio. He had this tune in his head and wanted to work something out. Joe stayed in the control room and listened. Thirty minutes later, Levi came back, thinking nothing of what he'd been doing.

Joe said, "Damn, DC, you never told me."

"Told you what?"

"What a beast you are." Levi smiled. "No, I'm serious. We've been working together for some years? I'm training you as an engineer, but you're an artist."

"Wait a minute, Joe. When we first met, I told you about playing with the Pershings. What did you think I was doing?"

"I don't know. I was impressed with the Nam piece. And I know if you played with that Pershing band, you had to be first class, but I guess I focused on you wanting to launch a studio, and I just never put it together. But, nigger, you're a beast—a motherfucking beast."

Silence. The word "nigger" was used colloquially within the black community as a playful term or even as an endearing term sometimes, but it had a whole different sound and effect coming out of the mouth of an Italian American.

Finally, Joe said, "Hey, DC. That was excitement coming out of my mouth, not disrespect. I'm sorry if you're offended. If you want, I'll never do it again."

Silence. Then finally Levi spoke, "Hey, Joe, here's what I know. That ain't the first time you've ever said that word, is it?"

Joe just dropped his head.

"Tell you what, Joe, let's let it go for right now. We got a session to get ready for."

"Okay, but I know I fucked up. What I wanted to get to was that I could use you on some sessions in New York, if you're up to it. If I haven't fucked it up between you and me."

Silence. The doorbell rang upstairs, and the two of them shifted into engineer mode as the next clients came for their recording session.

When Joe was dropped at the airport, Levi came back home and unplugged his telephone. He had abstained from drinking for several years now. Things had been going well for him. Isn't it funny how the mind works? Joe's inadvertent insult had triggered wounds that had nothing to do with being called a nigger. He was thinking about Big Sam and Marva Chance. He wondered how they would have strengthened him and taught him and protected him from these wounds that he carried deeply in his spirit. He thought about the fun and the love that he'd missed because they died too soon. Levi wept. And then Levi walked down to the corner liquor store and bought two fifths of Christian Brothers VSOP.

Over the next few days, he didn't answer the door. Paying clients came and buzzed at the security gate. They saw Levi's car outside and knew he was there. One local band leader became so upset that he started screaming and cursing loudly.

"You better not be in there, you son of a bitch. I booked this time and got all my people here for a session. This is fucked up. I'm going to look for another studio to do my work."

That's when Choc and Nilla came around from the backyard and started their signature low growls. The rapper cursed and went away.

***

Ben Parks hadn't been able to get in touch with his friend. After the fourth day, he left class and drove over to Anacostia. He saw Levi's car. Ben rang for a few minutes and then became even more alarmed. He went next door to Stu Cheeks' house.

"Have you seen Levi?"

"Yeah, he's over there. He comes out and walks the dogs, and then goes back in. He don't seem right, walking funny. And he don't speak or wave like he usually does when he sees me out on the back porch. There've been a lot of people coming to see him, but he don't answer. Maybe he's got a woman in there. I don't know."

Stu had made a joke, but Ben didn't laugh.

"Stu, I've never asked you to do anything like this, but I'm scared. Something's going on. Would you let me in over there?"

Silence. Then, "Yeah, I guess that's a good idea to check on him. Let me get the key."

Levi was on the first floor sitting at his kitchen table, staring at a picture of his parents on the wall. Stu and Ben counted seven bottles of Christian Brothers. Two of them had not yet been opened. Four were empty and the fifth almost drained. It was about seven at night. Levi was humming something. When he saw Ben walking in he smiled, "Hey, little fellow. You coming to check up on your big brother, your idol?"

"Yes, I am," answered Ben tersely.

"Stu, may I introduce you to my long-lost brother. This is going to be Doctor Benjamin Parks one day. Me and this guy grew up together."

Stu was agitated. "Thank you, but you know I know Ben. And you're a horse's ass neighbor. Wallowing around in this house for days, can't nobody reach you. What's wrong with you? You know I knew your grandfather for years. Stand up gentleman he was. Wouldn't stand for this from you. Wouldn't stand for it. You know I love your dogs, and I've always had my pistol and my shotgun ready for anybody tries to mess with them or your place while you're gone, but I'm ashamed of you right now, fellow. I'm ashamed."

Ben placed his hand on Stu's shoulder. "Thanks! You're the best, Stu. I'm going to stay with Levi. I'll get him cleaned up."

"Okay, young man. Did you know Levi's grandfather?"

179

"No I didn't, sir."

"Fine man he was. Fine man."

As Stu walked to the front, he spotted the telephone off the hook on a shelf full of books and odds and ends. He placed it on the receiver. Immediately it started to ring. He picked it up, "EAC Studio . . . No, this isn't Levi . . . No, I'm just in checking on the dogs. I saw the receiver off the hook and put it back . . . Levi's been out of town. I think he'll be back day after tomorrow . . . Sorry 'bout that. He had an emergency in New York he had to deal with. I know he's going to reschedule you when he's back, and take twenty percent off for your inconvenience."

Levi and Ben were listening. Ben gave Stu a thumbs-up. Levi sported a wry smile of resignation.

"Sure, I'll leave a message for him to call as soon as he gets back. Thanks for understanding. Bye."

As Stu put the phone back in the receiver, he didn't even look around. He just proceeded to the front door and closed it behind him.

Ben asked, "Can I pour those out?"

"Well, if you have to, little brother. Okay, sure. Maybe that's a good idea."

Ben started with the bottle that was one-third full. He poured it into the drain. Then he opened one of the full ones and did the same. He paused. He thought about taking the last bottle of VSOP home. Though he'd never actually tasted this brand, he liked cognac. But he had to preserve the symbolism. He opened the last bottle and down the drain it went.

Levi look wistful, but said nothing.

"Now what do you have in the fridge? Let me make you a meal. I see from what's out that you've done just about all the cold cuts known to mankind. Let's eat something hot. What do you say?"

"Yeah, yeah, yeah. You're in charge."

***

180

After the spaghetti meal, Levi and Ben went down to the studio and Levi put on some jazz: Alice Coltrane. He started talking about Big Sam.

"I was little, but I swear that man had the biggest hands there was. He could grab me in one hand and lift me over his head. He'd spin around and then toss me in the air. And he'd catch me with the other hand and do it again. I loved that."

"I wish I had known your old man."

"No, you wish you had known my mom. You would have had a crush the size of Virginia. You might not have been able to understand her, but she was the prettiest woman in Southwest. But Mom was strong too. Once I was in Bruce Wahl's practicing the piano with JT Ogelvie and this customer was acting up. A waiter asked him to calm down and he didn't. Then Bundy said something to him from behind the bar and the man cursed at him. Out of nowhere came Marva Chance out of the kitchen. She grabbed that man by the collar and he tried to turn around but her grip was so tight he couldn't. Then she walked him right out of the front door and shoved him.

"By then I was standing beside Ma. The man was out on the sidewalk trying to decide if he was going to try to come back. My mom just stood there with her arms folded. Eventually the man said some more curse words and walked away. Then Ma and I came back in and she went straight to the kitchen. When she came back out a minute later with a customer's order, she was smiling at them like nothing had ever happened."

"Damn, man. I guess nobody was going to mess with her."

"That's right. Probably the only person that could whip her ass was Big Sam Chance. And he worshiped the ground she walked on."

Levi's eyes were starting to droop. He fought it. "You know that honky motherfucker Joe called me a nigger?"

"What?"

"You heard me."

Ben didn't respond. He didn't have a response.

Alice Coltrane was playing "Blue Nile" off the *Ptah, the El Daoud* album. The two friends swayed and chair danced as they listened to the rich tapestry of instruments. After a while, Levi said, "Joe is a good white boy, and he's been good to me. His mouth just farted. He didn't mean no harm."

"You think?"

"Yeah, I think . . . Look at this place. We wouldn't be in this spot right here without his help. And he didn't know me from Shinola."

"So what you going to do?"

"I think I'll go to bed. Haven't had much sleep the past few days."

"Maybe I'll stay over with you."

"Yeah, you know there's a spare bedroom upstairs.

"That will do. But what are you going to do about Joe?"

"Think I heard Stu tell somebody that I'd be back day after tomorrow, so I guess I better get this studio straight and be ready to open up after that. The Joe thing will take care of itself, I hope."

"I'll make a big breakfast in the morning, and then I'll help you straighten up. That sound good to you?"

"Yeah, my friend. You my best friend, you know?"

"Yeah, I know, Levi."

Sitting side by side, they clasped hands and leaned toward one another. Their foreheads touched. Ben realized that he and Levi had played the dozens, shucked and jived throughout their long relationship, but they hadn't had a heart-to-heart like the one they just had.

"That's right, Levi. Now let me help get you up to the second floor."

Chapter 31
Moving On

Over the next few months, Joe called a couple of times each week, just to talk. Eventually Levi got past the shock from the "nigger incident" that had triggered his emotional retreat.

***

Then there was another turn of events in 1975. Joe introduced Levi to Arnold Luskin one day up at the Diamond Studio in Manhattan. Luskin was a famous record producer and executive who lived in Los Angeles, but he often travelled to New York to lay tracks with his East Coast artists. Diamond was Arnold Luskin's East Coast studio of choice.

By now, in addition to his engineering, Levi was doubling as a session player for some artists at EAC. He also was travelling to New York and playing piano and synthesizers on studio sessions for Joe Minolo. One day Luskin was working in Diamond Studios. After the session, Joe put on one of his tracks to see what Luskin thought.

"Who's that on synthesizer?"

"That's my man from DC. Name's Levi Chance."

"I want to meet that cat. Can you set that up for me?" said Luskin.

So, by the time they actually met, Luskin was already a Levi Chance fan. This led to him being hired not only for gigs at Diamond, but Luskin sometimes flew Levi out to LA to work with his West Coast artists. Levi's times in LA were not without problems, though. Females and liquor were constantly being offered to the session cats, especially the ones from out of town. A lot of the local guys were married or otherwise tied up. It was in LA that Levi first started mixing his drinking with working, and sometimes his work suffered, to the point that Luskin took him off one session and recorded over him with another keyboard player. After the session, Levi was furious. He untangled from some naked sweetie the next morning and caught a cab to Luskin's office.

"What the fuck, Arnold?" Levi said as he barged into his office.

"Wait a minute, bucko! You'd better slow your roll and think about who you're talking to."

Levi paused. Then slumped and sat down. "Can I get back, Arnold? I know I fucked up that track. Let me do it over. Let me go back in right now and do it over. Please."

"Motherfucker, you have more gifts than any human being deserves, but you're scary. You been coming into the studio smelling like liquor. The first time I noticed it, I almost kicked you out then, but I didn't, and you wailed on your part. I didn't like it, but I couldn't deny that the tracks were hot, so I let it go."

"Thanks, Arnold."

"Don't thank me, motherfucker. This is all business. That's all it is. Just business. It happened again on a couple of more trips, and you kept wailing. I was starting to think you were some kind of freak or something, but then yesterday you stank and your tracks sucked. I can't have that. I don't have time for that shit. I'm paying you good money and flying your dumb ass all the way from the East Coast for that shit. You know I've got bad motherfuckers out here just a phone call away any time I want them."

"Let me go back in and lay down over that other dude's tracks. As a matter of fact, if you have an extra track, keep that motherfuckers track and let me just cut next to him. Then you can compare mine and his."

Luskin looked at Levi. "Yours will be hotter. I know that. But not today. Let's give you a day to get all that shit out of your system. Stay one more day. I'm not going to the studio today anyway. Come in tomorrow before you go to out to LAX. Be at the studio at nine thirty a.m., and don't let me smell shit on you. You hear me, Levi?"

"I hear you, Arnold. Tha—" Levi caught himself. *Not thanks. It's just business.* "It won't happen ever again."

When Levi got back to his hotel room, a maid was in there cleaning, and what's-her-name from last night was sitting out on the terrace, drinking orange juice with buttered toast and marmalade. Levi walked out and sat down. She smiled and was about to say something.

"It's been really nice knowing you, darling. What's your name anyhow? No, never mind. Do I owe you anything?"

She stopped in mid-sip. Her eyes turned hard. "I'm no hooker, you sorry motherfucker. Fuck you!"

She got up and went into the room where the maid was trying to work and ignore their conversation. She picked up her purse and, without looking back, left the room.

Levi thought, *You did, my dear. You did that very nicely last night, whatever your name is. Thank you. Have a nice life.*

He drank coffee and ate an early dinner downstairs in the restaurant. He went to bed early, and at nine fifteen the next morning he was sitting by himself in the studio warming up. Arnold Luskin walked in at nine thirty sharp. Without a word, he entered the control booth and told the engineer to get ready.

Speaking into the microphone, he said, "Good morning, Levi. Hope you're ready."

"Does a fat baby fart?" came Levi's response from the studio.

"Roll it," Levi said, adjusting his headphones and turning back to the rack with the Synclavier II on the very top, an Oberheim OB-Xa Analog Synthesizer on the middle rack, and a Rhodes Stage 73 electric piano on the bottom.

One take! That's all it took. Levi went beyond himself. Arnold Luskin was in a trance and had to gather himself when Levi was done so he could look stern.

"I'll have to listen again and think about it," he straight-faced as Levi walked into the booth.

The engineer giggled, but then covered his mouth and busied himself with some knobs and faders. Levi understood, smiling inside but keeping his face humble.

185

"Okay, Arnold. Thanks for the second chance. You won't regret it ever again."

***

Within a few years, Levi Chance's credits as a session player ranged across genres, from blues releases, to R&B, to jazz and gospel, but he still wanted to produce. He wanted to call the shots in his own studio sessions, and he was deeply committed to giving more exposure to the many talented singers and musicians and songwriters from his hometown of Washington, DC. EAC sat dark for long periods of time while he was out of town, but when Levi got back to DC, he always had clients waiting to grab studio time before he went back out on the road.

Then one day he was in the music school up at Howard University. He was there to see Doctor Donald Byrd, who was leaving Howard to join the faculty at North Carolina Central University. Byrd wanted to give Levi some recommendations for students that showed promise as studio sidemen. That's when Levi heard the voice. Amy West was in one of the practice rooms near Byrd's office. She started up vocalizing and Levi stood up.

"Who is that?" he exclaimed.

"I don't know, man, but she's bad. You know I just work with the players, but I hear her all the time. I think she's a senior."

"Who do I have to go to if I want to meet her?"

"Shit, man, let's just go in. I don't know her, but I bet she knows who I am. Let's go."

Chapter 32

Recording Amy

The following weekend, Ben picked up Amy West and one of her giggly girlfriends at Meridian Hill Hall, the Howard University dormitory on Sixteenth Street NW. He drove them to Maple View Place Southeast. The young women looked suspicious as they inspected the ten-foot wrought iron fence. They both were startled when Nilla walked around from the back, eyed them, then came up to Ben for a sniff and a pat. When Levi buzzed the front door open from the basement, they entered up the steps through the massive first floor door into the wood paneled vestibule, and Geri (the girlfriend) whispered, "Damn, girl! This is fly."

To the right were steps that went upstairs to the bedrooms. Beside the steps was a hallway that turned left and seemed to go back to a dining room and kitchen area on that first floor. Right in front of them in the entrance was a wall plastered with a large painting of Duke Ellington in the center and a slightly smaller photo of John Phillip Souza, surrounded by photos of Levi with all sorts of artists, some of whom the girls knew.

"Hey, that's Chuck Brown. And that's Doctor Byrd. Who's that over there?"

"That's Keter Betts," responded Ben, relishing his role as tour guide, "and that one over there is Dick Morgan. On the other side is Shirley Horn, Buck Hill, and that's a group called The Young Senators." Conspicuously missing from the home's wall display of DC musicians was Levi's boyhood idol, Marvin Gaye.

Ben guided them down the hallway and turned them around to the right where they found another set of steps leading down. A sign above the steps read: "You are entering EAC Recording Studio. Bring you're A-Game!"

Descending the steps, they found a paneled doorway right in front of them. Through the thick glass, they saw Levi waving them in. Before pushing through, Amy looked behind her. Another thick panel doorway on her right-hand side hid an unknown chamber that became known when they entered the control room and viewed the mysterious contents. Over the knobs and faders and gizmos of the recording console, the girls looked out through a floor-to-ceiling plate glass window into the two-story-tall, all-paneled recording studio in front of them. Geri whistled. Amy blushed with surprise and wonder.

Ben said to Levi, "I got to make a run. I'll call in about an hour to see if you need more time. Okay?"

"Thanks, Ben!"

***

Ten months later, Levi was in Los Angeles shopping Amy West's demo tape to Arnold Luskin. They had recorded one half of an album (five songs). One in particular had Luskin swaying and licking his lips, but for the first time since the previous drinking incident, Levi had engaged in self-sabotage again the previous evening at the same bar in the same hotel as before. He seemed to inexplicably lose confidence at certain points. Arnold's nose had wrinkled the next morning when Levi came in, but Levi had rushed to Arnold's tape console before Luskin could stand from his desk. As the music started up, he had taken his seat.

Luskin intended not to like whatever he was going to hear, but that one song, "Leave Me All the Way," was so soulful, and Amy's rich alto voice colored it superbly:

Don't think it's over now, just because you're leaving.

Can't figure it out, where'd we go wrong . . .

When the song finished, Arnold Luskin looked at Levi Chance with a mixture of deep admiration and impending dread. Luskin had seen Levi at his best. He'd praised him for his chops on the ivory keys, but Luskin also had seen Levi Chance at his worst. Arnold Luskin was also a Vietnam veteran. He was part of the brotherhood.

If anyone would give Levi and his new artist a shot, it would be someone who understood, so Levi bit his tongue and waited for Luskin to finish his admonitions about drinking too much.

"Hey, man! Don't I always come through?" said Levi.

"You usually come through on sessions, but you and I both know that's not always the case. Is this girl signed to you as her producer?"

"Of course."

"See, you say that like it's a good thing. I'm sure you think it's a good thing for you, and maybe you really think you're best for her, but now I'm speaking to you not as just another producer. Now the hat I'm wearing is Advance Records. I'm being pitched to sign to my label a somewhat talented voice who's signed to a producer that could binge at exactly the wrong time and fuck up my label and my money. I really don't like it. Leave me the tape. I'm really going to have to think and pray on this one."

"Come on, Luss. You know she's the truth."

"I'm not saying she is, and I'm not saying she isn't. I'm saying I'm going to think on it. Bye, Levi."

Before Levi could object further, Arnold Luskin picked up his telephone, dialed some numbers, and swiveled his chair around to face the window behind him. After hearing him connect and begin a conversation that had nothing to do with him or Amy West, Levi went over to the console and ejected the tape, placed it in the plastic holder, and put it on Luskin's desk. Then he quietly exited the office and hailed a taxi to LAX.

Back in DC, Levi waited several days. But then Luskin called.

"Hello, this is EAC Studio."

"Levi, it's Arnold Luskin."

"Thanks for calling me back, Arnold. Can we do a deal?"

"Your artist has a nice voice, Levi, but breaking a new artist is hard, especially for a new producer. Even if we give you a deal, I have to give you a dose of reality. You won't be a priority with Advance. We're about to release albums on The Players, Tony

Drake, and Big Bad Boss Man, and that's just the ones that are ready now. Our promotions budget is spoken for."

"Well, we've got to start somewhere."

"Why not start at the top?"

"What do you mean?"

"I played your tune 'Leave Me All the Way' for one of my artists who is just about ready to start in the studio. She loves it and wants to do it to complete her album."

Silence. Then, "Arnold, I wrote that tune specifically for Amy. Amy kills it. I don't want to do it on another artist. What would I tell Amy?"

"You haven't asked me who my artist is."

Silence again. Then, "Okay, who is your artist?"

"Veronica Sessions."

More Silence.

"Are you still there?"

"Excuse me, Luss, did you say Veronica Sessions?"

"Yes."

"Whoa! I love Veronica Sessions. You're saying she wants to sing my song?"

"Why don't I have her tell you?"

"Wha—"

"Hello, Levi. This is Veronica."

Silence.

"Are you there?"

"Yes."

"I love your song. Can I put it on my album? I'm in the studio right now, and your track would complete the package. As a matter of fact, it might bump its way up to the number-two track on side one."

"But..."

"Please, Levi. I tell you what. Let me give you back to Arnold, but I can't wait to meet you."

Luskin was back on the telephone, "Hey, Levi."

"You're shitting me, Arnold. That really was her, wasn't it? You're shitting me."

"No, I'm not shitting you, and yes, that was Veronica. She's sitting across the room looking at me with her fingers crossed. This is the right move for your career, Levi. Veronica has had three albums in a row on the Billboard top ten, and the last one went to number one. This next one will do the same, especially with your song added."

"What would I tell Amy, Luss? This isn't fair. Let me write another song for Veronica."

"She wants 'Leave Me.' Amy is new. You can write other songs for her. Maybe her time will come or maybe it won't, but with Veronica you have a platinum-caliber artist dying to sing your song now. We might even be able to use some of your tracks and give you partial production."

"Luss, this is rotten."

"Levi, this is business. Just business. You like this young girl, and I get that. She has a nice voice, but not a proven voice. You've got a bad-ass song that has potential to be great with a proven artist. What's to think about?"

Silence. Then Levi spoke softly. His voice shook as he said, "No, Luss. No! I don't have to think about it. We'll find another label for Amy. No!"

Levi hung up the telephone.

***

Nine months later, Levi still had no deal for Amy West. Veronica Sessions' new album came out and went immediately to the top of the Billboard R&B charts. It stayed there for six straight weeks. Soon it went gold and then platinum, and then double platinum. Amy asked to get out of her production contract with Levi.

Levi obliged her request. He tore it up right in front of her and handed her the pieces.

"No fuss, Amy. I understand. Good luck."

Levi took the telephone off the hook again, for a week this time. After seeing clients at the gate twice, Stu Cheeks went over on his own. When he went through the door and smelled the rancid odor of old liquor mixed with some vomit and God knows what else, he entered the kitchen, where Levi was slumped over the table.

"Boy, you got a real problem," were the first words Stu could think of.

"Stu, you can kiss my entire ass," was Levi's garbled retort. "I ain't bothering nobody. It's my business. Get the fuck out of my house."

Stu left and Nilla met him on the steps. Stu patted the beautiful dog, and Choc also appeared for some much-needed love.

"Y'all need feeding?"

They whined in unison. Stu filled up their bowls in the shed behind the house, and the two Dobbies tore into the bowls with a vengeance. Stu got water from the outdoor faucet and left, but he decided to keep an eye out for whether Levi was feeding them each day. Most of the time, Levi managed to feed and water the dogs, and sometimes even to walk them around the neighborhood on tight leashes, but sometimes Stu, from his porch, failed to see Levi all day. That's when he'd go over and take care of the beautiful dogs.

There was no reaching Levi. Janice Westbrook decided to make a surprise booty call one night at Levi's house, but she couldn't get in and went away pissed. She called Ben. Stu had also called Ben, but Ben was right in the middle of exam week. The following week, Ben and Stu came into the house. Levi was sitting at the dining room table again. He had his eleventh-grade yearbook open to the class picture in the back. He had circled the pictures of Emmanuel Freeze, Arthur Bostic, and Clyde Simms. He just stared at the page.

This time Ben didn't ask. He took the half-empty bottle of Christian Brothers VSOP off the table and poured the contents down the drain. Levi said, "Motherfucker, you leave my shit alone."

As he rushed at Ben standing at the sink, Ben whirled and slapped his friend. Levi stopped and held his face to the side, but then turned toward Ben again. This time Ben delivered three harder slaps that knocked Levi off his feet.

"That's enough, Ben!" shouted Stu.

Ben saw that Levi wasn't trying to get up, so he looked for still-unopened bottles and didn't find any. Ben cooked, cleaned, and went to class. A week later, EAC was open for business again. Ben knew that Levi binged when he was idle, but he didn't fuck up his business. That's when Ben felt safe to leave Maple View Place.

Chapter 33
Ben's Marriages

Ben was graduated in the spring of 1972 from American University with a master's in History, and immediately accepted a position with the District of Columbia Public Schools (DCPS). At the Northwest DC high school where Ben taught, he met a beautiful fellow teacher by the name of Victoria Barber. Victoria and Ben taught together for four years before deciding to get married. Two years later they had their first son, Anthony (Tony) Parks. On the weekends, Ben entered a certification program at Georgetown University's School of Continuing Education, and in ten months received a certification in organization development, a relatively new discipline focusing on how organizations become healthy human systems.

The couple had bought a fixer-upper on Shannon Place Southeast, very near Levi's home and the EAC Recording Studio. Ben briefly joined a black fathers support group that met once per month at Union Temple Baptist church in the 1200 block of W Street SE. He found it difficult to attend each month and eventually dropped out. But before doing so, Ben was approached by Bill Portis, a brother and church deacon. He learned that Bill worked for a quasi-governmental training organization (USTO) focusing on organization development in general and the development of leaders, from first-line supervisors through executives in federal, state, and local government. Though in a leadership position in USTO, Portis was trained in organization development, just like Ben. He liked Ben's mind, and especially liked Ben's insights on organizational matters and issues of leadership. Bill asked if Ben would like to come in and meet his director.

Ben left DCPS and accepted a full-time instructor position at USTO. There he met another instructor by the name of Ted Freer.

The year 1981 was one of big changes. Ben and Ted left USTO and formed PFA (Parks-Freer Associates), an organization development consulting firm. And having found the task of fixing up the Shannon Place house more than they could accomplish, Victoria and Ben found the toll it took on the marriage more than they could stand. It drove a stake through them that became irreparable. This was somewhat tragic, because that same year, Victoria and Ben had their second son, Rico Parks, but the couple agreed to divorce amicably with joint custody of the two young sons.

One evening, Ben was elated to receive a call from Lou Bonefant, one of the old Michigan Park gang. He'd been in Nam briefly, been wounded, and then been medevac'd to Korea to complete his overseas tour. Lou and Ben's paths had not crossed in Korea, where Lou had extended his tour. When he returned to the United States, he brought with him a new wife named Han.

After high school, but before Lou Bonefant was drafted, he had gone to school in the building trades. Back from the army, he got a VA loan and purchased a home on Elm Street in the LeDroit Park neighborhood of Northwest DC. It too was a fixer-upper, but Lou gutted it himself, and created a lovely three-bedroom, three-bath, open floorplan home that he and his Korean wife enjoyed immensely. Lou started a construction business and caught on, providing maintenance and repair services with some Northwest apartment complexes. Eventually he landed several big (for a small businessman) subcontracting contracts with some of the prominent real estate developers in the DMV (District, Maryland, and Virginia).

The call that Lou Benefant placed to Ben Parks was about the house next door to Lou's in LeDroit Park. It had been vacant for several years, and Lou had just had a chance to see it on the inside. He had found it in considerably better shape than the house he had just finished rehabbing, and on further investigation he had found that the heirs wanted to get rid of it very badly. With the proceeds from sale of Shannon Place, Ben and Victoria were both able to place 10-percent down payments on their new, separate homes.

They maintained a cordial relationship after the divorce and raised the boys together until the boys were men.

Four years later, in 1985, Ben was in Philadelphia's Thirtieth Street Station, about to board the train back to DC from a business trip. It was then that he ran into Addie Sherrie Isles, his girlfriend from his senior year at Middle State University. Divorced now, she was living with her son in New Jersey and teaching in a public school there. After a long-distance courtship, which renewed their relationship from college, the two married and Addie took a job with the Montgomery County, Maryland, public school system. She moved into Ben's house in LeDroit Park. Her son moved in with his father, who also had found work in the DMV after college. Ben started back to school again that same year, this time at Howard University in a PhD program in Human Communication Studies (with an emphasis on communication in organizations).

Five years later, in 1990, Ben Parks defended his dissertation on *Contrasts in the Use of Power between White and Black Executives in the Corporate World*. After his presentation and the question and answers, Ben was asked to leave the small room where his committee had been grilling him. He stood alone for about fifteen minutes. Gillian and Richard Parks, his parents, and Addie had observed the presentation. They came out of the room to stand with Levi while he paced the hall, waiting through the deliberations. Ten minutes later, one of the committee members came out and motioned for Richard, Gillian, and Addie. When Ben tried to follow, he was blocked.

"One more minute for you, Mr. Parks."

The door was closed again, but this time only for about two minutes.

When the door opened next, it was the chair of his dissertation committee, and he was smiling. Ben came into the room and, before sitting, he saw that Gillian, Richard, and Addie were also smiling. When Ben was in his seat, the chair said, "We now want to congratulate you, Dr. Parks. Fine job. Welcome to the academy!"

Dr. Parks! He called me Dr. Parks!

Gillian screamed and rushed over to hug her son. "Now we have two Dr. Parks in the family. Isn't that special?"

Addie rewarded the new Dr. Parks that evening, upstairs in their home in LeDroit Park.

Chapter 34
The Early 1990s

More random thoughts and word-markers signifying Levi's and Ben's experiences over time.

Levi Chance:

EAC Studio thriving with local jazz and Go-Go clients.

Ben Parks:

Parks-Freer Associates, reached the half-million-dollar annual revenue mark in 1992.

Tony and Rico Parks were growing into very fine, but very different, young men.

Adjustment to Davita Sheridan becoming Davita Ferrier.

Davita renames Dance-A-Lot, Davita's Place.

I introduce Addie to Davita's Place.

Addie and I resume up-and-down pattern (like we were back at Middle State U.)

***

Meanwhile, Addie had formed a nice friendship with the neighbors, Han and Lou Bonefant. Addie had taken on the task of coaching Han in English. She and Han also enjoyed gardening, and they often spent time together in each other's backyards on the weekends, planting, weeding, and just enjoying the fresh air.

Eventually Han had become proficient enough to find employment as a teacher's aide. One day Han was on an errand. She walked from the Kinko's in Chinatown back to Thompson Middle School. On these errands for her teacher, she normally didn't pay attention to street vendors and street musicians, but on this occasion the tinny music emanating from the old battered boom box she passed had a familiar Asian sound.

Han thought, *Who is that?* Then it came to her. She'd heard Yuk Kak Soo on a visit back to Seoul to see her family, but she'd never heard this music in the States. After the cognitive dissonance shock of hearing this music out of context, Han gradually shifted her attention to the little girl who was dancing by the side of the boom box. She had the stain of caked mud that looked to be several days old on one pant leg. Otherwise, she wasn't raggedy, but wasn't exactly kempt either. Soon Han was caught up in the girl's innovative dance moves. She'd seen break dancing on TV. This was something like what she'd seen, but it was more subtle and soft in appearance. Han reached into her purse and drew out a five-dollar bill. She dropped it into the open canvas bag beside the boom box and started to walk away.

"Oh, thank you, ma'am," came the gravelly voice.

"You're welcome," said Han, stopping again.

"Where did you find that music you're playing?"

"I first heard it on a disk that one of my friends had. I liked it so much, she gave me the whole disk. Ma'am, where have I seen you before."

"I don't know."

"Do you have children at Thompson?"

Han was surprised. "Thompson Middle School? No, I don't have children there, but I work there part-time. I'm an aide, and I sometimes watch classes for teachers when they have papers to grade or have to take lunch for a long time. Do you go to Thompson?"

"Yes, ma'am."

"Yes, I think I've seen you too. Do your parents know you dance out here?"

Suddenly the child was collecting her boom box and her canvas bag and walking away.

Chapter 35
The Beautiful Bird Sings

When Ben Parks got to the table at the Bayou that night of September 17, 1996, after being sucker punched on the George Washington Parkway coming from a work assignment in Rockville Maryland, he was mad. But even more, he was flustered because all the way from the incident he thought he was going to be late. The show had in fact started when he came in. Though he had missed some bands, he hadn't missed the main act. He related the incident to Levi, who was holding his seat.

"Man, where you been?" said his old friend as he sat down. "I've been here since before six. There was already a big line forming, and all these tickets are general admission. I wanted to make sure we got a decent seat. Doors opened at seven."

The Bayou was under the Whitehurst Freeway at 3135 K Street NW. This was the funky southern end of the very upscale Georgetown section of the nation's capital. Dixieland jazz had been the venue's specialty in the 1950s through 1960s. By the 1970s, its reputation and steady clientele from the military, as well as from nearby Georgetown University, caused entrepreneurial tour companies to start including it as a stop for out-of-town visitors. Big national and international acts started to be booked there, including the likes of U2, the Dave Matthews Band, Hootie & the Blowfish, Kiss, Dire Straits, Foreigner, and Police. Local blacks didn't frequent the Bayou in big numbers, but on this night, as Ben observed, blacks were sprinkled throughout the packed crowd.

As he started to calm down, Ben became aware of the group on the stage. They were playing the James Brown number "Papa's Got a Brand New Bag." The guitar player, with a huge receding forehead, was playing a solo.

"Damn, Levi, who are these white boys? They're funky."

"That's Tommy Lepson's band. He calls them the Soul Crackers. Ain't that funny?"

Just then Janice Westbrook came back to the table. She had gasped when she saw Ben and immediately had gotten up and left the table. Now Ben accepted the ice pack she had brought from the bar.

Ben thanked Levi's long-time friend-with-benefits companion from the old days in Michigan Park and Harrison Tech. The sting of the cold ice at first made him wince. But Janice made him put the pack back up to his face, and gradually it began to make a difference. Levi knew that Ben loved Fosters Ale and ordered him one. Although Levi wasn't drinking alcohol, he had no problem with others at the table indulging.

A retinue rushed past their table, anxious to get seated before the show began. Levi grabbled the trailing member and held on.

"Chuck! Knew you'd be here, my man. This is sad, isn't it?"

The gravelly voiced man said, "Hey, Chance. Let's enjoy it. Let's savor it. She's ready."

Levi said, "Know that's right. Hey, I want you to meet my best friend. Chuck Brown, this is Doctor Ben Parks."

"Pleased to meet you, Doc. Sorry! Got to step. My table is way over there on the other side."

And just like that, the Go-Go legend was gone. But now another band was starting up. "Oh shit!" exclaimed Ben. "That's Pieces of a Dream."

"Yeah, man. They're the truth, but I wish you'd been here sooner. I wanted you to meet Keter Betts. They already played."

"Damn, man! He's a legend. You mean I missed him?"

"Yeah. He's still around here somewhere. Maybe I can spot him for you. See that table over there? That's Ron Holloway. I've used him a lot of times over at EAC. Talk about a fat tenor sax sound. He's the truth."

Ben started to really take in the significance of this event. All these musicians wouldn't be assembled in the same place if this wasn't a big deal. He had only heard of Eva Cassidy from his friend Levi Chance. He had never heard any of the Bowie, Maryland, native's records.

Ben had arrived around eight thirty. After ten, Chuck Brown left his seat and went backstage. Another band was setting up on stage. It wasn't Brown's popular group The Soul Searchers. Ben looked at Levi.

In a low voice, Levi said, "That's Eva's group. It's about to be on and popping."

Ben wondered about the relationship between this young white singer and the rough-hewn, street-hardened Chuck Brown, who'd driven a furniture truck in 1966 while he was organizing the Soul Searchers. Brown had also served time in the Lorton Correctional Institute for manslaughter, but now he had become the standard bearer of DC's uniquely funky music style (Go-Go) for a whole generation of young people.

Sensing Ben's unspoken question, Levi said, "See the guy on bass? That's Chris Biondo. He and Eva used to have a thing, but now they're just good friends. He's the one that introduced Chuck to Eva by playing one of her tapes late one night up in his studio in Rockville. When I was building my studio, Chris gave me some ideas about soundproofing, and monitors, and stuff like that."

After a few minutes, Brown came out on stage and the crowd buzzed. He did a few numbers with Eva Cassidy's band backing him. Then, using a walker, Ben saw a young woman with some sort of black floppy hat or scarf slowly appear on stage. He looked at Levi, who put his finger to his lip to indicate that Ben should be quiet.

With Chuck's help, Eva Cassidy perched herself on a stool and picked up her blonde Guild Songbird guitar. Ben had missed it, but he guessed that Chuck Brown had brought it out for her and placed it against the stool. With the enormous effort it must have taken her to come out by herself, her nose appeared to be running and she wiped it. Then she said something into the microphone that Ben didn't hear, but which caused people near the stage to break out into nervous laughter.

Eva said, "Good evening!"

Then she was singing, and the night was hers. The first number performed was "Little Red Top," which she had performed with Chuck Brown in 1992 on the *The Other Side* CD. The CD had done almost nothing in terms of sales. After that number, Chuck Brown left the stage and soon was seen sitting back in the audience. All alone now, Eva Cassidy began to strum her guitar quietly and the crowd rustled in anticipation. For the next four or five minutes, she capped off the night with her unique version of the classic George Douglas and George David Weiss tune, "Wonderful World." It was incredible to Ben how quietly she sang and yet how much intensity she produced with that unique purity. To Ben, it was the closest thing to angelic that he had ever heard.

After the night was over, Levi explained to Ben that Eva had cancer. He told her that she was undergoing very aggressive treatment, but that her prognosis wasn't good. He also told him that her head was shaved, and that was the reason for the black head covering.

Two months later, Eva Cassidy died of malignant melanoma at the age of thirty-three. Many believed that exposure to the sun during her years working outside at a nursery in suburban Maryland may have contributed to her contracting the disease, but the phenomenon of Eva Cassidy was unique in the annals of modern-day music. Sadly, Eva only became a star after her death. Posthumously, her records sold in excess of ten million copies. Ben Parks purchased every Eva Cassidy CD that was subsequently released. Her rendition of Harold Arlen's and EY Harburg's "Somewhere over the Rainbow" is preferred by many, even over the beloved Judy Garland version of the 1940s.

Chapter 36
Therapy

March 1997

The incident on the GW Parkway in September of the previous year really scared Ben Parks. He looked back on his life and thought of all the times he had lost his temper. Later in life, it almost always had something to do with driving, but earlier, there was the stupid incident of challenging Tracy Brown back in junior high school. There were various other fights and skirmishes where his reactions were far out of proportion.

I actually pulled over hoping that the guy would follow me. I actually got out of the car and charged back even though I was blinded by the guy's headlights and couldn't see a damn thing. What the fuck? I'm going to get my damn self killed. You know, I actually teach conflict resolution. That's about as hypocritical as it gets. Need to do something.

It was actually Janice who found a therapist for Ben. Janice had gone to her therapist for several years. The fact that she was childless, still single, and had this off-and-on relationship with Levi (obviously drawn to him but also scared of some of his out-of-control ways), had messed with her mind. Her sessions with Dr. Jose Calderon had been sort of a pressure release valve for her. She sometimes had talked with Levi in an attempt to get him to come with her. He had stubbornly refused. But then after hearing the tale that night at the Bayou, Janice had begun to worry Ben insistently until he relented and agreed to go.

***

Sitting across from Jose Calderon, Ben couldn't break out of his silence. He was uncomfortable, but knew he needed to be there. Dr. Calderon read through Ben's registration information, pausing to make notes on a pad.

"I'm familiar with OD. You guys do a variety of things supporting organizational change and that sort of thing, correct?"

"Yes."

"The Gestalt Institute in Cleveland. Did you train as a therapist?"

"No, as an executive coach. In OD we have to have a variety of skills. Gestalt also comes in handy with mediations."

Dr. Calderon made more notes. Then he looked up and waited. Finally, after observing that Ben was not able to open the conversation, Dr. Calderon said, "Dr. Parks, what are we going to talk about today?"

"About how stupid I can be sometimes, I guess. Dr. Calderon, it would help me if you just called me Ben."

"Okay, Ben, I'll go with your description for now. Why and how are you stupid sometimes?"

Ben relayed an account of the incident on the George Washington Parkway. Dr. Calderon listened and took more notes. He didn't interrupt.

Ending his tale, Ben said, "My friend Levi Chance told me about you. His friend is Janice Westbrook. I believe you've seen her for a while and she raves about you."

"That's nice, Ben, but stay with your story now. Is this the only time something like this has happened for you?"

Ben turned a little red. He took some deep breaths. "No, sir. Well, maybe the first time to this degree. The first time with these kinds of consequences, but the first incident like this that I can remember goes all the way back to junior high school. I tried to pick a fight with my good friend who also was the toughest guy in the whole damn school. Luckily, he didn't do anything to me."

"How old are you, Ben, if I may ask?"

"I think you have it on my registration."

"Humor me, Ben."

"I'm fifty-three, no, fifty-four."

"And you'd have me believe that between about age fifteen or sixteen and age fifty-four, this has happened twice?"

"No, Doc. Let's not dance. I'll answer whatever you want. Shall I give you two more examples? I have tons."

"Apologies, Ben. Yes. Two more would be fine."

"In college, I went after someone who was trying to get to my girlfriend. That was kind of bloody. I wasn't sent home, but got three days out of class."

"Yes."

"A lot of examples cluster around public behavior, including driving. I rage at people who blow their horns at me. It's such a punk thing to do. They wouldn't walk up to me and yell in my face, but they'll sit in their locked cars and lean on their horns with impunity. I rage at groups who walk together all across the sidewalks, forcing oncoming folks or people who need to pass them to almost walk in the street. I rage at people who walk into a room and stand in the doorway, either watching or even holding conversations, instead of moving into the room to clear the doorway. Is that enough?"

"Yes, that's enough. But you don't try to fight these folks, do you?"

"In my teen years and into my twenties, I might bump them or yell at them. No, I make faces usually, or I just go all tight inside."

"You say you rage. Do you know the old saying about rage?"

"Yes, it's like drinking poison and expecting the other person to die."

"Do you really rage, or is that an overstatement."

"Maybe sometimes it's an overstatement, but sometimes I really rage. Surely when I jumped out of my car and ran back into those headlights to get myself knocked out, I was in rage."

"So, I'm hearing the following kinds of consequences of your temper: You luck out when your junior high school buddy doesn't beat you up for picking a fight; you beat somebody up and get a three-day probation in college; you rage and poison yourself inside over driving and other public incidents; and most recently you get yourself knocked out on the side of a dark road."

"Yeah, Doctor. Remember, I said it was stupid stuff."

The doctor checked his notes. "No, Ben, you said, 'how stupid I can be sometimes.' You didn't say the stuff was stupid. I said I'd agree with your description for the time being. Now I'm ready to fully agree."

Ben visibly tightened. Dr. Jose Calderon paused and watched.

The doctor said, "That was very interesting, what I just observed."

Ben looked away. Then he started to smile. "You trapped me, Doc. That wasn't fair."

Now Dr. Calderon eased a smile. "Pardon me, Ben. I'm working here."

Now Ben actually laughed aloud. "Yes, you are, Doc, but you have to agree that people can be real assholes sometimes."

"Well I do agree, but I don't have to. And here's the deal. I'll stipulate to that for these examples, and for any others that you want to bring up for as long as we work together. And you know what else?"

"What, Doctor?"

"We're not going to talk about real assholes anymore for as long as we work together. We're not going to spend any more of our conversations right there. Are you hearing me?"

"But..."

"No buts! If you want to continue with that, this session is free and you can find another therapist."

Ben suddenly stood. Dr. Calderon sat still, unflinching. Ben starting walking around the office. The doctor watched and waited.

Then, just as suddenly, Ben came back and sat again. "I'm hearing you, Dr. Calderon. So what are we going to talk about?"

"Dr. Parks, I understand that you do mediations, so I'm not going to feed you what you already know. You know what we need to talk about, so please tell me."

"Damn, Doc. I think I need to be taking notes on your technique."

Doctor Calderon allowed himself a brief smile and nodded. Then he deadpanned again and just waited.

After a very long silence, Ben said, "It happens too much." Silence. "That's it, right?"

"Probably."

"And you think I ought to be able to control it, right? So I'm the bad guy, right?"

"I'm sorry you seem to be choosing that kind of defensive reaction when I'm only trying to get some facts out and set some boundaries. Do you think you're the bad guy?"

After a long pause, "Sorry, Doc! I get what you're doing. I've done it myself. So here's my question: Can you help me control it?"

Doctor Calderon made some more notes. Then he looked up. "Yes, Ben, I can probably help if you're willing to do some hard work. Are you?"

"I am."

"Then let's get together next week."

Doctor Calderon opened his desk and extracted a bound journal, which he handed over to Ben.

"I want you to write in this at least once per day until we get back together. Open it up and write the following on the first page. Since you're gestalt trained, we're going to use that language. Is that okay?"

Ben nodded.

"Question One—what's standing out?[6]

"Question Two—what is/was my feeling and what is/was my reaction?

"Question Three—what do I need to work on?"

---

[6] "What's standing out" is a typical question that refers to the Gestalt concept of figure and ground . . . what you notice is figural . . . everything else is ground

Ben did as instructed, then looked up with a question. Dr. Calderon said, "Please, let's not go back to playing games. You understand, don't you?"

Silence. Then Ben nodded and closed the journal. "Yes, I understand."

"Then please let my secretary know that you're coming back in one week. She'll find a slot for you. And she'll also take your two hundred. Thanks, and have a wonderful week, Ben."

"Thanks, Doctor."

> *Oh, what peace we often forfeit*
> *Oh, what useless pain we bear*
> *All because we do not carry*
> *Everything to God in prayer*[7]

***

In three subsequent weekly sessions, Ben and Dr. Calderon worked together. Ben learned techniques for keeping control of his temper. He learned the "alter ego" technique and practiced mentally conjuring his alter ego as a friend who when presented with similar situations always had insight and better control. At the moment that Ben was about to flare, his miniature alter ego would appear on his left shoulder. Doctor Calderon had Ben verbalize conversations with the alter ego. How would the alter ego interject? What would he say to Ben? What would he ask Ben? What would he advise?

Ben learned and practiced relaxation techniques like counting to ten, deep breathing, shoulder shrug/release, and the internal scream/release. Dr. Calderon often intentionally did things to trigger Ben. Afterward the two would laugh briefly about these tests, but Dr. Calderon always quickly reined in the laughter and they went back to work.

At the end of their third session together, Dr. Calderon asked Ben about his family. Ben talked about Tony and his gym. He

---

[7] From the gospel, "What a Friend We Have in Jesus."

expressed his heartfelt pride and how well his older son was doing and about being a proud grandparent.

Calderon said, "I understand that one of your sons is a music artist."

"That's awesome Doc. Yeah, Rico goes by R Squared, but he's not into the conscious stuff, except for now and then. I wish he would get off the sexual and gansta mess. It's really not even his background. When you talk to him, he actually has some meaningful stuff to say about life, and politics, and family, but he pretty much stays in the gutter. I think he thinks that's what his people want to hear. Maybe they do. I'm just old, you know."

"R Squared, huh. I'll listen out for him."

Next Calderon asked Ben about his faith.

"I'm not much into denominations, Doc. Right now I attend an AME church. Don't go as often as I should. But I choose churches based first on the quality of the preaching, then the music ministry, then the feel of the people, and finally I don't want to go to a church that's dark five or six night per week. I like for churches to be open and reaching out to help the community."

"What about prayer?"

"I pray before meals . . . usually. I pray when I come off the road after a long trip driving. I pray when I'm down, but I really don't pray enough."

***

At the beginning of their fourth and final session together, Dr. Calderon produced two Bibles and handed one to Ben.

"Do you know Philippians?"

"No. Not offhand."

They read together and picked apart the verses. First, Dr. Calderon led Ben to 4:7. He suggested that this might be the theme that the apostle Paul is teaching about—the way to the peace that passes all understanding.

They jumped back to the beginning of the book and read portions together. They stopped on 1:2 that lifted up *grace* in addition to *peace*. 1:4 to 1:6, they decided, is somewhat of the beginning of a formula for grace and peace: "prayer" and "petitioning" with "joy" in the "confidence" that God answers.

They lingered on 2:3 that speaks of avoiding "strife or vainglory." They debated the likelihood of someone being able to "esteem others better than themselves." By the conclusion of the session, Dr. Calderon asked Ben for his takeaways.

"Well, Doctor, it's something like this: If I want grace and peace, I need to pray. But not just any old kind of prayer. Some of my prayers should be thankful. And when my prayers are asking for something, I need to expect that God will hear and respond, that is, if I remember to elevate or esteem others and don't judge them. It's something like that. Am I right?"

"Whoa, Ben. This is my sword as well as yours, but I don't profess to be able to pronounce your interpretation as correct. I have my own interpretations. We both seek truth in the Word, and this particular book is one that often helps me. That's why I brought it to your attention."

"That is so helpful, Doctor. I'll use a lot of the stuff that you've taught me, but especially, I know I'll use this. Your techniques aren't exactly all clinical, are they? You have an interesting approach to your work."

Dr. Calderon, for the first time in their four sessions together, broke into a loud laugh, followed by sheepish chuckles that went on for a while. After he got back in control, he said, "No they aren't, Dr. Parks. But you and I are men of both science and faith. With something as important as what we've been working on, why should we pretend that only one is relevant?"

"I take your point, sir."

Calderon paused and made some more notes. "Ben, I use whatever is useful. One day you should ask your friend Janice about our hip-hop sessions. I found out that she's into a lot of conscious rap, and after that she was always surprised when we would suddenly be spitting Chuck D, Nas, Jay-Z, and Biggie."

"Well you've certainly helped me, even more than you can imagine. I'll be eternally grateful to you, but I hope I don't ever have to come back."

"I do too, Ben. But if you find that you do, I'll be here for you."

"Thanks!"

"Bye, Ben. Good luck!"

Ben left and paid his final $200 on the way out of Dr. Calderon's office.

Chapter 37
Into the New Millennium

1996 to 2000, Levi Chance:

Giving up on the dream of being a nationally known record producer.

Arnold Luskin and Joe Minola pulling back because of Levi's drinking.

Moving from Anacostia up to Bloomingdale.

Living near Ben Parks again.

Building another in-home studio . . . this time all-digital.

Janice complains.

Fuck 'em. I'm not bothering anybody.

If I want to take a drink. I'm going to take a drink.

Living off my songwriting.

1996 to 2000, Ben Parks:

Storming with Addie.

Getting my doctorate at Howard University.

My business collaboration with Ted Freer.

Becoming comfortable with Ted's gayness.

The business gets a boost from the TPC (US Terrorism Prevention Commission) contract.

Teaching the Cross-Cultural Communication summer seminar at Howard University.

Teaching hand dancing as a way of giving back to wounded warriors at Davita's place.

Chapter 38

Bad Clients

The year 2000 in the Offices of Parks-Freer Associates

Though coproprietors of their firm, Ben and Ted Freer rarely worked together. Ted's clientele was predominately international, and Ben's was 95 percent domestic. The exception was when something came along that involved diversity, more specifically, something having to do with integrating attraction orientation into the client company's diversity activities.

But now they had taken on a rather large professional association as a client. The association's director needed to have an organizational assessment done ASAP. A board of directors meeting was taking place in three and a half weeks, and the board had complained that they hadn't seen a review since Director Archie Stanton had taken over three years ago.

Ben, on the telephone with Mr. Stanton, said, "Sorry. We are almost never able to respond to this type of request on such short notice, sir."

"I understand that, under normal circumstances, but these circumstances are not normal. What can we do to bring you in?"

"I'm not sure you can do anything. My partner, whom you're also requesting to be on this assignment, leaves a week from today for a week in Columbia, and I have regular clients that will be coming in. I wouldn't like to put them off with such short notice."

"But you could put them off if you really needed to."

"Let me give you the name of another firm that does excellent work."

"Would they happen to have done a presentation out in Denver in 1995?"

"I have no idea, sir."

"Did you and Ted Freer do a presentation on diversity at the Convention Center that year?"

"Yes. I guess it was 1995."

"Then Dr. Parks, the other firm won't do. Our board chairman happened to be in the audience in Denver. He's directed me to reach out to you to conduct an assessment."

Silence. Then Ben said, "I'll confer with Ted. Let me see what he says. If he can slide his commitments back, I certainly am willing to slide mine back also."

"Thank you so much, Dr. Parks, but I just want to impress on you the fact that time is of the essence. When can I expect to hear back from you?"

"I'll call you back by close of business tomorrow. If things are a go, I'll fax an agreement to you for signing. Let me say to you that the rates for our time will be two thousand five hundred per day for each of us. The only additional would be reimbursement for any travel costs and any materials we need to use. We would require a check in advance for the first five days. You can messenger it over to us with the signed agreement. The balance will be due when you receive our report, plus our time sheets and expense receipts. Is that acceptable to you?"

"Yes. Twenty-five thousand up front. Absolutely."

"Well then, Mr. Stanton, you'll hear back from us tomorrow."

"Thank you, Dr. Parks. I await your positive response."

***

Ben walked down the hall to Ted's office. Explaining the situation, Ben didn't lobby for or against the assignment. But after thinking it over together, they agreed that this professional organization had a big profile and it would be nice to count them as clients. They also agreed that they'd be able to calm the ruffled feathers of their existing clients who'd be put off about one month.

So it was a go. Papers were signed. Check was received, deposited, and cleared. Both Ben and Ted visited the professional association's offices for the first time, three days after the initial telephone call. The offices were in downtown Washington, DC, on K Street, a power address. Marble and burnished glass were all over the place. Archie Stanton greeted them as his secretary opened the door to his office. His suit along with his broad smile under a tanned skin and brushed-back white hair gave off an impression of success.

They quickly got down to business, with Ted taking the lead in laying out the PFA assessment process. Archie asked very few questions and agreed quickly to the way they'd proceed. He made notes to put his chief of staff to work arranging interviews with randomly chosen front-line staff, plus supervisory and managerial level employees, and the entire ten-person executive team. Additionally, PFA wanted to interview a dozen or so members of the association. They wanted these to also be chosen at random. Archie made more notes.

Finally, they asked if Archie had the time to do a thirty-minute interview on the spot. They wanted to record the interview and not have to take written notes. Archie had paused, but then agreed. The interview was more like forty-five minutes. Essentially the questions were about why the association's board wanted this assessment, what Archie thought the main strengths and weaknesses (internal) and opportunities and threats (external) were. Archie Stanton was cryptic about strengths and weaknesses and expansive on opportunities and threats. All smiles, Archie had walked them out to the eleventh-floor elevators and had promised to set his chief of staff to work. Everything would be set up by the end of the week.

***

For the next two weeks, Ben and Ted worked night and day to gather the information, analyze it, synthesize it into themes, and write and edit their report. The gist of the report was that the association drew on the prestige of its field to establish itself as a big player with local and federal officials who were their stakeholders, and that they had huge success lobbying for federal legislation that benefited their membership. However, the data showed that they indiscriminately left dead bodies in their wake when faced with opposing interests. Furthermore, the results showed a climate of fear among the staff and an undercurrent of racism, and especially homophobia, when it came to hiring and promotion practices.

The report was delivered along with an oral summary, three days before the board of directors meeting.

※※※

Six weeks later, PFA had heard nothing back from Mr. Archie Stanton nor anyone else at the association. After many unreturned calls, Ben went to the association's office and sat in the outer office to wait for Archie Stanton to return from lunch. After about twenty minutes, he came through and his mannerisms changed abruptly when he saw Ben sitting there in his lobby, but he quickly composed himself and smiled a quick apology.

"Uh, sorry for not getting back to you, Dr. Parks. Things have been really hectic. In fact, I can't see you right now because someone else is coming in that I have to see."

"Oh really! Your secretary said your calendar was open."

Stanton shot an angry glance to the secretary, but quickly pasted the smile back on his face and begrudgingly ushered Ben into the office. He sat behind his desk and steepled his hands in front of his face.

"What can I do for you, Dr. Parks?"

Ben paused and silently admonished himself to stay civil. "Well, first of all, I'd be interested in what your board had to say about the report and what they're doing now."

Archie seemed to be considering how to answer. "Actually, Dr. Parks, there was a very busy agenda at the meeting last month. There was no time for the report."

Ben was stunned. He'd had the impression that the report was the priority item for the board. He and Ted had gone through all kinds of machinations to make the time for this last-minute assignment.

"No time?"

Silence.

"Given how anxious you were to have it done, that seems rather strange, Mr. Stanton. So where are things now?"

"Well, to tell the truth, Dr. Parks, we're nowhere. Your report was not exactly what I had in mind. It wasn't very useful to me."

Ben was drawing on all the work he'd done with Jose Calderon back when he was learning to control his temper. He silently breathed in several times in a way he'd learned that wasn't noticeable.

"I hadn't realized that the report was for you, Mr. Stanton. You told me that your board of directors had directed you to have the assessment done."

"Well, that was originally the case, Dr. Parks. But come on. You didn't really expect me to show that trash to them, did you?"

There it was! *Trash.*

Deep breaths.

"Mr. Stanton, I'm not going to dignify the characterization. However, I realize that I'm witnessing the kind of abusive behavior that Ted and I heard about over and over in our interviews. I'm just going to move past it to the second matter, that of the payment upon delivery. You are five weeks late, sir."

"You've been paid more than sufficiently."

Now the breathing was not enough, but fortunately the alter ego appeared on Ben's left shoulder. Up close in Ben's ear he whispered, *If you explode, Ben, he can dismiss you or even call security. Is that what you want? Exactly what do you want?*

Dammit, I want to be paid. I moved good clients around for this jerk.

Then what's the best way to that goal?

Ben often disliked these little exchanges with his alter ego. Then finally, "Mr. Stanton, I'm very sorry that you couldn't find a way to learn from the information in the report. I fully expected that, after the rush of getting prepared for your board meeting, we'd have had a chance to come in and talk about next steps. Yours is not the first case where this kind of information has come out of an assessment. These moments of self-reflection can be critical incidents that lead to huge positive transformations. All of the telephone calls that you ignored were about just that."

"But the decision, after the fact, that you're not going to pay what we agreed to is not one that you have, sir. You have to pay me for our time, even if you don't value the product. Check your contract and you will find that it is for time and materials, and then you can messenger the payment over to my office tomorrow. If we don't receive it, your board will be hearing from our attorneys. Thanks for your time."

Ben stood abruptly and walked out.

The next day, a courier showed up at the offices PFA offices. The check for the balance of the eleven and a quarter days on the PFA time sheet cleared. As professionals, PFA's calculations were based on only eight hours per day, regardless of the fact that Ben and Ted had worked twelve- and fourteen-hour days to discharge the assessment assignment.

Chapter 39
Early to Mid-2000s

Still more random thoughts and word-markers for Levi and Ben.

Ben Parks:

Older son Tony begins career as a gym owner and personal trainer.

Younger son Rico graduates from high school and goes off to college for two years.

Rico becomes R Squared, the rapper.

Beginning of clumsiness and forgetfulness.

Sister, Penny Parks Tomkins, moves back to DC to help Ben's dad with mom.

Ben's mom dies of Alzheimer's.

9/11

Parks-Freer Associates loses the TPC contract and closes up shop in Dupont Circle.

Remaining business: Ted has his, Ben has his.

Addie breaks her foot.

Addie and Ben split.

Alone, but not really lonely.

Levi Chance:

"Can't believe that even main-man Ben started fucking with me about drinking too much."

I sing at Ben's mom's funeral.

Rico Parks starts running the studio in Levi's house and doing most of the engineering.

Chapter 40
Up to New York and Back

June 2007

Addie and Ben had separated without much fanfare. He moved out of their home in the LeDroit Park section of DC and up to Harlem, where he and his business partner Ted Freer had invested years ago in a two-bedroom walkup for business purposes. To the seller's surprise, they had paid cash and the place had served them well, even though of late Ted rarely used it. Ben had a number of New York-based clients, and the ease of living in his own space was something he relished. Now more than ever, this place gave him some modicum of comfort, having been squeezed out of the DC house on Elm Street that he loved.

Ben Parks walked up the steps in the brownstone condominium on Hamilton Terrace. As he approached the second landing, the door opened and he prepared to greet his neighbor Beverly, the temptress, the lovely ballerina. Instead, a young girl in cornrows with a bat and ball came running past him, giggling. She vanished out the front door. Ben stood on the landing as a black man with an attaché case rushed after his daughter.

"Wait, Aisha! I told you not to run on the steps."

"Hurry up, Daddy, we'll be late," said the girl, poking her head back inside.

Passing Ben with his two rather large bags, the man asked, "Do you need help, sir?"

"No, you need to catch your daughter. I'm your neighbor upstairs, but we'll have time to meet. Enjoy your day."

***

Solitude and peace!

***

A week later, Ben was in the second bedroom on Hamilton Terrace, working on a training design for his midtown Manhattan museum clients, when he got a call from his old friend at USTO, Bill Portis. He smiled when Bill's number showed up on his cell phone. "Hey, Bill, if I live and breathe, I can't believe it. How are you, my brother?"

"Fine, Ben. Just fine. How are things up in the Big Apple?"

"Not bad. Not bad at all. To what do I owe this unexpected call?"

"Here's the deal, my friend. Do you remember when you were at USTO and I came into your classroom one time when you were running that simulation?"

"I think you did that more than once. Refresh me. What simulation are you talking about?"

"Blue-Green."

"Oh yes. I used to love to run that one. Haven't done it in years though."

"But that doesn't mean you couldn't bone back up to speed."

"Just like riding a bicycle."

"That's what I thought. Well, I described it to Amy Schoonover on my staff, and we think it's the perfect way to start off a four-day retreat for an organization she and I are starting to work with. The client came to USTO about a month ago at his wit's end. We signed on to work with him and did an assessment. Can I give you a high-level summary of what we found? Do you have time now, or should we schedule another call at a better time?"

"Let's do it now."

"Great! Well, the client is JJ Starns. He's chief of staff for the attorney general in a state government. I'm not going to identify the state just yet, until we have a deal. Okay?"

"Fine by me."

"So, there are attorneys, investigators, and litigation support teams across the various divisions of the state's department of justice. The various divisions specialize in all kinds of cases from discrimination, to criminal, to civil, to voting rights, and so forth. Got the picture?"

"Keep talking."

"Amy, JJ, and I worked together to review documents, design a survey, and conduct random interviews in the one division the AG is pulling his hair out over. Again, I'm not going to name the division, okay?"

"It's irrelevant to me at this point."

"So, when we'd boiled down everything we learned, we delivered a report to the AG identifying these themes: uncertain leadership, fuzzy vision, accountability issues, mistrust, and poor communications. Without getting too much in the weeds, this new division chief has been onboard about six months and is flailing because there's all sorts of resistance to his attempts to clear backlogged cases, even though that's exactly what the AG wants her to focus on. And when I say backlogged, I mean serious backlog. There are ten-year-old cases still on the books. There are all kinds of new cases that beg for attention, but can't be looked at until some old ones are cleared out. Attorneys point fingers at leadership and investigators. Investigators point fingers at attorneys. Litigation support teams don't know who to point fingers at. They're just miserable."

"You know, Bill, that might be all I need to know for now. Basically it's a food fight instead of working together toward the mission, which is basically closing cases and achieving justice. Is that about it?"

"That's about it."

"And you, JJ, and Amy have a design for unpacking all those issues and figuring out how to climb out of the funk, but first you want me to come in and shake them up with an experience that gives them a taste of their own unproductive behavior."

"Bingo!"

"I'm down. When?"

"Week after next."

"Okay, at the end of that week I start teaching my summer seminar up at Howard U. So earlier in the week would be better than later, so I can have some time to prep."

"We're figuring it'll be all day that Monday."

"Perfect. Can you do four thousand plus expenses for the day?"

"Yes, I can."

"Then shoot me the paperwork and details and I'll suit up and show up."

"Oh, you've discovered suits in your old age?"

"Just a figure of speech, Bill. Just a figure of speech."

"My man!"

"Talk to you soon, Bill."

"Take it easy, Ben."

The two hung up.

***

A week after Ben's call with Bill Portis, Ben's cell phone rang as he was about to put a forkful of fluffy pancake in his mouth. He was at Amy Ruth's on 116th off Malcolm X Boulevard in Harlem. Ben didn't cook a whole lot anymore, especially since the move to New York. At least one meal per day was always out of the house, and Amy Ruth's was great for any meal, but especially for breakfast because the cook knew how not to mash down the pancakes with his spatula. So they were just as light and fluffy as the ones that Ben used to fix back in DC when he was doing Saturday breakfast for his boys and as many neighborhood kids as wanted to show up.

"This is Ben."

"Hey, Cuz! It's Corinne."

Ben's real estate broker cousin was even closer than ever to Ben's sister Penny now.

"Hey, this is a surprise. How you doing? What's up?"

"Penny tells me you've got a gig in DC next week, and I understand you're teaching that seminar again this summer at Howard. It's going to be hard to do all your DC work from up there, isn't it?"

"Naw, Cuz, I commuted up here when I lived in DC. This is just the reverse."

"Where will you stay when you're down here? You won't want to be cooped up with Uncle Richard and Penny, will you?"

Ben started to get suspicious. "What's up, Corinne?"

"Well, someone asked me to find a nice condo in the U Street area, and I found just the perfect one. As a matter of fact, this person put down thirty percent in your name. That was a really big check. It's just one block off U Street, NW. You like that area, don't you?"

"Yes, I like that area, but I live in New York now. What the hell are you talking about? And nobody puts up that kind of money as a surprise . . . or a joke. This isn't funny, Corinne."

"Well, I'm not allowed to say who, but if you get down here on Friday, you can see it and move in over the weekend. Your big consulting gig is next week, right?"

"Right."

"See you then, Cuz. I love you!" The telephone line went dead.

The Sequel to *Forgetful*

Trapped in a bottle
Salvation springs from friendship
Life on the far side.

Chapter 41
Stock Taking

Davita Sheridan Ferrier and Levi Chance were walking on First Street in the Bloomingdale section of Washington, DC. They both held large, to-go coffee cups from the local barista out on Rhode Island Avenue, NW. Levi was a coffee-of-the day person. He had loaded his up with eight sugars. Davita had ordered a half-caf soy mocha. They walked as Davita talked. Levi didn't seem to have much to say. Davita's message to Levi was that, whatever he was going through, he was loved.

Davita had arrived that morning in her red Jeep Renegade and had parked outside Levi's row house around eleven. She noted a Nissan Altima outside with the personalized tags: *Musician.* She also noted that two tires were flat. She smiled inwardly.

Levi never did like to drive, she mused.

Davita didn't go up to the door. She didn't want to interrupt if Levi was in there with a woman. She'd been trying to get hold of him for a few weeks and hadn't been successful, but she was on a mission. She would wait an hour maybe. Maybe more. Just depends how she felt. She was going to talk to Levi, if not today, then she'd keep coming over until she did. Then about eleven thirty, just like that, he came out in pajamas and sat on his top stoop. He was disheveled, as Davita would have expected. He didn't bring something out to read. He didn't have a cell phone to make some calls. He just sat and stared around.

After about three minutes of observing him and the fact that he didn't notice her right across the street, Davita called out, "Hey, sir."

Levi didn't respond. Then louder, "Hey, sir."

Then something. A searching look. The head turning. Then eyes focusing. Then squinting against the sun. Then slow recognition and a slight smile. Then Levi held up a finger indicating he wanted

Davita to wait. He reappeared a couple of minutes later with some ripped jeans and a tee shirt with the lettering: I just pretend to be Crazy. Levi gathered himself, descended his steps unsteadily, and walked over to Davita's car.

"That you, Vita? Yeah, that is you. Damn girl, you know how to surprise a brother. Sup?"

"What have you been up to, Levi? You don't come up anymore. I don't hear from you. It's like you've cut me and everybody loose."

"Naw, Vita. It ain't like that. I just been busy, you know."

***

After their walk up to the avenue to get some coffee, they came back to Levi's house and at first they stood. Then Levi said, "House is kinda messy, Vita. But . . ."

"Don't worry about it, Levi. Let's just sit on the steps and talk a minute. Then I gotta go."

Davita sat on the step just before the little landing (third step up). There were another four steps above the landing that led to the front porch. Levi appeared to sit as far away on the same step as he could. Davita pushed back a rueful half smile.

He knows I can smell him all the way over here. Oh, my goodness. Oh, my Father, help me to know what to do to help my poor friend.

After a bit of silence, Davita asked, "Have you heard from Benjamin?"

"Naw, Vita. I embarrass Ben. Rico says stuff about what he's doing from time to time."

"Rico still works the studio downstairs?"

"Oh yeah. That's my little play nephew. Love that boy, and he's got skills that I never had behind a console."

"That's good. One day you're going to have to let me come in and see the studio. I've only heard about it."

Levi's voice was dripping with poorly concealed sadness and regret. "One day, Vita. One day."

For a minute they sat in silence. Then Levi spoke, "I don't want to keep you, Vita. Know you got stuff to do. But it was nice of you to . . ."

"You know Ben is moving back to DC."

Levi turned sharply and stared. "What?"

Davita wouldn't be baited into repeating herself. She knew Levi had heard her. She just let the words sink in. After squirming and glaring for a while, Levi starting crying. Davita still said nothing.

"That niggah left me. He couldn't stand being around me so much that he moved to a whole new city."

Davita scooted across the step so she was nearer, but not touching Levi. Then she placed the flat of her right hand on his back and patted softly.

"You had nothing to do with Ben going to New York. You know he had business there. Didn't you stay in his flat a few times when you were working up there with that Joe guy? What's his name?"

"Joe Minolo. He don't want nothing to do with me either."

Levi wiped at his face with his shirtsleeve.

"Also, you know that Ben and Addie split."

"Yeah, I know."

"What'd you expect him to do? Stay over there with her? She was never the right fit for Ben. It was a temperament thing. You know that, Levi. Except for me back in the day, our friend has never had good judgment about women."

Davita had said this in jest, but then they both laughed and it broke some of the terrible tension that was building up.

"Why'd you put my boy on lockout, Vita? You know he's always loved you."

"By the time Ben got his shit together, Levi, I'd already fallen in love with someone else. Did you know I've only been intimate with two men in my whole life: Ben, only once, back in high school, and my husband?"

Now Levi turned and stared with wide eyes. It was as if he were looking at an alien. Levi had been with hundreds of women of the one-night-stand-or-a-little-more variety. He knew that his off-and-on friend-with-benefits woman, Janice, had probably been with just as many men as he'd been with women. He knew that his old friend Tracy Brown had been an even bigger hound than him at one point.

"Only two, Vita? You shitting me."

"No, I'm not."

Davita was pleasantly surprised that Levi was engaging. She wanted to keep him going.

"I forget. You got any kids, Vita?"

"Oh, yes. My girls. The oldest is a doctor already, and the youngest is about to finish up at Meharry."

Levi's face showed a lack of comprehension.

"It's a medical school in Nashville."

"Oh. I know Nashville. At least I know the clubs in Nashville."

"Her big sister met a Kenyan at Howard Med. Now both of them are practicing medicine in Kenya. You know Tracy's wife, Deanna?"

"Yeah."

"Tracy is the only one she's ever been with."

"The only one?"

"The only one."

"That's a trip."

"They have two boys and two girls. The boys are natural, and the girls are adopted from Vietnam. The oldest is already a major or maybe a lieutenant colonel."

"Really?"

"And when the younger boy finished at West Point, he could have played pro in basketball or football, except that he owed the army three years, or maybe it's five years."

"Damn!"

"The girls are from some kind of indigenous tribe over in Vietnam. Their facial features are Asian, but their skin is as dark as mine."

"How old?"

"Oh, I don't know, a few years younger than the boys. Beautiful girls. Tracy felt so beholding to this particular tribe that he insisted on going to an orphanage after the war. Deanna insisted that they adopt girls."

Levi was beginning to fog. Davita shifted back to more familiar territory. "Maybe if Jackson hadn't come into my life, me and Ben might have tried again once he got back from the army, but it just wasn't to be, and I don't look back. I know he looks back sometimes, and I'm sad about that. I love him, but not in the way he'd want me to love him. The timing just didn't work out for me and Ben."

"That's sad, Vita."

"No, it's not. I love my husband. That's all there is to it."

Levi just nodded.

"My first love and the man of my life are two different people. I've never been unfaithful to the man of my life and never will, but I still love my first love. I'm basically here because I hurt so much when I know that he can't have you in his life because you're a drunk. He's so much better in so many ways when he can have you in his life. So I divert him, but I don't want to do that. Anyway, Ben will be back here soon."

"He won't come see me."

"Maybe he will, Levi. Don't be surprised. Maybe he will."

Davita leaned over and kissed Levi on the cheek. His skin tasted rancid, but she didn't show any sign of it. Levi leaned away. Davita gave him a few more pats on the back, then stood.

"I gotta run now, my friend. Praying for you."

And Davita was gone, jogging back across the street to her Wrangler.

"Bye Vita," shouted Levi."

But he didn't get up. From across the street he heard another voice. It was his neighbor, Mrs. Allen. She always sat on her front porch. Levi had often wondered if she had any furniture inside, because she always seemed to be out there scanning the block.

"Yo, Mrs. Allen," he said, waving as he stumbled back up his steps and into the sour-smelling house.

Chapter 42

U Street

I don't know what to think! I don't know what to feel! I'm definitely off my game and I've got an assignment on Monday that I need to be sharp for. Corinne could have filled me in a little more. What's this big mystery all about?

***

Benjamin Parks stared out the window as the train stopped at the Wilmington, Delaware, station on its way from Penn Station in New York to Union Station in Washington, DC. It was early afternoon on a Friday. Corinne would pick him up at the train station and take him somewhere on U Street to some condo that she claimed had already been purchased in his name for some amount that came to 30 percent of the purchase price. Ben knew that the U Street area was full of yuppies and buppies. It was becoming one of the hip night spots in town. Ben, somewhat of a night owl, spent time at various nightclubs there. He liked Twins near Fourteenth and U and Busboys and Poets at Fourteenth and V. He knew that 30 percent of the purchase price had to be a sizable amount of money.

He imagined that they wouldn't have had any credit information on him. So someone had either cosigned in order to buy it with his name on it, or there would be some quick-claim deed process to go through. That is, if he went along with this scheme. He wasn't sure what he was going to do, but the big questions were who and why. The logical answer would be his dad, Dr. Richard Parks, but Dad was ninety-plus and wouldn't have had the energy to get out and shop for a condo. Logic would suggest that Corinne and maybe Penny, his sister, had done the legwork. Were his sons, Tony and Rico, involved? Probably not, although they probably were part of some cheering section for whoever was driving this scheme.

Would Addie Parks, his estranged wife, have been a part of it? Again, probably not. Addie and Ben had been going through court-ordered mediation, and, as recently as two weeks ago, they had signed off on the settlement agreement to be presented to a judge for a no-contest divorce. Ben imagined Addie on Elm Street. On the sly, he had asked Lou Bonefant (from the old Michigan Park crew) who lived next door to keep an eye out for her. He thought of Lou and Han, his Korean wife. He had found out that Han had gotten them to take in a homeless Korean girl that went to the school where Han was a teaching assistant. The two of them were happier now with a youngster in the house.

Ben knew Addie had the locks changed. Ben welled up with resentment every time he thought of that, since he still paid the full mortgage check every month. Addie had never paid a dime for the mortgage on the Elm Street house. Lou had let him know that Addie was having the roof replaced. This was one of the things the real estate agent that Addie had found had advised, but Ben reflected on the fact that Addie had never really liked the neighborhood.

Selling Elm Street was one of the negotiated agreements he and Addie had reached through their mediation. She had had the temerity to ask for more than 50 percent of the sale proceeds, but, just to get things over with, Ben had gone along. Expedience rather than fairness was the standard he had gone by. Ben knew that, as bad as they were for each other, there was some emotion on his part that wouldn't go away.

Turning his attention to U Street, Ben was conflicted. He was curious about the new place, but he was also somewhat disappointed about the interruption of his new NYC persona. Also, he was leery about being thrust back into close proximity to Addie. Anything involving Addie Sherrie Isles Parks had almost always involved mixed emotions for Ben Parks.

He was also excited about two pieces of work back in DC. For one, he'd received an out-of-the-blue call while in NYC from an old friend whom he'd met at Union Temple Baptist Church, Bill Portis, from USTO. Bill had a client who was in big trouble. An intervention had been designed to support them. Though an accomplished OD person in his own right, Bill had sat in on Ben years ago when Ben conducted a particular simulation. Bill had been blown away by how much the simulation brought out. He'd wanted to run it himself, but after considering long and hard, he had realized that it would be a very delicate part of the whole assignment. Bill didn't feel he had the confidence to run it himself, so he wanted to plug Ben into the team working with this new client. Ben had accepted on a telephone call while up in New York.

Ben was also going to do the seminar on cross-cultural communication at Howard University for the fifth time since the first one back in the summer of 1999. He'd already seen the list of new students for the seminar. Their papers on why they wanted to take the seminar were impressive. Ben and Dean Prescott of the Graduate School at Howard University had convinced the governing committee of the Consortium of Washington Area Universities after the second session in 2001 to cap the enrollment at sixteen. That is, just as long as at least one from each of the nine member schools was admitted.

It's so much more competitive getting in now for new students, Ben thought. *But thankfully the dean's office takes care of that.*

***

Corinne expertly steered up North Capital Street from Union Station; she took the cut to the right just past Florida Avenue so she could turn left on Rhode Island Avenue. Then, just past Third Street NW, she made a slight right, which put them back on Florida. Soon, they crossed Seventh Street and suddenly Florida Avenue was U Street. In the early afternoon, the street was bustling with commerce. Then, within a few blocks past Vermont Avenue, Corinne turned right, and in another block she turned into an alley, produced and pressed a remote for keyless entry, and guided them down a few levels and into space seventy-one.

Ben was silent. He hadn't been paying attention on the street to the exterior of whatever complex they now were under.

Corinne got out and said, "Come on, Ben! Show a little interest, if not enthusiasm."

Ben forced a smile and got out. He followed her to a bank of elevators, which took them up two levels to a well-appointed lobby with soft carpeting, muted oil paintings, and plush chairs in a sitting area. Corinne waved at the receptionist, who seemed to know her. They walked past a bank of mailboxes and came to a set of elevators just as one opened and a white man in a business suit carrying a briefcase exited. He smiled and nodded to Corinne without noticing Ben. She simply stepped in and held the door as Ben slowly entered. She pressed the eighth-floor button and in a few seconds they arrived and exited to the left down a hallway. Corinne led them to the last door, which was 801.

"Well, here you go, Cuz."

She opened up and stepped back so Ben could enter first.

Highly polished terra cotta flooring was the first thing Ben noticed. Then, in the living room he spotted a small but attractive carpet, and three armchairs around a glass coffee table.

Corinne said, "This is just some of my staging stuff. I figured I'd leave it here, because I knew you wouldn't bring anything but an overnight bag."

Ben nodded and walked over to the bank of floor-to-ceiling windows and gazed out to the north, up the hill to Cardozo High School. A sliding door allowed him to step out onto a small balcony area surrounded by brick walls that came up to his waist. An oval metal table and folding chair were the only items out there.

Corinne came out after him and said, "This is one of my favorite features. You can sit out on your balcony in privacy from being viewed, but when you stand you can see across the city."

Ben agreed and began to warm to the place.

Neighborhoods of red, brown, and beige row houses stretched from west to east. Off to the east, Ben spotted something very familiar: the library clock tower. Over there was his alma mater, Howard University. He pictured Frederick Douglass Hall, where he would begin teaching his course on cross cultural communication starting in eight days. Déjà vu!

"Come on, Ben, I'm showing another place in about an hour. Have to get going."

He followed her back toward the front door and then off to the right, where he saw a huge kitchen. This kitchen was much bigger than at the place he and Ted Freer owned on Hamilton Terrace in Harlem. It was even bigger than the kitchen at the house Addie still lived in on Elm Street, just ten or fifteen blocks away. This kitchen was appointed with granite countertops, a Sub-Zero refrigerator, Jenn-Air gas range, other high-end equipment, and plenty of cabinet space. He blew out, "Whew!"

Corinne laughed. Next, down the hall, there were facing doors, opening up on the side by the kitchen to a guest bedroom, and on the other side to a master suite with walk-in closet. He saw the full bath with tub, shower, plenty of cabinets, as well as other necessities. This time he whistled. Then, at the end of the hallway, facing back toward the living room, was another door opening up to a second full bathroom about half the size of the one in the master bedroom. Rather than both a tub and shower, this one had only a shower. There was also closet space in that bedroom as well as in the hallway and in the living room vestibule.

"Well, Doctor, what do you think?"

"How much was this place?"

"Six ninety-five"

"Six hundred and ninety-five thousand dollars for a two-bedroom condominium?"

"That's right."

"Is that the market rate in this area?"

"Usually a place like this in this area would be mid-seventies. But it was heir property and had been on the market for about ninety days. The owner wanted to move it."

"Thirty percent of six ninety-five is over two hundred thousand, isn't it? That has to be Dad."

"Yes, it's mostly Uncle Richard, but there are others. You'll learn about the others in time. I gotta run."

Corinne tossed a ring of keys with a remote high in the air. As Ben looked to catch them, she turned abruptly and left the unit. Ben called after her, but when he got out in the hallway, she was already stepping into an elevator. Ben turned back into the unit and walked into the master bedroom, sparsely appointed with a small desk, small chest with three drawers, and a double bed. This was more of Corinne's staging furniture.

He tossed his overnight bag on the bed and went into the kitchen. He opened the fridge, where he found a small jar of mayonnaise, an uncut tomato, a loaf of twelve-grain bread, a dozen eggs, a package of maple-cured bacon, an unopened package of bologna, and one of honey-cured ham, a jar of Welch's grape juice, a six-pack of Fosters Ale, and a note saying: "Cuz, you might not want to shop tonight, so these few things will get you started. Have a good weekend and good luck with your assignment on Monday."

In the freezer, Ben found a half gallon of butter pecan ice cream. Ben roared with laughter. Then, after a bio break, he went back out and sat on the balcony for a moment. Standing, he looked out to view the activity of the day as it began to be time for the neighbors to come home from work, the school kids to come out for play, some businesses to close but others to begin to pick up traffic. Somehow, it was busy, but it wasn't noisy.

Ben thought of some things he wanted to do, but mostly he wanted to get to the bottom of the mystery. His mind flashed from subject to subject. Then a thought jumped forward. He took out his cell phone and dialed the digits.

"EAC."

"Hey, Levi. What you up to?"

"Pop, it's me. You don't even recognize your own son's voice?"

"Well, well, well! How you doing, Rico? You working a session?"

"Not yet, Pop, but my clients should be here in about ten. Yeah, I heard you were back in town."

"Yep, you and Tony were next on my call list."

"We get it. Your sons aren't your priorities anymore."

"Aw, Son, you're killing me with that pity line. You guys are grown men."

Laughter.

"Pop, I'm just kidding you, but I gotta go. There's the doorbell."

"Wait, I called for Levi."

"He's asleep, Pop."

"At five p.m.? Wake his ass up."

"Can't, Pop. I'll leave a note. Gotta go."

Phone dead.

Ben worried.

Chapter 43

The Weekend Flurry

Saturday morning after Ben's arrival back in DC

Ben's cell phone was ringing. He thought he was dreaming. It stopped. A minute later it started ringing again. Ben pulled the covers down and picked up the phone. The indicator said it was 8:14 a.m. In a very groggy voice he managed to get out a word, "Hello."

"I'm down the street at Starbucks, at Thirteenth and U. Treat you to coffee and a pastry. What do you need? Ten minutes to get over here, maybe fifteen."

"Davita?"

"Of course."

"Why are you up bothering me so early on a Saturday morning?"

"You're in a new place. I know your cousin put stuff in there and she needs it back. You've got today to buy whatever you need. Then I assume you need tomorrow to get ready for this big-deal assignment you're going to work on. I love to shop. So I'm here as your personal shopping assistant. Bring credit cards."

The phone went dead. Ben fell back on the pillow.

What the fuck? I don't need this. Then the realization: *Davita!*

Ben sprang up from the bed like he'd been revving and someone just popped his clutch. Fourteen minutes later, he was walking into Starbucks at Thirteenth and U Streets.

From a small round table in the corner, Davita looked up and pointed him to a barista, who noticed her gesture and nodded for Ben to approach.

"What are you having, sir? Your friend left me a gift card, and I haven't rung her up yet. We've been waiting for you."

Ben turned and stared. Davita smiled and motioned for him to turn back around.

"Mocha with soy milk. Two butter croissants, heated."

"Yes, sir!"

Five minutes later they were sitting across from each other.

"Good to see you, Ben."

"Good to be seen, I guess. I suspect something's up. Is this where it's going to be revealed? Are you the ringleader in this story? I knew it wasn't Corinne by herself."

"Yes, I'm fine too! Thanks for asking, my friend!"

Silence.

"All we're doing today is shopping. I know you have a big assignment on Monday, and I know that you go into some kind of laser zone before you work on whatever you have to work on. So we're not going to talk about anything but furniture and home goods today. Then, on Tuesday morning, I'm fixing you breakfast up at my place. Maybe a little later. Maybe eleven. We won't be rushing. That's when we talk about what we need to talk about."

"Damn, damn, damn. I feel like a damn marionette."

"Okay. And you're a very cute one, I might add. Eat up!"

Twenty minutes later they were back at Ben's condo. Davita took pictures as he walked her through. After seven minutes, she said she would use the restroom and then she'd be ready to go. Ben stood at the front door, waiting.

***

Seven hours later, Ben had spent a little over $3,900. On Sunday he had several phone calls with Bill Portis, whom he would be meeting early in the morning to coordinate with. He looked forward to Monday for a full day of potential fireworks.

Chapter 44

The Assignment

A Monday morning, June 2007

The arrangement he'd struck with Bill Portis of USTO was that Ben would have the entire first day of the assignment to run his simulation with the state legal department. This was to take place on campus at Howard University. Bill, the client JJ Starnes, and Bill's associate Amy Schoonover would sit through and observe. The department head, Ozzie Jamieson, would give some remarks at the outset, but then he would leave and return later in the day before the simulation ended. Bill and Amy would then pick it up to wrap up the day, and Ben would leave before they adjourned. The following morning would be travel time for participants to get to Airlie House, in Warrenton, Virginia, for a one o'clock start to their retreat. Other associates with Bill's consulting organization would come in and share the facilitation from Tuesday through Friday at noon. Ben would be on-call for follow-ups later if needed.

At exactly 8:30 a.m., Bill welcomed the participants who were getting settled. Then, before turning things over to Ben, he asked Ozzie to offer a greeting. The department head came forward.

"I just want to say to everyone that I and my boss, the attorney general, consider this week to be critical for us. We all know that we haven't been working together as effectively as we should. That fact is among the reasons our case closures are running six months to a year behind schedule. As everyone in this room knows, we are in violation of our court order to close cases within one hundred and eighty days. According to the interview notes that Amy and Bill shared with me, you agree that major improvements in the way we work are needed, so I hope we won't waste time debating that fact.

"I take a lot of the blame for not addressing things sooner. A number of you have privately indicated to me that you were getting fed up and were thinking of leaving. I don't want that. Every person in this room is talented, and I value you greatly, but as I've said before, things have to change. I'm hoping this will be the start of that process, so let's give our attention to Bill and his team. I've looked at their design and I think it's a good one. I won't be here this morning for your warm-up simulation due to obligations that I couldn't change, but I will rejoin you this afternoon to see where things are and to participate from that point on. Any questions of me before I bug out?"

Nobody spoke.

"Good luck!"

And just like that, Jamieson left. Portis said, "And now I want to introduce you to an old friend and colleague of mine."

He introduced Ben, who came forward and did about ten minutes of pleasantries; for example, finding out that two of these executives (Charles Wormley and Claudia Ali) were Howard U. grads.

Ben acknowledged Charles Wormley. "Pleased to meet a fellow Bison. I took a graduate degree at Howard in the 1990s, and later on I taught part-time for a few years at the School of Business, but you would have been gone before I came."

"Sorry I missed you, Ben."

Both men smiled. When Ms. Ali introduced herself, Ben said, "My attorney, Giles Harris, may have been in your class at the law school."

"No, he was a class ahead of me," she replied, "but I knew him casually."

After intros, Ben got right into the prep for the simulation. He turned on the projector and the title at the top of the screen read, BLUE-GREEN: A SIMULATION.

Below on the slide was a set of instructions and ground rules. Before reviewing the instructions, Ben gave this introduction using a laser pointer, "As far as I can tell, Blue-Green was first written up in this book."

From the materials Ben had placed on the lectern, he held up a tattered copy of the "1977 Annual Handbook for Group Facilitators" from what was then called University Associates, out of La Jolla, California. Then he got into logistics. "Before I ask you to work together on this simulation, I'd like to mix it up a bit. So I'd like for you to count off now by fours."

The execs complied and very shortly they were organized into four groups of four. For the next hour, the execs worked in their designated groups to decide on whether they would play blue or green in each of ten rounds. They passed slips of paper with their decisions for each round to another group as shown below:

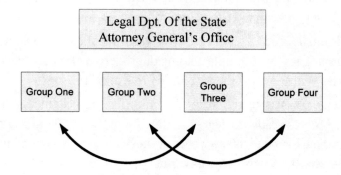

The scoring Instructions given to the groups were as follows:

(a) If you decide green and they decide blue, you get +10 and they get -10.

(b) If you decide blue and they decide green, you get -10 and they get +10.

(c) If you decide blue and they decide blue, you get +5 and they get +5.

(d) If you decide green and they decide green, you get -10 and they get -10. (e) Scores for rounds 6, 8, and 9 are doubled. (f) Scores for rounds 7 and 10 are squared and negatives remain negative.

And so it began. The four execs in each of the four groups deliberated. The folks in group two, for instance, easily reached agreement that they would always play blue. Other groups came to other conclusions. The accumulated scores at the end of five rounds looked like this:

Group 1: = -20; paired with Group 3: = zero

Group 2: = -50; paired with Group 4: = +50

The groups did some face-to-face negotiating after round five. The results were mixed in terms of improving the overall score.

After all sixth-round slips had been exchanged, the four team scores were as follows:

Group 1: played blue for +10; total = -10; paired with Group 3: played blue for +10; total = +10

Group 2: played blue for -20; paired with Group 4: played green for +20; total = +70

After round nine, the scores were:

Group 1: played blue for -20; total = +50; paired with Group 3: played green for +20; total = -50

Group 2: played blue for -20; total = -210; paired with Group 4: played green for + 20; total = +210

Group two had asked for a negotiation for every round from six on, but after continuing to play green in round six, group four never again wanted to negotiate, but before playing round ten, both groups one and three asked for another negotiation. In their final negotiation at the far corner of the hallway, Julissa Netzky from group three and Matthias Cohen from group one eyed one another.

"We thought we could trust you guys and you screwed us," said Netzky.

Cohen looked like he'd eaten a bug. Finally, he shrugged and said, "How can we make it up to you?"

"What were you thinking?" asked Netzky in a louder voice.

"The thinking was that we wanted to get back in the black, but we didn't think it through enough. We're sorry! This is another squared round. So what if we play blue again and you play green again?"

Netzky thought. Then she said, "No, that's not the answer. We've been playing green for the last two rounds because we were pissed at you, but if we do it again this round, we'd just switch places with you in the red and us in the black with a net zero effect."

Cohen's expression was forlorn.

Netzky said, "No, we'll go back to playing blue, and hopefully you will keep playing blue. It won't get us out of the red, but we'll be close, and you won't take a nosedive."

Cohen gulped. "Are you sure?"

Netzky nodded.

Cohen offered his hand and Netzky shook it.

"We owe you guys, big time."

Netzky didn't reply. She turned and walked back to room 325.

After the final round, all groups had played blue, with the exception of group four. The scores were as follows:

Group 1 = +25; total = +75; paired with Group 3 = +25; total = -25

Group 2 = -100; total = -310; paired with Group 4 = +100; total = +310

***

At the end of the one-hour exercise, Ben said, "Let's all take a fifteen-minute break. Then we'll debrief."

Then, when all sixteen executives were back in room 322, Ben walked to the easel on which he'd drawn the rough chart with "Office of the Attorney General: Legal Division" at the top, and modified the diagram as follows based on each group calling out its scores.

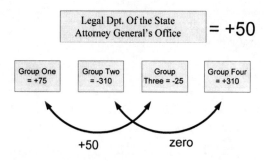

Ben's debrief commenced from that point. Very shortly, having been shown to be the group that played all green's, Carrie Brooks from group four said, "Wait a minute! No! No! No! This isn't fair. You didn't tell us we were playing together. You put us in teams and we won the competition with a score of three ten."

Ben looked at her but didn't reply.

Katie Collins and Tran Nguyen nodded in visible agreement, and Nguyen spoke. "You tricked us, sir. If you had said we were supposed to play *with* the other team and not *against* the other team, we would have done that. This is crap! What a stupid game. This is crap!"

Ben Parks looked back passively. Finally, he nodded toward group four member Claudia Ali, who hadn't spoken yet, "Do you have anything to add, Ms. Ali? Do you think I've unfairly tricked you?"

After a long pause, Ali spoke. "No, sir. I don't think you tricked us."

"I'm surprised, Ms. Ali. Your group members are pretty upset with me right now. You're not upset with me?"

"No, sir. I'm upset with us, and especially with myself."

"What?" screamed Collins. "What are you talking about, Claudia?"

Continuing, Claudia said, "Just look at Dr. Parks's chart. It has four groups that are part of the same organization. That's the organization, and we're all a part of it. It's right there on the chart. All sixteen of us are in the same organization. We're saying we won the competition with plus three ten, but what we're not admitting is that we did that at the expense of the other guys, who had a minus three ten. So what good was our plus three ten to the overall legal department?"

"That's crap!" said Collins again, even more loudly. She came back at Ben Parks with a question about why he'd broken them into teams. This led to a big discussion about whether Ben had ever used the word "team."

Seeing an expression on her face, Ben called on group three's Julissa Netzky. "You have something that might enlighten us, Ms. Netzky?"

"You never said the word 'team,' Dr. Parks. You consistently said we were in groups, and that's what's on your chart. Furthermore, you never used the word 'compete.' You said group one would communicate with group three and group two would communicate with group four. You never said it was a competition."

Ben looked back toward Katie Collins. "Ms. Collins?"

She looked defiant. "I thought . . . I could swear you said 'compete,' Dr. Parks."

Now, Ben asked the whole group to raise their hands as to whether he'd said "compete."

The tide started to turn when Tran Nguyen from the fourth group said, "My bad, Dr. Parks. You said 'communicate'."

Ben Parks took his time. He panned the entire room. Then he scratched his bald head as if he were also confused. Charles Wormley was smiling and seemed to be loving it.

Finally, Parks looked at Wormley and said, "Mr. Wormley, perhaps you can shed some light on what's going on here."

Wormley smiled even more broadly. "You are a sly dude, Dr. Parks, but you didn't lie to us. You didn't say 'compete.' You said 'communicate.' And you never said anything about 'teams,' which would have subtly implied a competition. Not only that, I forget exactly how, but somehow you said something about us 'working together' at one point. If there was any tricking going on, we tricked ourselves."

"Pray tell, Mr. Wormley. How did you trick yourselves?"

"It was our assumptions, Dr. Parks. Some of us, or a lot of us, assumed it was a competition, but you never even implied that it was a competition. We did that to ourselves."

Now some were nodding.

Then Ben interjected. "I'm looking at this score of positive fifty up here at the top of the chart. Again, I'm not really good at math. Can anyone calculate what that score would be had all teams played blue for ten rounds straight?"

248

Meaghan Greenberg from group two spoke up. "I've got positive eight twenty, Dr. Parks."

"Wow, that was fast, Ms. Greenberg. So the potential was positive eight twenty and you guys did positive fifty. Let's say that the State Department of Justice's Legal Division was to be assigned a grade for this activity. What grade would be appropriate?"

"I'd say we'd all get an F, Dr. Parks," said attorney Adib Deeb, who hadn't spoken in the full group until this point.

"Oh my! An F. We can't have that, can we?"

Everyone in the room said some version of "No" or "No, sir" or "No thank you, Dr. Parks."

"Ah, what to do? What to do?" said Ben with a pensive expression. A far-ranging conversation about competition, conflict, and assumptions ensued for the balance of the morning, and took up again in the afternoon. At one point late in the afternoon, Ben proposed a distinction that competition and conflict aren't the same but they are related, and that competing with a competitor is healthy and that conflict with an enemy was natural. But either, with an entity with whom we should be cooperative, was problematic. Then, at what seemed to him to be the right time for a hand-off, Ben stopped and panned the room. He looked to the back where Ozzie Jamieson had quietly entered and stood at the back near JJ Starnes. "My time is just about up."

As prearranged, JJ Starnes came to the front. He and Ben passed each other on the side as Ben moved to shake hands with Amy and Ozzie at the back.

Then JJ spoke, "Amy and I are going to step in for Ben at this point. He's a busy guy and he's given us the start I think we needed. We're coming up on the end of the day, but before we stop, we'd like for you guys to pair up and share some of what you're scribbling in your journals. Then we'll also share some of those select observations in the room. After that, hopefully, we'll all be able to wait until rush hour is over in the morning before heading out to Airlie House. They're allowing us an early check-in to our rooms and they'll have lunch for us starting at noon. Then we'll begin our retreat at one p.m. But first, before he gets out of the door, would you join me in giving a round of applause to Ben Parks? I think he's given us some insights that will come in very handy as we turn our attention to how we may play blues and greens with each other at the legal division."

There was some applause. Then most of the room, including Katie Collins, stood and joined the applause. Katie Collins came back to the door as Ben was about to turn.

"Thank you, Dr. Parks!" She hugged him tightly.

"You're welcome, Katie. And good luck." He hugged her firmly, but not tightly. Then he exited to leave the legal department of the state attorney general to their work.

Chapter 45
Mystery Solved

A Tuesday morning, June 2007

"I needed you back here. I didn't see how you could do what needed to be done from New York."

Davita Sheridan Ferrier was behind the bar at Davita's Place on upper Georgia Avenue. Ben was sitting on a barstool eating a hearty breakfast she'd prepared just for him: link sausages, soft scrambled eggs, grits, and a hot buttered biscuit, with orange juice and black decaf coffee.

"This was rather an extreme move. I'm going to have to pay you back, but I can't in one fell swoop."

"If you do, you do. If you don't, you don't. I don't really need the money. Anyway, your father put up most of the money. My contribution was just a drop in the bucket compared to his. And Janice Westbrook put some in, as well as Lou Bonefant and Tracy Brown. Even Bart and Brian Stokes chipped in a little. Bart comes through here pretty often and he tells me about things going on with the adopted side of Levi's family."

"What are you talking about that needs to be done so bad?"

"Slow down Ben. How are you? How's the place coming? How was the consulting assignment?"

Ben had just moved into a two-bedroom condo on Eleventh Street, NW in Washington (just a few blocks from the popular U Street corridor).

"Fine, great, good."

"Oh, you got jokes. You know you got to give me more than that."

"Okay, so I've got one agenda and you've got another. And whenever that happens, I can just forget about what I want to talk about."

Ben finished off his biscuit and took a final sip of his coffee. Then he used a paper napkin to clean his lips and said, "I love the place, Davita. I love the area. Haven't decided how I'm going to set up the second bedroom . . . an office, guest bedroom . . . probably both. So I guess it'll take me a while to get settled, but again I have to say thanks. That's just not enough, but it's all I have right now."

Davita bused Ben's dishes from the bar and then poured him and herself another cup of coffee. They were alone in the bar, as often was the case when Ben came up to Davita's Place in the mornings before she officially opened for lunch.

"We can talk about the assignment, but you're killing me. Why is it so important for me to be here? You know there's a certain amount of Addie vibe that I pick up when I'm in DC. I don't feel that when I'm up in New York."

"Oh, Ben, she was never for you. You know that. Your parents knew that. Penny knew that. Your cousin Corinne knew that. Your boys knew that. The only one in the world who didn't know it was you, but I know for some reason that you loved her, or love her. Whatever. And that'll just take time to wear off. In the meantime, you've got to get on with your life."

Looking at him through those beautiful light eyes contrasted against her chocolate brown skin, and taking one quick sip, now Davita answered Ben's question.

"Levi, dumb ass! Levi is the reason you need to be in DC. After your mom's funeral, when you two seemed to reconcile, I was hoping to see you get serious with him. The next thing I know, you're packing off to New York. Levi is in a deep, deep hole, Ben. He's wandering around in a valley of despair and probably doesn't even realize it. He needs an intervention. Tracy and Lou are down for it. Deanna and Janice would like to be involved, and so would I if Levi would respond okay to women being a part of the process, but you're the key player. You've got to help Levi. We'll help, but you have to take the lead. You have to take the lead. As soon as possible, all of us need to sit down together and strategize."

"You're talking about some heavy shit, Vita. We don't know what we're doing. I've been on Levi for years to go up to the VA for help. He won't do it. They have all kinds of programs and support groups. He won't do it. I don't know what to do."

"And that's why it's on us. Levi won't take help from just any old body. He won't take help from strangers. He'll only take help when he feels absolutely safe. He's got to know that folks love him. That's what he doesn't think he can get at the VA. It has to be us. The old Michigan Park crew plus the Stokes people from old Southwest. That's family for Levi. His dad being killed and mom passing broke his heart. Urban renewal broke his heart. Then Nam broke his heart. Arthur, Emmanuel, and Clyde broke his heart. Coming home from Nam to find that Sam Senior was dead and he hadn't been here to say goodbye broke his heart. Alma and Bundy Stokes both passing recently broke his heart."

"Levi's gift is his music, and I don't know if you even know about the rebuffs he's had, first by Marvin and then from his connections in New York and LA. Has Rico told you anything about that stuff?"

"Not really," said Ben.

"But still, his music is the only thing that keeps him out of the bottle. As soon as he stops playing, he starts drinking. Damn, Ben, you know his pattern better than anybody. We have to do this, and we have to do it now. He's killing himself. When can we start?"

Ben Parks stared at Davita Sheridan Ferrier with growing recognition that she was serious and absolutely resolute. His mind raced with all kinds of excuses; reasons why they would fail; reasons why he couldn't lead on this. Then, when he looked at Davita again, he knew none of his reasons would be good enough.

"I can't do it, Davita. I just can't."

Ben thought of Gillian, who would have brought up Galatians 6:9: "And let us not be weary in well doing: for in due season we shall reap, if we faint not."

Shit, he thought. *I don't need my mom from the grave teaming up with this woman in front of me.*

"I'll give you no more than a week to think about it. You're going to do this, Ben. And it's got to be soon. You can't procrastinate on this one, Ben. You can't take your sweet little time like you always do, thinking about this like one of your academic research projects. This is about action, and buster, you're going to drive this thing whether you like it or not. Is that clear?"

Ben didn't respond.

"Xavier Parks! Is that clear? You'll have all the help in the world, Ben, but you have to do this. Please say it's clear. Please say yes."

Ben never used his middle name. He shook his head, but didn't speak.

"No, Ben! We'll do it," said Davita with finality. "I'll be back in touch. Now I'm going upstairs. You can let yourself out."

Ben, the marionette, threw up his hands in exasperation. Davita stood and started toward the back stairs but then came back.

"By the way, Ben, when's the last time you had sex?"

"What?"

"You heard me."

Inside, Ben went on alert.

"No, Ben. We're not going to have sex."

Inside, Ben banged up against a brick wall.

"When, Ben?"

"Winter before last."

Ben flashed back. He and Addie had been to dinner at one of their favorite spots. It was the St. Petersburg House at the corners of Connecticut and Florida Avenue in DC. They had drunk top-shelf vodka together and shared caviar and borscht that was to die for. Addie had fussed. And she'd actually helped him tremendously. He was anguishing about his own forgetfulness, in fear that it might foretell his own slipping into dementia. He also was agonizing about Levi Chance, who had obviously become a hopeless drunk. Ben was dealing with his own inability to know how to handle his friend. He remembered one of her last lines before they'd gone home and slipped into fierce lovemaking. In typical Addie blunt fashion, Addie had shouted, "Deal with it, bucko!"

Standing there watching him remember, Davita finally interrupted. "Come back, Ben!" She was staring at him with considerable interest. "I'm going to do you a favor and not look under the bar."

Ben smiled sheepishly but couldn't help patting himself back in place.

"That thing that just happened to you, you need some more of that. You're too tense. It's not healthy."

"Any suggestions about with whom?"

"No, that's not my job, sir. I'm not a pimp. I'm just telling you to get fucked, in a nice way, I'm saying."

Without a word, Davita went to the back, and this time Ben knew the conversation was over. She'd go up to the apartment above the restaurant where she and her husband, Jackson Ferrier, stayed when they wanted to be in town instead of at their home out in Potomac, Maryland. This was the apartment that Davita's parents lived in for a while, when they first bought The Dance-A-Lot. That was before they bought their home on Monroe Street in Michigan Park, DC, back in the 1950s. The name, Davita's Place, didn't come along until her parents had passed.

Ben looked around, then toward the back where he knew the steps went up to the apartment. Davita was gone. He realized he'd better get going.

Chapter 46

Voulez Vous?

Davita's voice was in Ben's head. Then it came to him. He saw someone in his memory. About five foot six, with very dark skin, athletically toned (Ben had later learned that this was from spinning classes), bright smile, and striking features, with full lips. Seemingly she wore no makeup, but her skin glowed—always! This was Doris Smith, MD. On occasion, Doris had seemed to look out for Ben without warning, as in the way she had once referred him a new client, Jason Queen. Working out of lower Manhattan, the diligent and ambitious Queen was now one of Ben's top-revenue coaching clients. Living in Harlem had made it much more convenient for Ben to spend time with Queen.

Ben thought back to that time at the O Street Mansion in northwest DC. He had done countless jobs with the DC government's public health agency, where Doris was the chief medical officer. At the mansion, the city's public health agency had been holding a management retreat and Ben had been facilitating. These managers had all worked reasonably well with Ben, but Doris Smith had seemed particularly grateful for his presence. Some of her programs had been under attack. Quite the introvert, Dr. Smith would not have held her own so well had it not been for Ben's intervention on her behalf.

But as an organization development consultant who was used to accurately sizing up clients, Ben knew that she was beyond smart and that she was a capable leader. He also knew that, at least as of the last time he'd worked with her agency, the widowed Doris was not attached. Finally he knew, just from unspoken vibes, that there had been a mutual attraction between them. On the other hand, they hadn't so much as spoken to one another in over a year, and they had only ever spoken to one another in professional settings.

What the heck! Why not? Why not just see what's up?

Ben called. Surprisingly, she quickly agreed to meet him, just for lunch.

***

This woman was fine. The meet was at Tony and Joe's Seafood on the Georgetown waterfront. On the way, Ben got caught on a phone call that lasted way too long. He came into the restaurant about twenty minutes late. He saw Doris at a table and smiled, until he noticed she didn't smile back. Now he was on edge standing by the side of the dining table. She looked up and said with a sharp tone, "I almost left. I thought we said one thirty. I don't like to be kept waiting."

Ben took a breath. "Well, I got here. And now I'm gone. See ya!"

***

She caught up with him at his car parked on a two-hour meter on K Street under the Whitehurst Freeway.

"Dr. Parks, I'm damaged goods."

"So am I."

"Sorry for being so snappy. I'm guessing you were thinking twice about whether this was a good idea."

"Yep."

"Me too."

Ben turned to face her. He put his hand lightly on her shoulder and started walking toward the Potomac River waterfront. Without resistance, she went along. In about fifty steps they were at a little bench. They sat in silence for a long while, looking straight ahead out at the Georgetown University crews (male and female teams) working out. The teams stroked smoothly together, almost as if they were in some sort of water-propelled ballet.

Ben spoke. "We've got to somehow move from Dr. Parks to Ben. Do you think that's possible?"

Doris thought for a moment. "Sure, Ben. Why not?"

Ben smiled and she returned the smile.

"I've always been just a little off in terms of romance. It probably goes back to an old requited friend of mine, and also to my dad, Richard. I wasn't quite grown enough for the friend at the time in our lives when I think I might have had a chance with her. And as for my dad, he's a perfectionist in all things, even when it comes to relationships. He and my mom were married for more than sixty years. Not without some fights along the way, but perfection nonetheless."

"If I recall correctly, your dad's still alive, right?"

"Yes he is. In his nineties and still pushing."

"What a blessing."

"Yep."

They sat together in silence some more.

I wasn't quite grown enough for Davita and could never match the perfection of Richard. This ghost was with me through countless women up through Yvette and Addie.

Ben's determination with Addie not to fail again was misplaced from the start, but he couldn't acknowledge it because of the memories of failure.

"These ghosts of my parents' relationship and of all of my failed relationships stay with me."

"We all have ghosts, Ben."

"If anything happens between us, we still won't be as close as you might like."

"I haven't decided how close I want us to be."

Now Ben smiled broadly.

"Look, Ben."

She stopped for his recognition. Ben did a thumbs-up gesture to indicate he was listening.

"Look, Ben, we're beyond grown, and we've known each other for a long time. I think we've even flirted with each other from time to time. Or am I wrong about that?"

"No, you're not wrong."

"I recall a time when we'd been in a meeting together down at my office. I got excited because I actually thought you were going to make a move."

"When was that?"

"I don't know. A couple of years ago. The time isn't important."

Ben just looked and waited.

"A couple of times during the meeting I thought I caught you taking a peek at the girls."

Ben stared blankly for a few seconds, then smiled when he realized what she meant. But still he kept quiet.

"At one point, I turned and tried to give you the most alluring smile I could muster, just as my boss distracted your attention with some question about something."

"I might have been thinking about you, and the girls have caught my attention many times, but I probably wouldn't have said anything, even if Sonja hadn't distracted me. I wouldn't have been that confident."

Doris nodded with understanding. "Well, I was really happy when you called and asked to see me. I've often thought about what it might be like for us to go out, but now I think I'm way past being entertained by flirting."

"Okay."

"And I know you pretty well. I'm not sure how much more I need to know about you."

"Okay."

"Are you still hungry? We blew our lunch date, but we still should break bread together. Don't you think?"

"Okay, back to Tony and Joe's we go!"

"No, I took off for the rest of the afternoon, and I have a suite at the Four Seasons."

A raised eyebrow and silence.

"Did you hear me?"

"Yes. But I'm on a meter." It was the only thing he could think of to say.

"Well then, that just stops everything, doesn't it?"

Her crack caused the first outright laugh between them. It was clear to Ben that Doris had taken control of the date. That was fine with him. She said, "Before we get up from this bench, would you mind kissing me?"

Ben slid over on the bench and turned. She turned toward him and leaned in. They kissed lightly, lips open slightly. Tongues brushed each other, but they resisted the temptation to open more. Then Doris pulled back and said, "That's enough for now. I just wanted to break that ice."

"Good idea," said Ben.

***

Her car was already valet parked at the hotel. Ben found a lot near the cinema at Thirty-First and K Streets. They walked several blocks over to the hotel at Twenty-Eighth and Pennsylvania Avenue. It was about three thirty in the afternoon when they arrived and Ben really was hungry by now. They dined together in the lavish suite she'd rented for the night. There was music from the in-room entertainment center. The room service fare included two delicious nicoise salads and a nice bottle of pinot grigio. With some salad still on her plate, Doris stood from the table where they'd been sitting together. She walked into the bedroom. Ben used the bathroom and then followed her.

She was standing on one side of the tufted bench at the foot of the California king-sized bed. She wore a black business-style shirtdress. At the moment, the buttons were undone from top to bottom. This allowed Ben to observe what he already had known would be glorious. Not humongous, but very ample breasts were barely covered by the sheer bra that revealed the tone of her ebony skin underneath and the hint of dark nips mounted on a supple areola.

The girls, thought Ben. *Aw, those beautiful black girls.*

The bra, he thought, had to come from Victoria Secret. Standing in the doorway. Ben thought, *They are delicious. God bless you, Victoria.*

Doris's panties weren't those stringy thongs that you see in the magazine advertisements. They were low-waisted French-styled briefs, but also with a sheer material. The little things stretched down so as to afford the illusion of cover to Doris's nicely proportioned north-south facing ass region. Ben liked the intoxicating effect.

"Is this all right with you, Dr. Parks? I know where I want this to lead, at least for today. I don't want to wait the mandatory three dates. Okay?"

"Okay."

"Then walk over here."

Ben began unbuttoning his shirt as he walked toward her. He started around the tufted bench and she stopped him.

"Stay on the other side, please. Finish unbuttoning your shirt, and then I'd like you to kiss me from over there."

Separated now by the width of the bench, Ben had to lean forward. He rested his hands on the bench in order to lower himself to her height. Doris leaned toward him but kept her mouth closed. So Ben also kept his shut. Their lips touched lightly and Ben pressed forward just a little, but Doris backed away so their lips remained in contact but without pressure.

"Just there, Ben. Just there."

Ben got the idea. He wet his lips with his tongue and then began to brush her lips lightly with his.

"Yes," she murmured.

Now their heads slowly moved from side to side, brushing each other's lips lightly.

"Yes, that's right," sighed Doris.

After a while, she moaned and opened her lips for his tongue. He obliged. Now he licked her lips outside and reached his tongue inside to find the fleshy inside parts. In return, she did the same with him.

"Please take your pants off, Ben."

As Ben stepped out of his things, Doris walked over to one side of the large bedroom where there was a blonde hardwood desk and plush leather swivel chair. With her shirtdress still on and open, she wriggled out of her panties, reached around behind herself and popped her bra. Then, turning to watch Ben disrobe, she simultaneously bent to manipulate one of several levers on the chair. The first one she tried controlled the forward and backward motion of the chair's back. She made sure it was straight up, locked it into place, and placed the back so it rested against the desk with the seat part of the chair facing out into the room. Ben was almost finished undressing, but wondered what Doris was up to. The next lever Doris tried raised and lowered the seat of the chair. She first pulled the seat all the way up, and then she lowered it again to about a midway position. She locked that into place. The final lever controlled the swiveling action of the chair. She locked it so there was no swivel.

Turning, she said, "Too busy watching me. You're supposed to be ready by now."

Ben kicked his last leg out of his boxers. Now, Doris stood and dropped the shirtdress behind her to face Ben, gloriously naked. Ben's nature was now furiously erect. Doris mounted the chair and her knees sunk into the plushness of the leather. She bent forward to place her elbows on the chair back for support. She could see him approaching through the mirror above the desk, but she turned and looked back at him. He stopped his approach. Doris motioned him forward.

"Inside me!"

Ben walked forward and reached out toward her with his lowered hand.

"No, Ben. I don't need your hands. I'm already wet. I couldn't be wetter. Come around so I can feel you."

Ben came around toward one side of Doris. She took him in her hand and squeezed. "Ooh, I see you don't need much help either, old man."

"I guess not. I don't know what's gotten into me."

Squeezing his member anyway, she guided him back behind her and placed the throbbing part exactly where she wanted it. He leaned forward and then took the final half step for deep penetration.

"Oooooh! Oooooh! That's how I knew it would feel. Oooooh! So good!"

Ben thrust himself forward once. She reached back and firmly placed a hand on his chest. "One more thing, Ben, and then I'll let you take this wherever you want. For now, can we just be still like this? Can we not move until we just can't help ourselves? I wonder how long we could just be joined together like this without moving."

"I'll try, Doris."

"That's all I want right now, my friend. I don't want you to move inside me until you can't stop yourself. Then you can do anything you want."

But Doris began to squeeze him from the inside. His response was reflected in an involuntary gasp.

"Shush yourself, Dr. Parks. Shush, Benjamin. We're not going to technically consider this as movement."

"If you say so, Dr. Smith."

Ben had stood still for as long he could. The sensation was one of quivering anticipation surrounded by the sensuous warmth, feel, and smell of her. He felt himself swelling in spite of not being allowed the traditional in-and-out. He listened to her soft moans interspersed with what sounded like low humming. Whatever muscles she was using from inside, they were certainly well developed. He had never experienced a lovemaking moment like this.

Eventually he could no longer stop himself. He had to move. Ben began to thrust back and forth and around and around inside her pleasure places. As promised, Doris lustily joined the movement and moaned and cried until Ben came out and lifted her to the bed. He mounted her in the missionary position as she spread wide. She thrust and squeezed with a force that startled him. Still deep inside, he elevated his upper body onto his elbows until he could take her left breast in his mouth. Then her right one. They were sweet to the taste and he carefully sucked and licked on the nips as well as the broad encircling areola. Now Doris alternated pushing up with her pelvis to feel his thrusts below, and then with her torso to bring her breasts deeper into his mouth.

Four or five songs from the entertainment center later, Ben began to moan. She looked up at him with obvious interest. He tried to look away or close his eyes, but she somehow was right there smiling in front of him every time his eyes opened. Doris was deliciously enjoying Ben as she watched his expressions chronicle the storm mounting inside him. Finally, it came thunderously for Ben Parks. Simultaneously, Doris Smith let herself come.

Later entwined together, they talked about life, philosophy, popular culture, and all manner of unconnected topics.

"May I ask when the last time you were with someone was?"

"Only if you say first."

"That's easy. It was with my wife. We're separated. It was maybe about two years ago."

"Well, my husband died in 1997, so that was ten years ago."

"Astonishing."

"Why?"

"You're very skilled, to say the least. And maybe a little wanton."

Doris chuckled. "What's Usher's song? A lady in one place but a freak somewhere else. I guess that's me. Actually, Ben, I'm a visualizer. And after about five years of mourning and doing nothing, I started visualizing making love to one faceless person. He and I have had some steamy nights together. Because of him I'm sure I'm freakier than I ever was with my husband. And wouldn't you know? The faceless man I've been making love with turns out finally to be you. You're not bad in the sack. Actually, when you were working with us and DHS, I used to sit and try to visualize whether you were wearing boxers or briefs."

"What—"

"You heard me. Now, that's enough with the questions, Dr. Parks."

They channel surfed and watched TV until well into the night. Then the TV watched them sleep. Early in the morning, they woke, used the remote to turn off the TV, and made a sweeter, less athletic love this time.

Later, in the shower, they soaped each other generously, showering and embracing together. They small-talked through a fruit breakfast with yogurt, hot coffee, and pastries. Downstairs, Ben stuck with Doris at the front desk while she settled her bill and then walked her to the front door, where she handed her validated parking ticket to the valet. She leaned forward and kissed Ben on the cheek.

"This was nice," was all she said.

When she was safely inside her Escalade and pulling away, Ben waited a beat. Then he turned and walked alone the several blocks back to where his car was parked. He had no idea how things would play out. After that day, he just waited. Then he waited some more. Finally, he just settled into his routine. And it was a full two weeks before they had any further communication.

One morning Ben called Doris. She said, "No."

He simply said "okay." Then he said "goodbye."

A week after that he called again. This time she said, "Yes," and later that night Ben introduced Doris to his cooking, his wine, and his queen-sized bed on Eleventh Street.

About one month after that, Ben and Doris had freshly caught, parmesan-crusted grouper with mashed potatoes, asparagus, and a bottle of Domaine Savary Chablis at the Legal Sea Foods in Bethesda, Maryland. Afterward they luxuriated in Doris's backyard hot tub listening to music. Then they went to bed at Doris's home in DC's Shepherd Park neighborhood. When they were finishing, they heard a buzzing, but they weren't distracted until they heard it again after they were finished. Then they saw it and Doris screamed.

Ben got up in his birthday suit, picked up a paper towel from the roll in Doris's master bath, walked over to the plush drapes at one of Doris's windows and, with a swipe, caught the critter and crushed it.

"Come on, darling! It's a stink bug, not a saber-toothed tiger."

She laughed, but said, "True! But Orkin is going to be hearing from me the first thing in the morning. If they want to continue working for me, I'd better not see any more of them."

She and Ben laughed and Doris stopped being embarrassed.

***

The two rarely called or emailed each other in between occasions, but the next month they took a four-day weekend together and drove to Virginia Beach, Virginia, where they stayed at the Barclay Towers right on the beach. This inspired them to talk about taking two weeks in the Caribbean together as soon as they could settle on an island.

And so it went.

Chapter 47
Richard Parks

They were sitting in the den at the Parks' residence near the Carter Barron amphitheater in Northwest Washington, DC. Richard's desk was cluttered with books and papers surrounding a laptop computer. He was seated in a slightly worn leather armchair and, even though it was over eighty degrees outside, the air conditioner was turned off. Richard had a small blanket over his shoulders.

Ben's sister, Penelope Parks Tompkins, had said to her brother recently that their dad no longer felt heat. He was always cold. His ninety-plus years had apparently robbed him of the ability to get warm enough. They'd only been sitting a couple of minutes when Ben heard keys in the side door near the garage. Penny appeared at the door to the den.

"Hey, brother," she said.

"Dad, do you want something to drink? I'm going to make some ice tea. Want some, Ben?" all in the rapid-fire style Ben's younger sister was known for.

Penny worked in the kitchen while Richard and Ben settled. Penny came in and placed a decaffeinated iced tea by their dad's side table. Then she brought in two more, one for Ben and one for herself. She took a seat on the couch next to Ben.

"Okay, what's the topic of the day?" she asked with absolute faith that she was immediately included in the conversation. And she was. Penny had lived in the basement of their dad's home since about eight years before their mom, Gillian Parks, had died of Alzheimer's disease. Penny was divorced, with five grown kids spread across the country. After her marriage, she had no reason to stay in the Midwest, where she'd lived for thirty years, and Richard had needed help caring for Gillian.

"Your friend Davita is quite something," said Richard.

"Yep, I know. I've always known that, Dad, but she's even more than I knew. What happened?"

"She called me one evening and asked if I remembered her. She reminded me of some of the times we had met and finally I did remember. Then she asked to come over to see me and I said okay. When she got here the next evening, she was straight and to the point. She wanted you to come back to DC. Why didn't you and she ever get together?"

Penny turned and with an impish smile said, "Yeah, big bro. Why didn't you and Davita ever get together?"

"Shut up, instigator," said Ben with a wave of the hand.

Penny winked at Richard. Suddenly Ben was emotional. He choked back something in his throat.

"Dad, I really wish . . . I think I've always loved her, but by the time I got my head on straight, after I got back from Korea, she was already happily married. That makes me sad, so it's something I don't want to talk about."

Richard Parks stared at his son. Penny was silent for a change. Richard and Ben Parks didn't talk much or for long. Phone calls usually lasted two minutes or less; they always got right down to business with whatever the topic. When Ben came over, it usually was to get up on a ladder to change a light bulb, to dig a hole for a new shrub Richard had bought, to wash a window, or to hang Christmas lights out in early December. Sometimes he shopped for his dad when Richard felt too tired or weak to do so for himself and Penny wasn't available, but on these occasions, it was "What do you need, Dad?", do it, and gone.

Now Richard sensed turmoil in his son, and he imagined that if his dear wife, Gillian, were still alive, Ben would share with her things that he might not share with him. Richard continued, "Davita seemed to know that your cousin was in real estate. She wanted to get in touch with her. Penny got up and came back with one of Corinne's business cards. Then Davita made the pitch. She said she had ten thousand to put toward a down payment on a new place in your name."

"What?"

"Ten thousand dollars"

"Dad, I know you're not kidding because you don't kid, but . . . I don't know what to say."

"She said that a few others from your old circle around here were willing to put in a total of fifteen thousand more."

Ben was overcome with emotion. He walked out of the den and down the hall to the bathroom. Tears and sobs had overtaken him. He ran cold water and splashed his face over and over. He looked up into the bathroom mirror. He saw a face that used to be lean and tight. No longer. His eyes weren't bright like they used to be. He noticed moles growing on his face that hadn't been there the last time he'd studied his face. More water and deep breaths. He toweled off and went back to the den.

After sipping and checking his son out, Richard said, "Should I continue?"

Ben nodded as he downed the glass of tea in one frantic motion for relief.

"Davita said that she was going to call Corinne and begin to look for someplace they thought you'd like. She asked if she could come back in a few days to give a report, and I said certainly. She thanked me and left. Within a week, she was back with details on the Eleventh Street condo. I wanted to see it and she took me and your sister that very day. We liked it. Davita gave me some financial details, and I asked if I could contribute a modest amount."

Penny screamed, "Modest? Are you kidding me, Dad? Modest?"

Richard's eyes twinkled.

Ben waited, and when Richard showed no sign of elaborating, he just laughed.

"Davita and Corinne took it and ran with it. I don't know about your sister, but from that point on I had very little to do with it, other than to sign a few papers and write out a check."

"No, I didn't get into it," said Penny. "It was just the two of them."

On the TV, Jon Fortt, who had grown up in the DC church the Parks' family had been members of many years ago, was reporting on some stock development. This was one of the financial programs that Richard always watched in the middle of the day. Richard turned his attention to his laptop computer and hit some keys. He read something and hit some more keys. Then he waited for a moment, read something else, and smiled.

Ben stood and crossed to his dad, grabbed his big bald head with two hands, and placed a kiss on top with a loud sound.

Richard chuckled, then just smiled and looked back at the television.

"Bye, Dad."

"I put up a modest amount too, Ben. Aren't you going to kiss my forehead?"

Ben ran over and bear-hugged Penny. "It goes without saying that you would have something to do with it. Thank you, thank you, thank you, sister," said Ben as he placed a big wet one on her cheek.

Penny said, "Euwww, Ben. That was nasty. Don't ever kiss me again."

Ben had turned toward the door, but stopped and stepped back toward his sister, who screamed and rushed out of the den.

"No, no, no! Stop it, Ben. Leave me alone."

Ben chuckled. "Bye, family."

He exited and locked the door behind himself.

Chapter 48
Son Number One,
Thirty-Two-Year-Old Tony

Ben's Second Weekend back in DC

After the Monday assignment and the hand-off to Amy Schoonover and Bill Portis, Ben had a busy week. He'd had breakfast with Davita, setting off a whole unexpected tangent of worry about whether he could do what she was asking. He'd spent a day and a night with Doris Smith. That improved his spirits, ya betcha! But this pleasantness left him without a plan for anything beyond their day together.

He'd gone to visit his father and learned more of the depth and width of the conspiracy to entrap him. And he'd spent the rest of the week prepping for the fifth biannual running of his summer seminar on cross-cultural communication for the Consortium of Washington Metropolitan Area Universities.

The sixteen grad students from various universities had proved to be just as astute, eager, and challenging as the previous four summertime groups, going all the way back to 1999, when Dean Ralph Prescott of Howard University had first talked him into doing these intensive sessions. This particular Saturday session had baked him. That evening he ate at Dukem, an Ethiopian restaurant on U Street. Then he came home after eight o'clock, set his alarm for the next morning, and crashed. No sooner had he began to drift off, when the phone rang.

"Pop, I gotta see you. Can I come over?"

He was tired and wanted to rest for the Sunday session, which would begin at nine in the morning.

"Tony, I'm worn out. Can it wait until midweek?"

"Pop, I been waiting for months. You been gone up in New York all this time, and I've got something I gotta show you and tell you. Why'd you have to go up there all that time anyway?"

"Long story, T. Long story. I think you know what life with my wife was like. Long story."

"Yeah, Pop, but I sure am glad you're back. When I heard Cousin Corinne was on your case, I was so happy."

Ben Parks had two sons by his first wife, Yvette. Tony, the eldest, had owned a gym in the Adams Morgan section of Washington, DC, since he broke his hand in his fifth amateur boxing match some years ago. Tony's son, AR (Ashton Richard), was born to Tony and a baby-mama named Coral Peterson. She was a nice young woman. Unfortunately, Tony and Coral just hadn't clicked enough for them to stay together. Ben wasn't sure who was the oil and who was the water, but they'd sparked over and over again. Then they mutually decided to stay out of each other's way for the most part. But Tony had obviously observed Ben's and Yvette's joint custody and joint parenting, which had seemed to turn out pretty well. He'd committed himself to the same model with Coral and AR. Then, for a number of years, Tony had struck out to hit every skirt that came near. Many young women seemed to be attracted to his big muscles and the lure of hooking up with a young black entrepreneur.

"I need to close my eyes for a while, Tony. Can whatever you want to talk about wait one hour? I think I'll be okay by then. Just need to lie down."

"That's perfect, Pops. I'll be there at nine thirty. Get some sleep. I have a surprise for you."

***

Ben thought about Tony. *Tony lives in the world of protein shakes, and wheat grass pills, and fifty push-ups five times each day. Doesn't think he has time to think about signing up for the Affordable Care Act. Doesn't have time to think about serious relationships.*

Is Tony me? Is Rico me? I hope not. I'm a bad example for my sons in terms of making serious relationships with women work.

When the doorbell rang around nine thirty, Ben was indeed up and feeling somewhat refreshed. Always the clumsy one, he'd dropped the last of his favorite snifter glasses while mixing his go-to Ballantine's Scotch whiskey and Rock Creek Ginger Ale drink. So now he came to the door in his pajamas clutching his mixed drink in a mayonnaise jar in his left hand. He opened the door with his right hand, and in a flash Tony stepped across the threshold to hug his father tight, pinning Ben's arms to his side.

Ben was stuck. His son held him so tight, he could move neither hand. The left hand was pinned in a right angle holding his mayonnaise jar drink, and his right hand was pinned down to his side. Anyway, his attention was caught between the embrace of his eldest son and the *Vision* behind his son that was standing in the hallway. One of the people standing there with a big smile on his face was AR, Ben's first grandson. Then there was the other person. She was gorgeous—athletic looking but with an exotic smile and tawny brown skin. This person just watched. Even her eye contact was mesmerizing for Ben.

Finally Tony let his father go, and Ben went to move him aside to shake hands with his grandson. That's when the mayonnaise jar slipped from his left hand, and his second drink of the night splashed to the floor. Springing into action, AR leapt past Ben to the kitchen and came back with a roll of paper towels to clean up the mess. Tony was beside himself with laughter.

"Pop, you're still dropping things all over the place. Now you're messing up the floors in your brand-new condo. What about being forgetful? Are you still forgetting things too?"

"Mostly no, because I write things down. I've learned that when you make mental notes, the ink fades pretty quickly. So I don't try. I write things down."

Knowing that this was his second spoiled drink in the last ten minutes, Ben lied, "Well, I'm not as clumsy as I used to be. This was just a rare accident."

AR looked up from his work scooping up the last little pieces of broken glass on the floor. "Grandpop, should I just put this glass in the kitchen sink with the other broken glass I just saw in there?"

Tony looked from his son to his father. He ran to the kitchen sink to see what AR was talking about. Then he just couldn't stop himself from side-splitting laughter.

Finally, the Vision stepped into the room from the hallway. She grabbed Ben's hand softly, and suddenly all Ben could think about was that he was standing there in his pajamas.

"Dr. Parks, I'm Vashti. It is so good to meet you. I'm in love with your son, and we have something exciting to tell you. Can I come in?"

***

Thirty minutes later, Ben had changed into some cargo pants with a loose Ghanaian-made work shirt buttoned over his chest. He was sitting on one of two wicker armchairs facing a long wicker couch, all with deep cushions bought on the shopping spree with Davita. Ben had endured all the ribbing that AR and Tony could heap on their embarrassed elder about his chronic clumsiness, including some stories from the past that Ben would have rather not heard for the umpteenth time. Although he had not yet touched a drop of liquor to his lips, Ben had mixed his third drink of the night for himself in a clean jelly jar and had found some nice plastic cups for his guests. He served them a mixture of grape juice and ginger ale on the glass-topped wicker table between the facing wicker couch and chairs. Tony was next to Vashti on the couch and AR was on the chair next to his grandpop.

"Okay, okay! Enough!" said Ben. "What in the world was so important that you had to come here to see me in the middle of the night? I've got class again in the morning."

"Middle of the night," said AR, looking at his watch. "Grandpop, it's just a little after ten o'clock on a Saturday evening. You're not only still clumsy, but you're also really, really old now, aren't you?"

The Vision didn't laugh, but the two male Parks people broke up again. Finally, the Vision poked Tony in the side. Observing, Ben saw that she packed a punch. Macho, macho man Tony winced.

"Let's tell your father our news."

Her voice was music.

Suddenly the mood in the room shifted. Ben stiffened. AR smiled like the Cheshire Cat. Now Tony looked anxious and Vashti poked him again.

"Okay!" he protested, rubbing his side.

Finally, Tony muttered, "You're going to be a grandfather again, Pop."

Silence.

"I know that Rico and his lady just had a kid, and now me and Vashti are pregnant."

Ben just stared. He looked back and forth between his son, this gorgeous Vision sitting across from him, and his senior grandson, who seemed to be pleased as punch with the proceedings. Finally, Ben could think of nothing else to do. He turned the Concord grape jelly jar full of his third drink of the night up to his lips and just chugged.

In some ways, it rescued Ben when AR decided to jump in with a request. "Hey, Grandpop, I'm doing really well in school. Want me to bring you my report card so you can see?"

Instant alert!

"No, seriously! I got all B's and A's last semester."

"Since you said B's first, can I assume that there were more B's than A's?"

"It was almost even."

"Hmmm!"

"So, Grandpop! I was wondering what you'd think about the idea of me getting a car."

Tony sputtered, then laughed. "Now I know why you wanted to come with V and me, boy. This will be fun to watch."

AR held up his hand to his father in a "please, no interruptions" gesture. Vashti smiled but kept her eyes focused somewhere out of the window. Ben just looked and then licked his lips.

"AR, I don't seem to hear from you until you want something. It was looking like this night was an exception. Coming along with your pop and his new lady to take part in the introduction to his grandpop. Isn't that a nice story?"

"Naw, Grandpop. It's not like that."

"I know. It obviously isn't like that."

"No, I mean I did want to see you meet Vashti and hear about the baby on the way. Isn't that cool, Grandpop?"

"Very cool, Grandson."

"But I also thought it would be cool to see what you thought about the idea of a car."

"Have you gotten a driver's license yet?"

"I have my learner's permit. I can drive with Pop if nobody else is in the car."

"Good."

"So, starting in September you'll be in twelfth grade, right?"

"Yup."

"A lot of country kids drive to high school. It's also kind of common out in the suburbs, but as far as I know, it's not very common for inner-city kids. How many others in your class will be driving their own cars?"

"Uh, I don't know, Grandpop. I wanted to be the first."

"Oh, I see. You wanted to be the first. That would make you real cool with the young ladies, wouldn't it?"

"Well, I'm already cool with the young ladies, Grandpop. Heh, heh, heh!"

Ben broke up and Vashti couldn't hold back a giggle. Tony held his gaze and kept up his intense listening. Then, getting control, Ben managed a little, "Heh, heh, heh! I'm not down with that, AR."

"Aw, Grandpop."

"No."

"But Grandpop, it's inconvenient getting the bus and train to school every day."

"And I guess it's been inconvenient for three years now. One more to go."

"But with a new baby coming, I could help out with shopping and stuff."

"You could. And you probably will, car or no car."

"But Grandpop."

"AR, do you happen to remember coming to me about a month ago asking for a loan to get some new shoes?"

"Uh. Uh, yes, Grandpop."

"You said you wanted a loan. Is that correct?"

"Yes, Grandpop. These are the shoes."

"They're very nice."

"Thank you, Grandpop."

"No, it's not about thank you, Grandpop. They were paid for with a loan from me, correct?"

"Ummmm."

"Has anybody ever explained to you about the difference between remember and recollect?"

"What?"

"Remember versus recollect."

"I don't know, Grandpop. They're the same, I think."

"No."

"Can you use them in a sentence?"

"Sure! I remember loaning you some money to buy new shoes, but I don't seem to recollect you paying me back."

Now the room erupted. Tony's face broke from his strictly listening mode. Vashti asked to use the restroom. Even AR couldn't help himself from a stupid smile, but he regrouped and tried again.

"Grandpop, they gave all of the incoming seniors forms to fill out over the summer. One of the questions was about who would need parking on the school lot starting in the fall."

"Ah, and that's what gave you the idea of asking me about a car. Are you trying to get a new car?"

"Well, that would be nice."

"No."

"But it could be a used car."

"No."

Tony broke in, "Pop, you weren't this good when me and Rico were coming up. We could always break you down."

"I guess you're right, Tony. I remember you standing on a street corner for a half hour one time because I had turned you down for some money. You must have called fifty times. You were positioned on the street, right where I could see you from my desk."

"I remember that. And you finally gave me the money."

"Yes. Now I know that you were training me for this guy."

AR started back, "Aw, come on, Pop. I'm your oldest grandson."

For effect, Ben blew out a long breath. Then, "You never really knew your great-grandmother, Gillian. She was a wonderful woman."

"I remember her. She had Alzheimer's."

"But she didn't always have Alzheimer's, AR. She once was a very sharp woman, with a country wisdom that was hard to compete with. You know what she used to say to me sometime?"

Tony said, "I think I know what you're going to say, Pop."

"Yes, you heard this a few times from your grandmom."

"What Grandpop?"

"Your great-grandmom Gillian used to say: 'Boy, I think you're about to experience a serious case of disaccustomcy.'"

"Of what?"

"You heard me, AR. She'd tell me that I was going to suffer a case of disaccustomcy."

"What's that?"

"It meant that I'd gotten accustomed to certain things that I needed to be disaccustomed to, and that she was going to be the one to disaccustom me, to break me out of a bad habit to which I had become accustomed. Well, I'm about to disaccustom you from the idea that you can nag me into giving you a car. Don't ask me again. Do you understand?"

The word "but" almost formed in AR's mouth, but he looked carefully at his grandfather and thought better of continuing. "Okay, Grandpop. I love you."

"Yeah, right!"

"We better be going," said Tony.

"Right. This would be a good time."

"You really worked this one, Pop."

Ben winked.

The Vision stood and walked up to give Ben a hug. That was more than fine with Ben, but he remembered to maintain an appropriate tent space between them. The sweethearts walked out chuckling to themselves. AR walked behind them. He had a slight smirk, but said nothing else but, "I love you, Grandpop."

Chapter 49
Son Number Two

Twenty-Eight-Year-Old Rico, October 2007

Everything about seven-month-old Lenny (Leonard Benjamin Parks) was a fascination for Ben Parks' younger son. When Joni Morris had told him a year and a half ago that she wanted to get pregnant, Rico had told her no at first. They'd been friends since they entered the Washington High School for the Arts together as ninth graders back in September 1996. Both Joni and Rico had been in the visual arts program, and they'd kind of competed with one another for a while. Then Joni gravitated toward sculpture and metalwork, while Rico began to focus on photography and sketching. From that point on they became each other's muses and biggest fans. After graduation, Joni had gone off to SVA (School of the Visual Arts) in Manhattan, while Rico had left town for Chicago's Columbia College of Art.

Rico had dropped out of Columbia after completing two years, realizing that his real interest was in recording, not visual arts. Joni finished at SVA and began to help out one of her SVA teachers in his studio in the Bowery District of Lower Manhattan. Omar Pleast was well-known for large brass pieces, several of which were on display in public plazas in New York, Los Angeles, Dallas, and even in Washington, DC. From that point, for over two years, every commissioned piece delivered by Omar Pleast had Joni's hand on it. In return for her meticulous behind-the-scenes artistry, Pleast generously shared a reasonable amount of his large commissions with Joni. But after three years, Joni got homesick. Her desire to get back to DC was facilitated by Washington High School for the Arts, when they offered her the opportunity to come back to teach, now as a successful sculptor.

So Rico, who by then was practically running Levi Chance's EAC Recording Studio, and Joni were reunited. Rico was fast becoming the go-to engineer for many of the local hip-hop and rap artists. At one point Rico had envisioned himself as the next big rap star out of Washington, DC. His CDs and downloads were released and sold in the hundreds and sometimes thousands, but he never reached national acclaim, and he had refocused. He set his sights to learn everything he could about recording others. Levi had even taken him up to New York to see Diamond Studios and meet Joe Minolo. That trip had blown Rico's mind. It sealed the picture that had started to form in his mind of the kind of place that he would eventually like to build and run.

This time when Joni and Rico hooked up, it quickly became much more than the friends they'd been in high school. And it was with that history that they had come to the agreement to have a child together. They made the decision to talk later about whether or not to get married. Rico had agreed to their son being named after Joni's father, Leonard Morris. In return, Joni had agreed to the baby having Rico's father's name as his middle name as well as Rico's last name.

***

Sitting in the paneled control room in the basement of EAC Recording Studios, Rico often pushed back from the console and rolled his chair over to the corner where Lenny was sleeping or playing in his playpen. It all depended on whether artists were doing live sessions or Rico was alone mixing or mastering. If artists were there, Rico couldn't keep Lenny because it would be too loud. Then Joni would keep the baby with her in the loft studio she shared with two other sculptors near her two-bedroom apartment out in the Route-1 Artist Corridor in Brentwood, Maryland.

For the hundredth time, Rico observed that Lenny's facial features looked just like Joni's. He was a beautiful child. In this moment of staring down at his sleeping son in the corner of the EAC control room, Rico felt happy and a sense of fulfillment. But at the same time, Rico had realized that, though he really was in love with

Joni, his reluctance to marry her had more to do with his feeling of not having reached some of his personal goals than with any doubts about her. In fact, Rico knew that Joni's reluctance came from the same place as his.

Chapter 50
Hitting Bottom

An autumn Tuesday night around ten o'clock.

The doorbell rang upstairs at the home of Levi Chance, who was upstairs conked out in bed. When Rico Parks came up from EAC studio in the basement to answer the door, he was surprised to see Joni Morris and baby Leonard.

The Digga-Man, one of Rico's up-and-coming hip-hop artists, brushed by Rico on his way out of the house. "What up, Joni!" he said. "Later, Rico. Let me hear something when you're done mixing."

Rico was dealing with too many sources of stimulation. "Easy, Digga! Hey Joni, I thought you were staying home. Hey, my little man."

Joni looked frazzled. "Babe, I'm sorry. I know I said I'd be home all night with the baby. Liz, my girl, is in the hospital. She's at Washington Hospital Center. I gotta go see her. You gotta watch Lennie again tonight. Please!"

"What happened?"

"I guess it was a car accident. Anyway, her mom called me and said Liz wanted to see me."

"But I need to concentrate tonight. I'm tryna mix these tracks down for Digga."

"He's real tired, Rico. I woke him up and just fed him. He's knocked out. Just put him in the crib. You're gonna mix with the earphones, right? He won't wake up. I just don't want to take him to the hospital. I don't want him around all those germs, and I don't want him around no drama tonight. Liz is tripping. Her mom is tripping. Please, Ric."

Rico relented.

They went downstairs into the control room. Rico opened the playpen and Joni deposited him on the soft foam cushions and covered him. Then she gave Rico an extra juicy kiss and rubbed herself between his legs. He started to respond and abruptly she pulled away.

"I gotta go, babe. You know I love you. And now I owe you. Don't you like it when I owe you?"

Joni knew how to work on Rico. As a matter of fact, it might have been genetic. Lately the Parks men all seemed to be at a disadvantage with their women. Rico checked briefly on Lenny and, sure enough, he was in his favorite position in the crib, with his knees drawn up. Rico readjusted the cover on top of his son, then walked Joni back up the stairs and tried to grab her for some more quick loving.

"Naw, babe. Gotta go. I'll call you later to let you know 'bout Liz. I'm going to be real good to you tomorrow night. I promise."

Rico stood at the door as Joni ran down the steps and jumped into her silver Kia. Then she was gone.

***

By midnight, Rico was really pleased. The Digga-Man's gravelly voice fit perfectly over the synthesized beats that he'd put down for him. He continued to fiddle with the mid tones and highs to add some edge to the basically low-voiced track. He had in mind that he'd do some finger drumming on his AKAI MPD226 to add some more percussion in certain places. Suddenly there was a loud noise outside the control room. Startled, Rico stood. Reflexively he glanced over in the corner. Then he was horrified. Lennie wasn't in the playpen. Then, outside the control room, he thought he heard crying. A man's crying.

Through a fog, Levi had seen that a light in the basement was on. On shaky legs, he'd made his way down the stairs and peeked into the control room, where Rico was hunched over the console with his headphones on, adjusting EQ and moving faders up or down ever so slowly. He'd opened the door, and that's when he'd spotted Lennie asleep in the Nuna playpen in the corner behind his dad. Levi had quietly walked behind Rico, reached over, and picked Lennie up without waking him. Then he made his way back out of the control room.

On the fifth step, Levi had not stepped high enough. Losing his balance, he'd fallen backward and tumbled until he was back on the basement floor, feet over head. He'd been cradling Lennie on his soft belly, so when Levi hit bottom, the baby was cushioned for the initial hit. However, when Levi's arms went to the side at the bottom of the stairs, the freed baby bounced forward, landing his torso across Levi's mouth, nose, and eyes. Lennie's head hit the floor just past the groggy musician.

Throwing off his headphones, at first Rico only heard Levi's moaning. And then came his son. Lennie was wailing in distress. It was the loudest he'd ever heard his baby cry. It wasn't a cry for attention. It was a wail from pain—excruciating pain.

Rico burst out of the control room door to find Levi feet-over-head on his back at the bottom of the stairs with Lennie splayed across his face. The stench of Levi's liquor almost blew Rico backward, but instead he stepped over Levi to scoop up his child, and that's when he noticed there was a substantial red area and bump on Lennie's chin, and some puffing had started.

Coming back to consciousness, Levi spoke, "I lost my balance. I came in to see what you were doing and I saw him in the corner. I wanted some company. I wanted to take him upstairs. I lost my balance. When I felt myself falling, I tried to keep him on my chest, but he slipped away."

"You drunk motherfucker. You goddamn drunk motherfucker. I'll kill you, Levi. I'll kill you if you hurt my baby. What the fuck!"

"I'm sorry, Rico. I'm so sorry. I lost my balance."

Now, with Lennie in his arms, Rico actually did kick Levi. Once. Twice. Then he stopped. Lennie was still crying, and now Rico noticed blood between his fingers. Rico let out a wail of misery.

"You bitch, Levi. You goddamn bitch!"

Rico stumbled past the still-prone Levi on the steps. He almost lost a grip on Lennie himself, but managed to keep his balance. He fished for his car keys in his pocket with one hand while maintaining his grip on Lennie with his other. He was halfway to his car when Mrs. Allen, who lived across the street from Levi, intercepted him. She quickly assessed the situation.

"That damn drunk hurt my baby, Mrs. Allen."

Rico was fumbling with his car key.

"Give him to me, Rico. Call 911. Let's go back in and wait for the ambulance."

"I don't want to go back in that drunk's house, Mrs. Allen. I don't ever want to go back in there."

"Then we'll go over to my house and wait. Come on, son. Come on."

Now they looked back as they heard Levi coming out of his house and falling again, this time down the brick steps of his townhouse. Mrs. Allen, baby in hand, didn't pause. Rico started back, but then just shouted more obscenities at his uncle.

"The call, Rico. Make the call."

He bound up Mrs. Allen's steps and through the front door. He knew her landline was just inside in the foyer. The wail of the sirens came seven minutes after he placed the frantic call.

***

From the hospital, Rico's first call was to his mom, Yvette. Now it was approaching two in the morning. She said, "Have you reached Joni?"

"Mom, we're at Hospital Center. Joni is up here somewhere with her friend Liz, but she's not answering her cell phone."

"Call your father. I can't drive at night. Call your father. If he can't get there, call me back."

When they finally located Joni Morris on another floor in the hospital, she tried to rush into the pediatric ICU and was barred by a nurse. She turned on Rico and punched him again and again. Rico threw up his hands but didn't resist. He turned toward Joni and just let her pummel him until the same nurse and an attendant came and restrained her.

And that's how Ben Parks, who arrived at the hospital at 3:27 a.m., just as the doctors were coming out to speak to Rico and Joni, learned that his second grandchild had been injured in an accident at the hands of his best friend, Levi Chance. Ben and a woman from the DC Department of Child Welfare stood back behind the parents. Ben had his hand on his son's back for support and comfort.

They said that they were "cautiously hopeful."

"When there are falls like this, the seriousness of the injuries can be a matter of inches or even millimeters when it comes to exactly how the patient lands or glances," said the lead doctor.

Joni screamed, "Is he going to be all right?"

Ben and Rico both reached their hands toward her, but she brushed them away.

"We don't know for sure. We understand that he fell across someone's face. Is that correct?"

"Yes, doctor," answered Rico. "My uncle was going up some stairs and was holding Lennie at his chest. When he fell backward, he kept ahold until he landed on his back. Lennie bounced off his chest and landed mostly on my uncle's face, with just a little bit of his head on the floor."

"Well, that's remarkably lucky."

The doctors went on to explain where things stood. The first thing they had done with Lennie upon admission was to perform a CT scan to look for internal bleeding. They had found none. They had then sent the baby to Pedi ICU for careful monitoring, and that's where he was now.

Worst case, the doctors said, would be that if over the next few hours they detect any evidence of swelling, then they would know that bleeding had appeared (usually a subdural hematoma) and they would call a neurosurgeon. The surgeon would assess if surgery was needed. If so, the baby would go through OR and have a craniotomy where part of the skull is removed to reduce pressure from swelling and to remove the hematoma. The circular piece of skull would not be replaced because it may take days for the swelling to go down. The baby would go to Pedi ICU for careful monitoring and would remain sedated and incubated for days. Once the swelling improved, the baby would go back to the OR for the bone to be put back on the skull.

***

None of the worst fears materialized. Lennie was observed for two additional days and then released to Joni. Rico was demur and penitent about his lack of vigilance, but he and Joni talked it through. Ben and Yvette had been shocked, and Yvette wanted no more to do with Levi. Ben had several conversations with his muse Davita Sheridan Ferrier and eventually knew what he had to do.

Chapter 51

Arrested

Early the next morning after the incident, Detectives Upsala Rogers and Valentino Turré of the Metropolitan Police Department knocked loudly on the door of the row house on R Street NW. Detective Turré called out, "MPD."

No answer. Across the street, Mrs. Allen looked up and came down off her porch. She slowly crossed the street, and when she got to the bottom of Levi's steps she called out, "Officers, he's in there. It just takes him a while. He'll come out. Want me to call his number?"

"Ma'am, what is your name?" asked Detective Rogers.

"I'm Dorinda Allen. Mr. Chance is my neighbor. If you're here about that thing last night, I saw what happened."

That got the officers attention and they descended the steps until they were standing on the sidewalk again.

"What did you see?" asked Detective Rogers, taking a step toward the lady, but then stopping abruptly when Mrs. Allen retreated. Detective Turré kept his eye up the stairs on the still-closed front door.

"Well, I saw that boy Rico Parks coming down the steps with baby Lennie, and the baby was wailing up a storm."

"So you didn't see how the baby was injured?" called Detective Turré over his partner's shoulder.

"No, sir. I got Rico and the baby into my house, and that's where the ambulance picked them up."

"Did you see Mr. Chance at all?"

"Yes, sir. He came out after Rico, but he wasn't in no shape. Rico was shouting at him, and I told Mr. Chance to go back in the house. He did. He wasn't in no shape to cause any trouble."

Just then, the front door of Levi's house opened and Detective Turré called out, "Metropolitan Police. Are you Mr. Levi Chance?"

Levi's voice was soft. "Yes, sir."

"Please step out on the porch, sir."

Levi did as bidden.

Detective Rogers said to Mrs. Allen, "Thank you, ma'am, you can go on back across the street now. If we need anything else from you, we'll come over."

"Yes, officer. Just remember what I said. That man don't mean no harm. He just ain't right sometime. That's all."

"Yes, ma'am, we heard you. Thank you very much. We'll see you back across the street if we need anymore."

"Okay, officers. He don't mean no harm."

"We heard you, ma'am. Go on across the street now."

Mrs. Allen crossed the street, ascended her steps, and took her seat on the porch. Everybody in the neighborhood said that Mrs. Allen had the eyes of an eagle and the hearing of a cat. Now the officers walked up to the landing between the bottom four steps and the top four.

"Come on down here please, sir."

Again, Levi obeyed.

"You can sit, sir."

Levi sat on the landing and Detective Rogers stepped behind him while Detective Turré stepped down and faced him.

"We'd like to hear what happed last night with that baby," said Turré.

"I fucked up . . . I mean, I messed up, officer. I dropped him. I didn't mean to. Is he all right? Do you know if he's all right?"

"He's being evaluated at the hospital. That's all we can tell you, sir. How did you drop him?"

"I was carrying him up the steps. I think I wanted to play with him. I stumbled and fell. I tried to keep him from hitting the floor.

Then I don't remember until Rico was kicking me and the baby was screaming."

"Were you drinking, sir?"

"Yes."

"How much had you had?"

"I don't know."

"Two drinks? Three drinks? Four drinks? How much?"

"I don't know. I didn't mean to hurt him. I hope he's okay."

Then Detective Rogers said, "We don't know. I think we're going to have to take you in, sir. You have the right to remain silent. You have the right to an attorney. If you decide to answer questions, or waive the right to an attorney, anything you say can be used in court against you. Do you understand these rights, sir?"

"That boy didn't mean no harm, officers. I told you that," interrupted the vigilant Mrs. Allen from across the street as she saw Levi being lifted up and handcuffed. "He's got problems. He didn't mean no harm."

"Do you understand these rights, Mr. Chance?" repeated Detective Rogers.

Levi only nodded. After that Detective Rogers walked the cuffed Levi Chance to the cruiser and had her hand on Levi's head, helping him into the back seat. Detective Turré said, "Ma'am, we've heard what you said. Please don't interfere anymore."

Detective Turré then walked around the cruiser and jumped into the driver's seat, while Detective Rogers got into the shotgun seat. They turned off the cruiser lights that had been flashing during the whole incident and Detective Turré pulled away.

***

When Levi got to the Third District police building on V Street NW, he blew a .31 on the breathalyzer. He was put in a holding cell for seven hours. At that point he blew a .20. He never requested an attorney. He was further questioned, and then he was held overnight. In the morning, he was questioned yet again. The detectives heard from the District's Child and Family Services people who'd determined that Joni had custodial care of Lennie and was fit. Finally released that afternoon, Levi walked from Seventeenth and V back to his home on R Street near First.

***

After reviewing the evidence collected by MPD, the DC Department of Child Welfare's decided not to remove Lennie from his parents. They barred them from taking him to Levi's house for a minimum of six months, after which they would conduct another review. The vigilant Mrs. Allen told lawyers from the DA's office that the detectives definitely began questioning Levi before giving him his rights. In light of Lennie's full recovery, the DA decided to not bring negligence or endangerment charges against Levi Chance.

Chapter 52
Organizing

Ben, Tracy, Deanna, Janice, and Jose Calderon were seated at the bar. DaVita had outdone herself with this early-morning breakfast. The biscuits, in particular, made with biscuit mix, Havarti cheese, garlic flakes, and butter, were being wolfed down almost before landing on the old friends' plates. The menu was one of Ben's favorites. In honor of the occasion of Ben's willingness to lead the intervention with Levi, Davita was serving Conecuh Sausage from Evergreen, Alabama, with scrambled eggs and biscuits, coffee, and either cranberry or orange juice. The Conecuh was sold at the Walter Reed Hospital's Commissary in Silver Spring, MD. Many of Davita's wounded warrior customers from across the street at the Walter Reed Army Medical Center at Georgia Avenue and Aspen Street shopped there.

Davita's parents had been military and had introduced her to the delicacy as a child. Davita had insisted that they not get down to business until after eating. There were not regular customers at eight thirty in the morning. Her staff usually got in at around ten thirty, and they opened for lunch at eleven thirty. So as the little breakfast party began to wrap up and Tracy and Deanna led the way in gathering up dishes and stacking them back in the kitchen, Davita brought in a fresh pot and led the party to a large round dining table in the corner where the five could be more comfortable.

Jose Calderon had never been to Davita's place before, but Janice had asked him for his help. Since both she and Ben were patients of his psychology practice, Dr. Calderon was happy to attend the meeting off-the-clock.

Now serious, Davita directed the first salvo to Ben. "I think the rest of us have talked about this for a long time. Ben, why don't you summarize the facts for Dr. Calderon."

293

"That would be helpful," said Calderon.

"Well, we all grew up together in Michigan Park . . ."

"Excuse me, Ben. I didn't say give our life histories. Start with the night at Levi's house and the hospital."

"Damn, woman! You're the bossiest person I know."

"And you love it."

"All right, Davita. Doc, my son works in a professional recording studio that's in the home of my best friend, Levi Chance. Levi is a musician, and my son Rico has been his play nephew for pretty much all of Rico's life."

Ben stopped and looked at Davita, who gave him the swirly finger sign indicating that he should keep it moving.

"How old is your son?"

"He's twenty-seven or twenty-eight. I can't always remember."

"And what about Lennie, your grandson?"

"He's seven months old."

"Thanks. Please go on."

"Two nights ago, Rico was mixing a hip-hop tune in the studio. Levi had been drinking, probably all day. He was upstairs conked out in bed. Rico's lady, Joni, had an emergency and needed to drop their son Lennie off. My grandson was asleep, and they just deposited him in the crib and Rico kept working."

Jose Calderon was listening and asking no questions. Davita still thought Ben was giving too much detail, so she blurted in, "Levi woke up, came downstairs, took Lennie out of his crib, and dropped him going back up the stairs."

She looked over at Ben and wrinkled her nose. Ben tried to look angry, but he was really never angry with Davita.

"Go ahead from there, Benjamin."

Turning back to the doctor, Ben said, "We've been trying to get Levi to kick the drinking off and on since he came back from Vietnam. He's never owned that he had a problem, and he's never wanted any kind of treatment. He's fucked up his life in all kinds of ways, and his blessing is that: a), he's gifted as a musician, and b), he's somehow made some good money decisions over the years, so his drinking hasn't made him homeless. He dearly loves my son."

"And he dearly loves you, Ben," said Janice.

"Whatever."

"Go ahead."

"So Davita wanted me to lead an intervention. At first I said no way, but now it seems like I have to. The only thing is that I'm not comfortable, and I'd be willing to pay you whatever it takes for you to walk me through my role in an intervention. Also, if you would have the time and inclination, it would be great if you would actually be there."

"Okay," said Jose. "I've got it so far. Would each of the rest of you just tell me how you connect up with all of this?"

Janice introduced herself as Levi's lady friend. She didn't embellish beyond that, except to say that she'd been in love with him since high school. Tracy said that he and his wife, Deanna, had grown up in the same neighborhood and that he'd also been in Vietnam at the same time that Levi had started down the slippery slope to alcoholism.

Davita jumped in, "Tracy is a retired army general, was a big man on campus back in the day, and all of us, including Levi, have always looked up to him."

Deanna spoke. "I also grew up with all these guys, including Levi. I married Tracy when he came back from Vietnam the second time, but I wasn't ever really close with Levi and probably shouldn't be a part of whatever you think needs to be done. I'm just here with my husband and to see if there's a role for me."

"Hey, Doc! I've always got a big roll for my wife."

"Tracy, will you ever get your mind out of the gutter? Please excuse him, Doctor."

Faces were smiling but with no commentary.

The doctor spoke to Ben. "So what about your son Rico? It seems like he and what's-her-name are the closest thing to injured parties, other than your grandson."

"Joni."

"Yes, Joni. Would Joni also have a role in this intervention?"

"Rico, yes. Joni is too done with Levi," said Ben.

"Whatever we do, we need to do without her. Rico is furious, but he wants to be in on this."

"That's good. So let me get this straight. You're talking about meeting with Levi to get him to go to the VA, right?"

Everybody said yes.

"Where would this meeting be?"

Davita answered, "Well, it could always be here, Doctor, but we serve alcohol, and that symbolically might not be so good. I think Ben should invite everyone to see his new digs down on Eleventh Street."

They hadn't talked about that, and Ben looked surprised. Then his expression changed. "Yeah, that would be cool. Do you think you'd be willing to moderate this thing for us?"

"I think so. And I'm not interested in you paying me. I have a lot of respect for both you and Janice. I'd like to help you."

In unison from Janice and Ben came, "Thank you!"

"So let's count. Who would be there besides myself for this meeting?"

Everybody except Deanna raised their hands. Then Davita spoke, "Actually, now that I'm thinking about it, I don't have to be there. Only if you think I should, Doctor Calderon."

"Do you have strong connections to Levi?"

"Not really, although I've known him as long as Ben has known him. I'm just Ben's friend, and I got all this stuff started because I hate to see Levi in the state that he's in. I didn't want Lennie to get injured, of course, but I'd been trying to get Ben to do something. After the accident, Ben is stepping up, so I can step back."

"That might be good," said Calderon.

"So now it's Ben, the close friend. Tracy's the respected fellow-Vietnam vet. Janice is the love interest. And Rico represents the aggrieved parties. Did I get everyone?"

Nods. Then Ben said, "That makes a lot of sense, Doc. So what do we need to do to prep?"

"I want each of the participants to write something to Levi. You're going to give it to him, but you're also going to read it to him at our intervention. Not more than one page. I'd like to see what you have to say before that night, so maybe I can coach you a little. You can be too soft in these letters, and you can be too harsh. You can be too direct, and you can be not direct enough. There aren't really any rules, but I've done this enough that I kind of know it when I see it. That's the only reason I want to help. But other than that, I think we just need to agree on a time and date."

"Can you give us an example of what to say in our letters?" asked Janice.

"Sure. I brought a couple of examples with me, just to give you a feel, but make sure you understand that these are about someone else, from someone else. You can't just go by these. The most important thing will be how deeply heartfelt you can be about why you want Levi to take this step, and about how supportive you'll be if he does."

"Yes. Yes, Jose," said Janice. "I get it. I can do that. This man has been the love of my life. I can't lose him."

"And that's what you'll tell him," said Jose Calderon.

Janice nodded and Davita got up, went around the table, and hugged her from behind.

Suddenly Ben had another thought. "Actually, Doc, there are two more people I might want to add. If it makes sense to you, I want to give them a call tonight. Levi has an uncle in South Carolina named Homer. He's blood with Levi, and I wish they were closer, but they're not. So Bart Stokes is probably the closest to an almost blood brother that I could find. Bart and Brian were a lot older than

Levi, but since his Aunt Alma and Bundy aren't with us, Bart might be the one to say something representing Levi's old Southwest DC connections."

Ben looked around for confirming looks. Nobody registered approval or disapproval. Then Calderon said, "Okay, but just keep in mind that more isn't necessarily better. When you talk to this Bart, just express to him the importance of the writing assignment. You're trying to gauge whether he'd be committed to writing something heartfelt from that part of Levi's life that would enhance the intervention. Who else?"

"Well, there's this guy in New York that might fly down in the morning. He was instrumental in getting Levi's studio off the ground when he got back from Vietnam. They worked together for years and finally tailed off when Levi's drinking started to wear thin their relationship. His name is Joe Minolo, and I'm pretty sure I have a couple of phone numbers where I might reach him."

Expressionless faces. Then Calderon said, "Tentative okay, with the same cautions as the other guy. Okay?"

"Okay, Doc. I'll be real careful."

The meeting ended with the doctor reading the two sample testimonies that he'd brought with him. They were dripping with emotion and feeling. They might even have been intimidating, but this group was ready. They ended and the party quickly broke up with the understanding that Ben would drive the scheduling and getting Levi to the meeting under the pretext of showing off his new condominium.

As Ben was walking out, Davita caught up with him and they walked out on the sidewalk. When others had passed out of earshot, she turned and asked, "How you coming on that assignment I gave you?"

Ben looked puzzled.

"You know, isn't that what we've been talking about all morning? I'm actually going straight to Levi's right now to surprise him.

Hopefully we can hang out a little and then I'll invite him over for a meal sometime next week."

"Great! And that's not the assignment I'm talking about."

Now Ben was agitated . . . then, slowly, he started to blush.

Seeing that he now remembered, Davita said, "Yeah, that one."

Ben freed his arm from her grasp and started to back away. Then, smiling, he said, "Oh, it's going pretty well. Goodbye, Davita."

"With whom?"

"If we decide one day not to be incognito, you'll be the first to know. Goodbye, Davita."

Davita let it go at that.

***

Levi resisted and dodged for a couple of weeks. Then . . .

Chapter 53
The Intervention

The beginning of wisdom is to call things by their right names.

—Chinese proverb

On an October evening in 2007, Ben had been cleaning his place for company all day. As he cleaned, he also toiled in the kitchen preparing a gumbo with the Conecuh smoked sausage that he'd become addicted to. Steps leading up to this had included the morning planning session at Davita's place on upper Georgia Avenue and an afternoon of wrangling with Levi at his combination residence and studio on R Street in Bloomingdale.

Meanwhile, the previous day, Levi had worked a session that Rico was supposed to engineer. There were two more sessions scheduled for this evening, so, consistent with his pattern, Levi was not drinking. He wasn't really confident working with rappers and hip-hoppers. So he was being vigilant and was hearing things he hadn't appreciated in this music of a younger generation. Yet Levi hadn't wanted to talk about what Ben had come to discuss. He deflected when Ben opened up about the need for him to get help from the VA. Instead, he turned the talk to Janice.

"That gal. Ben, I love her. Both of us are whores. You know me. And she's had more dick than the legal law allows. You probably don't think I know, but I know that she even gave you some pity pussy that summer before you went off to school with those pink people. Told me she actually enjoyed it, even though you couldn't bring the hammer like me, but she said you were a really good kisser."

Ben had started to open his mouth in denial. Then stopped and just stared at his friend.

"It's okay, son. I've always known. It's always been okay. You're still my boy."

For the balance of the afternoon, they had bobbed and weaved like two prize fighters training under ropes in a gym. At five thirty in the evening, the doorbell rang.

"Okay, partner, time to go to work. You've gotta go."

"Why can't I stay and watch you work with the youngins?"

"Get the hell out. You make me nervous!"

As the two reached the front door to let Bubba-Rubba and his Nasty Crew in, Ben said, "I'm leaving on one condition."

Levi told the rappers to go on downstairs and he'd be down in a minute to start.

"I'm listening."

"You haven't been over to my place yet. I want you to come over for dinner tomorrow night. It's the perfect time. I've been messing around with a new gumbo recipe, and I think it's pretty good. You used to always talk about New Orleans cooking. I want to see what you think."

Levi stared for a beat. Then, "Okay. What time?"

"How about seven?"

"I'll be there."

Ben had expected resistance and was caught by surprise. He stared carefully at his friend. Levi's eyes only showed anxiousness to get downstairs to his clients. Finally, Ben said, "Okay, it's a date."

***

At six thirty, Dr. Jose Calderon was the first to arrive. Within the next fifteen minutes, the place filled up. Joe Minolo came in just before Janice and Rico, who arrived at the same time. In short order, Bart Stokes was rung in. Tracy was the last to come. By seven thirty there was still no Levi.

Rico said, "I have a key. Let's all go over there. It's only five minutes away."

Spontaneous agreement. Ben was disappointed that he wouldn't be showing off his gumbo that night, but he wanted to get on with this. He'd ladled out a generous portion into a large to-go container, along with a second, smaller container with rice. Then he was ready.

They all piled into cars and drove the dozen or so blocks to Levi's house. Parking was difficult in that neighborhood at that time of night, so they assembled on the sidewalk on the corner and waited for everyone to get there. Then they walked in line to the middle of the block where Levi lived. Ben spotted Mrs. Allen. Nobody had told her anything about this, but the wise old woman instantly sensed the meaning of this unusual congregation on her street. She rushed down her steps, and when she'd crossed the street she grabbed Rico and hugged him tightly.

"Bless you, son. How's your boy?"

"He's fine, Mrs. Allen. He's going to be okay. Thank you for everything that night."

"Oh, you know you're welcome, Rico. Bless you, boy. And bless y'all. I don't know you, but I know what you must be here for. Bless you."

The group responded with "Thank you, ma'am" and a variety of other expressions before filing up the stairs after Rico, who opened the door with his key and led the group in. He started to head down to the studio, but realized that Levi was sitting in the kitchen, staring out at his backyard. He wasn't drinking. Ben approached him with the food.

"Hey, partner. I guess we got our signals crossed. But I wanted you to have this."

He set the food containers down on the round ceramic table in front of Levi. His friend looked. Then smiled. Then looked around at the crowd behind Ben and Rico.

"Nigger, I knew you were trying to set me up for something."

Joe Minolo, standing at the back, smiled inwardly as he remembered the fracture they'd had in their relationship some years ago over the word *nigger*, but he said nothing.

"Guilty, my friend. Now get your ass up and let's go down to the studio. You have enough chairs in the big room for everybody to be able to sit."

Slowly, Levi stood with a wry smile on his face. Ben swung his hand with the palm up in that ushering gesture that polite people usually use. Rico led the way and hurried ahead to turn on the lights and arrange a circle of chairs in the studio. After him, Levi hit the stairs, followed by Janice, Jose, Joe, Bart, Tracy, and Ben bringing up the rear.

Bart whistled in approval when he saw the light-paneled convex walls reaching from basement floor up to the subfloor of the second level. Joe, Levi's studio guru, said, "Very nice, Levi. Very nice."

"Thanks, Joe. You know you taught me everything I know."

"Not everything, but you're welcome."

After some walking around, which included trips into the control room, everybody was finally seated, with Janice and Ben on either side of Levi.

Ben started, "So, Levi, as you so astutely guessed, I was trying to set up this meeting without you necessarily having a chance to duck it. Well, you ducked it anyway over at my place, so we've brought it to you. Thanks for being good-tempered about it . . . so far."

Chuckles. Levi nodded.

"So, what we have here are people who love and care about you. And I want to introduce you to Jose Calderon, who has helped us to figure this out and who will speak in a minute about what we're going to do."

Levi looked at Dr. Calderon, who stuck out his hand. Levi shook it and said, "I've been hearing your name for a few years from Janice. Thanks for taking care of her."

"You're welcome, and I guess I'll take it for a little while now, Ben."

"It's all yours."

"So, without wasting any time, Levi, this group of friends and family have all expressed to me that they've been concerned. And now they're starting to become afraid. They want to help you with your drinking problem, and there seems to be no doubt that it's a problem. They want you to get help beyond them. Let me just check for nods as to why we're all here."

Everyone nodded. Levi held his right hand up parallel to the floor with the palm down.

"Anybody see any shaking?"

Smiling, he turned the hand toward each of the seven to show them that his hand was perfectly steady. A few applauded lightly.

Levi turned back to Jose and said, "Thanks so much, Doc. I guess this was really worth it. Now I don't mind showing y'all the door."

Ben said, more sternly than he'd practiced, "We're not going anywhere yet, Levi."

Trying to keep the tone down, Jose quickly stepped in. "So, Levi, I think you probably know this . . . or maybe you don't, but for the sake of others, let me explain briefly. There are two categories of problem drinkers."

"Funny, Doc. You say problem drinkers instead of calling me an alcoholic to my face."

"Are you an alcoholic, Levi?"

"I think I like problem drinker better. Hadn't heard that one before. Has a nice ring to it."

"Okay, until you say it, we'll stick with problem drinker."

"But you need to speak to my hand. You still haven't said anything about my hand."

"Your hand is steady, and people have applauded that Levi, but all that does it put you in one category instead of the other."

"Tell me about these categories."

"The maintenance drinker is the first category. That's who most people think about when they visualize a problem drinker. These folks wake up to get their first drink of the day, and can't go to sleep at the end of the day without a pull. They may hide bottles all over the place so a drink is always nearby. Their drink of choice is whatever is at hand, but if they're buying it's usually a bottom-shelf vodka like Ambassador. And they may take something like Black Beauties, which are a combination of amphetamine, commonly known as speed, and dextroamphetamine, in order to get themselves started when they need to function. Or lately, methamphetamine has become more popular as a booster. For them, if one drink is good, then five or ten is probably better. But you appear to not be one of those."

"Never touched any of those boosters, to my knowledge. Dark coffee does me just fine. So, what's the other?"

"It's called the binge drinker."

"Binge?"

"Yep."

"And that is?"

"A binge drinker can go days, weeks, or even months without drinking, and they do so whenever they need to. They have a compelling reason not to drink for the time being, so they don't drink . . . for the time being. Someone meeting them during that period when they aren't drinking wouldn't have a clue."

"So why are they alco—I mean problem drinkers?"

"Simple. It's because once they have one drink, they can't stop, just like the maintenance drinker. That is until the binge is over and it's time for them to straighten up for that compelling reason, whatever it is."

"Interesting. And you think that's what I am."

"That's what I know you are, Levi," interjected Janice. "You binge until you have a reason not to binge. Then you binge again once that reason is over. And you've been binging again and again since you got back from Nam."

Holding up his hand, Jose gestured for quiet.

"In a couple of minutes, everybody in this room is going to speak to you, Levi. I think Rico wants to go first. Then Janice wants to be next, but let me just ensure this distinction is understood, even if it's not accepted."

"Once you start, you go from one drink to ten or twenty. That's pretty easy to understand, Doc," said Levi.

Everyone else nodded their understanding.

Levi glanced across the circle at Rico. He realized that Rico was staring at him with a fierce intensity. He focused. Then he said, "I miss you, nephew. I miss you so much. I'm so sorry. You've got to know I'm sorry, Rico. Your boy Bubba-Rubba was in for a session last night. He was surprised you weren't here, but I did the session and he seemed okay. Digga-Man called this morning. I told him you were on vacation."

Rico was quiet and controlled. "We ain't talking about Bubba or Digga."

"Is Lenny all right?"

"Lenny will be fine, no thanks to you."

"I'm so sorry, Rico."

"I heard that."

Jose interrupted again. "The fact that you're sorry right now while you're sober is a good thing, Levi. I think it's safe to say that nobody would be here if they didn't believe that when you're sober you'd hate the idea of injuring a seven-month old, much less the grandchild of your best friend and son of Rico. But drunk, you did it, Levi. As a drunk, you did it. And you could do it again or something, believe it or not, even worse."

"Fuck you, Doc," said Levi Chance, menacingly rising to his feet. Jose kept his seat, but Ben sprang up and took one step forward. Tracy twitched, but remained seated.

Frozen, Levi glared at Ben Parks. Then he took a step back and sat back down. "I seem to remember you slapping me around one day over on Maple View. Not sure you could do that today."

"I'm surprised," said Ben. "I'm surprised you remember anything about that day. You could smell that nasty-assed house a block away."

Now Rico interrupted his father, "Pop!"

Jose jumped back in. "So, Levi, the people in this room want you to do something that will be really, really hard. In fact, you'll hate it. So the question comes down to this: Will you hate it worse than losing everybody here? Worse than losing everybody who cares about you?"

Sulking now, Levi snatched a glance at the others. He sunk in his seat. Then he lowered his head and closed his eyes. After a long silence, he spoke barely audibly. "I'll stop. I can st—"

"No you can't!" shouted Janice. "Don't lie. You can't stop. Like Jose says, you can stop to do something, but you can't stop binging."

Janice got up and ran out of the room. She didn't want to use the restroom in the studio. Everyone sat in silence for almost five minutes.

Ben asked, "Should I go and check on her, Jose?"

Just then, Janice reappeared through the door and quietly walked to her seat. There was both strain and determination etched on her face.

Levi stared at her for a long time. Then finally he said to Jose, "So what do you want me to do, Doc?"

"For right now, Levi, we only want you to listen. That's all. Just listen. Are you willing to just listen? These people love you. They've written some letters, and we'd like to ask you to sit and listen to them without comment."

Levi scanned around again. The faces he met weren't smiling, yet he knew they were there for him. Totally there for him. He couldn't deny that truth, even to himself. Very softly he said, "I'm willing to listen."

The mood in the room lightened ever so slightly. Dr. Calderon nodded to Rico, who reached into a back pocket and pulled out a folded-up sheet of paper. He shook as he unfolded it. Then he had to turn it up the right way to read. When he started, his voice was shaky but he strained to stay quiet.

"Uncle Levi, I want you sober. Sometimes I think you're so sick you were bit by a cobra. And when I come over to use the studio, sometimes one of your songs is on the radio and I'm so proud. But the house is so bad it stinks, and I want to take all the liquor and pour it down the sink. I do what I can to spray and clean things up so clients won't complain when they come in the door."

"You're my idol, my inspiration, and my teacher, but I just don't want to watch you die. I don't want to watch you go down to your end. And I want you to be able to play with my son. I want Lennie to know you. I want Joni to get over how angry and hurt she is with you. And I want to be able to say to Joni that it's all fixed so she and I can get back to our lives. Right now, when Joni looks at me she sees you. Sometimes she can talk to me, but sometimes she can't. And I need her so bad, Uncle Levi . . ."

Rico's voice tailed off and he began to audibly weep. Ben started to stand but Rico said, "Let me do this, Pop."

Ben sat. Rico turned back to Levi, took several deep breaths, and continued, "So please, Uncle Levi, do what's right. Get treatment. Make that promise to all of us, right here, tonight."

Silence for one minute.

Tears were in Levi's eyes. Rico had stopped crying. Jose said, "Rico, would you like for Levi to have your letter?"

Without speaking, Rico stood and walked across the circle. He held out the letter. Levi looked up and stared at it. Rico appeared to be ready to go back to his chair.

"Please, Rico. Let me have it."

Rico placed the crumpled letter in Levi's hand and then turned silently and went back to his seat. After a moment, Jose pivoted and nodded to Janice, who had been crying all through Rico's turn, but suddenly she was in absolute control. She pulled an envelope from her purse, unfolded the letter from within and began reading.

"Levi, when we were graduating from Tech back then, I was so in love with you. That was more than fifty years ago. Back then, there was no way you could have convinced me that you and I wouldn't be married by now, but here I am, an old spinster. I have no kids because I never wanted to have a kid with anybody but you. I've been with more men than I can count, but only because I couldn't be with you the way I really always wanted to be with you. I've been thinking about this so hard, and the way I guess I want to say it is: Levi, you've been my drug."

"Now, I'm not even cute anymore. I was cute and sexy back then. I'm just old and shriveled up. And here I am, still waiting for my man to be the man I want to be with forever. I love you, Levi. I think I almost always have. But don't get me wrong, I've hated you too. I've hated you."

Janice's voice started to rise. "I've hated you so bad. You can be such an asshole. Tired of your meanness and lack of consideration. Tired of your toxic masculinity. But when I've hated you for wasting our lives, I'm sure what I really was hating was that alcohol."

Janice lowered the letter and shouted, "You've wasted both our lives, Levi Chance! Do you realize how fucked up that is? You piece of shit, do you realize how fucking tragic that is?"

Now before anyone could stop her, Janice rose and turned to face Levi. She slapped him three times as hard as she could. Levi sat perfectly still. Janice ran out again, but this time she returned more quickly. Nobody had spoken while she was out of the room. A suddenly composed Janice Westbrook finished her letter.

"Either you're going to get treatment, get your ass sober, and then ask me to marry you, Levi Chance . . . or I'm ready to leave this city and you'll never see me ever again for the rest of your miserable life. And good riddance! Fuck you! I'm serious, Levi Chance. I'm dead serious."

Janice placed her letter neatly back into the envelope and softly reached over to place it on Levi's lap without turning to look at him.

Jose said, "Is there water? Would anyone want water?"

In a flash, Rico was out of the room and up the stairs to the kitchen. He came back with a flat wicker basket full of twelve-ounce bottled waters. He handed one to Janice. Then he stood in front of Levi with his offer. Levi barely looked up to grab a bottle, but he downed more than half before taking it down from his lips. Everyone else took a bottle of water.

Then Jose asked, "From here we don't have a planned order. Who'd like to go next?"

Bart Stokes raised his hand and Jose nodded. Bart was always nattily dressed. He was wearing a brown and burgundy sport coat. He reached into the inner pocket and removed a folded sheet without an envelope. He cleared his throat.

"Levi, when Ben called me early this morning and asked me to participate in this meeting, I was scheduled to be flying to Chicago for a conference that's going on as we speak. But I'll get up early in the morning to catch the first flight out of National. It was that important for me to be here, because my mother and father loved you so much. I miss them every day and they talk to me from wherever they are, and I thought I heard my mother's voice telling me that I had to represent the family."

"I asked my mom, your Aunt Alma, what she wanted me to say, and she told me she wanted me to tell you that I've seen your alcoholism hurt you in many ways. But she told me that I first should tell you that I understand. She told me that I should say how deeply I know about the hurt you felt when Big Sam was killed so tragically. She told me to tell you that I know how much you loved your father and what an awesome man he was. And she told me to tell you how much Big Sam loved you and your mother. And . . ."

Now Bart started to be emotional, but fought back tears. "And your Auntie Alma told me that she and your Uncle Bundy wanted me to express how deeply all of us hurt for you when, less than eight years later, your sweet dear mother succumbed to that dreaded tuberculosis."

Levi screamed a low scream that grew louder and louder in the room. Janice got up, picked up her chair, and moved it closer so she could hug him.

"Oh sweetie. Oh, my sweet baby. You've never talked to me about this. And I'm sorry. I never asked you about your parents. I never knew. I never knew. Oh, Lee, I never knew."

After the storm of emotions subsided, Bart continued. "My mom spoke to me this afternoon from heaven. She told me that I'd have to remember to you that you weren't the only ones hurting when the government took our little home. All of us were hurt. Brian and me were already on our own, but we still hurt for you and my mom and dad. Those motherfuckers took what the Stokes and Chance families and many other Southwest families had worked for all their lives. She wanted me to say to you, 'How dare them? Those bastards. How dare them!'"

Janice and Levi rocked together side by side.

"But finally," said Bart, "my mom told me to tell you to forgive. She told me that you can't get well unless you forgive. She's praying up in heaven right now for you to be able to forgive. That's what I want to tell you, because, little brother, that's what Alma and Bundy Stokes would say to you if they could."

As Levi took the letter and he and Bart hugged in the middle of the room, others stood and stretched. Then Levi said, "I gotta pee."

That brought laughter in the room. Levi crossed to the door in the corner of the studio and disappeared. Others were directed to the other four bathrooms in the house. Ten minutes later, people were settled back.

Joe Minolo said, "I'll go next, Jose. Mine will be short."

"Okay."

"First of all, I want you to know that I was probably a last-minute addition to this meeting, sort of like what Bart talked about, but I too got the call and immediately dropped everything to come down here. After I talked to Ben this morning on the phone, I also called Arnold Luskin to see if he had anything to say to you."

"You talked to Arnold?" said a surprised Levi.

"Sure did. He said to tell you that you're one of the most talented musicians he's ever worked with. He also said that you are a terrific songwriter and that he wished you'd get back to writing. He said it's becoming harder and harder to find good songs. These R&B artists of today don't understand the simplest things about writings songs. Things like verse and chorus. Things like modulating the melody, or even how to write a melody with more than two or three chords. Things that make songs interesting. He wants you to know how much he'd like to start using you again."

"So that's what Arnold wants you to know. As for me, it's pretty much the same as Arnold. When we met, I really didn't know why I was attracted to helping you out. Probably it was a combination of your being a veteran plus the enthusiasm you had for starting your own studio down here. Through you, I've come to know DC as a hidden gem of musical talent. And I'll always be thankful for that."

"But then one night I heard you play in your studio over on Maple View. I really don't have any idea of where that is from here. But that night, listening to you on the keyboards in that studio, I just imagined us working together forever. I'd still like to do that, Levi. Get some help. First of all, just say it. You're a drunk, regardless of your hand being steady right now. You're an alcoholic. Just say it. Believe it or not, that will feel good to just name it what it is. Once you're in recovery, trust me. You'll be hearing from me."

Levi sat quietly through most of Joe's speech. Then he asked, "Is all of what you just said in that letter?"

Joe smiled. "Most of it. I improvised a little."

Levi rose and walked across the room to the other side of the circle. "Can I have it?"

"That's what I wrote it for. It's yours."

Taking the letter, Levi offered a handshake. Joe rose from his chair and bear-hugged Levi. Then Levi went back to his seat. After a moment, Jose said, "Looks like we have two more to go. Which one of you wants to be next?"

Tracy said, "I think Ben should go last, so I'll go next. I'm here, Levi, because I know that you still mourn the same three guys that I mourn, and because I know what they'd say to you if they could. So my job is to say it to you."

At first missing the reference to Emmanuel, Arthur, and Clyde, Levi spoke up. "My man! Tracy, do you know that I looked for you all over the place back in Nam. I always heard tales of you, but I never could find you. People called you a ghost."

Tracy waited. Then catching himself, Levi said, "Oh! You know this studio is named for them. Thanks for reminding me."

Tracy pulled out a folded piece of paper, opened it, and looked down for a moment. Then he put it down before continuing. "Levi, I'm glad to hear that, 'cause most of what I want to say to you involves Nam. First of all, you are my brother in ways that civilians cannot understand. I know you were in the rear echelon, and some vets put that down, but I don't. You were there. In your case, you were there voluntarily with the band. Actually, we missed each other by only a couple of days at China Beach. They told me you had been there performing when I came in for three or four days of rest. I was really sorry to miss you."

"Is that right? I never knew. I thought I was chasing you."

"We were chasing each other, my brother. But I know I was hard to find. That was because of what I was doing."

"What the hell were you doing, Tracy? That's what I want know. I'm assuming that you did all kinds of nasty stuff in Nam. Why didn't it bother you? Why didn't it mess you up?"

Tracy thought for a long while. The letter was on his lap, but he didn't refer to it.

"Well, Levi, you assume it didn't ever bother me. Sometimes it bothered me a lot. I never had much of a personal beef with the Vietnamese people or even the Viet Cong. At the Point, we studied the process that preceded all this conflict. I didn't particularly see anything wrong with the 1954 Geneva Accords, which eventually would have had elections take place in two years. And if the people had voted in a communist government, so be it. Privately, I never was too much of an anti-communist, just the same way that I don't believe democracy should be forced on some societies in the world today."

Tracy paused. Then he held up his hand. "Excuse, me. I didn't know I was going to get all political here. Let me get back on track."

He looked at his note and then looked up.

"But my theory on why it didn't mess me up is, number one, I was a soldier. And number two, there's a genetic thing inside of me that had to come out, simple genetics. It's kind of what I was born to do. A lot of guys over there were trained and forced to do what wasn't natural for them. And many of them did it very well, don't get me wrong, but it wasn't natural. I didn't agree with everything I was ordered to do, but my ancestor needed to see whether I met the test as a warrior. I'll never know what he thought, but I needed to do it in part for him. I come from a family of warriors. That's what my ancestors were. That's my theory."

"A family of warriors? I don't understand."

"Levi, it's too long a story to get into now. And it's off topic. Once you're in recovery, we can talk about it one day. Okay?"

"Okay."

"So, I was a soldier like you, but I was a different kind of soldier. I was a commando. You never knew where I was over there, because most of the time I was where we weren't supposed to be. We were around the Ho Chi Minh Trail in Laos or Cambodia, and we weren't supposed to be there."

"Damn!"

Tracy laughed inwardly, knowing that nobody in the room had a clue as to what that meant.

"I want you to know that I've spent the past thirty-eight years giving vague answers to questions about what I did in Vietnam. As a soldier, I went where I was sent. And in the course of whatever mission I was on, I did everything I could to keep my fellow soldiers safe. I know there are people who fundamentally hate what I am. Even though I'm retired now, I am, at my core, a career soldier. That's their right to hate that, and in return, I have a bunch of mixed feelings about them. I respect them, but I also feel sorry for them, because I know that they don't have acceptable answers about alternatives to war."

"When somebody attacks you, if fighting back is a bad thing, then what do you do instead? I've asked that question when being booed on college campuses. I've asked that question in political circles. I've been sneered at and been called a murderer, and, believe me, I take no personal pleasure in admitting that people have died at my hands. But when I ask the question about what is the alternative, most people sputter and have no answer. They just hate what I've done. They say stuff like 'turn the other cheek.' Okay, that's their right."

"I look up to you Tracy. Always have."

"Thanks, Levi, but I want to get back to my letter. There's stuff that I've written that I think is the most important stuff I have to say to you today."

"Okay, I'll stop interrupting."

"The army has all sorts of support, as does the VA. I've been in contact with some buddies down in Virginia Beach. They say there are so many liquor stores in that town, that Virginia Beach is really just a liquor store with a zip code. But there are a lot of retired military in the area, with Norfolk right down the road, and probably hundreds of meetings a day, all within a small radius from one another."

"If you agree to get help tonight, I'll take you there tomorrow morning. I'll hook you up with the right people to take care of you, and you'll have the benefit of being away from DC while you get sober. Of course, when you come back to town you'll need a support group like AA or something, but the initial hard work will be done around people who probably won't know you."

"Truthfully, Tracy, I'd like to stop. I can't."

Janice screamed, "Thank you, Jesus!"

Ben said, "That sounds like organic fertilizer to me. It's like when John Coltrane was complaining to Miles Davis about not being able to stop practicing and blowing his horn, Miles said, 'Man, just take the damn horn out your mouth.'"

Jose jumped in, "Well, Ben, that's a good story, but let's not oversimplify. No, Levi, you probably can't stop by yourself, but the route Tracy is offering you is a way that you can, if you decide right here tonight to commit yourself."

Ben said, "Now I need to say just a few things to wrap this up. Don't want to jump in on you, Tracy."

Tracy said, "I'm done."

He walked over and handed Levi his letter. Before returning to his seat, Brigadier General Tracy Brown, US Army (retired) snapped off a salute to Levi. Levi was totally caught off guard. His return salute was nowhere near as impressive, but he meant it nonetheless.

"Okay, you're on," said Jose to Ben.

"Not much to add, really, that I haven't said to you a dozen times or more. Levi, I love you, and I cannot continue to enable what you do to yourself. Remember the Plaza? Remember 'Why Do Fools Fall in Love?' Remember 'You're a Thousand Miles Away?'"

Levi was smiling.

"Sure you do, and that's how long you and me go back. Now you've become probably the most dangerous kind of drunk there is, because you're so skilled, Levi. You know how to not drink if it will interfere with your wife. Sorry to use that term, Janice, but I'm referring to Levi's music."

Janice nodded. Ben continued, "Will you get some help today? That's all I want to ask. Please, my friend. Will you? Will you take Tracy up on his offer?"

Levi sat and took his time. Then he turned to Janice. "Will you marry me?"

Her answer came instantly. "Of course I will, if you promise to get sober and stay that way, but you're going to have to ask me again when that time comes."

Levi nodded and turned to Rico. "Will you let me back into your life? Will you let this studio back into your life?"

Jose jumped in. "I don't like all these conditions you're trying to lay out. I see what Ben means when he talks about how skilled you are, so I'm going to stop Rico from answering. This is not about anybody else in this room but you, Levi. You either want to get help for itself or you don't. His answer will come in due time, but for now, the only question is: Will you get help?"

"Yes."

The old friends from Michigan Park crew erupted. Levi was mobbed. The evening ended with Ben giving Joe a ride back to Union Station to catch a late train back to New York. Janice hadn't stayed with Levi in months, but she stayed with him that night and they just held each other. That's all.

Chapter 54
DAP (Drug and Alcohol Program)

Before noon the next morning, Tracy was driving. Ben was riding shotgun. Janice and Levi were in the back seat of Tracy's Cadillac Deville. Later that day, Rico Parks entered the house on R Street and took over the operating of EAC Studios. He resumed his role of engineer for rap and hip-hop artists, but over the next three months, Rico would engineer for jazz artists, R&B artists, and even for a gospel artist who usually worked with Levi.

In the meantime, the departing party cruised across the Fourteenth Street Bridge, which was once known as the Highway Bridge back in the days before Levi was born. That was when Big Sam Chance first reunited Levi's mom with her blood family by driving her down to Aiken County, South Carolina. Now these travelers with a purpose continued down I-95 toward Richmond, VA, where they picked up I-64, which took them all the way down to where Tracy pulled into the Veteran's Administration Medical Center in Hampton about three hours later. Instead of off-loading at the main entrance, Tracy navigated around to the back. They parked at an unmarked entrance. The party walked into the red brick structure, which was the VA's treatment facility for substance abuse patients.

Two people inside appeared to be waiting specifically for them and instantly recognized Tracy. They rushed up to introduce themselves as Dr. Vance Proctor and Dr. Laila Kassis. Dr. Kassis wore a long gray tunic that went down past her hips to merge with a black skirt that stopped just at the heels of fashionable brown boots. Her hijab, covering her head but not her face, was adorned on the side with a simple gold pin. There was an appearance of no makeup. On the car ride back, Janice was asked about it, and she told Ben she really couldn't tell because the doctor's skin was so flawless.

The gray-bearded Dr. Proctor was in a faded-blue business suit and tie. He was tall enough to look Tracy straight in the eye. Probably mid-fifties, Proctor's handshake was firm, but his smile was relaxed.

"Welcome, General," he said in a low baritone voice. He looked back and forth between Levi and Ben, finally deciding correctly that Levi was the incoming patient. Tracy introduced everyone and handshakes dominoed around the group.

With a barely detectable Middle East accent, Doctor Kassis said, "We've discovered, Mr. Chance, that you have never registered with the VA. Is that correct?"

"I guess so," said Levi. "I never thought of it."

"Is that a problem?" asked Tracy.

"No, General. Your reputation is apparently well known around this hospital and up through the VA. The Pentagon has even sent us a copy of his DD-214, assuming that Mr. Chance might not have thought to bring it with him. We've been allowed to prepare some papers for Mr. Chance to sign, and it will be taken care of."

Used to having doors opened for him without asking, "Thank you" was Tracy's simple response. Doctor Proctor said, quite abruptly, "So we'll take it from here. Thank you for driving Mr. Chance down. We're anxious to get started. Please say your goodbyes now so we can get him enrolled before dinner, which starts," the doctor checked his watch, "in about thirty-five minutes, at seventeen hundred hours."

Even Tracy was surprised at how quickly it had come to this: hello, welcome, goodbye. No frills. No muss. No fuss. Janice gasped and then hugged Levi tightly. She turned her face upward and he kissed her quickly but gently.

"I'm ready, girl. Don't worry. I'm ready."

"I know."

Janice turned toward the door. Tracy followed. Ben had said nothing to this point.

"See you in ninety days, my man. I'll be waiting right outside those doors."

Levi simply waved his hand and then allowed himself to be ushered to a desk where he was given papers to read and sign. The two doctors turned him over to a younger man in green scrubs, who never smiled as he took charge of the rest of Levi's process of entering the VA's Drug and Alcohol Program (DAP).

***

As promised, the administrative tasks were quickly dispensed with and Levi was taken across a plaza into an area called the domiciliary. It seemed to be just another name for a barracks, and it looked no better, no worse. The room he was shown was perhaps nine feet by twelve feet or so. Two single beds were on either side of the room, one made up and one not. A four-drawer chest was against a wall. The green-garbed assistant said, "I'll find your roommate in the mess. He said he's using the two top drawers, so you've got the bottom two."

On the window side of the room were two metal desks facing each other, one with a picture of a white woman, probably close in age to Levi.

Levi reached into his brown leather overnight bag and took out an unframed picture of Janice. He kissed it and placed it into the seam of the other desk's blotter. *You're still cute and sexy,* he thought as he stared at it.

Also on the desk was a pad with scribbling that Levi didn't try to read. Finally, there was a small closet that Levi opened to discover wire hangers that were mostly empty. Two of the occupied hangers held blue jeans, and one held a heavy black coat with hood. There was a small roller bag on the floor underneath a green partially full laundry bag. That was all.

Green Scrubs was watching him from the door. Levi asked, "What do you do around here?"

"I'm a clinician."

"What's that?"

"I work with the members on a whole lot of things. You and I are going to get to know each other pretty well, if you last. You'll see what I do. For now, better wait to do the rest of your settling in later. I'll get you some sheets and a blanket, since it doesn't look like you brought any with you. What about towels?"

Levi shook his head.

"Okay, compliments of the house, but now let's get over to the mess. You'll have about forty-five minutes to eat and meet your roommate. Then you've got to get to evening meeting. After that, Doc Proctor wants to meet with you. You must have some kind of pull going. The docs don't usually stay back to do assessments at night, but he wants to see you right away. I'll take you to his office after evening meeting."

"Okay," said Levi.

Levi had no idea what evening meeting was, but figured there was no use in asking. He'd know soon enough. He threw his overnight bag and his Williams Model 8 bone case on the unmade single bed. The more than sixty-year-old instrument had been given to Levi by his first music teacher, JT Ogilvie, back in 1951 at Bruce Wahl's Restaurant and Beer Garden in Southwest Washington, DC. Now Levi Chance sighed and followed Green Scrubs back out to begin whatever was in store for him.

After dinner, Green Scrubs took him to a big room with metal folding chairs in rows. Levi slid into the back row at this, his first evening meeting. There were about one hundred men and women present, mostly men. He saw Green Scrubs walk up to the front row and speak to a large white man. The man stood and looked back to where Green Scrubs was pointing at him. The man seemed to spot Levi, nodded at Green Scrubs, and then sat back down. Green Scrubs left the room. Someone had introduced himself and another man as "counselors."

Okay, so they have doctors and clinicians and now they have counselors. That's a lot of titles, thought Levi with amusement. Now the second counselor was calling out names and people were answering "here" or "present" or sometimes silly shit like "in the room" or gung-ho shit like "hurrah."

Levi slumped in the uncomfortable metal chair until he got shocked out of his reverie. It came as a shock when Levi heard his name.

"Chance, Levi."

Levi sat up and looked around. He didn't answer right away. He hadn't expected to hear his name. This was his first meeting.

"Chance, Levi."

Now the big white man in the front row was looking back at him and gesturing.

"Here."

The counselor marked his clipboard and then looked back. "Your first meeting. Everybody say hello to Chance, Levi."

People turned and said, "Hello Chance, Levi."

Some had turned toward him, but most spoke mechanically as part of a ritual.

"So, Chance, Levi. Please try to answer right away from now on."

"Okay."

Silence.

Then the old army muscle awakened. "Yes, sir!" said Levi.

He hadn't called anyone sir in decades. It stirred something in him.

***

"Talk to me about your drinking."

In this first private meeting with Doctor Proctor, Levi had decided he wanted to downplay his need to be there.

"This was mostly my friends' idea." He was ready to talk, or rationalize. "I take a drink, Doc. I don't hurt anybody. I don't even drink much outside of my own home. I mostly drink at home, so I really never hurt anyone."

The doctor interrupted. He opened a file folder with "Chance, Levi" on the front. Scanning, he said, "According to what I see in this file, you dropped an infant. And let's see . . . this says you were in your own home."

Levi was frozen. No charges had been brought. Where had this come from? He thought of Ben. No, Ben hadn't been the contact here. That had been Tracy, but Levi had no idea that this kind of information had travelled down to Hampton, Virginia, and was already in a file they had on him.

"Don't I have a right to some privacy, Doc? You know, I might do better with that Dr. Kassis."

"No, not really. Not here. You want privacy, you can go back to DC, but if you want to stay here, you have to talk. Do you want to stay here?"

"You're tough, aren't you, Doc?"

"I am. And you have no chance with Dr. Kassis. She works with the female members. And that's not what we're going to talk about. You're going to tell me about your drinking. The more you minimize, the more you're going to eventually start pissing me off. Or if you don't really want to talk, you're going to leave my office and go pack your bag."

Realizing that he wasn't in a real advantageous position, Levi thought about the fact that this doctor didn't know him, but in some ways Doc already did know him more than a lot of acquaintances back in DC. Levi decided to play along for now.

"You know, Doctor Proctor, it's hard to admit it when you're depressed."

"Yes, I know. But okay, let's start there. Talk about your depression and why you think it's so hard to admit it."

For the next forty minutes or so, Levi talked. Doctor Vance Proctor listened and occasionally made a note on a white pad. He didn't ask a lot of questions. One of the few questions came as another interruption. "And what do you think you can do about all those reasons why you're depressed?"

The doctor sank back into listening mode for Levi's answers. Toward the end of the interview, he opened his desk drawer and took out a prescription pad. He wrote. Levi expected the doctor to hand him the several sheets off the pad, but the doctor didn't. He slipped the sheets into the file folder with the 'Chance, Levi" label and then closed the file.

"It's been a long day for you. Do you think you can find your way back over to the domiciliary?"

"Yes, sir."

"Do you shoot pool or play ping-pong? There are always games going on over there in the evenings. And we have TV in the social hall. Or if you haven't had a chance to settle into your room, maybe you can spend the first evening doing that. You'll find that morning comes early down here."

"Yes, sir."

Levi stood, expecting something else from the doctor. Maybe that this was a good first meeting. Or something.

The doctor opened his file again to the white pad and began to jot more notes. He didn't look up. After a count of ten, Levi stood, turned, and let himself out of the doctor's office.

Chapter 55

Divorce

January 2009

Meanwhile, arriving back in DC, Ben Parks wasn't feeling well. He had known for more than a few months that the next day was coming. Internal ecological issues had kept him running back and forth to the bathroom constantly. Now the day was here. Addie Sherrie Parks and Benjamin Xavier Parks sat beside their attorneys on either side of the courtroom. Judge Delano Douglass was presiding, and there were perhaps a dozen other people in the courtroom. Their cases would be heard after Parks v. Parks. As the plaintiff, Ben was being questioned by his attorney, Giles Harris, about the facts of the almost two-year separation, while Judge Douglass sat quietly listening.

"Is it true that you and Addie Parks separated on or about April 17, 2006?"

"Yes," answered Ben softly. There was a lump in his throat that he couldn't clear. He spoke carefully, because he didn't want to start coughing. Yet the impulse couldn't be stopped. The timing was always inconvenient. There was that drip at the back of his throat that always preceded one of his bronchial coughing spells.

"Argh, argh, argh, argh, argh, argh, argh."

Giles grabbed a pitcher of water. Addie looked over with concern. The judge patiently waited. Ben drank and eventually composed himself before Harris continued.

"And is it true that you have lived separately from that point until today?"

"Yes."

"This separation has been continuous and unbroken?"

"Yes."

"Do you still live in the District of Columbia?"

"Yes."

"And as far as you know, does Mrs. Addie Parks still live in the District of Columbia?"

"She does."

"Is it the case that you and Mrs. Parks have not cohabited since the separation in April 2006?"

"That is correct."

"And is it true that the two of you have used the services of the District's Alternative Dispute Resolution Division to negotiate an agreement reflected in the document that I have just tendered to the court?"

"Yes."

"And does this agreement resolve and bring closure to any outstanding issues or disputes, to include alimony, retirement, future income, and property, that might have existed between yourself and Mrs. Parks?"

"Yes, it does."

"And did you sign this agreement without coercion of any kind?"

"Yes, I did."

Ben had warned his attorney that he wasn't feeling well and that he might need a bio break at any moment during the proceedings. Attorney Harris had been observing Ben as his questioning was coming to an end. At this point, he turned to Judge Douglass and said, "We rest, Your Honor. Nothing further. And may we request a ten-minute break, Your Honor?"

The judge looked surprised and perhaps a little perturbed. Attorney Harris said, "My client will do what he needs to do as quickly as possible, but I assure you, Your Honor, that things will go more smoothly from this point with a ten-minute break."

Now the judge understood. He looked over at the other table as Addie's attorney stood and said, "No cross, Your Honor. And we have no objection to a short break."

The judge then said, "We're taking a break for ten minutes. In other words, we're starting up again in ten minutes. That's it."

Without further word, Ben stood and ran out of the courtroom. The judge let himself have a little smile. Nine minutes later, Ben came back. The judge spoke, "Is everything okay now, Mr. Parks?"

"Yes, sir."

Then the judge asked, "Let me confirm, this document that I'm holding resolves all matters between you and Ms. Parks?"

"Yes, Your Honor."

"And as the plaintiff, let me confirm that you view the differences between yourself and Ms. Parks as irreconcilable?"

Ben's throat caught again and he could barely get out the word, "Yes."

Judge Douglass stared at Ben intently before turning to Addie's table. To Addie, the judge asked, "Does this document resolve all matters of concern to you, Ms. Parks?"

"Yes, it does, Your Honor."

The judge addressed Ben again. "The District of Columbia grants an automatic thirty-day period for appeal. What is your intention regarding appeal?"

Ben looked at Giles for assurance before answering. "I want to waive the thirty-day appeal, Your Honor."

Looking back at Addie, the judge asked, "And what about you, Ms. Parks, concerning your right to appeal within thirty days?"

Very softly, Addie answered, "Waive, Your Honor."

The judge stared at his computer screen as he made various notes while these exchanges were taking place. Finally he looked up.

"These being the facts before me, I will certainly accept the agreement and motion for divorce, as well as the waiver of the thirty-day appeal process. If you'd like to wait in the back while the clerk finishes and files the documents, you can walk out of here today with your divorce. Is that what you want?"

"Yes, Your Honor," Addie and Ben spoke in unison.

The judge spoke to the clerk, who shuffled various papers, looked up, and called the next case, and as those parties came forward, the clerk exited the courtroom through a side door. About ten minutes later, she came back, swore in the next parties, and placed a stack of papers on the judge's side table. He was occupied on his computer, presumably finding the record for the next case, but when he saw the documents, he paused and read them over quickly before signing. The clerk took the papers and stamped and stapled them before coming out into the back of the courtroom and handing copies first to Addie's attorney and then to Ben's.

Giles, without looking, turned the papers over to Ben, who looked somewhat in shock.

"Is that it?" he asked Giles.

"That's it. You're divorced. Congratulations."

Ben sat in silence. The next case was already being heard by the judge. Ben couldn't move. Finally he said to Giles, "Thanks for everything. I'm not sure I feel like being congratulated. It's not necessarily a happy day for me."

As they stood and exited, Giles said, "Yes, I know, and I apologize for not being sensitive. I know you loved her, and you may still love her, or at least you care about her. The two of you were married for a long time, but I also know that you're sure you've done the right thing, and in time both of you will move on. Thanks for being a wonderful client."

"Thank you, Giles."

Giles and Ben moved into the hallway outside the courtroom, passing Addie and her attorney, who were standing and talking quietly. No eyes met.

Chapter 56
Sobriety

Back in Hampton, Virginia on the next day, Levi was not used to being up that early. His roommate, Early Jessup, from Suffolk, Virginia, whom he'd met the night before at dinner and at evening meeting, called and then shook him at that early hour. When Levi didn't respond, Jessup shook him hard until he did.

"Everything's on a schedule here, Newbie," said the roommate.

"Your clinician will be in here shortly. He's the green scrubs guy you met yesterday, and his job is primarily to bug you about things like getting up on time and taking your meds. Guessing that you don't have meds yet, but once you've had your initial interview and assessment with Doc Proctor, you'll get some meds."

"I had that last night."

"At first they won't trust you to take them on your own. That's where your clinician comes in. Thought I'd give you a heads-up this morning, but after this it'll be you and Reggie. I like to be in the gym by about five a.m. so I can pretty much have the equipment to myself. Breakfast is from six thirty to eight. I like to get there early because I like to get the fresh eggs. When the eggs sit in those warmers too long, they get hard."

"What if I don't want to eat breakfast?"

"The clinicians will notice and tell the counselors. Then you'll have to talk about it with a counselor. They want you to eat breakfast, so after a while, if you still won't eat breakfast, they might invite you to leave. I don't know. Reggie's actually a pretty good clinician. He notices stuff. He'll pay attention to where your spirit is every day. Everybody's disease is different, and so everybody's journey is different. It's all based on your assessment and how you're presenting."

"I don't have a disease."

Early laughed. "Alcoholism is the disease that tells you that you don't have a disease. If that wasn't so sad, it would be funny."

"Damn!"

"Better get used to things now. These folks don't play. They'll tell you to get your stuff and get out in a gnat's-hair minute if you don't seem like you're working like everybody else. You have to have a desire to get well. A desire to accept help. A desire to do what's necessary and to wake up the next day and do it all over again."

It took a few minutes for all this to register. Then Levi sat up in bed, swung his feet to the floor, and said, "My name is Levi. Can you call me Levi instead of Newbie?"

"No problem, Levi. You have a right to be called by the name you want to be called by. Some people want to shorten my name to Earl. I don't like that. My parents named me Early, and that's what I want to be called. Your parents named you Levi, and that's what you want to be called."

"Right."

"Done. Now, you stink. Go get a shower and get dressed. I'll wait until six twenty so we can walk over to breakfast together. Now understand, at six twenty I'm leaving, with or without you."

Arriving in the mess hall at six thirty-one and going through the line, the two DAP members sat in the mess and ate. Levi only picked at his food, but Early's appetite was ravenous. But he also was doing most of the talking.

"I'm a big man. I've gained back almost twenty pounds since I came in here forty-five days ago. Once I got all that whisky out of my system, I realized that I like to eat, so I eat. But I also exercise now, every day. I want muscle, not fat."

Early flexed an impressive bicep and grinned. As the two ate together, other members came and went from their table. Early introduced them to Levi, and most shook hands, but Levi and Early sat the longest, getting to know each other. They talked about Nam.

Early had been with the 7th Battalion, 15th Field Artillery. He had done one tour back in 1970-1971. They figured out that they'd just missed each other. Early had even been to Long Binh once or twice, where Levi had been stationed.

He said, "Aw, a REMF. If I'd knowed you back then, I'da made fun of you, but I don't make fun of people anymore. We're both just blessed to be back. As a matter of fact, there are a lot of things I don't do anymore. I don't curse anymore. I don't ever go a single day anymore without praying to my God. I'm changing my life, Levi. I was in a twenty-eight-day private program paid for by my trucker's insurance some years ago, and I stayed sober for a few years. Then I relapsed. I used to have a wife."

Then he shifted the topic. "In the war I was an ammo handler and assistant driver in Gamma Battery. We had those M110 Howitzers at An Khe. Our Michelles were over fifty thousand pounds apiece, and whichever ones were hot for that day's missions could drop two-hundred-pound bunker buster shells out of their eight-inch tubes into a top hat from a pit over eight or nine miles away."

"Your Michelles?"

"Oh yeah, that just what we called our beauties: Michelle One, Michelle Two, and Michelle Three. They were sweet, pretty, and deadly."

Just like Levi, it was in Nam where Early became a problem drinker.

"When we weren't fighting, we were drinking. Simple as that. If one or two was good, five or six had to be better."

Levi learned that sometime in 1970, Early's battery had become a target near An Khe because for some time they had successfully been limiting the enemy's ability to move their ammo resupply convoys over Highway 19. So they went after Gamma and other batteries that were consistently pummeling the highway.

"One day we dropped a shell right into the bed of a truck carrying ammo for their mortars. We heard our explosion and then we heard their ammo going off all that ways away for almost an hour."

Early told Levi that he and his Gamma buddies knew they'd been targeted after that. Infantry support was on the way one day, but before they arrived Charlie hit them with a vengeance. In a stroke of karma, one of the Charlie mortars dropped a shell right into the middle of a pile of residue (spent brass from Gamma's firing) and popped some hot brass up into a live ammo stack that was too close to the residue. All of a sudden, a live round went off on its own and stayed low, right out of the firing pit into the tree line a football field away. Luckily, nobody in Gamma was hit, but Early had been too close to the detonation, and instantly he was thrown to the ground. When he came to, his driver and ammo handler partner was standing over him yelling. Early couldn't make out a word for that day and for ten days after that.

That's when he received the diagnosis of "artillery ears." Partial hearing started to come back enough for Early to finish his tour, but the damage to his ears from sustained loud noises got progressively worse and worse. He came back to the States, got out of the army, and never saw to his increasing hearing loss. He got married, had some kids, and started doing long-haul trucking. His first brush with the VA had been after getting fired from the trucking job.

He talked loud because he couldn't hear. A waitress at an overnight truck stop got offended by his screaming and told her boss, who came after Early. Early put him in the hospital, and that got back to his company. Laid off, he started back drinking and did so heavier and heavier. He registered for help with the VA and was placed on disability. The help he got was an artillery-ear diagnosis and some hearing aids. However, the VA hadn't done anything about his drinking, probably because he was sober at the time and they never knew about it.

Early was still wearing the same transistor hearing aid by Philips that he'd gotten from the VA back in the 1990s. He'd found himself enjoying music again. One source of happiness was not having to say "huh?" over and over again.

"I didn't have a job anymore. I just drank. I was starting to have flashbacks. I couldn't sleep. I had to take a drink every three hours to keep from shaking. I had PTSD, what they used to call being shell-shocked, but I didn't know it back then. Sally's insurance paid for me to go through another twenty-eight-day private program. This time I stayed sober until I relapsed again. She left me. That's her picture on my desk. I want her back. I walked around in a fog for a long time, so it took me a long time to realize that, but I do.

"So I decided to come to the VA for a longer program. I saw other people getting sober, and I wasn't. So I knew I must have it worse than they did. So I knew I needed more than they did. Sally knows I'm here. I hope she'll take me back, but she probably won't. Even if she doesn't, though, I don't want to relapse ever again. The hard lesson that I've had to learn is that recovery is more than sobriety. Sobriety is what I have now. I've been sober since I came here, but I've been sober before. Now I want recovery, which happens one day at a time."

"That's deep."

"Not really. But you'll learn as you go."

Chapter 57
Meetings, Counseling, and Classes

Suddenly, Early checked his watch. He'd finished off Levi's plate and they'd just been talking for about fifteen minutes. "We've got to get over to morning meeting."

So that began one of the many patterned activities that Levi was subjected to: morning meetings and evening meetings. He soon realized that the main purpose of these meetings was to call the roll. They wanted to know if anybody had left campus, thereby leaving the program. His counselor was named Gene. Sometimes Gene led the meetings, and sometimes other counselors were in charge. There seemed to be six or seven counselors coming in and out, but Gene was the one he worked with in private sessions.

After reciting the twelve steps together, this first morning meeting for Levi was adjourned. They'd ended last night's the same way. Most seemed to close their eyes and just speak out. Some were reading off laminated cards. When they were done, Gene called out for Chance, Levi to stay back. Other program members were filing out as Levi moved to the front.

"Here's your schedule and some other program information, including your twelve-step card. Always have that with you."

The first odd thing Levi noted about his schedule was that he seemed to be expected to be at graduation that Friday morning.

"Thought this was a ninety-day program. What's up with this graduation thing?"

"It's not you graduating. We have two members graduating this week. Most weeks we have somebody ready for graduation. All the members are required to attend until finally it's their week."

"Oh."

"Also, you'll see that anger management class starts in twenty minutes. You won't be there this morning. You and I are going to get to know each other. Sometimes I'll pull you out of a class for a one-on-one. Those are the only times you can miss a class: when I pull you out or when Doc Proctor pulls you out. Is that clear?"

"As mud."

"So you're saying you have bad eyesight?"

"No. It's clear."

"Okay, for future information, you should know that I don't have a sense of humor. Is that clear?"

"Clear."

Then the two men walked in silence out of the room, clicked out the lights, and proceeded out of the building and over to the back door of the main VA hospital, climbed some steps, and entered a tiny office with one desk, three file cabinets, and three chairs. Gene moved around and took a seat. Levi faced him in one of the other chairs facing out past Gene and into a courtyard between the wings of the hospital.

"What did you tell Doc Proctor last night?"

"A lot of stuff."

"Tell me the same stuff."

Reluctantly, Levi began to talk about old Southwest, his parents, Nam, and the ups and downs of his music career. Counselor Gene just mostly listened and took notes. Finally, after almost one hour, he handed over a plain white bag. Levi ripped it open to find three vials of pills. Levi read the labels: Antabuse, naltrexone, and Campral. Counselor Gene noted that Levi didn't bother to read the dosage instructions.

"Those are the meds you'll be taking for now. Doc Proctor put them in last night after the two of you got together, and I picked them up when I came in this morning. I just wanted you to see them. Now I'll take them back. Reggie will be into your room every morning about five forty-five to make sure you're up and to start administering your meds in the proper intervals and dosage."

Counselor Gene reached out his hand, and reluctantly Levi surrendered his pills. He really hadn't even had a chance to study what they were.

***

By the second week, Levi thought he was coming apart. He was throwing his things back into the leather overnight bag after dinner. Early walked in, took a look, and sat on his bed to watch. After a minute, Early spoke, "So, that's it huh?"

"Gotta get outta here."

"You know if you leave, you can't come back."

"Don't intend to come back."

Early was quiet again. Levi's head was hurting. He wanted to drink. Early stood and walked over.

"Take my hand, brother."

"What?"

"I said, take my hand. You say you were raised Baptist, so you know how to pray, or at least you did at one point. I want us to drop to our knees and pray together."

Levi turned and stared. He saw a resolve in Early's face.

"I don't want to pray. I want to leave."

"I know you do, but I want you to pray to be able to stay until tomorrow. Leave tomorrow evening if you still must. Just pray to be able to stay one more day. I'll pray with you."

Early prayed out loud. It was a rousing prayer of calling on God to give Levi strength and to remove his doubts that he was fully able to conquer his disease. Levi then prayed, more hesitatingly at first, but he'd been inspired by Early's genuine concern for him. He squeezed Early's hand and then prayed some more out loud: "Early didn't have to do this for me. And yet he cared for me enough to stop what he was doing and offer his support. I want to be able to do that for someone else in the future, but right now I need and want to accept this good man's love for me, and I humbly ask you, Father, to help me learn how to love myself enough to let this demon liquor go."

At the morning meeting the next day, Levi and Early sat together, and Levi felt a sense of pride to be able to answer to roll call.

***

6:30 to 8 a.m. - Breakfast

8 to 9 a.m. - Morning Meeting

9 to noon – Anger Management Class

Noon to 12:45 – Lunch

12:45 to 1 p.m. – Domiciliary Time

1 p.m. to 2:45 p.m. – Addiction Class

2:45 to 3 p.m. – Break

3 to 4:45 p.m. – The Twelve Steps Class

4:45 to 5 p.m. – Domiciliary Time

5 to 6 p.m. – Afternoon Meeting

6 to 7 p.m. – Dinner

Evening – Recreation

Lights Out at 10 p.m.

Rewind and Repeat (over, and over, and over)

By midway in the program, Levi had started to appreciate the structure. He felt a mixture of sadness and pride when the Friday came that Early Jessup graduated. Levi now had his room to himself for one week. Then he came in one evening and found out that a newbie had moved in. No one had told him, but Levi stepped up to the responsibility of doing for this new member; for taking care of another human being as Early had done for him. He had responsibility. Having responsibility was a powerful driver in the recovery process. He couldn't remember doing this before, or at least not for a long time.

Just before his graduation, Levi wrote a letter to Early:

> *Thank you, my friend. You meant the world to me. I wouldn't have stayed here without your inspiration. Probably*

more than anything else, I just tried to do what you were doing, including praying to God and trusting his will. That was the biggest lesson you taught me, not the counselors and not the psychologists. You taught me with your actions, Early. And for that you will have my gratitude for the rest of my life. Hope you're well. If I get down to Suffolk one day, hope I could look you up. If you're ever in DC, you'll have a place and a friend.

Thanks,

Levi Chance

Chapter 58
Recovery

Twelve Steps[8]:

Admit we are powerless over alcohol and that our life is unmanageable.

Believe that a higher power, greater than ourselves, can restore us to sanity.

Make a decision to turn our lives over to the care of our higher power (God, if that's how we understand our higher power).

Search ourselves and make a moral assessment of who we are.

Admit to our higher power, to ourselves, and to at least one other human being the exact nature of our character and misdeeds.

Turn over our character issues and defects to our higher power to be removed.

Humbly ask our higher power to remove our shortcomings.

List those we have harmed and promise to ourselves and them that we will make amends to each of them.

Release the past by making direct amends and by doing no harm to such people or others from that point on.

Repeatedly take personal inventory and admit problems as soon as they are found.

Seek conscious contact with our higher power through meditation and prayer for knowledge of His will and for the power to obey.

After our spiritual awakening, practice these principles in all our affairs and share them with other alcoholics.

***

---

[8] Ronald Rogers, Chandler McMillin, and Morris Hill, _The Twelve Steps Revisited_. (New York: Bantam Books, 1990).

On a particular afternoon in mid-February 2008, after the morning graduation ceremony, Levi said his goodbyes and packed his one bag. He hadn't left the campus in ninety days. Even on weekends, he'd not joined member field trips to various places. Early hadn't gone on field trips, so Levi hadn't either. Instead, he sometimes had read in the evenings and on the weekends, sometimes he played bid whist or shot pool in the recreation room, but most times he played his bone or wrote music on a piano he'd found at the end of one of the domiciliary halls. By this day, he had about a dozen new songs that he really liked and was ready to send to Joe Minolo and Arnold Luskin.

He had been thinking about seeing Ben again. He'd developed a sense of humor and wanted to play an innocent joke on his friend when he was picked up, but he couldn't think of that perfect killer joke. He'd settled instead on writing and reciting a limerick the moment he saw his friend:

I want you to know my decision

I've made it with the utmost precision

No spirits I've found

Can challenge my jazzy new sound

I'm sober and my friends I'll astound.

He knew it was corny and not very good, but as he walked out of the treatment center, he had his head down reciting his limerick silently. When he looked up, instead of Ben, there stood Janice.

"Where's Ben?"

"That's all I get?"

"Sorry, babe."

They embraced and then Levi asked again. "Where's Ben?"

"I wouldn't let him come. Wanted you all to myself."

"Oh. That works. Will you marry me?"

"Are you clean for good?"

"With God's help and your love, I'm in it for one day at a time, but yes. That is my prayer. Not planning on slipping. I'm prepared to make amends to you for years of stupidity. When I get back, I've got to find me some meetings I can go to."

"Been looking for them for you. Found a lot of help at my Al-Anon meetings. Here's a list."

Levi took the piece of paper but didn't look at it. He just stared. "That's the group that has addicts as family members?"

"Yes."

"And you've been going to their meetings?"

"Yes, since the day after we got back to DC after dropping you off."

"I love you."

"I love you too. And yes, I will marry your sober ass, one year from today."

Noting the qualifier, Levi went into bargain mode. "One month from now."

"Split the difference. Ten months from now."

"That's not splitting the difference."

"It's not splitting it in half, but's it's splitting."

Studying Janice's face to gauge her resolve, Levi admitted the logic of her standing her ground to himself. "Deal."

Levi was really committed to his recovery and began working at it daily through the twelve steps.

Chapter 59
Finding Purpose

In early May 2008, Ben picked Levi up from his "lunch bunch," AA meeting at the church in Southwest DC. When he'd gotten back from treatment, he'd decided that he wanted to fix the flat tires on his car and start driving again. As a requirement, he had a breathalyzer installed that would allow him to start it up only if he were sober.

Levi didn't live in Southwest DC, but as often as possible he tried to make this particular meeting in his former neighborhood to be closer to his roots. Also, this lunch bunch meeting stressed the concept of responsibility more than others he'd tried. His responsibility for taking care of the group was to always bring napkins. He liked that. He even got there early lots of times, because he wanted to be there with the napkins as soon as people walked through the door. If he decided on a particular day to go to another meeting somewhere else, he asked a member of this meeting to meet him somewhere so he could hand over some napkins.

He liked the structure of the conversations that talked about how it was, what it was like, what members in the meeting had gone through, and where they were now. He liked helping the tribe members figure out how to do stuff: how to buy a car, how to look for an apartment, how to stay with their significant other in some cases, and how to get away in other cases. This was his new tribe and he got energy from being with them. He also joined Ben's American Legion Post on Capitol Hill and was soon far more active than Ben.

At one thirty on this particular afternoon, Ben inhaled deeply when his friend got into the car and was pleased to not smell liquor. Since Levi had just come out of a meeting, Ben knew he wouldn't smell anything, but this was one of his rituals and it gave him satisfaction each day Levi was verified sober. He turned over the ignition, focused on the new adventure he had in mind, and, as he pulled off, began explaining.

"This is something I think you're going to really like as a Vietnam vet. We're going to a place where there are several of them. And they're homeless."

"If they're Vietnam vets, it doesn't matter if they're homeless. We're brothers."

"Yes, I know that, Levi."

Ben pulled off and drove for a few minutes in silence. They pulled into a driveway in Southwest DC and drove underground, where they parked. They then went up on the escalator to the Safeway store, and Ben said, "Grab a basket."

They went to the miniatures aisle. Ben emptied the deodorant baskets and the lotion baskets. There were probably thirty to thirty-five products in each. Then he went to the beverage aisle and hefted several cases of bottled water.

"That's all," announced Ben.

"Let's check out."

"Oh, I see. You're going to try to turn me into some kind of Florence Nightingale. That's funny."

"Let's call it Floyd Nightingale. How's that?" responded Ben.

"Dig it!"

Back in the car, Ben said, "Look in the back seat. See that cardboard box. Pull it up here and read what it says."

Levi was starting to get in a good mood. "Okay, what do we have here?" He read, "Readybath Select. Total Body Cleansing System. Quantity equals thirty."

He looked over at Ben in the driver's seat. "Putting two and two together, we're going to do hygiene kit handouts, right?"

"Yup! Did I ever introduce you to Dr. Doris Smith?"

Levi thought and recognition soon came to his face. "Is that the phat midnight-skinned sister? Works for the city?"

Inwardly Ben smiled and even blushed a little. He and Doris were still private.

"My man! Never forget a fine woman, right?"

They exchanged a pound.

"Yeah, she's been with DC Public Health Agency forever. Anyway, I got her to hook me up with one of her field-workers under the bridge over by the steps where you guys in the Pershings used to play Tchaikovsky at night."

Levi took it in. He opened a booklet attached to the Readybath and read intently. "So, they can use these and not have to shower?"

"That's what I understand, Levi."

Levi nodded up and down. "Well, the mysterious Ben Parks. Drive on, my man. Drive on."

They proceeded through the streets of DC in silence for about fifteen minutes. Ben navigated from the Safeway, past the waterfront near where Levi had grown up. He saw Haines Point across the Washington Channel. Levi spotted something and grinned.

"Damn, that fish market is still booming, ain't it? Don't look that different from back in the day."

Ben smiled and let his friend remember. He drove through an underpass and made a quick left. They merged onto another section of Maine Avenue and soon were passing national monuments. Levi saw off to the left across the Tidal Basin the Jefferson Memorial.

A few more swerves and Levi spotted the famous steps. Then there was a park police car, and he was surprised to see Ben pull off onto the grass and the officer walk over with a lanky brother sporting locks under a rastacap.

Ben and Levi got out as the officer was asking, "Are you Dr. Parks?"

"That's me."

"Well, I can only give you one hour to park here. I'll stand by."

"Whatever you can, Officer. Thanks!"

Ben turned to the other man. "You must be Mr. Belliard."

"Das me, suh. Nigel Belliard, atcha service," said the man, reaching out for a brother shake. "Call me Nigel."

Taking the man's hand, Ben said, "This is my friend Levi."

The two of them shook as the park policeman wandered off. Then Nigel said, "By ma count, dere's four Vietnam vets plus seven Gulf War vets oberdere."

They all looked over to a bridge crossing the Potomac to Virginia. There was an encampment of tents and lean-tos under the bridge, with perhaps thirty people, mostly men, milling or sitting around.

"See de tall dude watchin' us? Das Frank Carson. Two tours 'n Nam plusa tour 'n Bosnia. Got out 'bout ten years go. Im say 'e had a couple a inside jobs, but just couldn't 'just."

Levi's enthusiasm was starting to show. "Let's go meet Frank."

He hoisted the box of Readybath and a case of water. He took off with Nigel. Ben tried to follow, but then had to go back to pick up the Safeway bag and the other water.

As they approached the encampment, Frank smiled and extended his hand to Nigel. "What's happening, rasta man!"

"Everyting's what everyting is, soldier," sang out Nigel as he smiled and embraced Frank.

"Wha's up wit dose feet?"

"They getting better, I think. Just can't keep on these boots day-'round. Have to change socks more. All those things y'all's doctor said. Where is she? I like it when she comes out with you."

"Know ya do, my mahn. Know ya like Doc Smit. Shi tol me ta tell ya hi."

"She say anything about our date?"

"Matter fac, said she cahn't wait."

"Yessir!" said Frank.

"That's some woman. Thanks for lying to me, man."

"Ya welcome, suh."

"So who you got here?"

"Dis Levi . . . Sorry, ah didn't catch ya lass name."

"Chance," said Levi.

"Levi Chance. Ah tink he was in de country 'bout da same time were you."

Frank studied the tall, thin Levi. He moved in closer to him before he spoke. "Where were you at, soldier?"

"In '67 and '68, I was mostly at Long Binh and the Tonsonut area."

Frank closed his eyes and thought for a long time. Then his eyes opened. "Tet."

Levi nodded. "That's right, man."

"Come here, my brother. I don't think I stink too bad this morning. Give a brother some love."

Levi enthusiastically grabbed Frank and they held each other for what seemed like minutes. Then Levi stepped back and said, "Frank, I want you to meet my brother. He's not a brother like you and me, but he's the only real friend I've had for fifty years or more. This is Dr. Parks."

"No, it's Ben," said Ben, stepping forward and shaking Frank's hand.

"Frank," said Levi. "This whole thing is Ben's idea. He's been trying to think of a way to do something every time he drives by you guys. But he didn't feel qualified."

Levi laughed and poked at Ben, who jumped back.

"So he finally decided to bring me down. Don't know why he didn't think of that at first. He's a doc, but he's slow."

Frank, Levi, and Nigel all had a laugh at Ben's expense. Silently, Ben was loving what was happening. He had had no idea that Levi would take to his cockamamie scheme so enthusiastically. He thought of Davita, who'd said before the intervention, "Levi just has his music, and when he's not playing, he's drinking."

He'd actually dreamed this idea at first. He'd dreamed of Levi connecting with homeless Vietnam vets and doing something to help them. After waking, he gradually assembled a plan in his mind involving Levi, who had always been fastidious about his appearance and hygiene when not drunk. As he'd hoped, Levi was keen on the idea of bringing products to his brothers and getting to know them. He'd thought that Doris Smith would be able to hook him up with contacts. She'd come through in a big way. He broke out of his reverie and realized that the process was proceeding without him.

He caught the tail end of Levi explaining to Frank, "Now I want to come out maybe twice a month and bring you guys this kind of stuff, if it's all right. I heard you say something about your smell. This might help. Matter of fact, if it's all right with you, I'm going to come back sooner and pass out some bigger bottles of deodorant. My friend Ben is cheap, but you all will probably run through these little bottles in no time."

Ben didn't interrupt.

"But the best thing is these Readybath packets."

Levi had torn open the box and was showing Frank the drawings on the cover.

"Sorry I can't afford one for every day for you and all your friends. They're kind of expensive, but maybe twice per week you can open one. There are eight sheets in each pack. See here on the cover how you use one for each part of your body. Then you throw them away, soak up some deodorant and lotion, and you're ready to go work up on K Street."

Frank laughed a long laugh. Then, as Levi handed out packets, deodorant, and lotion to the vets first and then to the other homeless folks, Frank broke out in a loud sob. Nigel walked over and put an arm around him. Frank took his time and then wiped his eyes.

Ben just observed. A siren bleeped. They looked over at the park policeman, who was standing by his car pointing at his watch.

"You go on, Ben," said Levi.

"I want to stay and get to know my brother some more. I can find my way back home."

"You sure?"

"Totally. Thanks, my friend."

Ben and Nigel walked away. After about fifty feet, Ben looked back. Frank and Levi were walking from person to person and Levi was shaking hands. Ben stood there for a while and had to be reminded by the officer to move along. He noticed his friend's expression. There was gratitude and a sense of purpose there that Ben hadn't seen in Levi for a very long time, maybe even since Vietnam.

Acknowledgements

My first novel, *Forgetful* (2013, SPBRA Books), was written mostly out of my head. As many writing instructors admonish, the watchwords were "write what you know." And so the character Benjamin Parks was created as someone who did work very much like the kind of work I had done for over forty years. That didn't make *Forgetful* easy to write. But, in comparison, it was so much easier than *Wounded*.

When the trajectory of this new story directed me to go into areas that I had no direct knowledge of, as a researcher, I initially spent time online and in libraries, and those activities yielded good stuff, but not enough. So, it's important for me to acknowledge some people (knowing that I cannot name all), but these are some key folks without whom I couldn't have completed this project.

For instance, I had only a vague knowledge of the urban renewal that was visited on the Southwest quadrant of Washington, DC, in the 1950s and 1960s. So, without the help of people like my dearest friend and love, former Southwest resident Katherine Duncan Warner, I couldn't have proceeded. Kitty is the daughter and granddaughter of Mary Green and John Green, who are listed on the urban renewal letter from the DC government in Chapter Thirteen. Thanks, Babes, for being my muse and for all your creative ideas. Similarly, former Southwest resident Bonita V. White (great-niece of Bruce Wahl) provided me with invaluable tips, for which I am truly grateful.

Tom Lewis's book, *Washington: A History of our National City*, was invaluable because it contained details that were needed to make the fiction that I was writing not necessarily accurate, but at least contextually believable. Similarly, when eventually Sam Chance Senior, Levi Chance, and even Ben Parks in his first marriage to Yvette Parks, all took up residence in the neighborhood known as Anacostia, I needed to stay believable. Many newcomers to the DC area seem to think that Anacostia is anything east of the river. Anacostia is a rather small neighborhood tucked in one corner of Southeast DC. I learned so much about that section from Dianne Dale's excellent history: *The Village That Shaped Us: A Look at Anacostia DC.*

I took great license with Levi Chance's time in Pershing's Own, the army band headquartered at Fort Myer, Virginia. As with most license I have taken, this was done simply for my own sensibility as a storyteller. First, I haven't found anywhere that this band was simply called the Pershings. Every account I've read has referred to them as Pershing's Own, including in my conversations with Harold Summey, currently a drummer in that prestigious band. Also, Harold was amused at the idea that Levi would have been accepted into the band in the time of the book. "There were none of us until at least ten years after that." Apologies to any who might take offense at this revisionist history for the sake of the story.

As another example, when it came to writing about Vietnam, although I am a veteran of the Vietnam era, I was never in-country. I was stationed in 1968 with the 92nd Psychological Operations Company at Fort Bragg, North Carolina, and sang as a member of the Green Beret Chorale before being deployed to South Korea. I expected to go to Nam, but it is only in retrospect that I have any appreciation for the kind of work that I might have done with a PsyOps or Special Forces unit had I been in Vietnam.

So, first props in this regard go to my cousin Arthur Reagin and my high school friends Donald Rowe and Calvin Tildon, all Vietnam vets. Thanks for your tips and your valuable advice as readers as well as for your heroic service. And secondly, I found the invaluable resource by John L. Plaster: *The Secret Wars of Americas Commandos in Vietnam.* New York, Simon & Schuster, 1997. Major Plaster's book was a godsend for me, and though I've never met him, nonetheless I thank him profusely.

Also, a tribute. I was honored to know First-Lieutenant Jerry Lynn Pool. Jerry and I graduated in Class 4-69 as second lieutenants from the US Army Officer Candidate School at Fort Benning,

Georgia. At Fort Benning, Jerry was the captain of our flag football team that won the brigade championship that year. I broke my finger in that game, and it is still crooked.

In Vietnam, Jerry was Fifth Special Forces and then became an SOG commando. He died on a top-secret mission in Cambodia on March 24, 1974. Jerry was posthumously promoted to the rank of captain and rests in Arlington National Cemetery in Section 60, and his name is listed on The Wall in Washington, DC (Panel W-2, Line 40). Bless you, Jerry. I looked up to you at Fort Benning and even more so now.

Thanks to Ron Holloway, whose presence that night with singer Eva Cassidy inspired me to do online research. I wanted to tell a version of an event that many relative newcomers to the city don't know about. The event took place in the city's Georgetown section, one of the most historic in the whole city.

When the story demanded that I tell the story of Levi Chance's path to sobriety, I had no clue. First, I want to thank my friend Russ Linden, who introduced me to Steven Schwartz. Steven convinced me that the direction that I had in mind for Levi Chance's intervention was not credible. Thus, I knew that, while the Michigan Park crew could do an intervention, they could not help Levi to recovery on their own. And second, thanks to Kate McPhall (a member of my church, Westminster Presbyterian), who turned me on to her friends Maggie and Ben Downing. Thank you, thank you, thank you Maggie and Ben for telling me your stories. And even more thanks to Maggie and Ben for introducing me Joe Harrell and Danny Fuentes. All these folks opened up to me about their continuing recovery processes. In so doing, they helped me understand something of what Levi would have to go through in order to traverse the difficult process of recovery.

Thank you to co-pastors Brian and Ruth Hamilton of Westminster for supporting me in my writing and for the uplift you give to us all every Sunday and throughout the weeks and years.

Thank you to the members of the Jazz and Cultural Society's (JACS's) writers group for your encouragement and for travelling with me on this journey of putting words into thoughts and feelings. You guys are very special to me.

And finally, when the story came to the injuries sustained by Lennie, the son of Rico Parks, I owe a deep debt of gratitude to my niece, Kelley Carroll, MD, who reviewed that chapter and made suggestions about how the wounds would be treated. Also to my longtime friend Manny Geraldo, Esq., who gave me valuable advice about the most likely legal process and its implications for Levi.

Points of Reference

The massive Lyndon Baines Johnson Building of the US Department of Education covers the footprint where Bruce Wahl's Restaurant and Beer Garden stood during some time periods in this book.

Dixon's Court was located between 3rd and 4th and between G and I Streets, SW.

Canal Street previously extended over to Fourth Street near Fort McNair.

The Marvin Gaye birthplace has been reported online at several different places, but the most references this author could find pointed to a long-gone site near First and Q Streets in SW DC.

Though the Alaska Highway work was actually executed in 1944, it has been presented here as happening in 1943 for reasons of literary license.

Big Sam Chance's time training at Fort Huachuca is probably a little off the actual historical timeline.

From the 1860s, when General Joseph Hooker set up shop there, into the 1920s, the slum section known as Murder Bay (containing brothels and the scene of numerous criminal activities) was approximately in the area that is now known as the Federal Triangle (Constitution Avenue on the south, Pennsylvania Avenue on the north, Fifteenth onset on the west). While this designation may not have been used during the time of this story, Sam Sr. might have taught the term to his son. There were still theaters, dance halls, and peep shows on and around Fourteenth Street into the 1970s. The beginning of a decades-long transformation was probably mostly the result of President Lyndon Johnson's Executive Order number 11210, which established a temporary commission on Pennsylvania Avenue in 1965.

CPSIA information can be obtained
at www.ICGtesting.com
Printed in the USA
FFOW02n0756261117
43751638-42618FF